MY HOT HOUSEMATE

Susannah Hardy

HAWKEYE
PUBLISHING

First published in Australia in 2025 by Hawkeye Publishing

Cover Design by Lily Qistina

A catalogue record of this book is available from the National Library of Australia.

ISBN: 9781923105430

Proudly printed in Australia.

www.hawkeyebooks.com.au

For Liz

1

LIFE offers unforgettable moments of pure perfection. Discovering your fiancé had an affair isn't one of them. When did my life become a cliché?

Mark was in the shower when his mobile sprang to life with a text. A second and a third promptly followed. I never usually looked at his phone, but for some reason I picked it up, expecting his agent or manager trying to track him down. But the texter's name yelled at me like a car alarm on a quiet street. Kourtney. Or "Kourt" as it said. I couldn't think why she'd need to urgently text Mark three times in a row. Especially when he was so adamant that nothing had happened between them. Surely there was only one reason for three speedy messages mere days after I'd accused Mark of cheating on me. And for him using a shortened (and familiar) version of a not-very-long name to store her number. My breathing accelerated as I pressed on the first message.

Hey babe, does she know?

Followed by *Hope ur ok.*

And then *Call me xx.*

I stared at my phone as if it had been the one cheating on me, desperately wanting to smash it against the wall. But then I'd have destroyed the only evidence that proved my fiancé was a complete shit. Instead, I typed *Now I do* and pressed send. Fury seeped through every cell in my body, but somehow that was all I could manage in the way of angry retorts. At least I'd answered her

7

question. I should have said, *I hope you trip over your big boobs, break both your legs and can't work for 12 months, you pathetic fiancé-stealing bitch.* But I didn't think of that until later.

Mark appeared at the bedroom door and saw his phone in my hands and my eyes as big as frisbees.

'Okay, so I'm going to ask you again,' I said in a strangely calm voice despite the anger brewing deep down inside. 'Did you sleep with Kourtney?'

From the pathetic look on Mark's perfectly chiselled face, he knew he had no option but to come clean. 'It was nothing, she meant nothing—'

'Stop talking.' I didn't want to hear any more stock phrases coming out of his mouth. No wonder he was an actor and not a scriptwriter.

Mark was silent.

'More than once?' I asked.

'Yeah, I'm sorry, it was—'

'Just answer the question.' I sounded far more magnificent than I felt. 'And why is she checking in with you? Calling you "babe" and asking you to ring her?'

'Okay, we did initially have feelings for each other, I admit, but I ended it after the shoot. It was a terrible mistake. It's you I want. It's always been you.'

Despite my desire to scream and brandish some sort of lethal weapon, I kept my voice steely and strong. 'Maybe you should have given that some thought before having sex with Kourtney in Canada!'

Mark said nothing. Standing there in his boxer shorts with wet hair he looked vulnerable and slightly ridiculous, not his usual TV star persona. I threw his phone against the wall. It didn't break, but it felt fantastic. So much so that I stormed into the kitchen and picked up the first thing I saw (the remains of Mark's dairy-free acai bowl) and dropped it on the tiled floor. Even more satisfying. Then, before I caused any more damage, I tossed everything I owned (which didn't add up to much) into a case and left.

I slept on friends' floors and couches until I ran out of friends with spare floors and couches and bought a plane ticket to Sydney (on a credit card, I'm still not sure how I'm going to pay it off). My manager, Benji, was far from impressed, but I assured him it was just a quick trip to see my father who isn't well (small white lie) and that I'd return soon.

So here I am.

Back in Australia. Broke. Unexpectedly single. And dog-sitting for the next three months. Which was never part of the plan. But to be honest, I'm having trouble remembering what my plan was. Something about moving to LA like every other actor in Sydney, living the dream, waiting to see what happens.

And things *had been* happening.

Well, slowly happening.

Okay, about two things had happened. One: I fell in love. Two: I got incredibly close to an on-going role in a TV series. The future was looking rosy… until my fiancé went and cocked it all up.

Literally.

I needed to get away, so when my best friend, Jazz, said she was looking for someone to house-sit while she and Stu went overseas, I offered on the spot.

'Yeah right, like that's going to happen,' she scoffed.

'Seriously, I'll do it.'

'What?' Jazz couldn't believe *her* luck, but it was as if a gift literally fell from the sky into my needy lap. The chance to exit LA stage right and let my heart recover near family and friends until I was ready to go back and pursue my Hollywood dream… What more could I ask for?

But now, standing outside Jazz and Stu's cosy Bondi cottage, I'm wondering if this really was the right decision. I head around to the side gate as usual (no one uses the front door), but just as I put my hand out to open it an explosion of barking sends me running back to the front garden. A harsh reminder that while Jazz and Stu are away, I'm required to take care of their precious baby, George, an enormous and energetic labradoodle – a labrador crossed with, in Jazz's words, 'the biggest poodle in the southern hemisphere'. Tall as a racehorse and just as hungry. I'll have my work cut out for me, particularly as I have no dog experience at all. And Jazz and Stu take their dog parenting duties extremely seriously. You'd think they were raising a future prime minister.

'Hey, come in.' Jazz appears before I knock, a slightly manic edge to her voice, not that I can hear much over the barking. 'Why didn't you go around the side? George, it's Indie, what did Mummy say about loud barking… He's just excited that you're here. Sorry, the place is a mess. I'm trying to pack, and you know what an epic process that is for me.'

I know all about Jazz's packing, which is like a grand scale military operation. Every item of clothing is considered and categorised into what she calls "possible trip moments". Then she begins the culling process, which literally takes days. It's bigger than preparing for any theatre production I've been in, and certainly different to my "throw-in-the-case" approach to packing. But then, I don't have a wardrobe like Jazz. Right now, I can hardly see the floor for clothes.

'Come through, Stu's cooking. Some sort of chicken, not sure exactly what.'

'Something extraordinary, I think you'll find,' comes a familiar voice from the kitchen.

'Bet it will be.' I walk through to where Stu is stirring a pot on the stove, dressed in a hot pink, frilly apron.

If there's one thing for certain, you always eat well with Jazz and Stu. They're both foodies. Although I do tire of their lengthy discussions over which bakery in Petersham makes the best Portuguese tart, or the subtle nuances between varying types of pecorino cheese.

'Hi there, stranger.' Stu puts down his spoon, comes around their impressive island bench, and wraps me in a big hug. 'So good to see you.'

Spending time with Jazz and Stu is like someone taking a heavy pile of books out of my arms and offering me a comfy seat. We've known each other so long, there's no pretending. No one in LA makes me feel like that.

More importantly, Jazz and Stu are deliriously happy together. Jazz once said to me that she couldn't imagine being with anyone other than Stu – that he filled in her blanks. Maybe living in their house will have some transformational effect and enable me to live happily ever after.

Stu releases me, glides to the fridge and retrieves a bottle of wine in one smooth move. But before I can even say, *Yes, please,* I'm confronted by what must be the biggest dog I've ever seen. Much bigger than I remember. Was he always that rich caramel colour? I thought he was white.

'Now, George, remember, no jumping,' says Jazz.

Unfortunately, George doesn't remember. Instead, he leaps wildly into mid-air. Two giant (muddy) paws hurtle towards me, like some sort of land octopus from a 60s horror film, and I let out a scream. I just can't help it.

'Indie, he's just happy to see you.' Jazz laughs and pats George affectionately as I look down to see two dirty paw prints on my one and only decent top.

I look at George, his dark eyes staring up out of a mass of caramel curls and I swear he's laughing at me. Like he senses I'm the new babysitter and he's trying to show who's boss.

'How does one look after a dog anyway?' I ask, trying to outstare George.

The kitchen plummets into silence. Jazz and Stu look at me like I've announced my plans to embark on a solo mission to the moon. Whoops, I thought I said that in my head.

'I was under the impression you had some "experience". You said it'd be "no problem!"' Jazz over-gesticulates the air quotes while putting a protective arm around her mini horse. 'God knows what you'll do to George.'

'Probably let him play in the dirt, chase birds, eat out of a dog bowl, sleep in the laundry…' I pause because Jazz is looking at me, horrified, while Stu is about to crush the glass of wine he's poured me. Clearly, that's not how one takes care of a dog.

'Guys, I'm joking!' I prise the wine from Stu's iron-like grip. 'I know what I'm doing, don't worry… let's go into the garden.'

Maybe a space change will distract my friends from how little I know about dogs. I'm not even into dogs. Jazz knows (and seems to have forgotten) I never had pets growing up and have never been settled anywhere long enough to invest time into one. Jazz and Stu only acquired George a year ago, so I haven't spent much time with him. We took him for a walk when I came back over last Christmas, but I didn't do much, except chat to Jazz. And he certainly wasn't the size of one of Santa's reindeers back then. I was so keen to come home, I didn't really think about the whole "looking after George" part of the deal. Maybe there's more to it than putting out a bit of canned food and occasionally going on a walk.

As we take our drinks outside, Jazz stops in front of what looks like a child's painting in an antique gilt frame and sighs.

'Don't you just love it? A friend of mine is an artist and asked if she could paint George. I really think she captured his inner soul.'

'Mmmmm.' I nod, despite the fact it looks nothing like a dog, let alone George. Maybe you need to be a dog owner to appreciate pet art.

Out in the garden, we settle into a 70s style cane sofa. Despite her obsession with George, it's lovely to see Jazz. Although we regularly chat with a glass of wine over Zoom, it's never as good as in the flesh.

'So, where are you going again?' I ask. 'You mentioned France?'

'Yes, also Belgium for a spot of antique buying, then off to Spain. Stu's got some time between projects, and we haven't had a proper holiday together for ages.'

Jazz and Stu have exciting jobs, no kids, and a cool little cottage in Bondi with a modest mortgage. They tackled everything early in life. Marriage, career, financial stability. But that's Jazz – on top of everything with super speed. I'm surprised she hasn't yet organised a baby or two to complete the picture.

She met Stu in Orientation Week at uni. I told her not to fall in love with her first university boyfriend, but she did. And they were perfect for each other. It was ridiculous. They got married in their mid-twenties, bought into the mental Bondi property market, and are now living life to the fullest.

Jazz was always creative, even at school, but didn't know what to do with her skills. Until she put her love of home interiors (and her marketing degree) into a blog, acquired a massive following and, in no time, established a fabulous online interiors business called Jazz Hands. One of the perks is going on trips overseas to source new pieces and see what's happening. She's always off to

New York or the South of France but never for as long as three months.

'Great, but I'll miss you,' I say.

'Of course you will, but you'll be so busy once you get an amazing film role here in Sydney and become even more of a star than you already are.'

'Don't know about that. I just missed an amazing role in LA. It was my big Hollywood break and it passed me by.'

'Something else will come up. It always does with you.'

'Not lately. Besides, I'm just taking time to chill out, earn some cash, and get back to LA.'

'How's your mum?' Jazz moves on, something she does with constant regularity. Sometimes it's hard to keep up. In fact, if "changing the subject in the fastest time possible" was a career, Jazz would be a CEO by now.

'Good. Same. Except with purple hair. "Wisteria" she calls it.'

'God, I love Pam. I haven't seen her for ages.'

Jazz and Mum are quite close, even meeting for coffee when I'm not around. Jazz's parents divorced during high school, so she'd often hang at our place on weekends and come away with us on holidays. We became her adopted family.

Jazz grins. 'Have you told her you're running away from Pymble to stay here?'

'Not yet.'

'Coward.'

George wanders over and sprawls near our feet, chin resting on his paws. I admire Jazz's pretty garden and the tension in my shoulders falls away like water. I feel more relaxed than I have in a month. I'm going to enjoy dog-sitting if this is what it's like. I haven't even started and already I feel like a new woman.

'So, Indie, there's one tiny hitch with the house.'

My newly relaxed shoulders clench and my mood starts to wane. I know from Jazz's overly casual tone that "the hitch" will be anything but "tiny".

'Stu promised the house to Jem without telling me. Maybe you two can share? It'll be great. What do you think?' Jazz practically vomits out the words because she knows the answers to both those questions. I don't want to live with anyone. And, if I did, the last person on my list would be Jeremy Taylor.

'Are you sure that wasn't the plan all along and you just neglected to tell me until the final moment in case I decided not to come back?'

'Of course not!' Jazz says, mildly outraged by the accusation. 'I had no idea when I asked you. Honestly, I could kill Stu. Sometimes I wonder how we even function as a couple. Not through effective communication obviously… It's not going to be a problem, is it?'

'I can always stay with Mum and Dad and train it to auditions. It's not like I'll be going out much, and you know Mum, she'd love it.'

'But you might get a theatre gig or a night shoot. It's hard to get back to Pymble late at night. And you're not attracted to Jem, so no issues there. Purely a housemate situation. Although, I've always wondered if anything happened between you two at our wedding?'

'Of course not.' Goosebumps prickle my skin, despite the afternoon's warmth.

'Are you sure?' Jazz is clearly enjoying teasing me.

'Absolutely! Are you kidding? So not my type. We'd end up killing each other. In fact, we nearly did.'

I close my mouth so nothing more comes out. If Jazz had any suspicions, by now there'd be little doubt left. Especially as my cheeks heat up like the inside of a car in the height of summer.

'Okay, settle down.' Jazz has a cheeky twinkle in her eye. 'The lady doth protest too much methinks.'

'Maybe leave the Shakespeare to me!' I laugh, desperately trying to grasp control of my senses, which feel like they've been tossed into a head wind.

Jem was the best man and I was chief bridesmaid. We didn't really know each other before the rehearsal dinner and, apart from being single, we had little in common. He hardly spoke to me, except to refute whatever I said or make casual snaky comments about the frivolous lives actors lead. I don't think I've ever met anyone more arrogant. And, in my industry, you can imagine some of the super egos that come along.

The other bridesmaids were totally into him. In fact, every single guest at the wedding, male and female, even a puppy someone brought, were either fawning over him or giggling whenever he came near. It was pathetic. It's not like he's incredibly good-looking. Average, really.

Well, maybe slightly above average.

Okay, he's quite good-looking if you're into guys with honey brown hair, chocolate-coloured eyes, and a lean, yet surprisingly firm, body.

Oh, look, he's hot. Totally hot. Can't deny it. The mere sight of him sent tingles from the tip of my salon hairdo down to my satin kitten heels. I'm used to meeting outrageously handsome and charismatic guys in the acting world and have developed a protective force field to keep them at bay, but if Jem so much as looked my way, my insides melted like grilled cheese.

'This has worked out well,' Jazz chatters on. 'Better to share the George duties. Especially bath days. Which happen once every two or three weeks, unless he gets extra dirty, then we do it more often, of course. There's a very specific way to wash him. Even Stu doesn't do it quite right. Getting the conditioner out of George's fur can be tricky and sometimes he doesn't like getting blow dried.'

'You do realise that George is a dog?' I say firmly. 'And there are people you can pay to do that?'

Jazz ignores my comment. 'Plus, there's the grocery shopping; much cheaper having a housemate. And you never know where it might lead…'

'Jazz, I guarantee, it will lead nowhere.'

'I don't understand, he's such a great guy. And so handsome. There's always a string of girls following close behind him.'

'Which is probably why I don't like him.'

'What about that Liam Hemsworth look-a-like you left in LA?'

Jazz makes a fair point, but I'm not going to admit it. 'What does Jem think about living with me?'

'He's fine with it. He's broke, so I'm sure he'll appreciate sharing grocery bills. Not sure if he's single. We thought he'd found the love of his life, but the other day, Stu said, "I think it's over". No explanation! Honestly, men are hopeless with the finer details.'

'What's he doing for work?'

'He opened a bar with a friend but I don't think it lasted long.' Jazz pauses to think. 'Not sure why. He's been doing a few extra jobs. I think he's labouring for someone. Either that or he's been living at the gym, he's looking incredibly fit. Stu said he might be studying, God knows what, my husband doesn't tell me anything much these days. Anyway, you'll hardly see him. You'll be like two beautiful ships in the night. Perfect situation really.'

Ever the optimist, Jazz can see the bright side of anything. Once we went camping and it poured for three days straight, we got a flat tyre, the tent almost blew away – and Jazz said it was the 'best camping trip ever'.

I take a swig of my wine. This situation isn't at all perfect, but at least I'll have a day or so to mull it over before seeing Jem in the flesh.

'Anyway, you can discuss the finer details when he gets here,' Jazz says breezily.

'What?' I respond with a spray of pinot grigio.

'He's coming for lunch too, just running five minutes late.'

My insides knot like silver necklaces left loose in a jewellery box. Maybe I could make an excuse and leave. Quick, what's a possible ailment I could have legitimately developed in the last five minutes?

The side gate clicks and a tall figure appears in the garden, every bit as hot as the night of Jazz and Stu's wedding. Just when I thought I'd had enough of good-looking egotistical men, another one steps into the spotlight.

2

I STAND there, frozen, like I'm trapped on the side of a mountain. George, on the other hand, couldn't have been more delighted, bouncing around like an excited toddler in a fine bone china shop.

'Hello, my favourite boy!' Jem handles George with true dog-owner confidence and, annoyingly, the enormous dog laps up his every word. Not that I care if George likes him more than he likes me. It's not a competition.

Except, it sort of is, and I want to win.

'Hi, handsome.' Jazz gives Jem a kiss and he hands her a bottle of wine and some chocolates. Thoughtful. I didn't have time to get anything. 'Did you lock the side gate?'

'Of course. George is safe.'

'Hi, mate,' Stu calls from the kitchen. 'How you going?'

'Not bad, nice look,' Jem shoots back, spying Stu's apron.

'Hey, Indie's here too. Back from LA.' Jazz smiles a not-so-innocent smile. 'When was the last time you saw each other? Maybe the wedding?'

Our paths have crossed occasionally since that day five years ago, the odd party or birthday drinks, but we always avoided each other as much as humanly possible. In fact, I don't think we've said more than about three words to each other since the wedding. I thought I'd forgotten that night but now, one mention sends me into a panic. I turn to Jem and swear a similar expression flutters across his face. Then, nothing.

19

I step forward. 'Hi, it's been a while.' I'm about to offer my hand for a shake but lose confidence and end up doing a weird sort of wave. I think he's got even more good-looking since the wedding. Dressed in torn jeans and a soft grey t-shirt, he looks like he's off to shoot a men's fragrance commercial, not attend a casual lunch with someone he truly detests.

The thing I've never told anyone, Jazz included, is not only did we bicker incessantly at the wedding, but we also shared an incredible kiss. A kiss that would definitely have led to more had we not been disturbed by one of the drunken groomsmen, who needed help putting wedding presents into someone's car. The moment was stolen and, unfortunately, only added to our awkwardness at the picnic brunch the next day. I tried to act cool (with little success), but Jem ignored me completely. Which was probably a good thing because whenever he was near, all I could think about was that kiss, and the waves of sizzling heat it propelled through every part of my body. At one stage, it got so bad, I tripped on a bag of ice and nearly knocked over Stu's mother. I thought I'd filed the whole incident into the "what was I thinking?" folder of my brain, never to be talked of again. But now, that snippet-like memory has resurfaced like a precious jewel washed ashore.

Surely by now, I'm immune to whatever physical power he had over me that night. And sharing a house and everyday domesticity will be very different. Not quite as sexy as a beautiful wedding, with that kiss and its pesky tingles, our bodies pressed together, his hands creeping down my back, me wishing they would move a little faster—

'Watch out!' he grunts, looking at the ground. 'Too late.'

'Sorry?' I glance down and see I've trodden in a huge mound of steaming dog poo.

'Bad luck.' Jem's voice is completely deadpan, but there's a sparkle in his eye.

Jazz looks over. 'Sorry about that. I told Stu to check the garden. Just hose it off over there.'

Jazz returns inside as I wiggle my foot out of my shoe. Disgusting. Maybe I'm not cut out for dog-sitting after all.

'Here, give it to me,' says Jem.

'No, no, it's fine.' I hold my poo shoe like it's the last hope for living, horrified at the idea of Jem coming anywhere near it.

But I have little choice as he takes the revolting item out of my hand, turns on the garden hose, washes it clean, and leaves it in the sun to dry.

'Thanks.' Heat floods my cheeks. I take the other shoe off to even it up and am now in bare feet. Great start.

'No worries.' Jem turns and heads to the laundry, hopefully to wash his hands.

Utterly mortified, I wish a time machine would magically appear. Yes, that would be perfect. Or some sort of portal providing a quick escape to another dimension. Something that might happen in Marvel films but not in real life. Not that characters in Marvel movies generally stand in dog poo and embarrass themselves in front of someone they kissed once and barely spoke to again. Maybe in a bad comedy. Is that what my life has become?

I take a few moments to gather my thoughts, arriving in the kitchen in time to hear Jazz discussing the house situation.

'Yeah, sorry about the mix-up.'

Jem looks confused. 'What do you mean?'

'About the house.'

'What about it?'

Jazz whips around to Stu who looks like he forgot to turn the iron off before leaving home. 'You didn't tell him, did you?'

'Sorry, must have forgotten. God, I'm an idiot.'

'You really are, Stu. I should've done it. I knew you'd forget.'

'It's not like you don't forget things. What about the basil last week – that was pretty important considering we were having pesto. Honestly!'

Jem and I stand awkwardly while Jazz and Stu dissect the whole misunderstanding. Just as it tumbles into a fiery discussion about Stu's inability to carry out the simplest of errands and what this means on a deeper level, Jem gently coughs to grab their attention.

'Sorry, guys.' Jazz turns back to us, words somersaulting out of her mouth. 'So, Jem, I offered the house to Indie, but Stu, like the complete moron that he is, offered it to you without talking to me first. He was supposed to tell you before today. Obviously, he hasn't. But you're both welcome to stay. In fact, I reckon it's better to share the house-sitting – well, the dog-sitting anyway.'

Jem looks like he just got up on Christmas morning to find an empty stocking. A mixture of shock, anger, and extreme disappointment. At least I know how he really feels about the situation.

'Why don't I find somewhere else?' Jem says, without looking at me.

'No, mate, where would you go?' Stu looks concerned.

'I'll stay at Mick's place. It's no problem.'

'You can't stay on Mick's couch any longer.'

'I can stay with my parents,' I pipe up, wishing I was anywhere but in Jazz and Stu's kitchen with a guy who dislikes me so intensely he's prepared to sleep indefinitely on some mate's sofa.

'You'll both stay here.' Jazz's tone indicates the matter is closed. 'It's a big job looking after George and neither of you is very experienced, no offence. And not to put too much pressure on you, but if anything happens to George, you'll be cut out of our lives forever. It's better to share that responsibility. Just saying.'

'It does make sense,' Stu adds.

Jem looks as happy as a rain cloud, but maybe that's his natural resting face. Sullen and moody. Unfortunately, a little bit sexy.

'I guess it'll be fine. I'm working crazy hours, labouring all day and working in a bar at night, so I'll hardly be here. It'll be good for George to have someone who's home all the time.' Jem looks at me properly for the first time since he arrived. 'You don't really work, do you? Regularly, I mean.'

And suddenly I'm back at the wedding, trying to explain that actors work very hard, but there are often periods of unemployment (most of the time), which can be stressful. It's not brain surgery, but it's what I do. He knows nothing about it and is in no position to put me down. And I've been one of the lucky ones to work nonstop. At the wedding, this discussion led to a stand-up argument between entrée and mains, and then a passionate kiss an hour later, but that won't be happening again.

'I'll be looking for work while I'm here.'

'But nothing as yet?' His voice is tinged with sarcasm.

'Not yet.'

'Indie just missed out on a huge TV role in LA but she'll be working soon – she's only been in the country for a few days.' Jazz jumps to my defence. 'Anyway, let's eat. How's that delicious smelling lunch going, Stu?'

'Very well indeed, I think you'll find I've outdone myself once again.'

Jem musters a faint smile. 'We'll be the judge of that, mate.'

'Yes, and I'm sure you'll let me know.' Stu laughs and turns to Jazz. 'Why don't you get Jem a drink and top up Indie's, then go outside? It's al fresco dining today.'

I say nothing, still smarting from the dig about my lack of work.

How dare he say that? Before I went to LA, I had back-to-back jobs in Sydney. And after, I came close to the break of my life. Who's he to judge anyway? It's not like he's such a huge success himself.

Jazz herds us out to the back terrace, where the outdoor table is set for lunch. If Jem's feeling uncomfortable, you wouldn't know. He keeps the conversation flowing smoothly, although he barely acknowledges me when I speak. He compliments Stu on the roasted cauliflower and quinoa salad, and chicken and chorizo hotpot, and shows interest in Jazz's latest venture sourcing vintage doors as decorative garden pieces. He offers to clear away and pays close attention to the many instructions for looking after George. He doesn't even flinch when Jazz says we should brush George three times a day and be careful to limit his screen time. He's the perfect gentleman. Even George is all over him like his life depends on it. Still, I know the truth. It's all a front to get people onside. In reality, he's a rude and arrogant arsehole.

'Shall we do a bathing demonstration?' Jazz asks. 'It's a tricky process to get George completely clean.'

'I'm sure I can work it out,' Jem says smoothly.

'Me too,' I add, determined not to be outdone.

Jazz doesn't look at all sure.

'They'll be okay,' Stu says gently. 'Jem helped me bathe George the other day.'

'True,' Jazz says reluctantly. 'It's just that if he doesn't get brushed and washed, his fur will matt. You also need to bathe his eyes and—'

'Calm down, honey.' Stu puts an arm around her, which she quickly brushes away, a simple action that leaves the air slightly strained.

'I'm calm.' Her voice is anything but calm. 'Just please

remember, he only eats poached chicken for dinner, no other food. He has a very sensitive stomach.'

'Shall we pop the kettle on?' I ask, thinking we could do with a soothing cuppa.

'Sure.' Jazz eyeballs the boys. 'Tea?'

They shake their heads, scared by Jazz's demeanour. We go to the kitchen but before I can ask what just happened between her and Stu, Jazz marches on once again, this time to an even less heartening subject.

'What happened with Mark? You've been so cagey.'

I take a deep breath. 'It's over.'

'Oh, Indie, I'm sorry.' Jazz fills up the kettle with water. 'But not surprised.'

'What?'

'I was never sure about him.'

'You never met him.'

'I've seen pictures. Too good-looking.'

'Nothing wrong with good-looking. Besides I only really meet actors and they're all good-looking. Goes with the territory.'

'There's your problem.'

Jazz thinks actors only ever lead to trouble. 'Self-absorbed commitment-phobe narcissists' is the way she usually describes them and, I admit, she's been right on many occasions. But Mark was different. Or so I thought.

We were cast as leads in a pilot. My first big job in LA. It was an interesting script, great group of actors, attractive and talented leading man. My Hollywood career was finally taking off, and I was beyond euphoric. We shot the pilot and, naturally, I fell for the good-looking, talented leading man and bizarrely enough, he fell for me.

The pilot never got picked up, which happens all the time, but

I still felt like I'd found Willy Wonka's last golden ticket. Apart from being handsome, Mark was smart and successful. Did I mention he was handsome? He ticked all my boxes and I seemed to tick his. We moved in together after a few months, which, as my mother said, was typical. I've always been an all or nothing kind of girl. No half measures. Besides, I'd never felt like that about anyone before and it was intoxicating. I wanted to be around him as much as possible, which is why I said, 'Yes please,' before he'd even finished proposing.

All was perfect until he was cast in a film, shooting in Canada. He was away for three months but came home for the occasional weekend. Well, he started by coming back on weekends but soon he was either "too tired" or had "lines to learn". Totally legitimate excuses. Besides, we were "fiancéd". He should be able to go away for work without me being suspicious. I expected him to trust *me*, so I never questioned any of it.

Except I didn't consider his leading lady. Kourtney Layne. Stunning, with an incredible body, and apparently a real sweetheart who sends a percentage of her earnings to some orphanage in Uganda and protests against climate change. 'Kourtney with a K', as she always says in interviews. Yes, I should have clocked her. But as I say, we were "fiancéd" so I didn't think I had to.

'Are you going to fill me in on what happened?' Jazz is waiting impatiently. 'I need details.'

Previously, I was so embarrassed, I couldn't bring myself to tell anyone. Now, safely on the other side of the world, it feels good to unload.

'Months after he'd finished shooting that film, we were at some fancy party and I was chatting to another actress—'

'Who? Was she famous?'

'No, and please don't interrupt.' Jazz is always asking about celebrities, hoping I might pass on her business card. 'Anyway, this not-famous actress was saying that Kourtney broke up with her boyfriend because she'd had an affair on the set of a film.'

'Oh, God! Mark?'

'I didn't think about it until half an hour later. I was by the pool and just froze. Luckily, there were so many ice statues at the party, no one noticed. But suddenly it all made sense. Mark was different after the shoot, edgy and unsettled. I thought he was simply coming down after an incredible acting experience.'

'A bit too incredible by the sounds of it!'

'Exactly. Early on, he'd told me how amazing it was working with Kourtney. His eyes shone, and I thought what a passionate actor he was.' I pause. 'Just a little more passionate than I realised. And not about the acting!'

'Did you confront him?'

'Straight away.'

'Did he deny it?'

'Of course, but do you know what?'

'What?'

'Just before he denied it, he hesitated.'

'No!'

'Yes!'

'So guilty.'

'I know!'

'Then what happened?'

'We got home and had the biggest, and only, argument we've ever had. He was furious I'd even accused him of such a thing.'

'Maybe he hesitated because he had something caught in his throat?'

'Maybe, but something didn't feel right, so that night, I googled Kourtney.'

'Indie.' Jazz looks at me sternly. 'I've told you not to "google stalk" people, it only leads to disaster.'

I ignore her. 'A photo came up of her and Mark out one night looking pretty cosy in some bar.'

'They might've been having a drink as colleagues.'

'I also found an online interview of Kourtney, around the time the film was shooting, and she was going on about her "leading man", saying how close and "in-tune" they were and how that helped with her role.' I breathe in and release the air heavily. 'Jazz, I'm not an idiot.'

'So what if she plays it up to some journo? It sounds like she might've been the troublemaker, not Mark.' Jazz slowly sips her drink as if savouring the flavour on her palate. 'Not wanting to interfere—'

'But you're going to anyway.'

'Do you think running away was a good idea?' she asks carefully. 'I don't really like the guy, but maybe he was telling the truth?'

'He wasn't,' I say flatly. 'I know for sure. A couple of days later, she sent him a text. Three of them, in fact.'

'Really?' Jazz sits upright, almost spilling her wine. 'Were they sexy?'

'No, but they were intimate. Far worse.'

'That bastard.'

'I also found out that the TV job I nearly got went to, wait for it… Kourtney with a K. It's like someone waved a magic wand and poof, she got my life.'

'That's bad luck.' Jazz pauses. 'I don't even know who she is, but I already hate her and I won't ever watch that show.'

I smile ruefully. 'I'd like to say it'll be terrible, but the script was awesome.'

'Does he know you've come back to Australia?' Jazz asks.

'I sent him a message to say it was over and I was going home for three months.

'What? You didn't tell him in person?'

'I didn't want to see him. I was so angry.'

'Look, he made a mistake, but maybe you should see what he has to say. Try to work things out.'

I look at Jazz as if she suddenly grew a third ear.

'You're engaged, remember?' she continues. 'And that means talking to each other and working through stuff. Marriage isn't like what you see in the movies or those scripts you're always reading. If you run away the minute things get difficult, you're not going to get very far.'

Jazz is right. But I'm surprised to hear her speaking so vehemently on the subject. She and Stu make marriage look like a Sunday sail on Sydney Harbour. Maybe it gets a bit rocky after all.

'Hate to say it, but what you need is to meet a non-actor.' Jazz flips back to our usual bone of contention. 'Someone sensible. Reliable. Honest. Not quite so good-looking. Someone who'll give you the love and attention you deserve rather than being totally focused on themselves.'

'But I only meet actors, and it's such a transient life. It would never work if I went out with a nice, stable accountant. They wouldn't get it.'

'I'm not saying you should go out with an accountant. Although our accountant is hilarious, you'd love him. Stable, but not at all boring. He does stand-up at night. Pretty good at it too, *and* he's recently divorced… for the second time… but that's only because—'

I throw up my hands in exasperation. 'I don't want to date a divorced accountant. I actually don't want to date anyone.'

'Why don't you have a coffee with him and…' Jazz stops as Stu and Jem walk into the kitchen with a few plates. 'Thanks guys, about time you did something.'

'I cooked lunch,' Stu says. 'Jem's the one who needs to do some work.'

'I'll clean up,' I say, wanting to contribute to the afternoon.

'You both can.' Jazz smiles. 'We need to check we've discussed everything George-wise.'

She vanishes like a magician doing the final trick of a show, with Stu, her assistant, following close behind. I half expect to see a puff of smoke and glitter. Probably giving us "space" to "get to know each other better". Should be fun.

Jem stacks the dishwasher without a word.

I fill up the sink and put on the washing up gloves. 'I'll wash the big things.'

'Sure.' He heads back outside to gather the serving plates and salad bowl.

Well, this isn't awkward at all! Why on earth did I kiss him at the wedding? I must have had one too many glasses of bubbly.

With my hands deep in a sink of sudsy water, I can't find the sponge. Thinking it must be on the bench, I twirl around just as Jem comes back with the platters and we almost collide. My heart staggers as if blindfolded, spun around, and told to walk in a straight line. But Jem doesn't move. He stands there, our eyes connecting for what feels like an hour-long millisecond. He mutters something but I miss it, thanks to his handsome features quickening my pulse.

'What?' My voice comes out in a whisper.

'The tea towel.' He looks down at my un-shoed feet. 'You're standing on it.'

'Oh, sorry.' I bend down to grab the tea towel and give it to him, my fingers briefly brushing past his in the process, causing my stomach to cartwheel.

I turn back to the sink as quickly as possible. He gets on with drying and the silence is as comfortable as when you finish an audition and have to make the epic journey to the exit.

'Do you know where this goes?' he asks gruffly.

I point to an old French wooden dresser in the dining area. 'From memory, the right-hand side drawer. Although, who knows with Jazz. She likes to change things around when she's stressed, which is most of the time.'

He barely reacts to my friendly dig at our mutual friend. Perhaps a slight twitch in the corner of his mouth? Other than that, his face remains deadpan.

It's going to be a long three months.

3

I LEAVE Jazz and Stu's as fast as possible. I think Stu made chocolate torte for dessert but I ate so quickly it may as well have been bread and jam. Jazz wanted me to take George for a walk so she could check I "knew what I was doing", but I explained that Mum and Dad were expecting me back. I'm pretty sure I can walk a dog. And I had to get away from Jem.

I stare out the train window as the inner-city buzz melts into the leafy streets of Sydney's upper north shore. Usually, the sight of its expansive homes and immaculately landscaped gardens depresses me, but this afternoon it feels peaceful. Walking home from the station I hear the gentle chirp of birds, and the sight of my family home makes me want to happy cry. Very unlike me, but going over the whole Mark debacle with Jazz has left me feeling brittle.

'So, what do you think?'

Mum and I are in the laundry, sorting out my clothes, which are so dirty I'm surprised they haven't jumped straight into the washing machine themselves.

'I think you need a new suitcase. This one's in tatters.'

'Mum!'

'Oh, I suppose it makes sense. But I was hoping we could spend more time together. Do our morning walk, have chats over cups of tea.'

'I'm only going to Bondi, Mum. I'll still see you. I'm sure I'll come over for dinner, even stay over.'

'I know, but it's not the same.'

'Would you rather I not go?'

'Don't be silly, sweetie.' Mum puts on her brave face. 'I want you to go, have some fun. Dad thinks it's a great idea. Take your mind off things for a while. And you're right, it'll be much easier for auditions. If you still want to do that sort of thing.'

Mum pulls me into a hug. I know it's hard for her. She loves me but has always struggled with my career choice, never missing an opportunity to suggest other options. Forget that I was accepted into the National Institute of Dramatic Art (NIDA), secured an amazing agent after graduation, and have barely stopped working. It just never seems real to Mum, even when she's there on opening night, proud as punch. For her, the industry is fraught with poverty, depression, and a fair amount of self-absorption. Which is true to a certain extent. And, like Jazz, she thinks acting encourages big egos. Also true. Still, there are just as many egos in other professions. But when I explain this, Mum comes back with the fact that they earn regular money and help people with open heart surgery, things like that. This is when we launch into a heated discussion on the importance of entertainment and storytelling in society (me), and how I need to consider a real job (Mum).

To be fair, Mum has been right by my side, supporting me through the industry's many ups, downs, and heartbreaks. She hates to see me rejected by anyone and, when you're an actor, that's about 99.99% of the time. Not including your personal life. I can appreciate her concerns.

'I could get out of it. A friend of Stu's is staying too, so there'll be someone else to look after George.'

'No, darling, I think you should move in,' Mum insists. 'Just pop over now and again.'

'Definitely. But I'm not going until next week, so we've got heaps of time to walk, chat, and do yoga.'

'Yes.' Mum brightens up immediately. 'That's exactly what you need to get back on track. You look like you could do with a good yoga session.'

Mum lives by yoga. It's her answer to anything. Like a "good night's sleep" or a "glass of water". I remember being about fifteen and totally devastated because some guy I'd kissed at a party never called and then told his friend to tell my friend that he didn't want to go out with me. Mum forced me into yoga poses morning, noon, and night. Don't know if it helped, but it stuck and, like Mum, I now find comfort in yoga. Which has served me well in my choice of career. If there's one thing you need, it's comfort – and luckily in LA, the one thing you can find without too much trouble is a yoga class.

'Who's the other person moving in?'

'Stu's best friend, Jeremy Taylor. Best man at their wedding. Do you remember?'

'Oh, yes, lovely boy, and very good-looking. I thought you two looked charming walking down the aisle—'

'Okay, that'll do.' Mum remembers Jem alright. 'He's not for me, and the feeling's mutual. We did nothing but fight most of the evening.'

Mum smiles into her cup of tea, like she has a special secret. I know what she's thinking, but I let it go because there's no point trying to convince her otherwise.

'Where's Dad today? Working?'

My dad is a dentist who runs a local practice two suburbs away and I have to say, he's a bit of a celebrity in the area. He's particularly known for his unique method of teeth brushing and claims to have single-handedly raised a community of excellent brushers. Personally, I can't imagine looking inside people's mouths all day, but Dad finds it fascinating and relishes the opportunity to discuss the details of what he sees with his patients.

'Do you know the best thing about being a dentist, Indie?' he'd say to me. 'I can talk to my patients and they can't talk back, unlike you and Mum who don't let me get a word in.' At which point, Mum and I would tell him to be quiet and stop going on with a lot of rubbish.

But I guess our professions are similar, presenting to a captive audience. Although, I think his audience pays a little more for his services than mine do for mine. And with greater regularity.

'No, he had a doctor's appointment this morning,' Mum jolts me from my obscure musings on the similarities of acting and dentistry. 'Now I think he's in the study, watching TV.'

'Is he okay?' Oh my God, the fib I told Benji!

'Oh, yes,' Mum says dismissively as she pours the tea. 'Just a check-up. He's been put on a special weight-loss diet and I think the doctor wants to make sure he's sticking to it. Which he's not.'

I pop my head into the study but stop at the door. The television is on, but Dad is asleep in an armchair. He often snoozes in front of the telly, but not usually in the afternoon. And the look of him snoring with a rug over his legs twinges my heart. He looks frail, despite his large frame, like he shrank while I was away. I feel a pinch of emotion at the back of my eyes.

A memory of the two of us playing in the garden pops up in my head like an old movie reel. I must have been about three and he was holding my hands and spinning me around and around, like I weighed nothing. I remember laughing so much I wet my pants. Mum was furious. It was a day like so many, but that particular time,

I remember thinking I could do this forever. Not the wetting-my-pants bit, of course, that was embarrassing. But playing with my dad in the garden. Spinning around, carefree and young. I had everything I could possibly want. One of life's moments of perfection. They don't come up often but when they do you have to hold on tight, the way I clung to Dad's hands.

I go back to the kitchen where Mum has made tea. She hands me a cup and offers me a plate of dry-looking, misshapen biscuits.

'Try one, it's a new muesli slice recipe I made up, no processed sugar, no dairy, no gluten, and absolutely delicious. Exactly what your father should be eating.'

I decline as Mum bites firmly into one. I'm surprised she doesn't crack a tooth.

After at least a full minute of chewing, she asks, 'So, why didn't your fiancé come over with you?'

My heart backflips like a piece of popping corn. That word. Fiancé. My breath shortens at the sound of it. I was so excited to have a fiancé. Now it feels like a hole in the pit of my stomach.

I was never interested in marriage, always more focused on my career, but Mark changed all that. He made it feel like it was the greatest invention of all time and just like that, I was hooked on the idea.

Before I left for LA, I did a short stint on a soap opera and my character was getting married. Secretly, I loved it. Not that I'd have admitted it to anyone on set. The dress, the hair, the excitement. I barely had to act. Except my on-screen fiancé changed his mind at the last minute and eloped with the local librarian. I remember thinking how awful to be dumped at the altar. Who does that to someone? Now I know exactly who does that. Not that I was left waiting at the church. At least I found out before we arrived anywhere near the big day, but I now have a greater understanding of what my character went through. If I were to play that role today, my performance would be award-winning. Now I have to play it for real, not get paid, nor receive any award.

'Oh, he's busy, really busy, couldn't get away in the middle of a shoot, he's going to try to come over, see how it goes.' I cover my empty ring finger.

Mum's eyes widen slightly, just enough to indicate that she hasn't bought my diarrhoea-like bout of excuses. Nor my weirdly happy-sounding voice, which sounds foreign, even to me.

'Well, that means Dad and I get you all to ourselves.'

'Right,' I say, swamped with guilt that I'm about to move out.

'I don't know why you couldn't meet someone here in Australia.' Mum sighs. 'When will I see you? And what about my grandchildren? When will I spend any quality time with them? I'll be that distant grandma who sends presents at Christmas and birthdays that are completely wrong. They'll prefer their other grandma – or grandmom, I should say.'

'Mum! Can you stop? Who knows if I'm even going to have children, and we might live in Australia. Mark loves the idea.' Or at least he once said he did.

'You might meet someone while you're home who sweeps you off your feet.'

'Mum! I'm engaged, remember?' Not technically, but at least it will stop Mum from saying things like that.

'Yes, of course.' Mum puts on her annoying tarot reading voice, something she does when she has a "feeling" about what's going to happen. 'But life can change in a second.'

I can't argue with that. Mine certainly did. In less than a month, my life went from practically perfect to a total mess. My insides feel like a blow-up paddling pool with a slow leak. Soft, hopeless, and not much fun anymore.

Thinking back, the affair was obvious. I just didn't see it. Or chose not to. It's always hard to settle down after a job. Working every day is an elusive dream for an actor. Normally, your life feels like a half-finished jigsaw puzzle with the last few pieces eternally lost. You might chance upon one crucial piece precisely when another goes missing. When all the bits come together and you finally get a job, it's like standing on top of Mount Everest. Just for a moment. Then the puzzle is broken up and put back in its box, with no certainty of it ever coming together again. However, it wasn't the thrill of the job that Mark was missing. It was the lovely Kourtney Layne.

Working intimately with people for short, intense periods of time is part of the job and clearly Mark and I don't have the sort of relationship to withstand it. Jazz wouldn't understand. She and Stu trust each other implicitly, but they don't do sex scenes with colleagues or pretend to be in relationships with them. Lines blur. I mean, look at how Mark and I met.

What I need now is to get lots of work in Sydney and maybe a well-paid television commercial to fund my flight back to LA, where I can continue on my chosen path. I'll take up the dog-sitting offer, and maybe it's a good thing Jem will be around to help with George. It's a big responsibility and Jazz and Stu will be able to rest a little easier as they sip their *vin rouge* in Provence.

I'll spend my time running along Bondi Beach until I look like one of those people that perpetually run along Bondi Beach. Then, when I've sorted myself out and allowed my heart to heal, I'll go back to LA looking so incredibly hot that Mark will regret his philandering faux pas and beg me to come back. Naturally, I'll refuse because I'll be far too busy with my very happening career and preparing for my incredible upcoming film role (and a string of enthusiastic lovers).

That's my plan and – unlike the plan about falling in love and living happily ever after – I'm sticking to it!

4

'THAT went well!' The next day, Jazz calls to gush about the most uncomfortable lunch in the history of all social engagements. I'm up early, striding along one of Pymble's many tree-lined streets to clear my mind and get my life on track before 9am.

'Jazz, why didn't you tell me about Jem? Or tell Jem about me?' I'm still furious at how it all unfolded. 'You know I wanted to live by myself and it's perfectly obvious he'd rather jump off a cliff than share a house with me.'

'Not true. Jem just doesn't know you very well.'

'He was rude and made it quite clear that what I do is a total waste of time.'

'That's just Jem,' says Jazz dismissively. 'Never afraid to voice an opinion, but also totally hilarious. And he doesn't think your work is a waste of time. In fact, he's seen all your plays and has always been complimentary.'

'Really?' I walk straight into an overflowing, green wheelie bin. 'I didn't know that.'

'And he often came over here and watched that police show you were in. I used to think it was a coincidence he'd have dinner at our place every Tuesday night but now I'm not so sure.'

'That doesn't mean he wants to share a house and a dog.'

'He's quite creative under that moody facade. Stu reckons he wanted to be a writer at some point but never pursued it. He's also a keen Scrabble player, and you know how much you love that game. Maybe you have more in common than you think. Anyway, you're both our best friends, so it's about time you got along!'

I know Jazz better than my own body measurements and something tells me she engineered the whole "mix-up" just to get her friends on the one page. And now, I'm stuck. I could dig my feet into the soft lawns of leafy Pymble to prove a point. Or I could stay in a cool house, near the beach, close to bars, cafés, and casting agents. Not really a difficult decision. And maybe I won't even see Jem. We'll be working different hours and I'm sure there's a long line of girls at the ready, happy to tend to his needs.

'Relax, I'm still moving in,' I assure my friend. 'Just don't expect us to be best buddies.'

'Of course not! Wouldn't dream of it.'

Even though I can't see her face, I know Jazz has an evil twinkle in her eye. But she leaves it there and moves onto an even less heartening topic.

'Did you hear Emily's getting married?'

My shoulders slump. 'I did. I'm invited.'

'Me too. We won't be here though.'

'I didn't think I would be either.' I sigh heavily. 'I really don't want to go.'

'You should. You haven't spoken in years.'

'That's not my fault. She's the one who dumped us.'

Emily always hung out with Jazz and me at school. We made a tight threesome until she moved on to bigger and better pastures.

'Remember, we caught up before you went to LA,' Jazz says. 'That was great, like old times.'

'Only because my face had been on the telly, and your interior business was starting to buzz.' I frown. 'Suddenly, we were worth knowing. I didn't buy it for a second.'

'We catch up for a drink every now and again and she always asks after you. I think she wants to make up for lost time.'

In Year Nine, Emily forgot about us and started running with the cool group, all the tall, skinny, blond girls. Who had boyfriends. Jazz and I were none of those things but we had fun regardless. Obviously not enough because Emily switched groups and became someone we no longer recognised. Not physically. Although somehow her already blond hair looked blonder, her legs longer. But her personality changed from this great girl to someone who cared only for how she looked and how much money she had.

'I doubt that very much. Who's she marrying anyway?'

'Some rich banker. They've been together for a while and he finally proposed. They're living in a mansion somewhere in the eastern suburbs and the wedding's going to be huge. You'll go, won't you?'

'Maybe.'

There's no way I'm going. I'd rather stick rusty safety pins in my eyes. Hopefully, I get an acting gig and am unavailable. Or I find an incredible boyfriend as my plus one. Since that's the less likely of the two, I quickly hang up from Jazz and call the other leading lady in my life – my agent, Michelle.

I've been on Michelle's books since graduating from drama school, when we all performed on Agents Day in what's called the Acting Graduate Showcase. All the agents gather to watch the graduating year strut their stuff and see who they'd like to represent. Michelle's not the biggest agent in Sydney but she has a fantastic reputation. I met her that day and immediately knew she was the one for me. I had a few other offers but when hers came through I was over the moon.

I fell into work immediately. I'd been so prepared for a life of poverty, depression, and 99.99% unemployment that my back-to-back jobs came as a surprise. A couple of guest roles on a television series, six months on *Home & Away,* and a lead role in a fantastic ABC detective series called *Time On The Line*. When I wasn't on telly, I was on stage with plays at both Sydney Theatre Company and the Belvoir Street Theatre Company.

I was so scared it would all end when people realised I couldn't actually act and saw me for the fraud I always felt I might be. But miraculously, the work kept coming, so when Hollywood beckoned like a glittering piece of gold, just out of reach, I wasn't interested. Others had jetted off to sit it out in La La Land, trying to get work, but I wanted to stay put. Until finally, the time had come. I was young, single, and had a decent body of work on my show reel. I knew I had to try. When my name miraculously came up in the Green Card Lottery, I had no more excuses. A definite sign. So, with my agent's blessing (and my mum's reluctant one), I packed my bags and headed for Tinsel Town to join the thousands of talented actresses clawing their way to fame and fortune.

And we all know how that worked out. Now, I feel nothing but drained and uninspired, so I tap out the number of the one person who always lifts my spirits.

'Darling! Wondered when you were going to call! How are you?'

Michelle does everything with maximum energy, barely stopping to draw breath. And she always sounds happy to hear from me, even if she's not, which is why she's so good at her job.

'Oh, I'm okay.'

'Shame you missed out on that series. You were so close. And sorry to hear about Mark.'

'My life is a disaster, isn't it?'

'Not at all, just time to get some work here in Sydney.'

'Yes, but remember, I'm not—'

'Staying for long, yeah I know.' Michelle laughs. 'We'll see how that pans out.'

'You wanted me to go to LA in the first place.'

'I did, and still do. You've got every chance of getting work over there, making a name for yourself and earning some real money.' Michelle pauses. 'It's just good to come home every now and again so people remember you. Slow and steady. LA isn't going anywhere.'

As always, Michelle blankets my worries with a few calm words. Truth is, part of me wants to stay in Sydney for good. I may sound serious about hopping on a plane back to LA but deep down, I'm petrified of failing. After just missing out on that huge job, I'm not sure I can go through it again. But I don't want Mark to think he's the reason I never cracked Hollywood. So, for now, I'm planning to buy a one-way ticket, and… and then what? It's so much easier when you have a script. You know exactly where you're heading, what's going to happen along the way, and there's usually a happy ending or at least a sense of hope. I'm starting to doubt whether I'll ever play the main role in my own life. Just bit parts, guest roles in other people's stories.

'You're right, of course,' I say. 'Let's worry about getting work here for now.'

'I'm not going to worry, Indie, because you'll have a job in no time.'

I don't know how Michelle stays positive in this crazy old industry, but she does. And continually supports her actors through its many highs and lows. I remember our first coffee meeting, which lasted two hours. It was like we'd known each other for years. She told me it needs to be that way for her to take on an actor. 'It has to feel like family,' she explained. 'Otherwise, I don't care enough.'

'Is there much happening?' I don't usually ask that question, as it's one that agents dread to hear. If they say no, the actor becomes depressed because there's no work coming up, and if they say yes, the actor's even more depressed because everyone else must be getting the work.

'A few bits and pieces,' Michelle says tactfully. 'There's a movie being cast, shooting in the Blue Mountains, with a great role for you. There was some issue with the lead actress and they need to re-cast.'

'What about a TV commercial to get me out of debt and buy me a ticket back to LA?' I suggest hopefully.

'TVCs aren't paying much these days but I'll see what's around… hang on, how do you feel about working with a python?'

'Ah… fine.' Actually, terrified, but I'm not in a position to be fussy. Surely there'll be some sort of snake wrangler on set.

'Oh, no, I think that one's been cast,' says Michelle. 'Never mind, I'll get you seen for the film instead.'

I silently sigh with relief. The things we say we'll do.

'Oh, I just remembered, I've got tickets to the opening of *The Three Sisters* at the Sydney Theatre Company tomorrow night. Do you want to be my date? You know how hubby hates opening nights.'

'Yes!' I say before Michelle has finished the sentence. Opening night at the Sydney Theatre Company with my agent and favourite Chekhov. Right now, life doesn't get better than that.

Michelle's partner, Hal Franks, is a successful writer for stage and screen. He sees every play in Sydney but prefers to do so once a show has settled in. Opening nights are fun but frenetic as the cast delivers its first real performance, usually to an audience of friends and industry types. It's a totally different energy to the rest of the season. One I absolutely love.

'Tia Harris is in it. You know her, don't you?' Michelle asks.

'She's one of my clients now.'

My heart slides. Tia was in my year at drama school. Tall, beautiful, and such a diva. She was the one "most likely to succeed". Everyone thought she was going to be a star. Ironic, considering I've ended up getting more work than her. But I didn't know she was on Michelle's books. She went with a much bigger agency. Maybe it didn't work out.

Michelle reads my thoughts. 'She joined about six months ago. I was surprised, too.'

'I'm not surprised,' I say. 'Just wondering why it took her so long to see the light.'

'You're too kind. Anyway, she's doing well, and I think she'll be a great Masha.'

My heart drops to my feet. I can almost hear a clunk. Masha from *The Three Sisters* is one of my favourite roles, one I've yet to perform professionally. I was desperate to play Masha in my final year at drama school, which made Tia even more determined to play her too. Everyone thought I was going to be cast but, somehow, she snagged the part and never let me forget it. Among my close friends, it became known as the "Masha Fiasco". She wasn't that good but somehow, the show became all about Tia. Everyone raved about her performance. And now she's going to rub my nose in it once again. Not that she knows I'm even in the country, let alone coming to opening night. But I'm sure she'll be delighted.

After graduating, I often saw her at auditions going for the same roles. Not that she always got them. But if I walked into an audition waiting room and saw Tia, I had to fight hard not to let it affect my performance. It makes me wonder why Michelle took her on.

'She's a bit like me,' I say nervously. 'Am I being replaced?'

'Never, you two are completely different.' Michelle is adamant. 'I know you get seen for similar roles but that's because you're both terrific actresses, offering very different qualities. You'd make a great Masha too. But Tia's here in Sydney, so this time she got the part.'

'I know, I know.'

'Actors!' Michelle laughs. 'So insecure when they've got no reason to be, especially you, my darling girl. So, tomorrow night, I'll meet you at the Opera Bar around 7pm? We can have a drink and you can tell me how much of a shit that ex-fiancé of yours is. Gotta take this call now.' Michelle hangs up before I can say another word.

Back home, my excitement subsides as I mull over the few pieces of clothing in my suitcase. Opening night! I need to look totally fabulous. Especially if I have to talk to Tia. I always feel drab in her towering presence. Maybe Jazz has something I can borrow. She's the sort of person who goes into an op shop and finds a magnificent vintage dress in great condition for next-to-nothing and looks amazing in it. Whereas I pick the wrong pieces and end up sending them back to Vinnies. Still, at least I've donated some money, and then given Vinnies the opportunity to re-sell the items and make the money once again. It's the least I can do.

5

THE following evening, I arrive at Circular Quay train station dressed in a stunning pantsuit and silver stilettoes thanks to Jazz's treasure trove of a wardrobe. I totter towards the iconic sails of the Opera House where the glittering panorama of Sydney Harbour stops my heart. It truly is the most amazing corner of the world and never fails to set my spirits soaring. However, as I approach the bustling Opera Bar, I feel less comfortable in my surrounds. I scan the tables, crammed with bright, beautiful people enjoying after-work or pre-show drinks. I weave my way through and just as I'm starting to think maybe I got the time wrong, I feel a tap on my shoulder. I spin around to see Michelle wrapped in a fuchsia scarf, clutching an ice bucket, a bottle of bubbly, and two glasses.

'I've ordered a cheese platter. I know you probably haven't eaten yet. And by the looks of you, you could do with a bit of Camembert.'

I give Michelle a big hug. 'So good to see you.'

'And good to have you back in the country,' she says with a broad smile. 'I'm planning on making the most of it, starting with a few drinks right now.'

Michelle grabs the only free table in the whole bar and pours two glasses of bubbles. She hands one to me and chinks it with her own.

'Welcome home!'

'Thanks, and thanks for asking me tonight. I love this play.

48

Even if Tia is playing my role.'

'You guys aren't friends, I take it?'

'Oh, sort of.'

Not friends at all. Never have been. Back in drama school she was a princess who demanded so much attention. And usually got it because all the teachers loved her. We did a production of *A Midsummer Night's Dream* in second year – should have been called *A Midsummer Night's Nightmare*. I was cast as Hermia and Tia was Helena and, as usual, she sucked all the energy out of the rehearsal room, leaving little time or space for me. Then, during one of the performances, in the scene where Helena thinks Hermia has turned against her, Tia "accidentally" tripped me up. A complete mistake, apparently, but one the audience found hilarious. Everyone raved about it for at least a week afterwards. The reality was Tia wasn't paying attention onstage. I turned her mistake into a comic moment but somehow she came out on top.

'You know, I'd have put you up for this part, too, if you'd been here.' Michelle cuts through my sinking mood. 'You'd have played it beautifully.'

'That's okay, you don't have to say that.' I smile. 'I'm sure Tia will be fantastic.'

'And you'll be fantastic when you get your next job,' Michelle says gently.

As it happens, the play is amazing, as is Tia. I'm not sure I would have played it better. The way things have been going, I'm wondering if I'm actually any good at all.

I escape to the queue for the Ladies at interval. I don't really need to go, and I certainly don't have time to get out of Jazz's pantsuit (and back in), but I just want a moment to centre myself.

I've often dreamt of coming back to Australia – successful, victorious, and happily partnered up. But here I am, the complete opposite, too scared to venture out of a toilet cubicle.

I don't usually doubt myself. But I let my guard down for one second and fell in love with a total bastard who found someone better, younger (only by two years, but still), and more successful (not that you'd have heard of her, she's not that talented to be honest). Next minute, I'm sleeping on floors, fleeing the country, and embarking on a career as a casual dog-sitter. I don't even like dogs that much.

I push my inner monologue to the back of my mind and rush to find Michelle just as a loud dinging fills the foyer.

'Right on time,' she says as I approach.

'Sorry, pantsuit issues.'

'Enjoying the show?'

I force a smile. 'I am.'

An hour later, the play is done, and we're back in the foyer, enjoying another glass of bubbly and mingling with the who's who of the Sydney theatre industry. Michelle wants to wait to see Tia, and I don't want to be rude by leaving before that happens.

Eventually, the actors come out, and Tia makes a beeline for us.

'Michelle, thank you *so* much for coming, lovely to see you.' She kisses my agent… *our* agent… on both cheeks. 'And *thank you* for those beautiful flowers.'

'You were absolutely brilliant, my darling!' Michelle assures her. 'You know Indigo James.'

Tia greets me slightly less enthusiastically, only obvious to a fellow actor. 'Oh yes, Indie, you're back.'

'For a while.'

'So nice to see you,' she says in a voice that makes it sound as if seeing me is anything but nice. 'How funny I got to play Masha again.'

'Yes, congratulations.' I try to be generous. 'Such a fantastic role.'

'It really is, I feel so lucky, so humbled.' Tia puts a hand on her heart, making me want to puke. 'How's everything going in LA?'

'Great! Really well.' I try to sound as upbeat as Tia, which is hard when she's just come off stage after a remarkable performance and I'm about to start dog-sitting. Still, in six weeks, she'll be back to her call centre job or working nights in a bar. Everyone's in the same boat.

'So, what did you guys think?' she asks, even though Michelle told her she was fantastic about a minute ago.

'It was wonderful,' Michelle says. 'Not sure about the guy playing Andrei, apart from him, everyone was marvellous.'

'What was the director like?' I ask.

'Jen Edwards? Ah-mazing!' Tia gushes. 'Have you worked with her?'

'Um no.' I've never even heard of her but I'm not going to admit that.

'She's fairly new to the scene. She's done a lot of independent theatre and this is her second gig with the STC. Definitely one to watch. We clicked right from the start. We're already talking about working together again next season.'

'Great,' I said for about the millionth time. Great, great, great. Everything is great and all I want to do is run back to my toilet cubicle, curl up in a foetal position, and have a little cry.

Michelle and Tia start discussing the play scene by scene so I sneak off to the bar in search of something stronger than bubbles.

'Hello, you!'

I turn and squeal so loudly that a group of nearby teenage girls look up from their mobile phones.

'Lucy! How are you?' I throw my arms around a stunning

woman with a huge smile and a mass of blond curls. Lucy and I were at NIDA together and, unlike Tia, have been friends ever since.

'Good.' She hugs me back. 'When did you get home?'

'A few days ago.'

'Is Mark here, too?' Lucy asks, looking around.

'Ah, no.' I hesitate. 'We've had a few problems, looks like it's over.'

'Oh, Indie! Sorry to hear that. What happened?'

'Long story, tell you over a few glasses of wine sometime,' I say, not wanting to go through it again. 'So, what did you think of the show?'

'You'd have been a better Masha.'

'Thanks.' It's not true, but that's what friends say to each other in this business, especially if they're party to the Masha fiasco. 'Who are you here with?'

She gives a sly smile. 'My boyfriend, Jesse.'

'What? Boyfriend! Since when?'

'Since I realised what was good for me,' a familiar voice says.

I turn and give the scruffy-looking guy in front of me a bear hug. 'About time.'

Jesse was also in our year, and he and Lucy were always "just good friends" even though they were secretly in love with each other. Everyone could see it but them.

'I need details. I want to know everything.'

For the next hour, I chat easily with people who know me well. Such a change from the shallow LA life I've been living. On one hand, I loved that no one knew me before and I was starting fresh. But on the other, I missed old friends who really got me and my humour.

'So, where's the American?' Jesse asks before Lucy can stop

him. 'What? Have I said something wrong?'

I smile as Lucy desperately tries to indicate with her overly animated eyes that he's most definitely said the wrong thing.

'It's over.'

'Sorry to hear that, Indie.' Jesse gives a little grin. 'Although, I'm sure there are more than a few guys back here who'll be thrilled to hear that news.'

I roll my eyes. 'Oh, yeah, they'll be knocking down my door.'

Michelle appears and wraps me in a hug. 'Must go, darling, getting up early. Started boot camp, would you believe? Helps me deal with all the stress of my over-anxious actors! Present company excluded of course.'

Probably time I go too. I spot Tia in the distance talking intently to an extremely high-profile actor. She always knew how to work a room.

'Where are you staying?' asks Lucy.

'Home with Mum and Dad, but I'll be house-sitting for my friend, Jazz, in Bondi from Thursday. I'm looking after their dog.'

'Yay, we can do coffee, or lunch,' Lucy bubbles. 'Maybe yoga? I found a great new yoga centre you'll love. I'm frighteningly free at the moment. We can hang out pretty much all the time!'

'Fantastic.' I love Lucy's over-excited response. 'But now you've said that I bet you get booked for a job this week.'

'I doubt it.' Lucy sighs. 'There's a movie being cast. Shooting in the Blue Mountains. You should look into it.'

'Michelle mentioned it.'

'The script's fantastic and it's being directed by Nina Freeman,' Lucy says. 'Do you know her?'

'Yeah, she directed me in *Time on the Line*.'

'Of course! Hassle Michelle. Apparently, they need to re-cast the female lead in a hurry. It starts shooting pretty soon. You'll get an audition for sure.'

Normally, a piece of information like that would ignite a little spark in my stomach that slowly grows in size and fervour, spurring me on yet another journey to nab, not even a job but simply the chance to audition. Now, I can barely muster *any* enthusiasm. What's happening to me? Am I losing my passion? I push the thought into the shadowy corners of my mind. No, I'm just tired. Nothing more. And now, it's time for bed. In fact, I could go to sleep right here on this bar stool.

'We're going out for another drink somewhere, maybe grab some food,' Lucy says. 'You have to come. It's been so long since we've hung out.'

I want to say no but the thought of going home makes me even more depressed. On the other hand, if I stay out late, it's hard to get home and I can't afford an Uber.

'I'd love to, but I'd better start the long trek back before it's too late.'

'Stay at my place,' Lucy says. 'You'll have to sleep on the couch, I'm afraid.'

'That's fine, I'm used to couches.'

My mood and energy levels take an upward swing and I text Mum like a dutiful teenager, letting her know my plans. I half expect her to call back and ask to speak with Lucy, just to confirm I'm telling the truth.

We make our way to a bar in Darlinghurst where another actor friend is having birthday drinks. It's the best night I've had in ages. But hours later, I'm curled up at Lucy's on yet another couch, wondering if this new plan is going to make any difference to my life at all.

6

THURSDAY arrives and I prepare myself for yet another journey. Okay, so it's only into the city then over to Bondi. But I've been on the go for weeks and I'm looking forward to staying still. Jazz and Stu left early this morning, so no turning back now.

My well-worn case bulges a little more since fishing out left-behind clothing from my cupboards. Nothing like not wearing something for a few years to suddenly recognise its worth. I struggle down to the kitchen, say goodbye to Mum, and convince her I'm not leaving the country, only the suburb. I guess as far as Pymble-dwellers are concerned, that's pretty much the same thing. However, I assure her I'll come back to visit next week.

'Will you sleep over?' she asks, immediately cheered.

'Maybe.' I smile. 'I have to look after George and I'm not sure what Jem's schedule will be like.'

'Such a nice young man,' Mum says. 'We had an interesting conversation at the wedding about public education in Australia.'

Of course they did. 'Well, he wasn't so nice to me that night, nor the next day.'

'You seemed to be getting on famously when I saw you together.'

The sensation of Jem's soft lips, inches from mine, flashes in my mind like a neon light. 'Not my type, Mum.'

I don't mention he cleaned my shoe the other day, otherwise she'd think him even more of a saint than she already does.

'Whatever you say.' Mum pauses and looks mournful.

'It's only across the Harbour Bridge.'

'I know.' Mum pulls me into the fifth hug for the day. 'Now, you'd better go before I get teary, and then there'll be no stopping me.'

'You're off?' Dad's head appears around the corner.

'If Mum will let me.'

'Pam, release your daughter.' Something Dad has been saying since I started high school. If not for Dad, I'd still be living at home and coming down for dinner at seven.

I disentangle myself from Mum's clutches and tell my father I'm fine to walk to the station to catch the next train to the city.

'At least let me drive you to the station.'

'Dad, it's a short walk.'

'Happy to, love. Feel like I've hardly seen you.'

We set off, chatting about this and that. Usually, we discuss politics, podcasts, books, new recipes, anything really, just not feelings or relationships, unless Mum puts him up to it. Quite refreshing.

'So, how's Matt?' he asks.

'You mean Mark?' Okay, it looks like we *are* talking relationships. Mum definitely put him up to it.

'Oh yes, Mark, sorry, I've never managed to remember his name. Funny, considering it's not particularly complicated.'

'He's fine. Why?'

'Oh, just asking. You've hardly mentioned him since you got home.'

'Did Mum tell you to ask me?'

'No, not at all.' Dad hesitates. 'Okay, she did. You know how she worries about you. We both do.'

'There's nothing to worry about.'

'It's just, I couldn't imagine you marrying someone I didn't think was absolutely right for you,' Dad says. 'And I'm not sure he's right.'

My eyebrows shoot up like a high-speed elevator. This has to be the longest (and only) relationship conversation we've ever had. 'You don't know him very well.'

'Mum says you'll be living with that Jeremy chap from the wedding. Nice guy. Head firmly on his shoulders. Salt of the earth.'

'Okay, Dad, that'll do.' I nip the conversation (and the clichés) as fast as I can. 'Jem is a housemate, we're just friends. Not even that, if I'm honest. All we did at the wedding was argue.'

'Your Mum and I didn't get on when we met.'

'Really? You never told me that.'

'Couldn't stand each other but also couldn't keep away from each other.' Dad smiles. 'Well, I secretly adored her but she drove me crazy. Always saying we were too different. Had to marry her in the end just to prove her wrong. Best thing I've ever done.'

'Oh, and what about me?'

'Second best thing then.'

'Thanks.'

Dad pulls up at the station and jumps out to help carry my case, despite being in a "no standing zone". My parents seem to forget I'm in my thirties now and live away from the family home – overseas – successfully functioning without their constant supervision. I assure him I'll be fine from here. Fortunately, a police car drives by and he changes his tune.

'Actually, I'd better get going, love.' He makes a dash to the driver's door. 'Take care, and don't forget about us.'

He drives off and I make my way to the city-bound platform, feeling like I'm stepping into the unknown, despite the fact I've been doing this train trip since I was a teenager.

I open Jazz and Stu's shiny red front door to a stillness that tells me I'm alone. Jem isn't arriving until tomorrow, so I have some time on my own to settle in. I pop the keys on the antique table and make my way down the creaky hall to the living room, which is cosy and welcoming despite its lack of Jazz and Stu. I go to the kitchen and dump my bag when the sound of mad barking outside reminds me that I am, in fact, anything but alone. I tentatively open the sliding doors and step onto the terrace where George looks like he's about to self-combust.

'Hello, there. Whoa!'

George jumps up, his two front paws almost reaching my tummy but this time I'm prepared and don't even blink when he leaves dirty marks on my top. It's encouraging to receive such a big welcome. If that means a little extra washing, so be it. Maybe he remembers me from lunch. Or perhaps simply seeing a human who might offer food or a walk is enough to send him into a frenzy. It's all new to me.

But now I'm here alone with a great big, needy, jumpy, licky dog, I'm not sure what to do. Maybe take him for a walk? I hadn't planned on a walk straight up, but I probably need to get milk and bread, that sort of thing.

I stroll into the spotless kitchen to find a note from Jazz. "Eat whatever you like." I open the fridge and find it packed. There's even one of Stu's signature homemade pumpkin, ricotta, and basil lasagnes with a Post-it note on it saying, "Dinner for tonight".

Right, so there's no hurry for food shopping. But I do feel like a walk. Check out the neighbourhood. Clear my head. Apparently, George likes to be walked two to three times a day so I'd better get started.

I spy a thesis-like wad of papers on the kitchen bench, entitled *Read Me!* I feel like Alice in Wonderland with all these instructions. What with the enormous list she gave me at lunch the other day, I'll need some sort of filing system. I never knew how much was involved in looking after a dog. I glance at the list and see George needs his ears cleaned once a week with special drops that he apparently hates. That should be fun. And his teeth? I didn't know you had to clean dogs' teeth. He also likes a bedtime story before he goes to sleep. It looks like he prefers saucy romance as his current favourite is *Fifty Shades of Grey*! And his dinner consists of organic poached chicken breast, which Jazz has prepared and frozen in single serves. It's like I have a child (with inappropriate taste in literature) to look after, and a demanding, high maintenance one at that. My brain starts to whirl like a ceiling fan on its highest setting.

'Why don't we go for a walk?'

George jumps around madly, as if to say, 'Yes, yes, yes! You're so awesome, Auntie Indie!'

Okay, I don't know for sure he's saying I'm awesome, but he's definitely enthusiastic.

'Calm down, that's a good boy.' I look around. From memory, there's a leash somewhere and maybe a harness?

I look at George expectantly, unsure why I think a dog can help me out. Jazz spoke at length about the leash, but to be honest, I didn't absorb that many details. I'd like to blame the jetlag but deep down I know I was thrown by Jem's presence. And treading in dog poo right under his sarcastic nose didn't help. I wish I'd been more focused because now I have no idea what to do.

As it happens, George leads me to the front door and there, on the hall table, is the leash and what looks to be some sort of harness. After ten minutes of examining the harness and watching a couple of "How to put a harness on your dog" YouTube videos, followed by fifteen minutes of dog wrestling, I throw it aside and just clip the leash on his collar. Who needs a harness anyway? I grab the keys and head out the door feeling like I've already run a marathon.

'I can do this,' I tell George, trying to convince me more than him. He doesn't seem to have any doubts about my ability as he bounds down the street, just about pulling my arm out of its socket.

'Wait for me.' I break into a light run to keep up. I'll be as fit as an Olympic athlete if I keep this up every day. I'd imagined a nice leisurely stroll but this is like being swept away in a whirlwind. Except, every time we settle into a steady pace, George stops dead to sniff something, just about dislocating my shoulder. By the time I catch my breath, he's off again. I barely see the stunning stretch of Bondi Beach, let alone appreciate its beauty. So much for breathing fresh salty air and feasting eyes on the breathtaking horizon beyond. No time for that.

George seems to know where to go as we eventually arrive at a park with lots of other dogs roaming around off their leashes. This must be the dog park Jazz mentioned. I open the gate and carefully close it behind me. Should I let George off his leash? Probably another vital piece of information I missed over lunch. I remember once walking with Jazz and she'd let him off every now and again. As the park's enclosed, I figure this is the place to do it.

'Stay where I can see you,' I say, sounding frighteningly like my mother.

Naturally, George doesn't listen and runs around like a naughty toddler with selective hearing (and a lot more body hair). I look at the other dog owners in the park. They all seem to know each other and I feel them checking me out as if to say, 'She's new.'

I try to look like I'm used to hanging out with dogs but no doubt it's completely obvious that I'm the casual babysitter, not the mum. I spot a green rubber ball on the grass. George might like to play with that.

'George!' I call out. 'Fetch!'

George looks up at me like a bored teenager. I swear he rolls his eyes. Okay, so he doesn't do "fetch". Weird. I thought all dogs liked that.

'Sorry, that's Roxie's ball,' says a polite voice behind me.

I turn to see the tallest man in the world. With short dark hair. Dressed in smart black running gear with a sleeveless puffer jacket. Slick, stylish, and immaculate with nothing out of place. I feel so scruffy in my old top with muddy paw prints down the front (thanks, George!). I look at my feet to see I'm still wearing my short black boots. I didn't even put trainers on. I feel so unlike a proper dog owner.

'Pardon?' I suddenly remember that this tall dark stranger spoke to me.

'The ball, it's Roxie's.' He offers an apologetic smile. 'Sorry, she's just a bit particular.'

'No, I'm sorry. I just saw it on the ground and thought George might like it, but he wasn't interested.'

'You're looking after George?' he says. 'So, Jazz has left?'

'Yes, she has. And yes, I'm trying to. In fact, this is our first walk.'

'You didn't want to use the harness?'

I sigh inwardly. Of course, a dog person would notice. 'I ah… decided to go without today… does it matter?'

'It's up to you, but the harness is safer as dogs can slip out of collars more easily. It's also better for their throat.'

I look at George, terrified. What was I thinking by not persisting with the harness? Although I have to say, he doesn't look like he's suffering. And just to prove it, he chooses this moment to do one of his almighty poos right in front of us. Bigger than the one I stepped in the other day and that's saying something.

'Oh, George!' I look up, mortified. 'So sorry.'

The stranger laughs. 'It's no problem, we all do it.'

'Yes, I guess you're right.' I feel awkward at the sudden openness of our exchange. And the image it evokes.

Now finished his business, George runs off with another big dog that must be Roxie, leaving me to deal with the disgusting mound in front of us. What do I do?

'Did you bring a bag?' The stranger speaks in a calm tone. He must sense my panic. And as my hands are empty apart from the leash, he realises I didn't bring anything with me.

'A poop bag? To pick it up?' He points at the ground. 'A bag for the...'

I shake my head. It was probably on the list with succinct directions on where they're kept and how to use them but of course, I haven't yet studied the list. I do remember mention of a dog-walking bag, maybe the poop bags are inside? I blame Jem for being so distracting at lunch. We haven't even started living together and he's already ruining everything. Now I feel completely ridiculous in front of this nice-looking dog man.

'Here, take one of mine.' He waves a small black plastic bag at me. 'We dog owners have no issue with sharing.'

'Thanks.' I take the bag and look down dubiously. How do I pick it up? I don't want to touch it but I'm not sure how to get it in the bag. Dog Man takes out another bag, puts his hand inside, like a glove, picks up the pile in one fell swoop, peels the bag over, ties a knot, and hands it to me.

'It goes in that bin over there.' He grins. 'You really don't know much about looking after dogs, do you?'

'Is it that obvious?'

'Yes.'

'It's true,' I admit. 'I don't know anything. Just don't tell Jazz, else she'll fly back in a flash. Still, I'm learning, and now I know what to do with a number two. So, thanks for that!'

'I'm Alex,' he says with a crinkly smile.

'Hi, I'm Indie.' I smile back and shake his outstretched arm.

'I know, I recognise you. And Jazz talks about you all the time, so I feel like I know you.'

'Oh, right.' I wonder what on earth Jazz has been saying. 'How do you know Jazz and Stu?'

'I only really know Jazz. Through the dogs – Roxie and George are besties, girlfriend and boyfriend actually.'

'Really?'

'Absolutely besotted with each other. I was considering moving to another suburb but Jazz and I decided it would break the dogs' hearts not to see each other every day.'

Like Jazz, Alex obviously thinks Roxie is practically human, but I don't know him well enough to tease him like I would Jazz.

'Jazz told me you'd be looking after George and to say hi.'

'Check up on me, more like, make sure I'm looking after George properly.'

Alex looks like he's been caught sneaking a cookie from the cupboard. 'Yes, she did, I can't lie.'

'So how am I doing so far?'

'Pretty good for your first walk.' He pretends to be serious. 'But definitely room for improvement.'

'Oh, really! You wait, I'll be all over this dog-minding thing in a few days and giving you advice.'

'I shall look forward to it.'

'Apparently, I have to bathe George every second or third week. That seems a bit excessive, doesn't it?'

Alex looks at me with surprise. 'Not really. Sometimes I wash Roxie once a week if she's particularly muddy or sandy.'

Wow! Dog people really are mad.

'So, was Jazz okay when she left?' Alex continues.

'Yes, I think so. Why do you ask?'

'Oh, just with all that trouble with Stu and… well, I'm sure you know.'

I stare at Alex, confused. 'No, I don't. What's going on with Stu? They seemed fine. I had lunch with them just before they left.'

'It's nothing, nothing at all.' Alex shuffles his feet. 'I shouldn't have said anything.'

Panic rises in my chest. What's going on with my two best friends? And why don't I know about it? 'You have to tell me *now*.'

'Look, I may have misunderstood the situation.' Alex's words start to race. 'I don't really know Stu, but Jazz confides in me every now and again. It was probably nothing, she'd have told you if it was. You're her best friend.'

'Ah, yeah.' I scan the park, nervously looking for George. Clearly, not such a great friend if I know nothing about her marital problems. But there can't be anything wrong with her and Stu. They've always been very much in love. He fills in her blanks, doesn't he? They can't break up, it's not allowed. What about the rest of us? That would leave us with absolutely nothing to strive for. If Stu and Jazz can't make it work, no one can.

'Sorry, I didn't mean to upset you, forget I said anything,' Alex says. 'I loved that series you were in, by the way, the police one.'

'*Time on the Line*?'

'Yeah, you were great.' He smiles shyly. 'I've been dying to meet you, so I was thrilled when Jazz said you'd be coming to the dog park.'

'Hopefully, I'll see you around. I'm sure I'll be needing a few more dog tips.'

'Anytime, glad to help.' Alex calls Roxie, who bounds up with George close on his heels. Alex deftly attaches the leash onto Roxie's harness (must learn how to use one) who looks up with big sorrowful eyes as if to say, 'A little bit longer?'

'Come on, my girl, it's late. George will be going home too.'

'Yes, time for us to go, George, quick sticks,' I say firmly. What's happening to me? I've only been looking after George for a few hours and I'm already talking like a stern parent.

'See you, Indie,' Alex calls as he drags Roxie away.

I attach George's leash, despite his equally mournful eyes, and head for the gate. What was Alex talking about? The thought of my best friends having relationship problems is enough to send my world off kilter. It can't be true. Jazz would tell me something as significant as that. Still, something is going on and I need to find out what.

7

BACK home, George's tongue is just about falling out of his mouth. He pushes his (now empty) water bowl towards me and barks for at least a minute before I realise he must be thirsty. God! I hope I haven't dehydrated him on the first day! I quickly fill the bowl and he furiously laps up the water.

Disaster averted.

Now what?

I take my things to Jazz and Stu's room which looks like a picture torn out of a chic interior magazine, with a wrought iron bed (probably French) dressed in lush white linen and piled with pillows. Almost too good to sleep on. Jem will be in the spare room but we have to share the bathroom. Jazz isn't a fan of ensuites ('How close does your bed need to be to your toilet anyway?'), so they never put one in. Unfortunately.

I unpack a few bits and pieces, trying to make myself feel at home.

Funny word. Home.

I don't even know where mine is. There was pleasant Pymble, followed by a series of flats, group houses, then Mark's apartment. Sleek, modern, cold. I never felt completely comfortable there. Too much white. Nothing like Jazz's quirky vintage cottage full of warmth and eclectic French country pieces. Mark's place was like him. Perfect, you might say. But now, being so far away from his flawless face and overly positive personality, I wonder if he was ever right for me.

I grab my laptop and go outside where George is rolling around on the grass. It's probably time for one of his baths, especially after playing in the park, but the thought of it is exhausting. I take a quick photo of him happily playing with his squeaky toy and text it to Jazz.

I turn on my computer to find a string of emails from Mark, one from Benji, and a very quick one from Jazz, wondering if George is okay. Honestly, she's worried already. Doesn't she think I can look after a dog for a few hours without running into strife? Then I think about the poop bag scenario and the harness catastrophe. Okay, she's probably right to worry. Besides, it gives me a chance to ask what I need to ask. I tap out a quick response.

All fine here. I've even taken George for a very successful walk to the dog park. Met Alex. Nice guy. Although he seemed to think there's something up between you and Stu. What's going on?

I xxx

Who knows where they are right now and in which time zone but I'm sure they're fine and it won't be long before they post cute couple shots with the most amazing cheese, fruit market, or decorative window box. They probably had a bad day with one of their silly squabbles and Jazz confided in a fellow dog owner. But then, Jazz looked like she was going to explode when she realised Stu hadn't told Jem about me moving in. In fact, she was snippy with him most of the afternoon. A wisp of doubt clouds my mind. Maybe their life isn't as dreamy as I thought.

I scan Mark's messages, all wanting second-chance forgiveness, and delete them. Tonight's not about Mark. It's about enjoying my own space before my grumpy housemate arrives. And soaking in the beautiful freestanding claw bath that Jazz and Stu installed in their bathroom. I love baths, but we didn't have one in LA. I mean,

Mark didn't have one. I must stop the couple talk. It wasn't my place. There's no "we" about it.

The email from Benji is energised as always, checking in on me and wondering if I have a return date yet as there are some auditions for roles 'THAT WOULD BE PERFECT' for me. Benji always talks in capital letters. He hardly sleeps, lives on sugar, and is the most upbeat person I've ever come across. I'll worry about him later; I can't match his energy today.

As the afternoon fades to pinky dusk, I settle in for the night, pouring a glass of wine from a bottle with a sticker on it saying, "Drink me", and running a hot bubble bath where I stay until my fingers wrinkle. George keeps barking and putting his paws on the edge of the bath, trying to lap up the water. Not quite the solitary meditative experience I was hoping for. At one stage, he looks like he's about to jump in.

'George, what is it?' I wish he could tell me. 'Are you hungry?'

'Woof!' He looks at me with big pleading eyes. Oh my God. He's hungry. I haven't fed him. I jump out of the bath, wrap myself in a towel, and head to the kitchen with George just about tripping me up, no doubt relieved that the seemingly dense human finally got the message.

I try to read Jazz's instructions while George barks furiously as if to say, 'Will you just hurry up?' It's like I've given birth to a toddler. I can't hear myself think.

Heat up defrosted serve of organic poached chicken that you took out of freezer earlier.

Damn!

I retrieve a serve of poached organic chicken from the freezer, pop it in the microwave, and look back at the list.

Do not defrost in microwave! George doesn't like it.

Oops!

Heat up in a frying pan of simmering water.

Double oops.

Oh well, just this once won't hurt. Surely a dog won't notice how I defrost and heat delicious home-cooked organic chicken. Don't dogs eat stuff out of garbage bins and sniff each other's bottoms?

I pull out the steaming chicken, chop it up into "bite size pieces" (whatever that means for a dog), put it into George's beautifully hand-crafted bowl, and place his gourmet meal in the designated spot. George bounds up excitedly, takes a sniff, and looks up at me with questioning eyes.

'What?'

George still looks at me. I swear he raises his eyebrows.

'Okay, I admit I used the microwave. For God's sake, how can you even tell?'

George doesn't move.

'Well, that's your dinner,' I say nervously. 'Take it or leave it.'

We both stand there. George is good at this staring thing but I'm not giving in. Otherwise, where will it end? Cooking three special meals a day for a dog, that's where. And as the adult (and only human being), surely, I'm the boss?

After about thirty seconds, I fold like flimsy cardboard. 'Oh, alright, I'll do another one, but it'll take a while to defrost.'

I grab another rock-hard bag of chicken out of the freezer. Then I remember Stu's lasagne in the fridge. I look back at George. Do dogs eat lasagne? Why not? Surely it can't hurt. People give dogs leftovers all the time. And this lasagne is lovingly handmade by Stu. Neither parent could disagree with that.

'What about lasagne, George?'

George woofs enthusiastically.

'Don't tell your parents,' I whisper. 'Just a little bit of lasagne and maybe you can have your chicken later.'

'Woof, woof, woof,' George responds as if he totally understands and thinks it's a great idea.

I put the lasagne in the oven and take off the towel wrapped around me. Not that it matters tonight but from tomorrow I'll have to remember to wear a robe. I throw on some trackies and eventually George and I tuck into the very delicious veggie lasagne. Well, George is eating like he's been let loose at the butcher's and told to help himself. I'm a little more restrained.

A couple of hours of Netflix-bingeing later, I'm ready for bed. And George is too by the looks of things. I grab the instructions to see what happens next.

Take George out into garden to do his final wee.

Make sure indoor water bowl is full.

Settle him in his hallway resting station and make sure he has his toy lamb in his bed.

Read 2 pages of bedtime book.

I take George outside but I can't tell if he's been to the toilet or not. He tries to come back in but I block the door.

'Not until you've done a wee.'

George doesn't move.

I wait a few more moments then give in. 'Okay, into bed.'

George runs down the hall while I hunt for his toy lamb. Just as I start pulling apart the lounge room, I hear a weird choking noise coming from his direction.

I run up to find George dry retching. But before I can even locate the emergency section of Jazz's instructions, he lets loose with the most enormous vomit that looks a lot like Stu's lasagne.

'George! Oh, my goodness!'

He gets himself together and trots back to the kitchen and I hear him lapping up water from the indoor bowl. Maybe lasagne wasn't such a good idea after all. Come to think of it, I vaguely remember Jazz saying something about George's sensitive stomach. Definitely poached chicken from now on. At least the mess is on the floorboards and not one of Jazz's precious antique rugs.

I start wiping the floor with paper towel, realising I'll need more than that to complete the job. Should I call a vet? I head to the laundry to grab a bucket and mop and anything else that might help me out, and return to spy George happily curled up on the cream-coloured couch, not looking sick at all.

'No, George, get down from there.'

'Woof!' George "digs a hole" in the pile of throw cushions and snuggles into it.

'George, down!' I assume a confidence I don't feel. This is turning into a nightmare.

There must have been a tone in my voice because George jumps off and totters down to his hall bed, sorry, "resting station". Obviously, he knows he was doing the wrong thing.

With George happily settled and lasagne-free, I don't call the vet. And I think I'll skip the bedtime story. Not a great start to my dog-minding career but it's not like George can tell Jazz and Stu. Besides, I must face the disaster in the hall, a truly disgusting job I hope never to have to repeat.

Eventually, the hall is sparkling. I put everything away, only to spy a little puddle further towards the front door and have to get everything out again. Maybe George didn't wee in the garden after all. Tomorrow night, I'll stand over him with a torch.

I check in on him and he jumps up in a flash.

'George, it's time for sleep,' I say firmly.

But George has other ideas, walking up to a basket of dog-looking accessories, putting a paw on a paperback, and looking up at me with pleading eyes. *Fifty Shades of Grey*. Heaven help me.

'No bedtime story tonight, George.'

George doesn't move. We stare at each other once again and I last even less time than I did before. I grab the book and George returns to his resting station. I open to where there's a bookmark and start reading, unconvinced he has any idea what I'm saying. It's a raunchy passage and he seems riveted until slowly but surely his eyelids droop.

I creep away and climb into Jazz and Stu's king-size bed with its crisp white sheets. This is going to be harder than I thought. It's been one day, well only one afternoon, and I'm already over it. I haven't even given George a bath yet.

Having dozed off at some point, a noise wakes me. Like someone dropped a heavy book. Was that inside the house? My heart races and I keep as still as possible, listening to the silence. Maybe it was next door? This house is as safe as a bank, thanks to Stu's meticulous attention to security details. And wouldn't George bark if there were an intruder? I guess it could be Jem but he's not coming over until tomorrow. Wanting to be sure, I creep out of bed and ease open my door. The hall is quiet. George is sound asleep. See? Nothing at all.

I'm about to climb back under the covers when a rattle in the kitchen makes my heart nearly eject out of my mouth and onto the floor. I hear George get up and head towards the kitchen. What now? Go and check it out? But what if there's an intruder? I feel like I've been cast in a horror film and I'm doing a scene where the audience is screaming, 'Don't go in the kitchen! Oh no, she's going in the kitchen…'

I try to steady my breathing and haywire heartbeat. George isn't barking so it must be okay. I pad silently down the hall to the back of the house, grabbing a nearby broom with trembling hands. Not that it offers much in the way of defence but it's something. I creep up to the door, which is slightly ajar, raising the broom above my head. But as I edge in, the door flings wide open. I let out an ear-piercing scream.

'Shhh, jeez, it's okay. It's just me.'

And there he is. Jem Taylor. A sarcastic grin on his far-too-handsome face. And George excitedly jumping around, trying to lick him. Not such a frightening scene. In fact, far from it.

'Man, you scare easily,' he says with a smug smile. 'That was some scream.'

'I wasn't scared. I heard a noise. Wondered if someone had broken in – and I see that someone has!'

'Not broken in, I had a key.' He pauses. 'What were you going to do? Sweep me to death?'

'Of course not.' I look at the broom, my whitened knuckles stretched around it. 'I just saw this in the hall and thought I'd better put it away in case someone trips over it.' Damn, why didn't I come across something a little more impressive?

'Sure.'

George follows Jem around the kitchen. Fat lot of good he was in a crisis. He's positively delighted to see Jem. Let's hope it's because he knows him and not because he befriends any stranger who breaks in and gives him a pat.

'What are you doing coming in at this hour? Thought you were arriving tomorrow.'

'I finished up at work and decided to head straight over,' he replies coolly. 'I didn't realise I was supposed to follow a schedule.'

'Doesn't worry me, just wasn't expecting you.' I try to sound equally cool but fail miserably.

'Right, well, if it's okay with you, I'm going to crash.' And with that, he strides to the spare room and shuts the door.

How rude! First, he comes in this late and gives me the fright of my life – and doesn't even apologise. Then, he makes out like I'm particular about when he comes and goes, when honestly, I couldn't care less. And to top it off, I'm now totally awake with little chance of going back to sleep. I look at the clock. Ten past two. Ages until morning. Damn Jem and his weird hours. Why did he have to wake me up? And be so obnoxious about it. We've only been living together for about twelve minutes and already it's not working.

I decide to make a cup of tea and after fossicking around in the pantry I find something called Sleepy Time. Can't hurt. I make a cup, fetch my laptop, and climb back into bed to check emails.

Nothing from Jazz. Do she and Stu really have problems? And if so, why hasn't Jazz confided in me? She talks to some random dog park guy but not her oldest friend in the world. Unless he's not just some random dog park guy. Maybe he's a close friend. Maybe too close. You don't tell other guys about your relationship problems unless there's something else going on. Alex did talk about Jazz with a certain familiarity and he certainly knows more about her marriage than I do.

No. Not possible. I squash the thought to the back of my brain and flick through my messages. Another email from Mark. I want to delete it but my heart catches and I cave.

Hey, beautiful girl. Have you been getting my messages? I don't want to lose you. We can work this out, can't we? Please, please, please? xxx

What does he mean work it out? We were engaged and he slept with someone else. Not just any old someone, but Kourtney. When it comes to skinny, ridiculously gorgeous looking actresses, Kourtney is on top of the list, or at least in the top five. Why her? And then she goes and nabs my series? As if I can go back to Mark now! It would be like she was by my side all the time, directing my life, making me feel inadequate: 'Indie darling, do it like this, that's what I always find when I have sex with Mark.' Or, 'You call that acting? No wonder I got cast over you.'

Tears slide down my cheeks and there's nothing I can do to stop them. It's not like he forgot to get my yogurt when he did the grocery shop or left his wet towel on the bedroom floor for the hundredth time. How can we possibly recover from this? I grab some tissues and blow my nose.

I check out his Instagram account (can't help myself) and a photo jumps out at me, almost slapping me in the face: a happy laughing scene of him with friends at a restaurant. Posted only a matter of hours ago. He's obviously not suffering too much. My tears evaporate in a flash. How dare he say he's desperate for me yet be out having a great time? I turn off my computer in a huff and climb into bed.

I lie there for hours, fuming at the thought of Mark socialising while I'm stuck looking after a dog. I finally drift off into an unsettled sleep where Mark and Kourtney are having sex right in front of me. I'm about to ask if they wouldn't mind stopping but thankfully the sun creeps through the timber venetians, insisting I get up.

8

I FORCE myself out of bed, in desperate need of coffee and some sort of plan for the rest of my life. The first item is doable. I know Jazz has a fancy coffee machine and gourmet coffee in the cupboard. The second may take a little more thought. But coffee will certainly help.

I grab my dressing gown and tiptoe to the kitchen. Jem's door is closed. Probably still asleep. Then I remember George. That's right, I have a dog to tend to and right now, he's probably starving.

I go to the kitchen but he's not there. I check outside. No George. That's strange. Jazz said he's always up early, waiting for his morning snack and first walk of the day. In fact, she said he wakes her up by jumping on her bed and licking her face which sounds disgusting, but is, no doubt, heaven for Jazz.

I scan the house once more but George is nowhere to be found. I pop my head in the laundry and check behind the door, the cupboard below the sink, even in the washing machine (you never know). Still no George. Maybe Jem has him? I creep up to his door but I don't dare knock. It's firmly shut, with no light on, so safe to assume he's still asleep. Where could George be?

I feel like I've lost my footing on a hill and am slowly tumbling to the bottom. How can George be gone? What do I do? Call the police? The vet? My mum? I go to grab my phone, which seems to have disappeared along with George. I check the kitchen table and turn out my handbag. My stress levels build like a rollercoaster climbing to the top of a precarious ride, every passing second signifying yet another moment of pending danger. Phone, where are you?

A click at the side gate grabs my attention and George comes bounding through the sliding doors, jumping up on me and trying to lick my face.

'George! Where were you? I was so worried.' I try to avoid his licky tongue without offending him.

Jem ambles in, leash in hand. 'I took him for a walk. That okay? Jazz said he likes one first thing, remember?'

'Oh, sure.' I squeeze my hands into two tight fists. 'You might have left a note. I thought he'd got out or had been stolen or something.'

Jem smiles his sarcastic smile. 'You didn't see that the leash and harness were gone? And I was gone? And George was gone? If you looked, it was pretty obvious. I thought actors were meant to be observant.'

I take a deep breath and slowly count to three, smothering the wave of irritation mounting inside me. 'Just would have been nice. Polite.'

'Right, well, next time I'll write you a little note and deliver it personally under your door.' Jem walks away but then stops. 'Now, if it's okay with you, I'm going to have a shower, or do you want that in writing as well?'

I try to think of a good comeback but my mind is emptier than my current work schedule, so I turn and stride down the hall, which is frustrating because I want to go to my bedroom, the same direction he was heading. Now I'm stuck in the kitchen. What an arsehole! I was going to see if he wanted any groceries but I certainly won't bother now. Not only did he wake me up last night and give me the fright of my life, but he took George for a walk without letting me know, throwing me into total panic. And to top it off, he worked out the harness with no trouble whatsoever.

'Do you need the bathroom?' Jem calls after me. 'I'd better get going. Gotta get to work. Double shift. Some of us do it every day, you know.'

Even more of an arsehole.

'Go right ahead.' I storm to my bedroom, shutting the door behind me.

He's the most aggravating person I've ever met. Attractive, yes, but to be honest, anything he has in the looks department is outweighed by his unappealing personality. I really dodged a few bullets when we got disturbed that night at the wedding. God knows why he has girls following him around in hoards, not that I've seen any yet. Maybe they're all camping outside, waiting for him to go to work.

I sit in my room, determined to stay there until he's well and truly left the house. Then I'll relax with my coffee and plan my day. I should do some yoga, but I feel too edgy. Which is why I should do it. Maybe go for a run instead? Not with George, just on my own. I haven't been running in ages and next to yoga, it's one of the things that keeps me sane. Right now, it's exactly what I need.

With my first decision of the day made, I rummage through my case for a pair of gym shorts, a singlet, trainers, and baseball cap. No time for coffee now. I throw on the clothes in a flash, pull my cap firmly down over my messy hair, and dash down the hall. In my haste, I literally bump into Jem, dressed in nothing but a towel.

'Whoops, sorry.' Heat surges up my neck like a wave of bubbling lava. Probably because I'm inches away from a near naked man – and the bits I *can* see are nothing short of spectacular.

'No problem, lucky I remembered the towel instead of doing my usual nudie run.' Jem gives me a quick up and down glance.

'Where you going? Zumba?'

'Err… I was just… in a hurry… going for a run.' I'm painfully aware that I'm not really forming proper sentences but the whole nothing-but-a-towel incident has thrown me sideways. I don't know where to look so I focus on his nose, no doubt making me look like an over-anxious zombie. It's not like I haven't seen a great body in recent months. Mark practically lives at the gym, plenty of muscle there, but Jem looks more… what is it? Rugged? Australian? Maybe that's it. I haven't seen any Australian guys up close for so long I've forgotten what they look like. Great! Now I'm comparing the body of my ex to that of my housemate, whom I despise. Who cares about either of them, or their bodies?

A slight smile creeps up one corner of Jem's mouth. 'Okay.'

Damn! He obviously sees how embarrassed I am. My face, I imagine, is beetroot red by now. An unfortunate occurrence in certain moments of humiliation. He's so arrogant, he probably thinks I'm a prude. Which I'm so not. I'm used to naked bodies, I've worked in professional theatre for God's sake, it goes with the territory. Or maybe he thinks I'm still attracted to him? He's so used to women falling at his feet, he expects I'll do the same. Nothing could be further from my mind. All I want is to wipe that smug smile off his face.

'I don't do Zumba.'

'Sure.'

'I don't.'

'Yoga maybe?'

'Yeah, well, I usually do yoga, but now I'm going for a run. Probably about 10ks, maybe more.'

What am I saying? I haven't run that far in months. Have I ever run ten kilometres? I'd be lucky to do half that. Just stop talking, Indie, and move away from the semi-naked man.

'Good for you.' He saunters down the hall to his room, towel draped a little too loosely around his torso, exposing the topmost curve of his bum. I stand there, fixated, tingling from the waist down, watching the towel sway in time with his body, wishing it would slip off completely.

I shake my head like a cartoon character, mortified by the effect Jem has on me. I can't stand the guy but my body clearly thinks otherwise and now the image of him in nothing but a towel is imprinted on the forefront of my brain. I escape out the door and start a shuffle down the street. I take it slowly because I'm incredibly unfit right now. Not that I was going to admit that to Jem with his surprising muscle tone. But funnily enough, as I get going, I don't feel too out of breath. Quite the opposite in fact. I don't know if it's being pissed off with Jem or the world in general, but all I want to do is run. My speed picks up, my breathing falls into a natural rhythm, and I remember why I love doing this. I zip past rows of cute cottages and renovated beach apartments, dodging prams and hipster couples. I haven't felt so free in ages and it's exhilarating, like I'm burning up a bottomless supply of pent-up anxiety and anger accumulated over the last month. My annoyance with Jem is certainly contributing. Or was it the sight of him and his cheeky towel casually strolling towards the bathroom? Not wanting to unpack that right now, I keep running.

9

THANKFULLY, when I get back to the house, Jem has left for work. Jazz and Stu's wedding photo catches my eye like a beacon. Jem and I are both in it, smiling like we're the best of friends. I absolutely can't believe I kissed him that night. What was I thinking? Nothing very sensible, that's for sure. I lie the photo flat. Better not to have reminders flashing at me.

Unfortunately, even with the photo out of sight, the thought of that wedding kiss still sends a ripple right down to my core. So annoying. I like him less with every passing moment, but that night keeps flooding my thoughts and whipping my heart rate into chaos. Now I have to spend three months tiptoeing around the house, not knowing if I must endure another awkward conversation or dodge a towel-clad man jumping out of nowhere. But it's not like I have much choice.

Look, it's only Day Two. Give it a chance. If it's still unbearable in a week, I'll simply email Jazz to say that Mum wants me home as Dad's not well (sorry Dad, but I may as well keep my lies consistent). Jem seems quite capable of looking after a dog. He doesn't need my help, that's for sure. And we clearly don't get on, which can't be good for George. We'll end up like those parents who really should get divorced because they can't be in the same room without bickering. The last thing I want is to be googling dog counsellors. Although, knowing Jazz, George probably already has one. No doubt, the phone number is on that encyclopaedic list "just in case".

Before jumping in the shower, I turn on my computer and see two emails, one from Michelle and one from Jazz. To my delight, Michelle has got me an audition for Monday morning. My heart sinks when I see that it's for a television commercial for a breakfast cereal. Still, I did say to Michelle I wanted one and it's paying $10,000. Not ginormous but not too bad. It has come through a casting agent in Surry Hills who always used to call me in. It would be good to touch base with them. And the fee would certainly help my financial situation. Breakfast cereal. I can do that! At least it's not toilet paper, tampons, or (my worst fear) incontinence pads. Then again, I'm broke, so I can't be fussy.

I read over the script – if you can call it that. Being visual only, it's about half a page. In fact, the scene is quite ridiculous but hey, for the money, I'm prepared to momentarily throw any serious acting ambitions out the window. Then shut the window, throw away the key, and pull down the blind. Self-respect? No time for that right now!

I confirm my audition time with Michelle then open Jazz's email.

Bonjour!

Glad you met up with Alex, he's a big fan of yours. He's familiar with George's routine so can answer any questions.

There's no problem with Stu, just a silly argument. Alex was picking up Roxie after she spent the afternoon at our place. I might have said a few things but nothing to worry about. You know me, I can get carried away in the moment.

Aren't George and Roxie cute? They spend a lot of time together so maybe schedule some play dates. Socialisation is very important for labradoodles.

Has Jem arrived? Hopefully you two can be nice to each other!

JX

I knew it! Nothing to worry about. And yes, I've seen how Jazz gets carried away. When I next see Alex, I'll explain that he got it all wrong. Of course, Jazz and Stu are fine.

I read the email again. But why is Alex so familiar with George's routine? Doesn't that seem a little too intimate for pet owners? Plus, at the dog park, Alex said how he and Jazz decided he couldn't move out of the area. It's like they're co-parenting or something.

I get the feeling I don't know the whole story. I can't explain it, but something about Jazz's email isn't right. She brushed it all aside a little too easily. I'll have to go back to the dog park to do further investigating.

Later that evening, after a relaxing day of doing very little, I'm happily curled up in front of a new series I've been meaning to watch for ages, Jazz's fluffy throw wrapped around my legs. I hear the front door open and my heart sinks lower than the saggy vintage couch I'm sitting on. Damn, I was enjoying a quiet moment alone.

Jem saunters in and stops short when he sees me.

'Hi there,' I say brightly.

'Hey,' he mutters.

There's an awkward pause, which I naturally rush to fill. 'Just started a new Netflix series called *Sub Zero*, a friend of mine from LA is in it, supposed to be pretty good.'

'I'll leave you to it.' He exits the room like lightening.

'I cooked some pasta and there are leftovers,' I call after him.

No reply. But then I hear him clunking around the kitchen, the microwave whirring, and chair legs scraping.

Ten minutes later, I creep into the kitchen to make a cup of tea and find Jem sitting at the table reading. He looks up and our eyes momentarily lock, but just as quickly, he turns back to his book.

I pop the kettle on the stove and rummage around for another

Sleepy Time tea bag, trying to ignore the obvious tension and deafening silence.

'How was the pasta?' I eventually ask.

'Good. Thanks for that.' He doesn't even look up. 'Would have been even better with fresh tomatoes.'

What? Did he actually say that? Unbelievable! I may not be the world's best cook, but he's lucky to have food waiting in the fridge.

'You didn't have to eat it,' I snap back.

He looks surprised. 'Don't take it personally. It was a good sauce. I just prefer fresh tomatoes over canned. It really makes a difference.'

'It was the best I could do in the circumstances.'

'Sure, and it was good to have dinner cooked. Just saying.'

He goes back to his book, and I fume, almost as much as my kettle, which is now whistling steam. I pour the water into my cup and jiggle the bag violently. How dare he come in late and criticise the unexpected dinner that was waiting for him! I want to tell him what he can do with his love of fresh tomato pasta sauce but hold my tongue and focus all my energy on my teabag, causing it to break off from the string and me having to fish it out with my fingers. Just walk away Indie. Just. Walk. Away.

But I don't.

I put my tea back down on the bench and tackle the tension head on.

'Look, Jem, I know you don't particularly want to live with me. I promise you, the feeling's more than mutual, but it looks like neither of us has much choice. So, can we please get past whatever happened between us? I don't expect you to like me, but I'd appreciate it if you could at least be polite and respectful.'

Jem's face darkens like an unexpected storm that threatens but never eventuates. 'Sure,' he says, standing up. 'Sorry.'

'Oh, um thanks.' I'm thrown by his simple response. 'I'll try to keep out of your way.'

Jem looks straight at me for a moment, sending my nervous system into meltdown. 'As far as I'm concerned, there's nothing to get past.'

'Oh, sure… well, great,' I reply even more flustered, wishing I knew a spell to make myself invisible. 'I agree, nothing to get past.'

'So, we're cool?' His eyes drill straight into mine.

'Oh, yeah, we're cool.' I use my most breezy manner. 'Of course.'

Jem turns and walks out, and I let out a breath I didn't know I was holding. Somehow, by trying to be assertive, I've come out looking like the one with the problem. Like a person who has issues with things. Which I'm so not.

Two days in.

Only eighty-nine more to endure.

10

AFTER avoiding Jem all weekend, I get up at six on Monday morning to wash my hair and plan my audition outfit. I'm going for a mum role so after much deliberation (and the realisation I don't even know what mums wear, and if I did, it wasn't going to be found in my measly suitcase), I decide on jeans and a pastel pink shirt from Jazz's wardrobe. She won't mind in the slightest and it looks perfect. I go to the kitchen to make a quick cup of tea, checking my emails while I wait for the kettle. Mark has emailed three times. I press delete without reading them.

'You're up early.'

'Huh?' I'm so deep in thought, I didn't realise Jem had walked up behind me. 'Oh, I've got a casting this morning.'

'What for?' he says as if he couldn't care less.

'An ad.' I sincerely wish it was for a feature film or a Shakespeare theatre production.

Jem's eyebrows rise ever so slightly, which infuriates me. Honestly, he's so rude. I should just pick up my tea and walk away but he's so irritatingly arrogant, I can't help but take the bait.

'Lots of actors do ads. They're usually good money. This one's lucrative and I really need the cash right now.'

'You could get a job.'

'This would be a job.'

'Yeah, right, sure. What's the ad for anyway?'

'Breakfast cereal.' I don't mention that it's for sugar-laden

Breakfast Pops, as I feel this would only add to Jem's apparent delight in the situation.

'Good for you.' His voice grates like metal chair legs dragged across floorboards.

'Well, it's paying twenty grand for a one-day shoot. So yes, it would be good.' And with that little lie about a wage I haven't yet secured, I forget my cup of tea and head straight to the bathroom.

I shouldn't let him get to me, but I can't help it. Jem Taylor rubs me all the wrong ways. Not that I care what he thinks of me. In fact, I couldn't care less. But he makes me feel so dithery. I can't get my words straight or think of anything witty to shut him up. It drives me crazy. As does the mere shape of his seemingly perfect arms. I'm so angry, yet I can't stop this desire to simply press my hands on his skin to see if it's as smooth as it looks.

Okay, this must stop. Focus on the audition, Indie. It may only be an ad, but it's well paid and I need the cash. What does Jem know about the industry anyway? Actors do ads, especially if the money is good. George Clooney did Nespresso ads didn't he? And Cate Blanchett, Chanel No 5? And this one's only being shown in Australia so no one in the US would see it anyway. Won't harm my profile over there.

I bet Jem couldn't earn twenty grand in one day. Although, I'm not actually earning that either, I remind myself. It's ten, and I haven't got it yet.

The trouble with acting is it's worse than a fickle lover. Only interested in you when you're completely indifferent. If you're too needy, it walks away. But the minute you decide to get on with your life, plan a holiday or take a day job, it lures you back into its toxic clutches. It's great when you're working regularly and the pressure's off. You're no longer desperate for money or positive affirmations. The trouble is when you're not working, you pin all your hopes on a breakfast cereal commercial and they can smell your desperation a mile away. And the part will probably go to someone with red curly hair to match the very cute red-curly-haired eight-year-old they've already cast to play the daughter.

I arrive at the casting fifteen minutes before my audition time to calm my nerves and collect my thoughts. I fill out a wardrobe form with my contact details, measurements, availability – pretty much my entire life on a single page – and look around the room. There are four other actresses waiting. All different looks. No one I know.

The door opens and I hear the casting agent laughing loudly with whoever just did their audition. Thirty seconds later, a familiar face appears in front of me, lifting my spirits.

'Charlie Reynolds!' I throw my arms around my old friend from drama school.

'Indie James! You're back!'

'How are you?'

'Pretty good. You look amazing, as always. When did you arrive?'

'Last week, but I'm heading back in a few months.'

'We definitely need to catch up over a coffee or a beer or something. You free this week?'

'For sure. I'm so free.' I've finished my wardrobe form, so I return the pen and clipboard to the table. 'Are you going for Breakfast Pops?'

'Yep, Dad role. It's pretty straightforward. Just keep it natural. Nothing too over the top.'

I grin. 'That would've been hard for you.'

'Hey! I can be subtle.'

'Sure, like when you suggested Hamlet be played as an overweight footy player.'

'Okay, not one of my better ideas.'

The door to the audition room re-opens and a striking woman with jet black hair scraped into two space buns on top of her head walks out, looking at her list. She must be a new casting assistant here.

'Indigo?'

Charlie gives me a quick thumbs-up, mouths 'Call me', and heads out the door.

I take a breath to centre myself.

'Come on in, I'll take that.' The woman holds her hand out for my wardrobe form, talking non-stop. 'I don't think we've met before, I'm Maddi. Great to see you. Thanks for coming in. Fab shirt, love that. After you.'

As I step into the studio, I feel that familiar flicker of anxiety. It doesn't matter how many auditions I do, it's always the same. Over the years, I've learnt to manage my nerves, using them to energise my performance, but today I'm feeling more jittery than normal. And bumping into Charlie like that was a surprise I wasn't expecting. Luckily, I don't have time to think about it as Maddi gets straight down to business.

'Okay, I'll just grab a photo. Look straight at the camera and smile… one, two, three, great. Actually, not so great, let's do another one. One, two, three, hmm, that'll do. Now a quick chat, just your name and agent, any ads on air, any ads for a competitive product in the last three years, if you're free for the shoot date, if you have any allergies to wheat or gluten, and if you're prepared to eat the product.'

I do as I'm told, throwing in the fact I've been working in LA and have recently done a pilot. Okay, so maybe the pilot wasn't that recent, but Maddi doesn't know that.

'Right, so you've had a look at the script? Pretty funny, this one. Director is hilarious. You'll love him.'

I don't agree but smile and nod as if I do.

'They're looking for a real Aussie mum, warm, approachable, someone who's good fun but firm, strict but easy-going. Does that make sense?'

It doesn't make sense at all, but I nod once again. Are there any mums like that? Who gives their kids chocolate covered breakfast cereal anyway? Actually, I made Mum buy Cocoa Pops once. I pestered her relentlessly until she gave in. So maybe it's the mums with pushy kids who'll do anything for a bit of peace.

'All the family is eating the dull ordinary cereal and everyone is sad,' Maddi continues. 'You cheer up breakfast by serving Breakfast Pops and suddenly everyone is bright and happy.'

'Right.' Seems easy enough.

'And what the director would like, which isn't in the script, is for Mum to boogie around the kitchen.'

Uh oh, didn't see that coming.

'Feel free to try whatever you like, maybe start a conga line, maybe a bit of disco dancing. Or Flamenco. Whatever you feel comfortable with. Mum is a real live wire and it's all about what you can bring to the scene. Maybe grab the cereal box and shake it like a maraca. Just a celebration of how happy Breakfast Pops makes you and your family feel. Does that make sense?'

'Ah, sure.' Crazy dancing isn't my strong point, but I didn't think that would ever be a problem. Now I wish I'd done some sort of special workshop on it, instead of wasting my time on acting techniques.

'After you pour the cereal, I'm going to play some music to see how you go. Regular mum who breaks out with what she thinks are some super cool dance moves. Just go for it. But keep it real, okay? Fun, but not too over the top. Just warm and natural. Oh, and keep the box facing front, it's really tempting to put it side on but we need to see the front.'

I sigh to myself. Crazy dancing that's warm and natural. Clearly, one of those ads where they want the performance to walk in the door. They want the actor to create the script.

After the first take, which is just plain embarrassing, Maddi switches off the music and does a half smile, almost out of sympathy. She suggests having another go straightaway. I do it again but she's far from impressed.

'Mmm yes, why don't you, I don't know, wiggle your hips a bit more, have some fun, give yourself permission to have a good time?' She grasps at directorial clichés. 'And don't move out of shot. And keep the box front on. Do your dance steps right there in that spot. Does that make sense? Just let yourself go.'

I smile and nod as if to say no problem, while thinking that if Maddi, with her top knots, asks if it makes sense one more time I'm going to scream.

Judging from her unenthusiastic response after the next take, Maddi doesn't think I'm in the running. I want to explain that I'm actually considered a successful actress in some circles.

'Okay, I think that's good,' she says in a way that indicates that none of the takes is any good at all. 'Why don't we do one last one? And, this time, it's whatever you want. Surprise me.' I think what she really wants to say is, 'Just act better'.

Feeling like I have zero chance of landing the job, I let loose in the last take. Once I've served my sad family the cereal, I start moving slowly, channelling Baby from *Dirty Dancing*. I grab the cereal box (keeping it facing front) as if it's a sexy lover I'm trying to seduce. I twirl, I wiggle, I even throw in some Flamenco moves and toss my head back, laughing in delight. Then, on the spur of the moment, I stop as if my family is looking at me puzzled and confused. I put the cereal box down (facing front of course) and smile a warm and approachable smile. Unembarrassed, confident, and back to my normal easy-going Mum persona, I even pretend I'm eating the super unhealthy breakfast cereal and loving it to the point of almost orgasming. The things we do for money.

'That was great! Perfect! That's the one, I think.' Maddi seems genuinely pleased, surprised even. 'I don't think we need to do that again, I've got a few versions now.'

'Great, thanks, nice to meet you.' I head to the door as fast as I can.

The waiting room is now packed full of "warm, approachable, easy-going, Aussie mum" types about my age. They could cast it ten times over with the actresses waiting to go in and that doesn't count those who came before and the many more that will come in later. Why can't they just give me the job and be done with it? It would save everyone a great deal of hassle and help me get back to Mark… Mark? Why did I think that? Habit, I guess. I'm so used to being in that relationship, it popped out as naturally as breathing air. But not anymore. He isn't the one. Well, I wasn't his one, just one of many. And that's not good enough.

Time to let go and move on. Start a new Indie chapter. Get myself out of debt, buy a ticket back to LA, and become a huge success. Easy. Not that crazy dancing at an audition for a Breakfast Pops TVC is an amazing new chapter, but it's certainly a small (if slightly embarrassing) step in the right direction.

11

WITH absolutely nothing on the next day, I catch the train (actually two trains and a bus) over to Pymble to spend the day with Mum.

Mum opens the door with some sort of white goo on her face. 'Darling! So lovely to see you.'

'Hi, Mum… what's that?'

'A homemade facemask, oatmeal, honey, and what not. You pay over $100 for something like this and it cost me under ten dollars to make. Do you want to try?'

Next minute, Mum and I are lounging on the outdoor sofa with white goo on our faces.

'Doesn't this feel great?'

'It feels hard,' I try to say, but can hardly move my mouth.

'We'll wash it off soon and have a pot of liquorice tea. You'll look amazing.'

I'm not sure how amazing I'll look, but it's fun hanging out with Mum.

'So, are you going to tell me why you're not wearing your engagement ring?'

Until moments like this. My mind jumps to my teenage years, when Mum'd say, 'So, are you going to tell me why you spent the night at Beth's place when her mother was away and thought you were both sleeping the night here?' I guess some things never change.

'It's over.' There's never any point avoiding the truth when it comes to one of Mum's direct questions. 'Turns out he cheated on me.'

'Oh, darling, I'm sorry.' She pauses to think. 'I'm not surprised, mind you. I was never quite sure about him.'

First Jazz, then Dad, now Mum. 'But you hardly knew him.'

'Well, I know him well enough now,' she says primly. 'Trust is everything, and if you don't have that, you have nothing.'

It's a relief to tell Mum and have someone totally and unconditionally on my side.

'He wants to get back together.'

'You're not going to, are you?'

I say nothing and not just because of the ever-hardening porridge on my face. I don't know the answer. I'd hoped coming back to Australia might give me clarity but my mind is as jumbled as ever.

'You'll know what to do.' Mum brings me back to the moment. 'How's Jazz going?'

'Ah, good, I think. Can we wash this off? I think my face is going to break.'

'Hang on.' Mum looks at me suspiciously. 'What's up with Jazz?'

'Nothing, why do you ask?'

'Indie.'

'Nothing's wrong.'

Mum pauses very loudly. There's no way out of it. Honestly, she should work for MI5.

'I think she and Stu are having problems.'

I explain about Alex's comment, Jazz's response, and how nothing adds up.

'I'm sure they're fine, probably a silly squabble.' Mum isn't at all fazed. 'Right, let's wash our faces, have some tea, then we can make my eleven thirty yoga class.'

As far as Mum is concerned, Jazz and Stu are perfectly suited. Unlike Mark and me. She didn't seem at all surprised that my fiancé was unfaithful and we've separated, but she'd never entertain such a thought when it comes to Jazz and Stu.

'How are you getting on with Jem?'

'Well enough.' A huge exaggeration, but to be honest, I've hardly seen him as he leaves early, gets back late, and stays in his bedroom with the light creeping out under the door until all hours. 'Except he criticised my pasta sauce.'

'Can't blame him for that.'

'Gee, thanks, Mum.'

The day slips away and three o'clock rolls around in a flash. I'm so relaxed that George and his hectic schedule slip my mind. I almost choke over what must be our seventh cup of tea for the day. 'I better get back.'

'You can't stay for dinner and sleep here tonight?'

'I'm just not sure what Jem is up to. Someone has to walk the dog, feed him, and read a bedtime story.'

Mum laughs until she realises I'm not joking. 'How ridiculous!'

'Jazz is like some sort of tiger mum for dogs.'

I'd love to stay over at Mum and Dad's. I feel like I need to spend more time with them while I'm in Australia, but what if Jem doesn't come home either? Or gets in late and George hasn't had dinner? We need to work out a schedule. Who takes George for walks, who feeds him, who bathes him (not that either of us have done that yet).

I arrive back and thankfully, Jem is out, but I feel at a loose end. Normally, the thought of hiding in my bedroom streaming Netflix on my laptop is heaven but not tonight. I try Lucy and Jesse, who insist I join them for dinner, but I don't feel like crashing their date.

'Come on, it'll be fun,' Lucy says. 'We're going to a party later on – you could meet us there.'

'That's okay, you guys have fun.' I don't feel like turning up to some party on my own.

We arrange to meet for a walk in the morning. My heart feels like lead as I contemplate another night alone, creeping around trying to avoid my irritating housemate.

Until Charlie Reynolds leaps into my head like a superhero. Maybe I should take him up on his offer of a drink? Charlie and I were best friends at drama school. I always found him attractive but he was such a flirt and fell in love with every actress he met and I never wanted to be one of his many conquests. Anyway, that's all in the past and we're still good friends. It would be nice to catch up, so I send a quick text.

Surprisingly, the response is immediate and we arrange to meet at 7pm, Bar Max in Surry Hills.

Around six thirty, I'm ready to head out when Jem comes through the sliding door. Instead of grunting a few disinterested words, he briefly pauses, his eyes taking in the little black dress I found in Jazz's cupboard. Then he moves to the fridge.

'Where you off to?'

'Some bar.' I can't be bothered explaining, nor do I feel I need to. 'Actually, glad you're here, I was thinking we need to set up some sort of roster system for walking George, feeding him, and so on.'

'Sure, if you want,' he says. 'Which one?'

'Sorry?'

'Which bar?'

'Oh… Bar Max… anyway, I'll draw up a chart and maybe we

can fill in when we're available?'

'So, you're going on a date?'

'No, no, not a date, no.' The question sends me into a fluster. 'Just a drink with an old friend… I haven't fed George yet but I got a sachet of chicken out to defrost…'

'Is the old friend a guy?'

'Yes, but that doesn't—'

'Is he straight?'

'Yes, but I don't think—'

'If he's a heterosexual guy, and he suggested Bar Max, it's a date.'

'No, we're really just friends. We went through drama school together.'

'Right, well, have fun.' Jem pours some juice into a glass with a not-so-subtle smirk on his face. 'And yes, I'll feed George.'

Honestly, he couldn't be any more annoying if he tried. And that's saying something.

'It's not a date,' I say.

'If you say so.'

Once again, I struggle to find the perfect retort, so I strut down the hall with my head as high as it can be when you're only one hundred and sixty-three centimetres tall. How dare he assume I'm going on a date? And why can I never think of a good comeback? There's nothing between Charlie and me. And even if there was – which there's not – it's none of his business.

'Don't be too late,' Jem calls after me. 'I'll walk George in the morning if you're not back by then. Shall I put it on the roster?'

I ignore his remark and stride out the front door and down to the bus stop, glad to be free of Jem Taylor for the evening.

12

'WOW, Indie James, you look amazing!' Charlie is waiting for me outside Bar Max.

'Don't sound so surprised, Charlie Reynolds.' We always refer to each other by full name, a quirk of our friendship that started back in first year of drama school and stuck. Something about having a name that sounds like an actor. He insisted mine was great, and I always preferred his.

'I'm not surprised, it's what I've come to expect, but it's still worthy of comment.'

Charlie looks gorgeous himself, I have to say. He's incredibly attractive in an actorish sort of way, but definitely a better friend than lover.

Not long before I left for LA, we played opposite each other in a play at Belvoir St Theatre and, one night, we accidently fell into bed. And then the next night. And the next. We never said that we were boyfriend/girlfriend. He was so casual that I truly didn't expect anything. Charlie wasn't the sort of guy to commit to a long-term relationship and by then, I was set on going overseas. We never really talked about it and then I left and met Mark. Now, it's like it never happened.

'Let's grab a drink, and there's a party later if you're interested,' he says. 'You know Richard Miles and Duncan Walters?'

'Of course, I did a show with Richard once and Duncan was the year below us at drama school, wasn't he?'

'They're throwing a joint birthday party at the Waverly Bowling Club.'

'Sounds good.'

Charlie and I have a couple of beers and then find a cheap Thai place for dinner. I'd forgotten how funny he could be. And charming. He gives people absolute focus, unlike Mark, who was always looking around to see who else was at the party. Always popping off to introduce himself to some director or asking people to join us. Which I never minded at first. It was exciting, and I didn't know a lot of industry people in LA. But we were rarely alone and our life together was hectic. No time to stop and think. Off to try this new café, hike that mountain, we didn't relax very often. No wonder I needed daily yoga classes and was considering a meditation course. I was emotionally and physically exhausted.

Seeing Charlie is like putting on a favourite pair of jeans that always feels good and still looks great. No need for backstories about where I studied and what jobs are on my CV. I can get straight to the present and fill him in on why I'm now dog-sitting for Jazz.

'What an idiot,' Charlie says, when I explain what Mark did. 'He must be cracked in the head.'

'Actors! What can I say?'

'We're not all like that, Indie James.' Charlie looks at me with his perfect *Home & Away* face and piercing blue eyes and a wash of warmth spreads across my neck and chest.

I change the subject. 'Did you hear about that ad?'

'No.'

'Me either.'

'I think Tia Harris was cast as the mum. Sorry to break the bad news.'

I groan. Of course she was! All the work I used to get is now going to her because everyone in Sydney has forgotten who I am.

'Indie,' Charlie says in a stern voice, knowing exactly what sort of insecure thoughts are invading my mind, 'don't go there. It's just an ad.'

I smile ruefully. 'I know, I just wish it wasn't Tia.'

'You're not still smarting from the Masha Fiasco, are you? Come on, that was years ago.'

'I know, but she's so competitive and always makes out she's so much more successful than me.'

'Which she's not.'

'But now she's on Michelle's books, I feel like I'm being replaced. First Kourtney, now Tia.'

'Rubbish. You're completely different to Tia. And you can act rings around her.'

'See, that's why I like hanging out with you, Charlie Reynolds. You always make me feel good about myself.'

'That's my job.' Charlie pauses, his cheeky grin falling away. 'Remind me, why did nothing ever eventuate between us?'

I whack him on the arm. 'It did, if I remember correctly. Thanks very much, it mustn't have been very memorable.'

'Of course, I remember. But I also remember feeling disappointed because you quickly lost interest.'

'You were the one who didn't want to be in a relationship. Too busy dating every glamorous and successful actress in Sydney.'

'What?' Charlie gapes. 'I was not. I wish I had though, that sounds exciting…'

'Come on, you were always after some gorgeous girl and then you'd move on. You always thought of me as a mate, which was probably better. Yes, we had a fling but that's all it was. And I never fancied being yet another one of your adoring crowd.'

'Indie, you were never one of the crowd.'

'Well, that's something, I guess.'

'When you started going out with Mark, I never heard from you again, apart from the occasional like or comment on Instagram. We used to hang out so much and when you left, I really missed you. I still miss you.'

'I guess I lost contact with a lot of people.' I think of Jazz and her possibly failing marriage. And her newfound friendship with Alex, the Dog Man. And my parents, who aren't getting any younger. Maybe I haven't been there for the important people in my life.

Fortunately, the waitress interrupts my many thoughts of guilt and self-doubt to take our order. I'm hopeless with menu decisions. I know everything on a menu is probably delicious, but I find the pressure of choosing the perfect dish overwhelming. I leave it to Charlie, who seems to know exactly what to order, and escape to the toilet.

I rehash what Charlie just said. What did he mean? Did he want a relationship with me back then? He never said so, but then, I was so keen to go overseas, maybe I didn't read between the blurry casual lines.

I return to the table and in no time the waitress arrives with five dishes and a huge bowl of rice.

'How much did you order? Weren't you thinking two dishes and an entrée to share?'

'I was, but I threw in a few extras by mistake,' Charlie replies sheepishly. 'I'm so hungry, I'm sure I can eat for the two of us.'

'No need, I can hold my own.'

'I remember that about you.'

It's true, I eat a lot and I'm always hungry. Just one of those metabolisms. But right now, I'm busy looking at Charlie through newly-single eyes and I like what I see. Maybe he's not the ladies' man I thought he was. Maybe he's calmed down and is looking for—

'More rice?' Charlie snaps me back with a sharp jolt. I still haven't sorted out my last relationship and already, I'm contemplating another. Is Charlie even single? Don't ask, Indie, just leave it.

'Thanks, so are you seeing anyone?' Oops, didn't mean to say that. I see an edge of surprise in Charlie's eyes.

'Why do you ask? You up for the job?'

'Doubt it, too much like hard work.'

'Not at all, I'm great boyfriend material.'

'Is that what all the girls tell you?'

'They do, when they dump me. "You'd make a great boyfriend, just not for me".'

'Girls dump *you,* do they?'

'Yup.'

'You never told me that.'

'You never asked. You assume I'm the heartbreaker, but in fact, I'm usually the heartbreakee.'

'Poor Charlie.'

'It's okay, most of them are wrong for me anyway.' He looks at his phone and checks a few messages. 'Hey, we should get to this party.'

Charlie pays for dinner despite my protests. 'You can get it next time.'

'Next time? Like a second date? I might have to dump you before then,' I joke.

'That'd be right. Nothing new there.'

Out on the street, Charlie hails a taxi and gently takes my hand, giving my heart a slight jolt. That tiny bit of skin around mine feels smooth and exciting. Am I just looking for something to get over

Mark? Some strange sort of revenge for cheating on me? Probably, but that's okay, isn't it?

Sitting in the cab, we don't say a word but Charlie still has my hand firmly in his. Just that simple gesture and my body is inflamed. Or maybe it's his hair product. Like a caramel milkshake. Delicious.

Despite what Charlie says now, he wasn't interested in anything more than a fling back then. But here he is, all blond and beautiful, holding my hand in a taxi, and I just want to… Enough Indie, stop right now.

'You okay?' Charlie asks. 'Something wrong?'

'Yes, I mean no, nothing wrong, all okay.' Get it together, Indie, for God's sake.

We arrive at the party, which is filled to the brim with practically every Sydney actor I've ever met or worked with. Which is a good thing as it distracts me from weirdly lusting after Charlie. I see Lucy and Jesse almost immediately.

'Glad you made it in the end, and you're here with Charlie, I see.' Lucy raises her eyebrows so high they disappear into her curly mop.

'We're just friends, you know that.'

'I seem to remember something a little more.'

'Once or twice and that was it.'

'You two always got on well.'

'Charlie got on well with every girl back at drama school,' I say. 'But, yes, we did have a fling before I went to LA.'

'Well?'

'It was nothing serious. And right now, I need to recover from one relationship before launching into another.'

'We're not talking about a relationship,' Lucy says with a twinkle in her eye. 'Just have some fun. Can't hurt.'

'What are you two discussing?' Charlie chooses that moment

to come and put his arms around both of us. 'Looks intense.'

'Far from it,' I say.

'Then maybe I can interest you both in another drink?'

'Vodka tonic, please,' Lucy says.

I nod.

Charlie brings back drinks and then excuses himself to catch up with another friend. A little later, I see him across the room near the bar, chatting to a group of people. I'd forgotten just how damn hot he is. I certainly remember the sex being surprisingly good.

Our paths don't cross again for another hour or so. Maybe he feels embarrassed after our dinner conversation. Like he revealed too much.

Tia arrives later – she must have come straight from the theatre – and I keep out of her way. I don't particularly want to hear what a great show it was tonight, and how she's ten grand richer than I am. Besides, she makes an immediate beeline for Charlie and the pair of them are soon chatting quite comfortably. Obviously better friends now than back in drama school.

Apart from that, it's great seeing so many familiar faces in one space. I'd forgotten about the tight acting community here in Sydney. I wish I could stay and never go back to LA.

Eventually, the night winds down and just as I feel I should get going, Charlie bounds up. 'Share a cab? I can drop you off.'

'Sure.'

'Unless you want to come back for a drink at my place? Cup of tea?'

I don't really feel like going home, so I agree. We're just friends, I say to myself. Something I have to *keep* saying. Trying to convince myself maybe?

Back at Charlie's, we actually do share a pot of tea and some chocolate chip cookies. Absolutely fine. Nothing untoward here.

Charlie puts his cup back down on the coffee table. 'You were quite the talk of the town tonight.'

'Me? People hardly remember me, and if they do, they didn't realise I've been away.'

'Are you kidding? You were an instant success after graduation. Then went to LA. It doesn't get more glamorous than that.'

'What about you?' I ask flirtatiously.

'What do you mean?'

'What did you think back then?'

'Of you?'

'Yes, of me.'

Charlie pauses, and I think he's going to make some disparaging comment, as is his usual way of shying away from meaningful moments.

'I thought you were just about perfect, Indie James.'

'What? Don't be ridiculous!'

'I did. I still do. And you are. I wanted to say that when we were having dinner but didn't want to freak you out.'

'You never thought that back at drama school.'

'Yes, I did.'

'Charlie Reynolds, you did not!'

'Are you telling me what I was thinking?'

'No but—'

'But what?'

'Come on, I bet you've said that to just about every girl in our year. How many times has it worked?'

A faint look of annoyance flickers across his eyes. 'I haven't said that to anyone else.'

'Why have you never said it to me before?'

'I thought you knew. Clearly, you don't, so I'm saying it now.'

The voice in my head tells me it's just another line, but I'm here and sort of available, so I push the point.

'Well, what are you going to do about it?'

Charlie doesn't waste another second, pulling me towards him and kissing me on the lips. Slow, sensuous, sexy.

I don't know if it's the thrill of kissing someone different, or the fact that we've been down this strangely familiar road before, but I respond with enthusiasm. It's out of character for me, especially considering the Mark situation, but I'm feeling reckless. Free and uninhibited as Charlie's arms wrap around me. Like I'm on holiday in a different country. Which I sort of am. I also realise how little fire there's been with Mark lately. Somewhere along the way, it fizzled out. Probably the day Kourtney moved centre stage.

Our bodies inch closer and Charlie gives a faint groan of desire as our kisses become more desperate. Suddenly, he pulls away and looks at me, possibly sensing my rambling thoughts.

'What?' I say, suddenly feeling self-conscious.

'You okay?'

I nod, giving him a quick kiss on the lips, my stomach turning in anticipation. It's been so long since someone has been attracted to me, particularly a flirty actor like Charlie. My ego was badly hurt after Mark, and being around Jem hasn't helped, so this makes a welcome change.

'It's… well… you've just come out of a full-on relationship, engagement even, which sounds like it's not really over.' Charlie looks concerned. 'Maybe you need a bit more time.'

'Are you changing your mind, Charlie Reynolds?'

By way of an answer, Charlie grabs my hand and leads me down the hall to his bedroom.

'Nice sheets,' I comment.

'Egyptian cotton, 400 thread count.' He gently guides me down so I can feel them for myself and slowly starts to remove every item of my clothing. Luckily, I'm not wearing much so it doesn't take long.

'You definitely okay with this?'

'Definitely. It's well and truly over with Mark.' I try to tell myself more than Charlie. 'And what could be better than to move on and have some fun?'

That same hurt look clouds Charlie's eyes. 'Is that all this is to you? A bit of fun?'

'Not just that,' I say quickly. 'You're very special to me, but I'm not looking for a relationship.'

'Right.' His mood shifts instantly.

'Sorry, but I'm really—

'It's just I've always liked you, Indie James.' He leans back on his pillow, staring at the ceiling. 'I knew you weren't seriously interested back then, your career was always more important, but I kinda hoped one day it might work out. Until you got engaged, and I knew it could never happen.'

'Charlie—'

'Then you turned up at the casting and I feel the same way as I did back then.'

In a flash, I realise I've picked the wrong guy for my revenge sex. While I was having fun, enjoying the attention of my handsome funny friend, to whom I'm incredibly attracted, I didn't consider him at all. I feel absolutely rotten. And what does he mean about my career being more important? I didn't think I was that ambitious.

'You know what, Charlie Reynolds,' I run my fingers through his thick, honey-coloured hair, 'you're right, I'm not ready for this. Can we press pause?'

Charlie's shoulders drop. 'Yeah, of course, I get it.'

'I need to sort out my life before confusing it even more.'

'I'd be a confusion?'

'No, but I need to clear my head. Starting something now wouldn't be fair to you, or Mark.' I pull the lush sheets around me. 'Sorry, I shouldn't have let it go so far.'

'Are you sure that's the reason?'

'What do you mean?'

'Maybe you don't feel the same about me as I do you.'

'Charlie Reynolds, I adore you, I always have, but my head's all over the place, and I don't want to ruin our friendship.'

Charlie offers a faint smile. 'I don't mind if you do.'

'Well, I mind.' Fatigue hits like a lightning bolt and all I want is to close my eyes. 'Could I just stay over? I don't feel like going home now.'

'Of course.' Charlie lies down, cocooning his body around mine, as he's done countless times before as both friends and lovers, and we slowly drift off to sleep.

What seems like seconds later, morning light filters through the drawn curtains, gently nudging open my eyes and weighing on my aching head. Where am I? This isn't my room. Oh God, have I gone into Jem's room by accident? How much did I drink last night?

A movement next to me grabs my attention and blurry images from the night before jolt through my mind. That's right. Charlie. Not Jem after all. But why did I let this happen?

'Hey, you.' Charlie rolls over, facing me eye-to-eye.

'Good morning.'

Suddenly, the Egyptian sheets feel scratchy and I want to be out from under them.

'I better go.' I can't even bring myself to make an excuse.

There's nothing to say. I've been horrible to my friend. Did I think I'd feel better by sleeping with someone else? Just because Mark did that, doesn't mean I should as well.

'Yep, sure.' Charlie jumps out of bed and grabs his dressing gown. 'I've got a shift at the café this morning anyway, so I'd better get going.'

The mood descends into awkwardness as I throw on my clothes and fumble around for my shoes and bag.

'You okay, Charlie Reynolds?'

'Yep, fine.' He walks to the bathroom. 'See you, Indie.'

I let myself out and find myself on the street at seven in the morning, feeling wretched and hungover. Charlie didn't respond with my full name. Which tells me that he's definitely not fine. And considering the night's events, neither am I.

13

BACK home, I creep through the front door with the stealth of an undercover agent. The last thing I want is for Jem to see me coming in at this hour, asking how my "date" went. I head straight to my bedroom, where I find George stretched out across the bed, fast asleep. I didn't travel halfway across the world to exchange one snoring lump for another. And Jazz would be furious if she found out. What if I create some habit that won't shift?

'George,' I say, trying to whisper. 'Wake up, off the bed, there's a good boy.'

George stirs, going from zero to about fifty thousand, standing on the bed and barking excitedly.

'Shhhh, be quiet and get down.' I try to move vintage white lace cushions out of George's path with little success. 'I'll give you a treat if you calm down, or I'll take you for a walk later, I just need to change.'

George's doggie attention must have focused on the "treat" and "walk" bits of my sentence because he tumbles into a fervent licky frenzy. Clearly "later" or "need to change" were just white noise.

'Okay, okay, give me a chance, won't be long.'

The house is quiet. Jem must have gone to work already. My breathing calms and my body relaxes. Until I see the kitchen with a half-filled cereal bowl on the bench, a scatter of cornflakes on the floor, half a piece of vegemite toast on the table (my super expensive sourdough bread), and dirty dishes in the sink from last night. It's like a pack of teenagers just got home from school.

Mark was such a clean freak; there was never so much as a stray crumb in the kitchen, so this is a bit of a shock. I try to ignore it and make a cup of tea, only to find no milk left in the fridge. Too much wasted on cereal. Honestly.

'You're home.' Jem's voice behind me makes me jump.

'Can you not do that?' I say, already annoyed by the state of the kitchen and now even more so to see the person responsible. I'm about to lecture him on cleaning up after himself but a look in his eyes stops me. Is that disapproval?

'So, how was the date?'

I sigh. Here we go. 'It wasn't a date.'

'It went for a long time. What was his name?'

'Charlie, just an old friend from drama school, like I told you. We went to a party, I had a little too much to drink and crashed on his couch. End of story. Not that it's any of your business.'

I must have an edge to my voice because, surprisingly, Jem backs down. 'Okay, you're right, none of my business.' With that, he grabs his keys, mutters something I don't understand, and marches out the door.

Thank God! Although, he's obviously not planning on cleaning up the kitchen anytime soon.

I shower and put on some comfy trackie pants and trainers to go for my planned walk with Lucy. But it does little to ease the discomfort prickling my insides. Last night, I wasn't fair to Charlie but deep down, if I'm honest, there's something else. That expression on Jem's face when he saw me come in, having spent a night with another guy. Not that what I do, or with whom I sleep or don't sleep, have anything to do with Jem.

I walk back into the kitchen, fuming once again at its

dishevelled state. We need to set up a cleaning roster, as well as a roster for George. And I'm going to have to say something about the grocery situation. Not that I've done much shopping, but he's done none, and it's starting to drive me crazy.

Lucy texts to postpone our walk, as she's been booked for a voiceover. Happy that today went her way and relieved I don't have to dissect the outcome of the evening, I have the morning to myself. Until George looks at me with deep sorrowful eyes as if to say, 'I don't want to trouble you, but if you could possibly take me for a walk, I'd really appreciate it.'

'Haven't you been out this morning?' I ask.

Apparently not, judging from the way George is jumping up and down. I look shocking and need a shower. My hair is a mess and I could do with a spot of make-up. But I'm only walking a dog. Do I have to look glamorous for that?

Determined to get his doggy way, George is increasingly persistent, so I throw all caution to the Bondi wind. Who cares if I bump into anyone I know?

'Okay, George, seeing as you're asking so politely.'

I grab the leash (ignoring the harness), click it on George's collar and head out the door. With all this walking, not to mention regular running, I'm going to be as fit as ten fiddles. One thing for sure, it's tiring me out and helping me finally sleep properly. It's also getting my mind off LA and Mark.

We stroll along the promenade and immediately I realise that not only should I have had a shower and washed (and styled) my hair but bought a whole new wardrobe of cool chic exercise attire. Every single person looks amazing. Beautiful. Perfectly dressed, with a combination of up-to-the-minute chic and I-really-don't-care casualness. Neither of which is achieved by my mismatched running outfit. I put my head down and keep walking, which isn't easy to do as George spies a seagull every couple of steps.

'Just because you see a bird doesn't mean you have to run after it, and you probably won't catch it, as it has wings and you don't.'

'Woof!' says George, which translates as, 'I could if you ran a bit faster or let me off my lead. I reckon I could get it in one gulp.'

Great, now I'm having imaginary conversations with a dog. Becoming a dog person is more contagious than I realised. One week in, and I'm turning into Jazz. It won't be long before I'm setting a place at the table for George and sharing my dinner. Although, he only eats organic and I gave up that privilege when I became an actor. On my precarious income, it's a luxury I can ill afford.

George drags me back up the hill and I realise we're at the dog park. I look around for Alex, but George sees Roxie first. The two of them rumble and lick each other. Dating is so different for dogs. No dinner in a restaurant and awkward chit chat. You either like the smell of each other or not. If you do, then it's on, if not, you bark and they go away. Heaven!

'They're happy to see each other.' Alex strolls up. 'How are you?'

'Good.' I pause. 'Actually, not good at all, pretty bad to be honest.'

I barely know Alex but somehow, I feel comfortable opening up. He's so easy to talk to. Maybe he's a psychologist. If not, he should be.

'What's wrong? Is it the fiancé?'

'Ex-fiancé.' Emotion swells in my chest and suddenly all my woes tumble out of my mouth and all over my nicely dressed dog owner acquaintance. How my relationship fell apart and how I found out the truth. 'Then I left for Sydney, and as far as I'm concerned, it's over. Except he keeps emailing me, wanting to work things out.'

'Do you want to work things out?'

'How should *I* know?' My voice even scares me.

'Sorry.' Alex backs away. 'Just asking.'

'No, I'm sorry, I didn't mean to take it out on you. I nearly slept with someone else last night. An old friend. But I couldn't go through with it. It meant more to him than me, and I feel terrible.'

'Well done for following your instincts.'

I look at Alex suspiciously. 'Are you a psychologist?'

He laughs. 'No, a primary school teacher. I guess I get a lot of practice teaching Year Three.'

'Bit of a handful?'

'You have no idea.' He pauses. 'People always tell me I should go back and study psychology. Jazz is always saying that.'

'Is she?' I ask casually. 'Sounds like you guys have talked a lot?'

'Oh, just here and there, at the park,' Alex says vaguely.

'I asked her about what you said, and she reckons it was just a silly squabble with Stu.'

'Did she?' He frowns as if trying to recall the conversation. 'Yes, well it probably was. You know her better than I do, plus she'd had a few glasses of wine.'

'Oh? Where were you?' Surely "a few glasses of wine" is not normal between dog owners? Not that I really know, but Jazz is married, and Alex is, well, handsome.

'Over at Jazz's,' Alex says. 'The dogs usually have a play date on a Friday, I was picking up Roxie.'

'Oh, right.'

'Jazz was upset about Stu, they seem to fight a lot over George.'

'George?'

'Yes, stuff like how to look after him, where he sleeps, what he eats. Sometimes parents don't agree, a bit like with child rearing, and it causes conflict.'

Relief washes over me. That doesn't sound too bad. I thought they were having relationship problems. How to look after a pet? That's nothing. 'Well, their personalities are different. Jazz has always been super-organised. She categorises books, even hangs her clothes in alphabetical order in her wardrobe.'

'But it sends mixed messages and confuses George.'

'Really?' I had no idea having a dog was such a challenge. Not just the walking, feeding, brushing, and washing (Note to self: *must wash George*), but the emotional commitment. It really is like having a child. One that will never move out of home. 'I'm sure they'll work it out.'

'There's more to it.' Alex pauses, as if wondering how much he should say. 'We were having a glass of wine, as we often do after picking up from a play date, but she'd already had a few and was angry with Stu, and not just about George.'

'What was she angry about?' I wonder if I even know my best friend anymore, and why she wants to discuss everything with Dog Man. But then I just did exactly that, so who am I to talk?

'If I tell you this, you can't say anything to Jazz. Promise?'

I nod with my fingers crossed behind my back.

'She was crying because Stu said he doesn't want to have a baby.'

'A baby?' I knew they were in no hurry for kids but they definitely planned for one, down the track. Stu can't have changed his mind? He's had baby names picked out since he was a teenager.

'Look, maybe talk to Jazz.' Alex looks uncomfortable. 'She's not in a good way.'

I nod. 'Better go.'

'Yeah, me too.' Alex calls the dogs and they come running. 'Thanks for the chat.'

'Not at all.' He clips the leash to Roxie's harness. 'Give me a call sometime, and we can have a drink. I'd love to hear more about your work. Maybe without the "children".' He points to our dogs wrestling in front of us.

'That'd be lovely.'

I put George on the lead and turn towards home, feeling puzzled. I came back to Sydney to recover and relax, only to discover that my friend has relationship problems but hasn't confided in me. I selfishly nearly slept with a good friend and hurt his feelings. I keep having steamy wedding flashbacks of my cranky housemate. And now I'm making friends with a stranger at the dog park, who has some emotional connection to my best friend – how close, I'm still not sure. The plan was to escape heartbreak and confusion. But somehow, I've catapulted myself into a whole lot more.

When I get home, I'm about to call Charlie to apologise but get distracted by a text from my agent. *Things to discuss. Quick coffee?*

Hurray! Let's hope she has some good news that will get my mind off my disastrous personal life.

I walk into the kitchen and almost fall over backwards when I see a pile of empty green shopping bags on the kitchen floor. Jem must have been shopping. Not only that, but the Spray & Wipe is sitting out and has been put to good use because I can practically see myself in the stone benchtop.

This doesn't change anything. Jem is still rude and annoying. But a few groceries might help. I take a sneak peek in the fridge and like what I see. Fresh fruit and vegies, gourmet cheeses, and all sorts of interesting ingredients that would only be purchased by someone who likes to cook. Is that a jar of capers? Impressive. I wonder what he does with those? The next couple of months may be more bearable than I thought. One thing's for sure, they couldn't get much worse.

We meet in a tiny café, where Michelle knows everyone, and squeeze into a corner table as two coffees miraculously appear.

'Wow, good service.'

'I texted ahead,' Michelle says. 'They always time it perfectly, so my coffee's ready when I arrive. I think my caffeine addiction keeps their business afloat.'

We settle in and Michelle gets straight to the point. 'So, I have good news. Just secured you an audition for the film I mentioned, *Not Missing Out.*'

'That *is* good news.'

'Nina Freeman is directing, everyone wants to work on it. Very closed shop, and they need to re-cast their female lead in a hurry.'

'I heard that, why?'

'The actress they cast went out partying one weekend, got completely wasted and posted one too many photos on Instagram and Twitter that didn't show her in the best light.'

'Really?'

'Suddenly the photos were everywhere. The producers didn't want her associated with the film, so she got fired.'

'God!'

'But then it got worse. She went on a Twitter rant, complaining about how unfair it was, how the producers were wrong. Needless to say, she won't be working again anytime soon.'

'What's the character?'

'A fiery forensic scientist called Alyssa. Perfect role for you. I'll email you the script, but I've also got a hard copy at the agency if you want to borrow it. I'll just get you to sign a non-disclosure agreement. Let me know what you think, but don't take too long. I need to confirm ASAP. They want to cast the part quickly as the shoot is scheduled to start in three or four weeks.'

'Sounds good.'

'And now for the bad news.'

'Uh oh.' I hold my breath. Words an actor never wants to hear. Maybe she's decided not to represent me anymore? Maybe that's what this coffee is about. Letting me down gently, explaining how the industry is so dire she has to let people go. Maybe now Tia's getting my work, she doesn't need someone like me on her books. Oh my God, I'm being dumped!

'Breakfast Pops. It's a no go, I'm afraid.'

I let out a huge breath. 'No surprise there, I heard Tia got it. Naturally!'

Michelle looks at me sternly. 'It's just an ad. Next one will be yours. Focus on this film audition. You can get this.'

I smile as positively as I can, knowing Michelle has no time for insecure actors, but I'm really beginning to doubt my ability to get any job, Breakfast Pops or otherwise. And I genuinely thought my agent was about to drop me from the agency. I need to get a grip or I'm not going to survive.

Michelle needs to go, so I head to the agency to pick up the script. I know it will be in my inbox but I love having a hard copy to read. I find another café and order yet another coffee. Ten minutes in and I know the role is fantastic and want it to be mine. That familiar whirl of excitement sparks deep in my stomach, a feeling I haven't had in ages. I don't know if I've got what it takes, but one thing's for sure, I'm going to put everybody (particularly the male and canine variety) to one side and give it my best shot.

<h1 style="text-align:center">14</h1>

BACK home, I step out onto the terrace expecting to be bowled over, but the garden is as quiet as the rest of the house. I check every one of George's favourite hidey-holes and his assortment of "break-out stations", but nothing. I notice the leash isn't on the hook so he must be out with Jem. Should I text to check? No, he'll just think I'm neurotic. Even more than usual.

Half an hour later, Jem walks in the door. Alone.

'Where's George?'

'In the garden, I imagine,' Jem replies curtly.

'Except he's not.'

'What do you mean? Where is he?'

'I got home a little while ago and he wasn't here, so I thought he was with you.'

'Why didn't you call or text me to check?'

'Remember last time I got worried?' I say in a sarcastic tone. 'You thought I was over-doing it.'

'What about this?' Jem grabs the leash and waves it at me.

Damn! I didn't see the leash on the sofa. Clearly, Jem hadn't taken George out for a walk. Which I would have known if I'd returned the leash to the correct spot on the hall table.

Jem sprints out the back and looks around, calling for George. Honestly, does he think I'm not able to see if a dog is in a small backyard? He comes back into the kitchen, leash in hand, and walks straight past me.

'Where are you going?'

He turns with a grim expression. 'To look for George. Unless you want to explain to Jazz and Stu why he's not here when they get home. Where were you today? With your new boyfriend, I suppose?'

'No! Charlie is not my boyfriend.' I take a breath to calm myself. 'I had a meeting with my agent. I took George out this morning and put him back in the garden.'

'Did you shut the gate?'

'Of course I shut the gate.' My tummy quivers. George and I did come back through the side gate, but did I shut it properly? I thought I did, but my mind is a blur. Like when you can't remember if you've turned off the oven. I always have to go back and check I've locked the front door properly. What if this was the one time I actually hadn't done it? What if something's happened to him and it's all my fault? Jazz will never forgive me. Oh, why did I use the side gate?

'He might be around the neighbourhood,' Jem cuts through my panic. 'Let's split up. Start with his favourite spots. I'll head to the oval; I've been taking him there for walks.'

Jem is cool as a summer breeze, completely in control. I've been so irritated by his reassured manner, but now it's what I need. Irritating but somehow steady.

'Right. I'll go to the dog park.'

'Take your phone and keep in contact. And check the home answering machine every now and then. Someone might find him and ring the number on his collar. Let's hope Jazz and Stu didn't put their mobiles on his tag. We don't want them getting a call in the French countryside from some stranger who's found George on the street.'

A knot tightens in the pit of my stomach. Jazz asked me to do one thing, and I failed. She and Stu are likely to jump on the first plane home if they know George is lost. And considering what's going on for Jazz, they need all the time away they can get.

Jem strides to the front door, looking surprisingly strong and sexy. Keep your mind on the job, Indie.

'Are you coming?' Jem waits impatiently.

'Yes, sorry.' I follow him out the front gate.

He heads off at a rapid pace, but I can't move. Once Jem turns the corner at the end of the street, I duck down the side path and push on the wooden gate. It swings open, hitting the fence with a bang. I stare at it in horror. Oh my God! It's all my fault. Here I am, going on about how rude and ill-mannered Jem is, while I've possibly lost my best friend's dog. What's more, I'll now have to admit to Jem that I made a mistake. He's going to love this. And I'm going to feel even more of an idiot around him than I already do. Why, why, why didn't I check the gate?

I quickly make sure it's well and truly shut now. Jem doesn't have to know about this yet. No one does.

I run after Jem and we part ways at the end of the road. I hear him calling for George as I race in the direction of the dog park, all my fingers crossed. He loves the park. Maybe he's there right now, happily digging up a garden bed.

Please be there. Please be there.

I pick up my pace. It's lucky I've started running again. Adrenalin and anxiety kick in and I arrive in less than three minutes. That must be a record. Not that it matters now. I scan the park, hoping to see a flash of his caramel coat. But no George. I look in every garden bed and under every bush. Still, no George.

Despair swoops in like sudden rain clouds. Where else could he be? I pace nearby streets. I check the front garden of every home. I even ask a few people, but no one has seen a dog that fits

George's description. He's so distinctive, like a fluffy caramel coloured pony that's had too much red cordial, you'd remember if you saw him.

I text Jem. *Anything?*

His response is short but not so sweet. *Nope.*

I power along street after street in a panic, short of breath and drenched with perspiration. What if something terrible has happened? What if he's been hit by a car? I almost hyperventilate at the thought. Jazz will never forgive me, Stu neither.

Finally, I see Jem on the other side of the road. He shakes his head as he crosses to me.

My heart sinks even lower. 'What are we going to do?'

I think about Alex. He'd know what to do. I don't have his number but it could be in Jazz's wad of papers back home.

'I don't know. Maybe report it to the police, or what about the vet?' Jem rubs his forehead. 'Someone might have found him and dropped him in.'

'He's micro-chipped so they'll call us.' I groan. 'I mean, they'll call Jazz.'

'Not much we can do about that. At least we'd know George was safe.'

We start googling vets and find one in the area that's still open. Jem calls immediately, but sadly they haven't seen a labradoodle called George. They take down all the details and also suggest reporting it to the council and maybe putting a post on a local Facebook group.

Scanning the streets, I feel disconnected to the buzzing Bondi scene around me, like I'm watching a horrible movie play out. But for once, I don't know the script and there's absolutely no guarantee of a happy Hollywood ending.

Why on earth did I think that looking after a dog would make my life any better? Of all the things I could have done to soothe my broken heart and battered ego, I chose a job for which I have zero experience. And now I've failed, and apart from having to carry the guilt for the rest of my life, I'll lose my best friends forever. Surely misplacing a dog is a deal breaker for pet owners. Especially Jazz and Stu. There's no coming back from this.

My anxiety levels take flight. Tidal waves of emotion swirl in my chest, a hot heaviness in my eyes. Don't cry now. Here on the street with the last person I want to see me vulnerable.

But it's all too much. A massive sob comes out of my mouth and Jem looks at me, concern in his chocolate eyes.

'Hey, it's okay. We'll find George. Or we could buy a duplicate labradoodle and pretend it's George. Do you think they'll guess?'

Jem's comforting words, mixed with the notion of trying to trick Jazz and Stu by replacing George, turns my cry into a half laugh and then a bit of a snort. Which makes Jem laugh and me even more embarrassed.

'Indie, it's going to be fine.'

'I don't know about that. I've made a mess of everything.'

'Hardly. From where I stand, your life looks pretty good. Except for the George bit. That's pretty crap, but as I say, we'll buy another. Shall I google labradoodle breeders? Or costume hire shops? Maybe one of your actor friends would like a job?'

Now, I laugh.

'Want to grab a drink?' he asks.

'Are you kidding?' I almost fall over backwards. 'We've lost our friends' dog and you want to have a drink?'

'Calm down. We can stop for a break.'

I must look as doubtful as I feel because Jem starts walking away, towards a cool-looking bar.

'I'm going in there for a stiff drink, with or without you,' he calls back. 'Ten minutes isn't going to make much difference.'

I stare after him, desperate to follow, but spend three minutes agonising over the decision. I wish I had a whiteboard to list the pros and cons. I check the home voicemail one more time. No dog-related messages. May as well have a drink.

I walk into the dimly lit bar, which is even more cool inside than out, with bold coloured 70s furniture, vintage pinball machines, and an ultra-hip Bondi crowd to match. I look down at my baggy trackie pants, wishing Jem hadn't chosen somewhere quite so up-to-the-minute. I try to channel Jazz, who wouldn't care at all if it were her. 'Just pretend it's a fashion choice,' she'd say to me. 'All the celebs wear tracksuits out these days, you should know that.'

I spy Jem in a cosy corner armchair, looking completely comfortable in his hipster surrounds. Two drinks and a packet of Cheezels are sitting on a low coffee table in front of him.

'Gin & tonic?' he asks with a grin.

'Pretty confident I'd turn up.'

'I wasn't really, figured I'd drink the second one myself if you didn't.' Jem taps his glass against mine and takes a swig. 'But I'm glad you did. Cheezel?'

My heart jumps. Not at the offer of a Cheezel (although I take one immediately), but that he's glad I'm here. And it puts me on edge, more than the fact we've lost George.

'How have you stayed so calm through this debacle?' I take a seat in the chair opposite. 'My head's about to explode.'

'It's a front. Really, I'm freaking out. Stu's going to kill me. My life will literally be over.'

'Jazz is going to do worse to me. I might have to go back to LA sooner than anticipated.'

'At least you have an escape plan.'

'You can come too.' The words fall out before I can stop them. 'If you have no other option, that is.'

'I might take you up on that.' Jem smiles, and tiny dimples form on either side of his mouth. Have they always been there? I've never noticed. It's like I'm seeing an entirely different person. Or the same person through fresh eyes. Whatever it is, the transformation is enormous. Suddenly, Jem is funny, generous, and even more sexy. Maybe it's because we've been thrown together in the thick of a major catastrophe. Isn't there some study on that? People drawn together in times of trauma? Not sure if that refers to losing a labradoodle but it's certainly having the same effect.

'Indie?' Jem is looking at me questioningly, 'You okay?'

I realise I've been staring at him intensely as I sort out what's going on in my head (and deeper down). Surely nothing. This is Jem. The guy who thinks I'm a waste of time and not worthy of his famous charm. It's clearly some weird side effect from losing George. Like people lost on a mountain, turning to each other for comfort—

'Are you sure you're alright?' Jem looks worried. 'Maybe we should go.'

'No, no, I'm fine.' I try to block the image of us stranded in a snowstorm, bunking down in a makeshift tent with only our bodies to keep each other warm… I focus on my gin and tonic instead, and a few sips in, I relax a little. It's just the circumstance. Once we wake up tomorrow, life will be business as usual. Particularly when he finds out I'm the one who left the gate unlocked. He'll be his normal unpleasant sarcastic self, and I can continue to ignore him as much as possible.

Before I know it, I've finished my drink. I must have really needed it. And it has certainly lightened the mood.

'I just can't believe we lost George,' I say eventually. 'He's hardly a dog you misplace. You couldn't get a bigger dog.'

'I know. We're looking after the biggest dog in Bondi and we somehow manage to lose him.'

'And it's only been one week.' I giggle. It feels wrong, but it's like I've found myself in a real-life sitcom and I can't help but laugh. Except in a normal sitcom, the dog would be found within the standard twenty minutes of screen time, waiting on the doorstep, or delivered by some gorgeous stranger, maybe Ryan Reynolds doing a guest role. The dog would be fine and back home and everything would end with a raucous round of laughter and applause from a studio audience.

I don't think that's how this one is going to end. No wonder I love acting, screen endings are a lot neater and happier than real life. Except when I got left at the altar in that soap. That wasn't so happy, but at least my character went on to have a thing with the PE teacher at the local high school. Then they moved to the country and ran an Airbnb. Even that character got her happy ending after being dumped. My life doesn't have the benefit of a roomful of talented writers behind it.

'Has it only been a week?' Jem brings me back to the present. 'My God, it feels way longer.'

'Rude!' I laugh again, the tension in my body easing. Ironic. The worst possible thing has happened, yet the dragging weight in my chest is slipping away like water. Probably just the G&T on an empty stomach (you can't count Cheezels).

'So, what happened with your American actor boyfriend?'

Jem's question takes me by surprise. The only relationship conversations we've had consist of his annoying comments about Charlie.

'Sorry.' He obviously caught my reaction. 'It's just that Jazz told me you were getting married, but then it was all off?'

I take a breath. 'He cheated on me, so I left.'

'Sorry to hear that.' Jem does look sorry.

'But he's really remorseful and wants to try to work it out.' Even I can hear how pathetic this sounds. 'But I don't think I want to.'

'Has it got something to do with that guy the other night?'

'Charlie? No, I told you, we're old friends. There was something between us years ago, but that's over, and I don't need any more confusion in my life.'

Our eyes briefly connect, and that fateful wedding kiss streams across my busy mind. Suddenly it's all too much. My disastrous relationship, lack of work, potentially murderous best friend. So much for relaxing and recovering. My lips start to tremble as I fight back my very determined tears. I don't usually cry but since the Mark and Kourtney debacle (or Mourtney, as I've decided to call it), the tears won't stop.

'Hey, I don't know who your ex is or what happened, but you have to do what's right for you.' Jem's voice softens. 'He's a bloody idiot for cheating on you, that's for sure.'

And just like that, the floodgates fling open and I'm sobbing in a trendy Bondi bar with a guy I barely know and who doesn't like me much anyway. Only now, I'm making an even worse impression on him than I already have and am appearing even more pathetic. I grab a napkin to wipe my face, which is probably looking as red as a rash by now.

'Sorry.' I sniff and blow my snotty nose. So attractive.

'It's okay, sometimes crying is the best thing to do. Perhaps not so loudly in a public place, mind you, people are starting to look.'

I giggle despite my tsunami of sadness. 'Sorry about that. You can sit at another table if you like.'

'Would you mind?'

I whack his arm playfully. 'Sure, but people will think you've just broken my heart, and they might rush to my support.'

'True, they might chase me down and demand an explanation.' Jem smiles. 'I'd never break up with you in a bar. Not my style.'

'Really? How would you do it then?' I ask, mildly interested in whatever technique he prefers when breaking a girl's heart. I wonder if it's something he does often.

Jem looks at me, like he's about to answer but swiftly changes the subject. 'How about another drink?'

'I'll get the next round.' I'm not sure what just happened. It's like I got a little glimpse of the real Jem but then just as quickly, the window slammed shut.

I buy two more G&Ts and order some retro bar food to share. Not exactly what I feel like, but I'm so hungry and if we're having another drink, I must eat, or I'll keel over. In times of stress (and a couple of alcoholic beverages), my sizeable appetite quadruples.

When the waitress plonks the dishes on our table, Jem's eyes light up. 'Did you order this?'

'I wasn't sure what you liked and it's all very 70s, there's a cubed cheese and cabanossi platter, a serve of meatballs, and there should be some mushroom vol-au-vents coming. I drew the line at the cheese fondue.'

'You've changed your tune about taking a break from dog hunting.' Jem gives a sly smile. 'Suddenly there's time for a 70s banquet.'

'I don't know about you, but I'm starving. Maybe because we're in the middle of a crisis. Maybe it's your fault for suggesting a drink.'

'I'm glad I did, this looks great. I'll give you some money.'

'Don't worry, my treat.' I feign nonchalance even though I used an almost full credit card. 'You can buy milk next week if you want to make up for it.' I always prefer to have control on a date.

Except this isn't a date, I remind myself. Just two people who happen to be sharing a house, and who've accidently lost a dog they're supposed to be guarding with their lives. Nothing like a date at all. In fact, like no other situation I've been in before.

I never liked that I was living in Mark's flat. I tried to give him rent but he wouldn't accept it. Eventually, after getting engaged, I figured we were a team anyway. But I felt disempowered. Then it all blew up, and I had no control, nowhere to go. Except home to Mum and Dad.

'What's wrong?' Jem pauses, fork in hand.

I shake off my thoughts and look up to see him staring at me. There's no avoiding those eyes. Kind but magnetic. I can't look away.

'Sorry to mention your ex. None of my business.'

'That's okay. What about you? Jazz said you had a girlfriend?'

'Alice. It's over.'

'Oh, right.'

I wait for a little more information but it seems that's all I'm going to get. We descend into marginally uncomfortable silence.

'Look,' Jem speaks up, 'I just want to say I'm sorry I've been a bit gruff. There's a lot going on for me right now.'

'The bar you opened with your friend?'

'My ex-friend.'

'Jazz said it didn't go so well.'

'You could say that.'

'What happened?'

'We ran out of money. Well, he spent all the money, stole my girlfriend, and left me in the lurch.' Jem looks down at his hands. 'Sorry, I'm still angry about it.'

'God. No wonder you've been such a rude bastard.'

'Thanks very much.'

'Only joking.'

'No, you're right.' He sighs. 'I've been an idiot and I'm sorry. It's just they're still together.'

'Was he an old friend?'

'Not really. We met through work and always talked about going out on our own. He hung out with Alice and me quite a bit, they got on well. Funnily enough. Anyway, sorry.'

'Forget about it,' I say. 'Besides, I don't think I'd know what to say if you started being all cheery in the mornings, I might fall on the kitchen floor in shock. Maybe even hit my head on the way down and get concussed. I'd have to go to hospital, I might need stitches, and have to wear an ugly bandage on my head, so only able to audition for zombie roles.'

'Fair point. I'll try not to be too cheerful.'

'Won't be hard, I imagine.'

Jem laughs. Right, so he clearly has a sense of humour beneath the arrogant exterior. Jazz is always saying he's hilarious but I've never seen it. I dearly want to ask more about Alice and his friend. How did he find out? What happened? How much money did he lose? But it doesn't feel like he wants to share any more and I don't want to push.

Soon, we're standing on the footpath, back to reality. George is gone and panic sweeps over me once again.

'Let's walk.' Jem comes up with another sensible suggestion. 'It's not far, and we might see George somewhere. You never know.'

We make our way towards the park, where I'd frantically searched for George not too long before. We amble side by side. Not touching, but occasionally brushing against each other, as one often does when walking next to someone. Completely normal. But is it normal to feel an electric shock every time it happens? Step slightly away, Indie, keep a safe distance.

We arrive back home in no time. I walk up the front path, avoiding the side gate and the conversation it will bring. Jem unlocks the front door and we walk down the very quiet hall. The lack of frantic barking is deafening.

'I don't think I can sleep,' I say.

'Me either.' Jem looks worried. 'We'll have to get up early and keep looking.'

'Shall we put up some signs?' I suggest flatly. 'Maybe offer a reward?'

'Good idea.' Jem shows even less enthusiasm. 'I don't know what we're going to say to Jazz and Stu.'

A heavy silence wraps around us. Away from the noisy bar, the lounge room is empty and cold, void of atmosphere. And it's all my fault. Maybe Jem's right. I am a waste of space. I can't even remember to lock a gate, let alone secure employment in my chosen profession.

Before I can decide whether I should come clean, Jem puts his arms around me and gives me a hug. I tense, unsure what's going on. But he feels so calm and strong. I slowly relax against his body and creep my arms around his back, which, I have to say, is pleasantly taut and toned. We stand there for what seems like an hour, probably twenty seconds, chills running through my veins, despite the warmth of Jem's body. Rationally, I know he's only comforting me, but I could stay here forever.

Slowly, he pulls back. 'Do you want to play Scrabble?'

What? That was unexpected.

'Random, I know, but I saw it in the cupboard the other day. Jazz mentioned that you liked playing, and I thought it might help to pass the time—'

'Are you kidding?' I almost trip over the Persian rug in an

attempt to retrieve the box from the games cupboard. 'I'd love to play Scrabble. And a word of warning – I'm pretty bloody good at it.'

'Really? Challenge accepted.'

'Okay, but I don't think you know quite who you're dealing with here.'

Scrabble was a Sunday night tradition in our house when I was growing up. It was fiercely competitive. Once, Dad and I organised a tournament in the street, complete with semi-finals, finals, and a trophy. I didn't win but I came close. If not for Mrs Whatmore's last-minute ZIPPERS, which scored her an incredible fifty-seven points, I'd have been the champion.

'Choose your letters,' I say in an authoritative tone. 'Normally, I'd say no mobile phones but we might need to keep an ear out in case someone messages about George.'

'Very generous of you.' Jem chooses his seven letters. 'But what if I need to go to the toilet, is that allowed?'

Jem's tone indicates that he's not taking Scrabble as seriously as he should.

'We'll have a designated toilet break after twenty minutes, which we'll take at the same time.' What am I saying? 'I mean, we'll travel to the bathroom at the same time… um, not go at the same time.'

Jem looks at me, eyebrows raised. 'Glad to hear that.'

Mortified, I put my head down and try to focus on my first word. It doesn't take long before we're in the thick of it and I'm well out in front. Thanks to FOXES with a double letter on X.

'Come on,' I say impatiently. 'We'll have to set a timer if you take this long.'

'Don't rush me. Brilliance takes lengthy contemplation.'

Jem finally puts down his word, which I have to say is brilliant points-wise but definitely not a word. I'm about to contest it, when a knock at the back sliding door makes us both jump.

'I'll go.' Jem stands.

I follow close behind. Why would someone come to the back door at this time of night?

A tall dark figure is standing outside on the terrace.

Jem tentatively pulls open the sliding door. 'Hi, can I help you?'

I see who it is and get such a shock that I knock over George's water bowl.

'Alex!' My voice comes out louder and higher than expected. 'What are you doing here?'

Before he can respond, George bounds in and almost knocks me over, madly wagging his tail and licking my face.

'George!' I squeal even louder. 'You're home!'

Overcome with relief, I fight back tears once again. Jem looks emotional too. We're both hugging George like parents reunited with their lost child, rather than two incompatible housemates who've had their friends' dog returned to them.

'He turned up at my place, looking for Roxie,' Alex says. 'They've had a few play dates, so he must have worked out where to go. Jazz and I often take turns in minding each other's dogs when we're working. Not so boring for them being stuck at home when there's a friend. Anyway, I was late tonight as I had to help with a school music concert and when I got home, there he was.'

'He got out today,' I say sheepishly. 'We've been out looking for him all night.'

I suddenly realise Jem is standing there looking bemused.

'Sorry, this is Alex,' I say to Jem. 'We met at the dog park. His dog, Roxie, and George are an item.'

'It's true,' Alex says. 'When it becomes a thing for dogs to marry, these two will be first in line.'

I don't point out that Jazz and Alex appear to be equally friendly. And it doesn't escape my notice that George has been round to Roxie's place enough times to get himself there, and Alex seems comfortable using the back sliding door at Jazz and Stu's house.

'Mate, thanks for bringing George back,' Jem says. 'We've been fraught.'

I nod, guiltily recalling that a couple of hours ago we were at the pub looking anything but. Still, anxiety goes through different stages. Maybe that was our denial stage. Our "gin and tonic" stage.

'Yeah, thanks again, Alex,' I say. 'Jazz would literally kill me in my sleep if I lost George.'

Alex grins. 'She probably wouldn't have even waited until you were asleep.'

I giggle. 'For sure!'

'How'd he get out?' Alex asks. 'The side gate is usually closed. Is there a hole in the fence, maybe?'

Heat crackles across my cheeks and I look down, too ashamed to speak.

'Anyway, not to worry,' Alex continues. 'George knew where he was going, he's a pretty smart dog.'

'Yes, thank God,' I say. 'If something had happened to him… well, there are no words to describe that particular horror.'

'I'd have called to let you know but I didn't have your mobile number, and I didn't want to text Jazz because she'd have freaked out and jumped on a plane.' Alex takes a card out of his pocket and hands it to me. 'Here are my contact details, maybe text me your number in case there's another emergency.'

'Good idea.' I take the card, feeling strangely awkward in front of Jem. Come on Indie, he's not asking you out, he's offering help with looking after George because you clearly have no idea how to do it properly.

'Can I get you a drink, Alex?' Jem offers. 'Least we could do for saving our necks.'

'No, thanks, I'll be off. I've given George some dinner, by the way, so don't let him convince you otherwise.' Alex gives George an affectionate pat and moves towards the sliding door.

George watches him go, probably sad to say goodbye to the only person here who seems to know what they're doing.

'Can we maybe not tell Jazz that we lost George?' I give an embarrassed grin. 'Or at least not for a while.'

'Your secret's safe with me.' Alex smiles his crinkly smile. 'I'll see you at the dog park some time.' And with that, he disappears into the night.

'That was odd,' Jem says, once we hear the side gate firmly click and Alex's footsteps fade into the distance. 'He seems like a close friend. Funny, Stu's never mentioned him.'

George comes jumping back, leaping up like an oversized circus dog, clearly still excited by his day out and late-night return. Jem and I pat and cuddle him, our bodies edging closer together, but luckily the big, bouncy, fluffy barrier between us prevents too much random touching.

'Yeah, I'd never heard of him either.' I wonder if Jem's thinking what I'm thinking. 'We've chatted a couple of times at the dog park. I think Jazz instructed him to keep an eye on me. Make sure I was looking after George properly. Not that I've done that tonight. But I have to say, he's been a great source of dog owner information. Do you know I went on my first walk with George without poop bags?'

Jem pretends to look shocked. 'Unbelievable.'

The comment about Alex makes me feel uncomfortable. Stu has probably never mentioned him because he doesn't know about him. Jazz has never mentioned him to me either, which is highly suspicious. Is something going on between them?

I dismiss the thought immediately. She and Alex are friends brought together simply because their dogs get along. Like parents at school pick-up. It doesn't mean she's having an affair.

'I've learnt so much about dogs already,' I say.

'Like how not to lose one?'

My heart sinks. I have to come clean. As much as I don't want to. 'I guess I haven't learnt that part yet.' I take a big breath. 'It was my fault. The gate, I left it open.' There's a moment's pause, while my words float between us. I wait, dreading the negative reaction that will surely fire my way.

'It's okay, I already knew.'

'Really? Why didn't you say anything?'

'You were feeling bad enough already,' Jem says gently. 'And it was an easy mistake to make, could have been either of us.'

'Except you wouldn't have ever done it.'

'No, probably not.'

'Jem!'

'Only joking.' He smiles. 'But remember, I'm over here a lot and Jazz is constantly telling me to shut the gate. It's been drummed into me over the past year.'

'Can you imagine if we'd lost George for good?' I can't believe Jem said nothing when he easily could have given me a hard time. A week ago, he'd have relished the opportunity to put me down with his critical tongue.

'But we didn't.' His face lights up in a way I've not yet seen. 'So, we don't have to imagine.'

I look at Jem. He gives George an affectionate pat as he puts down the refilled water bowl. The same tingles I felt at the bar catch me unaware. Get a grip, Indie. You can't have a crush on Jem. That would be completely annoying. Especially since he can't stand me. Although, I have to say, right now it doesn't feel like he can't stand me. Maybe the whole incident has had a positive effect on both of us.

'Sorry to put you through this ordeal tonight,' I say. 'Probably the last thing you needed at the end of a long day.'

'Don't worry, it wasn't all bad.' He gazes at me with those heavenly eyes. 'There are worse ways to spend an evening.'

My heart leaps like it's jumping a puddle in the rain.

'But that's it for me, I have an early start in the morning.' He turns up the hall to his room. 'I'll have to beat you at Scrabble another time.'

'Good luck with that,' I call after him. 'Hey, you know we'll have to bathe George soon?'

'I know, maybe we should go halves on a dog groomer?'

'Jazz will freak out.'

'She doesn't have to know. 'Night.'

I watch Jem walk down the hall. Did he really enjoy hanging out with me? Or was he just being nice to make me feel better? Will he turn around and be rude again tomorrow? I can't answer any of these questions, but whatever happens, Jem is not the person I thought he was.

15

AFTER what feels like an eternity, I drift off to sleep but it's far from relaxing as the whole George debacle invades my dreams. One minute I'm running through the streets looking for George, the next Jazz is back from France and yelling at me, telling me what a bad friend I am. At last, Jem grabs my hand and puts his arms around me, like he did tonight, and presses his lips gently to mine. Suddenly we're back at the wedding, kissing in a back room with such intensity and passion that it wakes me with a start.

The room is a murky early morning grey. I look at the clock. Only 5:35am. I roll over and try to go back to sleep, knowing it's never going to happen. Thanks to Jem and his dream kissing, I'm well and truly awake.

I try to roll over, but my bed feels uncomfortable and cold. Whether I like it or not, it's time to get up. I creep into the kitchen, make a coffee and set myself up at the island bench to read the audition scenes Michelle sent through. I'm deep in thought, but not so deep that I don't notice Jem arrive in little more than his boxers, hair standing on end, rubbing his eyes and yawning.

'Sorry, did I give you a fright?'

I try to tear my eyes away from his almost perfect upper body. 'Not at all, I'm getting used to you slinking around.'

'I was worried you might have your trusty broom at the ready.'

'Yeah, you wouldn't have stood a chance.'

Jem offers a little smile. Just a smirk, which is a start. If he finds my jokes even the tiniest bit funny, we might be able to get through the next couple of months.

'Do you want a coffee?' he asks.

'I've got one. Thanks.'

Jem makes his coffee in silence and takes it out to the garden. I watch him through the glass sliding doors as he puts his mug down on the outside table to greet George, who is ecstatic. He throws a squeaky toy over and over for George to fetch. A very simple action, but for some reason, my heart melts like ice-cream in the sun.

What's going on? Yesterday, Jem was the most irritating person I'd met, and now I'm mesmerised because he's affectionate towards a dog. Probably the anxiety of losing George and the relief of finding him. We simply bonded through a cataclysmic situation. Natural to be feeling a little fluttery in the stomach. Normal reaction really.

Besides, it's hard to think straight when confronted by that well-defined body and sexy bedroom hair so early in the morning. Obviously, whatever feelings were brewing last night haven't faded as easily as I hoped.

Jem wanders back in and puts his mug in the sink. 'I'll wash that up later. Going to have a shower.'

'That's fine.' I remember the mess I found in the kitchen the other day. This is all so weird. Something has shifted in our friendship, if you can call it that, but I'm even less sure how to behave around him. Are we friends? These pesky tingles keep throwing me off course.

Luckily, I'm distracted by my phone ringing. I look at the time. Who'd call so early? It could be Mark, but I don't recognise the number. My hands tremble slightly as I swipe my phone.

'Hello?'

'Indie!'

'Jazz!' I look at Jem, whose face looks as shocked as I'm sure mine does. Why is Jazz calling this morning, just after we lost her precious George? Did Alex tell her? Or someone else from the dog park? They seem so tight I wouldn't put it past any of them.

'Indie, are you there?'

'Sorry, yes, I'm here.' I try to steady my breathing and focus on my friend.

'How are you going? How's George?'

'He's good.' My voice jumps an octave. 'Missing his mum, I think.'

'I just wanted to check in and make sure everything's okay and you haven't forgotten to feed him, or heaven forbid, lost him.'

What? Does she know? My eyes feel like they've expanded an inch in diameter, and Jem is looking at me, slightly pale and panicked.

'No, no, of course not.'

'Can you put him on?'

'What?'

'George, can you put him on?'

'Ah, sure.' I cover the phone and whisper to Jem, 'She wants to speak to George, do you think she knows?'

'What did she say?' Jem whispers back.

'She wondered if we'd lost George or forgotten to feed him.'

'If she knew, she'd be more upfront about it.'

'True.' I go back to Jazz. 'Sorry, just went outside to get him. He was in the garden.'

I put the phone in front of George, who sniffs it. I hear Jazz saying hello and asking him questions. He must recognise the voice because he gives a gentle woof.

Jem looks like he's about to crack up, which gives me the

giggles. I take the phone back.

'What's so funny?' Jazz asks.

'Ah, nothing, sorry.' I'm usually good at controlling corpsing on stage but today I'm having trouble keeping a straight face. 'George just looked so cute when he heard your voice.'

Jem indicates he's going to jump in the shower. Or maybe he's going hiking in the rain? Either way, he disappears into the bathroom and I'm left alone with Jazz.

'So, how are *you* going?' she asks. 'Got some fabulous job yet?'

'No, I missed out on an ad, but I have an audition for a lead in a film.'

'Great. And how's Jem?'

'Annoying.' Actually, a godsend in the last twenty-four hours but I'm not going to admit that to Jazz. 'Listen, I'm sorry I haven't been around for you lately.'

'What do you mean?'

'Alex told me how upset you were that night. Something about Stu not wanting a baby?'

Jazz falls silent. I can hear her breathing heavily, or is she crying?

'I don't know what's going on between us.' She gives a little sniff. Definitely crying.

'But you guys are fine, aren't you?'

'Oh, Indie. I think I've ruined everything.' Jazz starts to sob. 'I can't believe Alex told you about that night. It was just one kiss, and it didn't mean anything.'

'What?' Did I hear correctly? 'What kiss?'

'Maybe he didn't tell you everything.'

'Jazz, what happened?' I feel sick to my stomach. Like I'm onstage but haven't learnt my lines.

'Nothing, it was nothing. I'd had a few glasses of wine when

Alex arrived to pick up Roxie, and… I got really upset about everything. Alex is so understanding, and we share the same views on dog rearing. One minute I was looking at him, thinking what a great father he'd be and the next, I was kissing him, which is ridiculous because he's—'

'Jazz! What about Stu?'

'I know, I know, I love Stu, I do, but we've been fighting so much and now he's saying that if we can't look after a dog, how can we look after a baby?'

'Does Stu know?'

'No!'

'Jazz!'

'I know, I know, I have to tell him. And I will, but it's not so much about the kiss because Alex—'

'I can't believe Alex. Did he kiss you back?'

'I think so? But then he stopped, saying we couldn't do this.'

'What did you say?'

'I may have pleaded with him to keep going.'

'Jazz!'

'I was pretty drunk.'

I don't know what to say. After the Mourtney disaster, I can't believe my best friend is doing the same thing to lovely Stu, my other best friend. Anger swells like a balloon from the depths of my stomach, expanding into every corner of my body.

'Jazz, you'd better sort yourself out. Stu deserves better.'

'That's rich coming from you,' Jazz cuts through her tears. 'I don't need you telling me what to do, it's not like you've had the greatest relationships in the world. Maybe you need to sort yourself out before you lecture me.'

'Jazz, it's just that I—'

'And I'm not Mark in this situation. This is completely different.'

'I never said that. I'm not judging you, Jazz.'

'I think you might be.'

'Just talk to Stu.'

'I've got to go.' And with that, Jazz hangs up.

What just happened? I wasn't comparing her to Mark, but I do know what it's like to be cheated on. She's probably feeling incredibly guilty and took it out on me. I'll try calling her later when she's calmed down. Maybe send her an email. One thing's for sure, Jazz has got some working out to do.

'Well?' Jem walks back into the kitchen. 'Is our secret safe?'

'Sorry?' Suddenly I don't know which secret we're talking about.

'Jazz, did she know?'

'I think we got away with it.'

'Phew. I've gotta go, see you tonight?'

'Yep.'

Jem leaves.

I can't believe Jazz and I had a fight. We never do that. I also can't believe she kissed Dog Man. But before I unpack that scenario, I focus on Jem and how he seems to have transformed into a seemingly pleasant person. He didn't offer any rude comments this morning, and I have to say, I'm completely thrown. But for now, I sweep it into a cupboard at the back of my brain and get to work on my audition pieces.

Until my concentration wanes and it's time for a coffee. I call Lucy to see if she'd like to meet up.

'I can't believe you lost the dog,' Lucy says, as we sip lattes in a light and airy Bronte café, just up from the beach. 'Actually, knowing you and your experience with pets, it's hardly surprising.'

'Please, I don't want to even think about it.' I rub my forehead. 'It was awful.'

'Have you told Jazz?'

'No way, but would you believe she called this morning out of the blue?'

'Really? How weird. And who's this Alex guy who brought George back?'

'One of Jazz's dog park friends.' I don't want to go into too much detail. 'When you get a dog, it's like you gain entry to a whole different universe, a tightknit cult-like community with its own language, laws, and customs.'

Lucy giggles. 'And how are you fitting in?'

'I'm definitely an outsider. It's clear I have no idea what I'm doing. I don't even have a puffer jacket, which seems to be standard dog-walking attire.'

'How's Jem? Still super aggravating?'

'He's… he's actually okay.' I tap my foot nervously on the timber floorboards. 'In fact, he was great last night during the whole George crisis. Especially as it was my fault.'

Lucy studies my face. 'He doesn't sound so bad after all.'

'I'm sure it'll go back to normal tonight once the incident's forgotten. I'm still waiting for him to rub in the fact that I left the gate open.'

Lucy smiles but doesn't say another word. I know what she's thinking but she's wrong. There's nothing between Jem and me. If there were, it would have happened by now. Well, it did happen once but went nowhere. I quickly change the subject to my upcoming audition.

'When is it?' Lucy asks.

'Next Tuesday. Ten twenty.'

'Chookas!' Actors never say 'Good luck' as it's unlucky. 'Not that you'll need it, you'll be amazing.'

Back at the house, I look at the side gate dubiously. Come on, Indie, it's just an inanimate object. You can do it. I open it and carefully close it behind me. See? Nothing to worry about. George bounds up, tackling me as if I'd been away for a month.

'Hello there, get down, George. I saw you an hour ago.' I look at his muddy paws. 'Wow, you're absolutely filthy after your adventure last night.'

George woofs at me, as if to say, 'I know, isn't it great?'

There's also an offensive odour wafting around. I sniff his fur and just about gag. Okay. The time has come. I need to fulfil my dog-sitting duties and give George a bath. After last night, it doesn't seem so scary. Besides, I've dealt with much more frightening things in my life. Pretty much every audition I've ever done. Every opening night. Terrifying. Surely bathing a dog isn't as bad as that moment when you step out on stage in front of a packed audience, thinking, 'God, I hope I can do this.'

I study the copious notes Jazz left for me, outlining the whole process and describing how much George loves bath days. A dog groomer is a tempting idea, but maybe after the gate disaster, this is a way of showing Jem how capable I really am.

The notes say to bathe George in the claw bath, so I fetch his (organic) bath wash and conditioner from the laundry and fill the bath to the required depth. So far so good. Back to the notes:

Remove George's collar and tell him that he's having a bath.

Test the water with your elbow. Should be lukewarm.

Right. Here we go. I go into the garden, where George is sniffing around the flower beds, looking like he's having a lovely time. Maybe I should do it later. No, Indie, just do it now for goodness' sake.

'George! Come here, that's a good boy.'

George bounds over, no doubt thinking we're off for a walk. Little does he know.

I remove his collar, speaking very gently. 'So, we're going to have a bath now.'

And just like that, he takes off around the garden. Note to self: next time take collar off in bathroom with door locked. I try to catch George but it becomes like a game. The minute I get close to him, he runs to the other side of the yard, excitement all over his face. Ten minutes later, I'm exhausted and no closer to giving him a bath.

Fed up, I grab the bag of extra special treats that Jazz has labelled 'Strictly only one a week' to lure George into the house.

Four treats later, I have him in the kitchen, but with no collar around his neck, the only way to keep hold of him is on my knees with two arms firmly around his body.

I give him one more treat (okay, no more for a couple of weeks) and then carry him into the bathroom. My God he's heavy. And awkward.

'George, definitely no more treats for you, you weigh a tonne.'

I get him into the bathroom and put him down on the tessellated tiles for a break. George sees the bath filled with water and barks at it fearfully, the noise bouncing around the walls.

'Shh, George, it's okay, just a bath.'

I go to pick him up and despite his furious struggles, plonk him in the water, where he gives an almighty yelp.

Goodness, I didn't test the water! I drag George out, my back protesting under the weight, and put him back on the tiles. I dip my elbow in to feel ice-cold water. I turn the hot tap on full bore, only to find George has disappeared. Damn, why didn't I close the door?

I race down the hall, following the muddy paw prints that stop outside my bedroom door. I poke my head in to see George lying on the now-not-so-crisp white sheets. Looks like he's walked all over them, trying to find the perfect spot. Great. More washing.

'George! Get down from there immediately!'

'Woof.' George doesn't move a single doggy muscle.

There's nothing to do but grab the wet, dirty dog.

I do this, but George fights me every step of the way.

Struggling to breathe, I lug the biggest dog in Bondi back to the bathroom. 'I thought… you liked… bath days.'

When we finally arrive, I see I've left the hot tap running. I put George down and quickly lock the door. 'You're not going anywhere.'

In response, George does the biggest shake, covering me with droplets of water. I turn off the tap, put my elbow in the water and nearly scald myself. The bath is too full, but too hot to pull out the plug, so I turn on the cold. George furiously scratches at the door to get out.

'Not the paintwork!'

Finally, I pull the plug and the water drains to a more acceptable dog level. And yes, definitely lukewarm. Two arms around George, I lift him into the bath and glance at the notes sitting on the vanity.

Use scoop to gently wet his fur all over.

Scoop? What scoop? It must be in the laundry. Not wanting to leave George unsupervised – he might make a run for it out the window – I improvise with a china floral jug from the windowsill. Except it's so small, it takes ages to get him all wet. And he keeps doing his doggie shake, wetting me more and more.

Unable to get right around him, I strip down to my bra and undies and hop into the bath, scooping handfuls of water over his back. I can't see the notes, but I imagine soap is next, so I pour the delicious smelling, organic, rose petal bath wash all over him and rub it in. George doesn't mind this bit, so we have a moment of peace. Which ends the second I rinse him. He absolutely hates it and splashes around just to make sure I know.

By now the water is so soapy I'm having trouble getting the bath wash out of his fur. Plus, I'm now completely drenched and my legs are slippery with soap. I skip the conditioner, grab the jug, and use clean tap water to rinse his fur. Exhausted and slimy, I climb out of the bath and pick George up in my arms. A quick look at the notes tells me I forgot to bring his towels from the laundry. Damn.

I carry him out, struggling under his wet weight. Until he hears the side gate click and turns into an over-excited octopus, thrashing in my arms, and I have no choice but to let him go. He races outside, wet paws over everything. I run after him only to be confronted by Jem, who looks like he's trying to keep a straight face at a world-famous comedy gig. Double damn.

'Bath day, is it?' Jem says as George throws his dripping body against his. 'Down, George.'

I'm suddenly painfully aware of my wet, and not particularly attractive, underwear. 'Ah yes, but it didn't quite go to plan… no, George!'

Before I can even process the extent of my humiliation, George takes off around the yard, rolling in the dirtiest patches he can find. I race after him and it becomes some sort of running-around-in-circles type of game that George is definitely winning.

No longer able to restrain himself, Jem doubles over and bellows with laughter. I've never heard anything like it. As if someone's mowing the lawn in the middle of a thunderstorm. He wipes tears from his eyes and holds his stomach trying to catch his breath. Every time his laughter subsides, he looks at me and starts to roar all over again. To be honest, it's a little over the top and making me cranky. At least I'm trying to bath the dog, which is more than he's done.

However, Jem's raucous laughter gradually lifts my temper like sun shining on a morning fog. And if you think about it, it's a pretty funny scene to walk in on. I start giggling myself, uncontrollably it seems, which sets Jem off once again, and in turn makes me giggle even more.

'Funniest thing… seen for a long… time.' Jem attempts to speak but fails. 'Can't believe… George… through… dirt again.'

As do I. 'Bath… total disaster.'

'I… know.'

We continue to communicate via some sort of weird, breathless, laughing language, which proves completely contagious, sending us both into yet another fit. Finally, after about three exhausting minutes of intense guffawing, we calm down and steady our breathing. Lucky. If it had gone on for much longer, I might have passed out. Or wet my pants. Either way, it would have been embarrassing.

'You're hilarious,' Jem gives the broadest grin I've ever seen on his face. Or anyone's for that matter. My insides heat up like a croissant in the oven. But then looking at myself in my worst saggy baggy underwear, soaking wet, and an incomplete task on my hands, I'm not sure if this is a compliment or a put down. I grab a towel in the laundry, dry myself off and grab my clothes from the bathroom floor, hoping Jem is more focused on my hilarious antics than my near nakedness.

I walk back out to the garden. 'What do I do now? George is still soapy and dirtier than when I started.'

'I'll give you a hand.'

It's not long before the situation is under control. Jem and I get George into the old shower in the laundry and rinse him off there.

We throw a couple of towels around the wet dog and give him a good rub.

'We're meant to blow dry his fur.' I wonder if people really do that. 'His hairdryer's in the cupboard.'

Reluctantly, Jem gets it out and starts drying George, who barks the whole time, trying to bite the air coming out of the dryer. Eventually he's dry, but his fur is all matted.

'Maybe because I didn't use conditioner?'

'We'll just give him a brush.'

The brushing proves equally challenging. Jem pins George down, while I go into action. And at last George is knot-free.

Once everything is cleaned up, the hall is mopped, and my sheets are in the wash, I say, 'Definitely booking an appointment with the dog groomer next time.'

'What about next time we do it together?' Jem asks.

'It's a date,' I say without thinking.

A flutter of surprise crosses Jem's eyes. 'Maybe not in our underwear.'

Okay, so he did notice.

'Well, that's just the technique I use, not sure how *you* do it.'

Jem smiles. 'It seemed to go really well for you.'

'At least I gave it a try.'

'True, you were very brave, as well as funny.'

'Gee, thanks.'

There's an uncomfortable silence as I secretly wish I'd chosen nicer underwear this morning, but little did I know I'd be caught in my undies by my hot housemate while bathing my best friend's dog. Not really something you can prepare for.

I mutter something about going for a run, and with that I'm out the door.

Is Jem flirting with me? No, he just offered to help bath the dog next time. That's it. But he did see me at my absolute worst and didn't flee. In fact, the more mistakes I make, the nicer Jem is. And I certainly haven't laughed like that with anyone in ages. I should be thrilled that we're getting along, and I am. But for some reason, it's making me panic more than going onstage for an opening night, and, unlike those pesky performance nerves, I'm not sure what to do about it.

16

I DON'T actually go for a run, unless you count the mad dash to get out the front door away from Jem and his witty and confusing banter. Physically and emotionally drained from not just losing and bathing George, but spending far too much one-on-one time with Jem, I slow to an amble. Plus, I didn't have time to put on proper running clothes or shoes.

I arrive at the beach, where the salty air soothes my chaotic thoughts and the warm sand between my toes feels like heaven. I attempt to clear my mind and focus on my audition. Work is the happy escape I need right now.

After about forty minutes of therapeutic beach marching, I arrive at the sliding door to be met with the sound of clanging pots and pans. I follow the noises to what I'm pretty sure was the kitchen, now possibly a cyclone affected area.

The island is strewn from one end to the other with bowls, saucepans, and utensils, all of which have been used. Some sort of sauce has spilled over the Caesarstone and hasn't been cleaned up. Stu would pass out if he saw that – he's very particular about the benchtops, always following me around with a dishcloth and a set of coasters. The floor can barely be seen for the vegetable scraps, empty food packages, and bulging shopping bags, and the sink is piled high with dirty dishes. In the very heart of the disarray is Jem, earphones on, nodding his head in time to whatever he's listening to, chopping a bunch of something green and looking completely content in his private world.

I just want to keep staring, but he looks up.

'You're cooking?' I do a chopping action with my hands.

'Hi, I'm cooking,' he says loudly, pointing to his earphones.

'Bit of a mess,' I raise my voice, gesturing to the chaos around him.

'Sorry, it's a bit of a mess,' he says, even more loudly.

I give up. I was hopeless at mime back at drama school. Never saw the point. I head to my room.

Jem takes his earphones off and calls after me, 'You in for dinner?'

'Ah yeah, I think so.' Wow, last week we could barely have a conversation, and now, he's checking in with me about dinner. 'But do you think you've used enough bowls? There might be a couple in there you haven't got your hands on yet.'

'Very funny.' He goes back to his chopping. 'Maybe I won't cook dinner for you after all.'

'I'm joking, that would be lovely.'

'It's hard using someone else's kitchen when you don't know where anything is,' he continues. 'Is there anything you don't eat?'

'No, I eat everything, and I eat a lot. Except Turkish Delight. Can't stand it.'

Jem relaxes, his dark espresso eyes giving a sudden sparkle. 'I'll be sure to avoid any dishes containing that.'

I go to my bedroom to put my things down. Dinner? Together? What does that mean? I was hoping to work on my script tonight, but it's a nice gesture. I don't want him to think I don't appreciate it. And I've got to eat. He'll probably watch TV after, so then I can sneak away to work on my lines. I also need to email Jazz after that weird fight.

I bounce back into the kitchen, where Jem's head is buried in a cookbook. 'Just going to have a shower and work on my audition. Is that okay?'

'Sure,' he says, without looking up. 'Another ad?'

'Actually, no. This is for a film shooting in the Blue Mountains. The director's a big deal.'

'Sounds great.' He stirs a pot on the stove. 'Okay, you do that and let me create some magic here.'

I smile. 'Don't stress too much. I'm already starving, so your magic can be average and I'll still love it.'

I turn on the shower and realise it's the first time Jem didn't make a rude comment about me going for an audition. Maybe he wasn't really listening, too focused on chopping chicken and coriander. After I've showered, I throw on tracksuit pants and a comfy t-shirt. Should I put on something more presentable seeing as Jem is going to all this effort? No. We're still just housemates, and trackies are acceptable night-at-home attire. It's a bit late to be making any sort of impression in that department. Apart from the underwear incident, Jem never sees me wear much else. He might not recognise me if I dress up.

I take out my scenes and start reading, tummy bubbling with excitement. When I arrived in Sydney, I felt exhausted at the thought of preparing for another role, but this one is perfect for me and I'm ready to tackle it. Apart from being distracted by the most delicious cooking aromas. I pop my head into the surprisingly clean kitchen. Jem's there, with a tea towel over his shoulder like a professional.

'I'll have to call you Jamie Oliver from now on.'

'Wait until you taste it before you start comparing me to one of the greats,' Jem says in a somewhat serious tone. 'Glass of wine?'

'Sure.' So much for working on my lines. Still, one glass won't hurt. To be honest, I'm feeling slightly nervous at the thought of dining alone with Jem. I need wine to get me through.

Jem hands me a glass. 'Is white okay? It'll be great with this dish.'

'Perfect, thanks.' I clink my drink against his. 'Cheers.'

'To a successful audition.'

Our glasses lightly tap and our eyes lock for a microsecond. I glance away as a ripple of nerves runs down to my toes. Jem takes a sip of his wine, unfazed. Get a grip, Indie.

'I've set the table outside. You go and sit down and I'll bring the food out.'

I take a seat at the outdoor table, gulping my wine to help tame my nerves. Until I realise, I've almost finished my glass. Better slow down. The way I'm feeling, God knows what I'll do.

Jem arrives and places a bowl in front of me. I tentatively put a forkful of chicken into my mouth, realising in an instant that he certainly can cook.

'This is delicious,' I can't help but say through my mouthful. 'Oh my God, it's incredible.'

'Glad you like it. I enjoy cooking but I never get time.'

'You need to make time.' I take another bite. 'In fact, I insist you do all the cooking while we're living here.'

'Sure, if you do all the washing up and house cleaning.'

I nod as I chew, savouring every flavour and not quite believing this person is the same guy I've been tolerating for the past week. He even looks different. Just as handsome but there's something else, an openness, a warmth I've never seen before. A strand of his unruly hair flops over his eyes, and it takes every milligram of willpower not to reach out and gently move it back into place.

'You okay?' He frowns. 'Something wrong with the food?'

Oh God, I must be staring at him. 'No, it's perfect, it's just…'

Even though he looks at me expectantly, I can't possibly say what's on my mind. Especially when it's probably the furthest thing from *his* mind. Just as he's started to open up, I'll freak him out and he'll slam shut.

'What?'

My face heats up like a frying pan. 'Oh, nothing, just thinking what a nice night this is.' Honestly, Indie, is that the best you can do, "a nice night"? It's almost an insult.

'I couldn't agree with you more,' Jem says. 'Your chef is awesome.'

I giggle. 'He's okay.'

'Indie, I want to say something, but I don't want you to take it the wrong way.'

'I'll try not to.' My insides squirm. Clearly, he thinks I like him, and he's about to let me down gently. Have I been that obvious? I don't like him *that* much. How arrogant. I'm being nice, so now he assumes I'm head over heels in love with him. Honestly!

'I know I talked about it last night, but I just want to properly apologise for my behaviour when we first moved in. I was a bit of an idiot.'

Okay, so I wasn't expecting that.

'I was just so angry at the world,' he continues. 'Angry with Dean. Angry that I'd failed. Angry with Alice. Angry I was forced back into working for someone else. And I took it out on you.'

Jem keeps saying the most unexpected things. I can't believe I'm talking to the same guy. Has he always been this emotionally intelligent?

'So, you're not angry anymore?'

'I'm furious. Alice keeps texting me wanting "to talk". Dean says he has no money, says it all went in bills. A complete mess. But I feel bad that I took it out on you. I'm hoping you might forget all about it. What do you think?'

For some reason, I desperately want to put my hands on his perfectly sculpted face and tell him that all is forgiven in the form of a haiku. But that might possibly freak him out. Best keep it light.

'Hmm, I'm not sure. Maybe one day. Certainly, if you cook a few more dinners like this one, I'll think about it.'

Jem gives a comical sigh of relief. 'Phew! That's a start. How about I clean up and see what I can do for dessert? That might speed up the forgiveness process.'

I stand up. 'No, you cooked. I'll clear away.'

Thankful for a moment alone, I carry a pile of plates to the kitchen and start stacking the dishwasher. But before I can even gather my frenetic thoughts, Jem appears behind me.

'Just bringing this in.' He places the serving bowl on the bench. 'Do you want another glass of wine?'

I turn around and he's much closer than I anticipated. We almost bump noses but neither of us moves away. I couldn't if I tried, my feet seem to be locked to the ground by some super powerful magnetic force.

'Sorry?' It dawns on me that he asked a question but for the life of me, I can't think what it was. I also can't stop staring at his lips, wondering what it would be like to kiss them. Actually, I know what it's like to kiss them and the memory flashes across my brain in neon splendour. I shift my gaze to somewhere safer, only to find myself staring into his mesmerising eyes, which are like rock pools at night, bathed in moonlight. Yes, I know that sounds like bad teenage poetry but there's no other way to describe them.

'Just wondering if you want more wine?' He picks up a bottle off the bench, evidently unaware of my inner turmoil. 'I feel like a glass of red.'

'Yes, great, good idea!' I pull myself together. This must stop. Maybe I shouldn't have any more wine. One glass and I'm celebrating the beauty of every feature on Jem's face. Another one might end in disaster, or at least total embarrassment. For me more than him. But I'm enjoying the night and don't particularly want it to stop.

'I'll get dessert ready. Fancy some Turkish Delight cheesecake?'

'What?'

'Joking, but I have made a cheesecake.'

Is there nothing this guy can't do? Cheesecake is one of my all-time favourite desserts.

Moments later, we're back outside with vibey jazz music floating out from the living room, eating the most divine cheesecake I've ever tasted. Maybe because I haven't eaten cheesecake in about a year. Mark was particular about his diet, so we rarely ate processed sugar. Or dairy. Or gluten. What did we eat? I can't remember. In fact, I'm having trouble remembering what Mark and I even talked about.

I don't know if it's the second glass of wine, the gourmet food, or because the strain between us has lifted, but I feel so relaxed, as if I've known Jem for years. Which I kind of have in a weird way.

'You know something I always wonder about?' I say tentatively.

'What?'

I take a breath. 'Why didn't you want to dance with me back at Jazz and Stu's wedding?'

'We danced, didn't we?'

'We danced for about thirty seconds because we had to and then you made some excuse and left the dance floor.'

'Did I really?' Jem shifts in his seat. 'What an idiot.'

He stands, the silence between us fraught with unanswered questions. Where's he going? Have I embarrassed him? Indie, why can't you keep your mouth shut?

'It seems I owe you a dance then.'

I look at him blankly. 'You want to go dancing somewhere now?'

'No, let's dance here. Right now. I'll choose the music.'

Jem goes inside and puts on something strong but moody. He returns, takes my hand, pulls me close, and puts his other arm around my waist. I can hardly breathe, but I try my best. I don't want to hyperventilate in his arms. His body presses up against mine, igniting a fiery glow in the pit of my stomach, which quickly travels south, wreaking earthquake havoc down my thighs. I close my eyes, trying to quash the alarming intensity of the moment, but fail miserably.

The song ends and we're left standing there in each other's arms with no music to hide behind. Jem doesn't pull away and neither do I. He smells delicious, the shampoo in the bathroom. I look up, our faces mere inches apart.

'I'd better finish stacking the dishwasher.' I'm unable to trust that I won't suddenly press my lips against his in the hope of it being reciprocated. Or worse, just touch as much of his skin as I can. Either way could be disastrous.

Jem holds my gaze for another couple of seconds, although I swear it's longer, then releases me. 'Yes, you'd better get to it. The kitchen's a mess.'

I relax, my nerves instantly swept away by the gentle evening breeze. Once again, my imagination was running away with me. This isn't the kissing scene in a movie. This is two people dancing together after sharing a sumptuous meal, microseconds from each other's lips, caught up in the moment… actually it sounds exactly like a kissing scene in a movie. Except, life isn't like that. The two people aren't really suited. They're simply sharing a house and, up until yesterday, barely spoke more than a few random words to each other.

He doesn't let me go.

'We may not have danced that night, but I remember doing something else.' His husky voice knots my stomach. 'Well, almost doing.'

As much as I've tried in recent weeks to block that night firmly from my thoughts, I can't help but see that amazing kiss flash up like a well-lit billboard.

'I'm surprised you remember.' I hope we're talking about the same thing and not something like collecting all the petals from the tables for Jazz. 'You seemed to have forgotten by the next day.'

'I thought you were avoiding me.'

'Hardly. You couldn't get away from me fast enough. That night and at the brunch the next day.'

Jem looks away momentarily. 'I wasn't sure how you felt about it. You were so aloof. It was hard to read.'

'I kept trying to talk to you, but you ran away whenever I came near. At one point you chose to talk to Stu's Great Aunt Irene, rather than me. Didn't do much for my confidence.'

'Well, I'm here now.' Jem pauses. 'And to be fair, Aunty Irene's a fascinating woman. You should hear some of the things she's done.'

I want to giggle, but the world slows to a quiet halt. Before I know it, Jem's lips gently meet mine, the memory of the wedding night washing over me, the same feelings of longing flooding my veins. Time slips into slow motion, every second stretched beyond its capacity as I lose myself to what seems to be long lost desire.

Jem pulls away with a grin. 'Just how I remembered it.'

I smile shyly. It was exactly how I remembered it, too.

'I've wanted to do that ever since we lost George.'

'What? Not before?'

'I thought there was no chance,' Jem says. 'It was pretty clear I wasn't your favourite person.'

'True. You were far too rude to kiss.'

Jem laughs. 'Fair enough.'

His arms envelop me as minutes momentarily stop passing, like someone's pressed the pause button. What do we do next? Certainly not clean up the kitchen, that's for sure. This moment is so unexpected, so thrilling, I feel like I've been turned upside down and sent out to find north with nothing but a penknife and a packet of matches.

George breaks our silence with a resounding bark, jolting us back to the present. Rudely followed by my mobile ringing. I look at my watch. Ten thirty. My stomach twists. A call this late can only be Mark.

Jem keeps his arms still around me. 'You wanna get that?'

'Not really.'

The phone goes to voicemail. But then goes off again, sounding even more insistent.

'Sorry, maybe I should answer it.'

I slip out of Jem's embrace and head inside to grab my phone. I glance at the number and answer. 'Mum? Are you okay?'

'Indie, thank goodness I got you.'

'What's wrong? You sound upset.'

'Something terrible has happened. It's Dad… he's…' Mum breaks down into sobs and I can't understand a single word.

'Mum, what is it? What's happened?'

Jem walks in and looks at me questioningly, but all I can do is give an exasperated shrug.

'Sorry, darling, I'm here.' Mum's still crying but pauses to take a breath. 'We're on our way to Royal North Shore Hospital in an ambulance—'

'Oh my God! Mum, what happened?'

'We're not completely sure, but it looks like Dad's having a heart attack...'

17

'WHAT?' I clutch my phone, mouth so open a train could drive through. Of all the words I thought Mum might say in this moment, "heart" and "attack" did not spring to mind. Especially in the same sentence. Blood drains from my head and I feel like I'm about to pass out. 'Are you sure? What happened? Is he… is he going to be alright?'

'We don't know anything yet. We're almost at the hospital.' Mum is frantic. 'He'd been feeling a bit off all day, then tonight, we were sitting quietly watching *Would I Lie to You*, you know how we love that show, so funny and hardly stressful, I'm not really sure why that—'

'Mum!'

'Sorry, anyway he felt this awful tightness in his chest. He tried lying down but it wouldn't go away. He went into a cold sweat and felt sick in his tummy, it was awful.' Mum is rattling on, clearly in shock. 'I've been telling him to stick to his diet but he just won't listen. The other day, I walked into the kitchen and he'd made himself an ice cream sundae with marshmallows and chocolate sprinkles! I didn't even know we had any chocolate sprinkles—'

'Mum!' I speak firmly, despite a wobble in my voice. 'I'm coming right now. I'll meet you in emergency.'

'Thanks, darling.' The relief in Mum's voice is instantaneous. 'See you soon.'

I hang up, hands shaking uncontrollably, like when you have

fiddley props to deal with onstage but no strategy to control it. My darling dad is having a heart attack! No, no, no, it can't be true. My parents are never sick. I can't remember the last time either of them even had a cold.

'Indie, what's happened?' Jem is standing, waiting.

'My dad… it's his heart, I have to—'

'Go to the hospital,' Jem finishes my sentence in a calm voice. 'Of course, let's go, I'll drive.'

I look at him like he's just offered me a million dollars. My head's flying like an out-of-control rollercoaster, complete with children screaming to get off. Driving over to the north shore seems impossible.

'Right, thanks, um, what do I need?' I'm finding it hard to breathe let alone get out the door. Come on, Indie. Take a big breath in. And out. In. And out. You can do it.

'Bag, phone, and wallet.' Jem takes control like when we lost George, and while I don't have the headspace to fully admire it, I'm truly grateful. 'I'll just bring George inside, who knows how long we'll be.'

We speed up the Pacific Highway and soon pull up outside the emergency department. That last conversation with Dad on the way to the train station before moving to Jazz's replays in my mind. The image of my father smiling awkwardly, trying to discuss my relationship, skewers my heart like a knitting needle. Oh my God! The fib I told Benji. It's all coming true. That's why you should never tell lies. I let out an almighty sob. Jem has seen me cry a few times now, so I just don't care.

'Hey, we don't know what's going on yet, it may all be fine. Do you know that someone goes to hospital with a heart attack every nine minutes and most of the time, they pull through. Very common.'

I nod, unable to speak, wondering how Jem knows such a specific piece of information.

'Saw it on a documentary,' he says as if reading my mind. 'You go in, I'll find a park.'

I do as I'm told and walk up to the front desk. An older woman with cropped grey hair and kind eyes looks up.

'Hi, my father, David James, just came in, I think he's had a… a…' The word doesn't want to come out of my mouth. Maybe if I don't say it, then it won't be real.

'Just take a seat, I'll see what I can find out.'

I walk over to the plastic seats, but I can't possibly sit. The doors open and Mum comes out, white as a porcelain bowl and just as fragile.

'Indie.' She puts her arms out and we hug as we always do but this time, it's fraught with questions and worries.

'What's happening?' I can barely catch my breath. 'Was it… a heart attack?'

'Looks like it.' My mother's face crumples, tears running down her cheeks. I swear I hear my own heart crack.

She dabs at her eyes with a soggy-looking tissue. 'Sorry, sweetheart, thanks for coming.'

'Everything's going to be okay.' I'm not sure why I say that because I have no idea. I'm not a doctor. I had a guest role as the visiting cardiologist on a drama called *Country Doctors* but it was more about the breakdown my character had when one of her patients died, so not at all helpful right now.

'We don't know. Everything might not be okay…' Mum stops herself. 'Darling, would you stay for a while? Until we hear some news?'

'Of course, we'll… I mean, I'll stay.' I can't believe I almost spoke for Jem, like he's my boyfriend. What is it with emergency situations and their matchmaking powers?

Jem appears by my side. Mum looks surprised, even pleased to see him.

'Mum, this is Jem, you met at Jazz and Stu's wedding. He drove me here.'

'Yes, of course, I remember Jem, how are you? Sorry to be seeing you in this situation, things like this usually happen to other people, not us.'

Jem turns to me. 'Do you want me to leave you in peace?'

That's the last thing I want. I need Jem to stay and be normal in this crisis. 'No, don't go, we're just waiting to see what's happening. Well, you can if you want, but I need to stay.'

'Alright, how about I find some coffees?' He wanders off, leaving Mum and me sitting in silence.

My insides feel like they've been tossed into a blender. What if this happened when I was in LA and I couldn't get back in time? I'd never have forgiven myself.

Ten minutes later, Jem walks up and hands us each a latte. 'I wasn't sure what you wanted.'

'That's perfect, thanks.'

We perch on the uncomfortable chairs, time passing like it's stuck in traffic. I tap out a quick text to Jazz. I don't want to spoil her holiday, but she'd kill me if I didn't let her know.

Within seconds, my phone rings with Jazz's name flashing on the screen. My eyes prickle with tears. We haven't spoken since our disagreement, but in the heat of a crisis, that no longer matters.

'Tell me it's not true.'

Hearing Jazz's voice is too much. I've had to be strong for Mum, but a few words from my best friend tips me over an emotional cliff. I walk away and clutch a nearby railing, dizzy and unsteady, like the floor is falling away.

'Oh, Jazz, it's just terrible,' I sob. 'We don't know what's going on, he might recover but we don't know—'

'My God, he's not going to—'

'I don't know.' I can't bear to hear the question Jazz is about to ask. Instead, I cry like I'm never going to stop, while she waits patiently on the other end.

'Do you want me to come back?' Jazz asks when I stop to take a breath. 'I will if you need me.'

She would, too.

'No, it'll be fine.' I sniff, trying to control my tears that are now forming a gigantic pool on the lino floor in front of me. 'Look, I'm so sorry about our last conversation. I was being unfair and should never have said what I said.'

'No, I'm sorry, please don't think about it again. All forgotten.'

'I'm here if you need to talk about Stu.'

'Sounds like you've got enough on your plate.'

Mum waves at me, looking worried. 'I'd better go, I'll call you when I know more.'

I hang up and walk back to where Mum is now talking to the doctor, a magnificent Amazonian woman who looks like she's no older than me. Maybe Mum's right about doctors being more important than actors. Look what she's doing tonight. Saving my father's life. What have I done? Not worked on an audition piece that may or may not land me a film role.

'We've given him medication to clear the blockages,' the Amazon is saying in a calm soothing voice. 'Now blood is flowing freely to his heart, which is very good news.'

'Is he going to die?' Mum puts her hand to her mouth as the tears once again stream down her face.

'Not this time, it seems.' The doctor smiles. 'And certainly not on my shift.'

Mum half laughs, half sobs. Overcome with relief, I give her a hug as I blink away my own tears.

'Can we see him?' I ask.

'Not right now, I'm afraid. He's in the ICU. We'll monitor his heart overnight. You should be able to see him in the morning.' She pauses, checking her notes. 'He'll stay here for a couple of days at least. See how he's going. If he needs bypass surgery, a week or longer.'

'Oh my God!' Mum looks like she's about to keel over herself. That's all I need, the two of them in intensive care.

'Mum, that's fairly common.' That much I do remember from my *Country Doctors* gig.

'Yes, you're right,' says the doctor. 'And also, the best way to prevent another heart attack. After that, we need to look at David's lifestyle, exercise, diet, and set up a rehabilitation program. He's not out of the woods yet. Recovery can take anywhere from a couple of weeks to three months, sometimes longer.'

'Don't worry, Doctor, he'll be on a strict regime from now on,' my mother says firmly. 'No more secret chocolate in the middle of the night or sneaking a quick spoonful of cream from the fridge after dinner. He thinks I don't know, but I do.'

'Looks like he'll be in good hands.' The Amazon smiles. 'Why don't you all try and get some sleep. You're welcome to stay here and wait, but there's not much more you can do.'

The doctor leaves and Mum turns back to us. 'It's nearly four in the morning, why don't you both go home and get some sleep?'

I don't want to leave, but we should check on George, and Jem's got work this morning. I give Mum a hug and make her promise to call me later.

Driving back, we don't say much, and with so little traffic, we're home in a flash. George gallops to the door, his happy doggy welcome so heart-warming after a night like this one.

'Thanks for driving me,' I say to Jem. 'I really appreciate it.'

'No problem.' He pauses. 'Look, I'm going to crash. I'm working today so I need to grab a couple of hours of sleep.'

'Sure, me too.'

'You okay?'

'Yep… well, no… I don't know, I think I'm in shock.' I take a breath. 'About before when we… I'm really…'

'It's fine, you don't have to explain.' Jem turns to go.

'Well, it's just—'

'I've gotta go to bed. I'll see you later.'

He makes a beeline for his bedroom, closing both door and conversation in one fell swoop. I can't believe it's happened again. We take one step closer and he runs away.

I climb under Jazz's vintage quilt, my mind replaying the night's events. I finally kiss my hot housemate, just as my father has a heart attack. What are the odds?

Much like at the wedding, life intervened like a nosy neighbour, insisting that Jem and I not be together. And Dad? A clear sign that I should be in Australia. That I need to spend more time with my parents, rather than wasting my life trying to crack Hollywood. There's time for that later, but my parents… I need to make the most of them while I can.

I always knew what I wanted and where I was going. And my career unfolded like a dream, the future exciting and full of potential. But now? I don't know what to do. Which is not surprising after no sleep and a near family tragedy. But still, everything feels bleak, like the script of my life is no longer working. The beginning was promising, but now the middle has sagged. And the end? I guess no one ever knows how that's going to turn out. But one thing's for sure, mine definitely needs some imaginative re-writing and a thorough edit if I've any hope of finding my happily-ever-after.

18

I WAKE a few hours later with a start, stressed and in need of about ten cups of tea. So much for a quiet, relaxing night working on my script. It couldn't have been less quiet or less relaxing. I think of Dad and my stomach turns. I hope he's alright.

George, who's curled up on the end of my bed (sorry Jazz), rouses himself to deliver a disgusting good morning lick on my face and jumps off to stretch. No wonder we call it downward dog in yoga, it's exactly what George does every morning.

'I'm going to call Mum,' I explain. 'Maybe a W-A-L-K later.'

George bounds around me excitedly, obviously more than capable of spelling. I sigh and go to put the kettle on. One look at the kitchen reminds me I didn't finish the cleaning up last night. Not something you do before racing to emergency.

I quietly stack the dishwasher and fill the sink to wash the millions of pots that Jem required to cook dinner. Once that mess is cleared up, I decide to go for a walk to clear my head and sort out the rest of my life. Footsteps pad down the hall and my body freezes. Jem. My mind flips back to last night's kiss and although it feels a universe away, my insides ignite like a sparkler.

He appears in the kitchen, dishevelled and sleepy.

'Morning.' I try to sound casual.

'Hey.' He gives nothing away. 'Thanks for cleaning up.'

I wonder if we're going to address the awkward and embarrassing elephant that's taking up most of the room.

'Listen, Indie, you've got a lot on in your life right now.' Jem sounds removed and matter of fact. 'Your dad, this audition. I'll just leave you to it.'

Hello elephant.

I open my mouth to speak, but he cuts me off before I can sort my thoughts into a sentence.

'It's a hard time for both of us.' He pauses as if wanting to say something more but changes his mind. 'See you later.'

He grabs the lead, taking George out the sliding door, while I escape to my bedroom. Hot, heavy tears soak Jazz's crisp classic French linen pillowcase as I lay down to rest my aching head.

I don't move until I hear Jem return with George, shower, and leave for work. When I'm convinced he's gone, I creep out to the lounge room.

My mobile rings and I grab it quickly. 'Mum?'

'Darling, Dad's doing very well.' She sounds like a different person, or rather she sounds more like herself than she did last night. 'I'm with him now.'

My hands tremble and my eyes sting. 'Can I say hello?'

'He can't talk very well. He's still got all these tubes in his mouth and he's feeling a bit drained and sleepy. Why don't you come in tomorrow? They'll have removed the tubes and he'll be in his own room then. I'd better go now. He's trying to ask me something through hand gestures and for the life of me, I can't work out what it is.'

Mum hangs up. I text Jazz to let her know the news. God knows what time it is over there but she'll want to know.

The response is immediate. *Hurray!*

She must have been waiting by the phone. Such a good friend. I can't believe I haven't been there for her. Coming home was about recovering, but all I've done is wallow, so now I'm not going to waste another microsecond of precious time. Life is just too short.

My mind flips to Jem. With last night's kiss, Mark became a distant memory; I need to close that chapter once and for all. There I was judging Jazz when I wasn't being fair myself. Who knows what will happen with Jem, but I need to be properly "un-fiancéd". And I have to do it immediately.

Invigorated, I dial Mark's number.

'Babe?'

'Hi.'

'So good to hear your voice. How are you?'

'Not so good…' I falter. 'Dad… he just had a heart attack.'

'My God! Is he okay?'

'Looks like he'll recover, but it's been devastating, to say the least.'

'Do you want me to come over?' Mark jumps into superhero mode; I can almost see him standing on a building, hands on hips, in a Superman costume. 'I could be there in twenty-four hours, just let me—'

'No!' God, that's the last thing I need right now. Mark and Jem sitting around having awkward conversations.

'But, babe, I miss you so—'

'Look, we need to talk.'

One line that says it all. Even Mark must sense what's coming as he forges on like a desperate soldier, single-handedly trying to save his country.

'Babe, I'm so sorry about everything. Please forgive me and please, please, please come home.'

Home. That word keeps coming up. LA isn't home to me. Being so far away, it now feels temporary and transient. Mark's slick apartment, not mine. His friends, not mine. His life, not yet mine.

None of it felt like me. Maybe coming home was trying to work that out and find a true sense of the word.

'Indie, I've been an idiot. There are no excuses for what I did.'

Mark's deep velvety voice always made my heart melt, like a marshmallow on a campfire, but now it's leaving me cold as butter in the fridge.

'You're right, there are no excuses.' I feel tears loitering.

'It'll never happen again, you have to believe me. It's over with Kourtney. I haven't spoken to her in ages.'

'I don't give a shit about Kourtney. But what about next time you do a film? How will I ever really know if you're being faithful?'

'You just have to forgive me and trust me again, babe.' Mark pauses. 'Is this about that Jem guy with the dog?'

Fury bubbles up from the soles of my feet, like hot lava rushing to every corner of my body. It's like someone handed me supersonic glasses and I'm suddenly seeing the real Mark for the first time. 'How dare you ask that! You did this. You broke us the minute you had sex with Kourtney. No, the minute you *decided* to have sex with Kourtney. I loved you and you let me down – and you're asking if it has something to do with some guy I'm dog-sitting with?'

There's silence on the other end of the line.

'You're unbelievable, Mark. I don't know what I was thinking when I agreed to marry you, but it was the worst decision I've ever made. Thank God you hooked up with Kourtney. I should be rejoicing because it showed exactly who you are. Your true colours, that I thought so amazing, are horrible and offensive. In fact, please thank Kourtney for me next time you see her, which I'm sure will be soon. You probably just had sex with her. Is she there? Say thanks from me!'

I'm so angry, even I don't know what I'm saying anymore.

Mark probably has no idea.

'Um, so what are you saying, babe?'

See?

'I don't love you, Mark.' I speak slowly, so he doesn't miss the not-so-subtle detail. 'Trust is everything and I can't get past this.'

'Don't say that, babe. You can trust me again.'

'No, I can't.'

'Can't or don't want to?'

I think of my beautiful engagement ring sitting back in LA. I couldn't bear to even look at it, let alone keep it on my person. It means nothing now. I was never special to Mark. His smouldering charm wasn't just for me. It was for everyone. Every casting director, director, and producer. How many times had he told me some funny story, then I'd hear it another ten times as he re-told anyone and everyone we saw. He knows how to turn on the charm and he's devastatingly handsome, but now the idea of "our whole lives together" makes my heart sink like a coin in a fountain.

Another heavy silence descends.

'Mark?'

'I won't hold you up any longer.' He speaks in a detached business-like tone and hangs up before I respond. At least he got the message.

I wait for the inevitable tears but there are none. Not for him. Mark wasn't my Mr Right even before Kourtney arrived on the scene. We were fabulous on paper but paper is too fragile to last a lifetime.

I sit there, drained but relieved that at least one messy drawer of my life has been de-cluttered. Now I can focus on what's important – helping with Dad's recovery, powering through a big audition, finding out what's going on with my best friend's marriage, avoiding my aloof housemate who I accidently kissed, and trying not to re-lose one gigantic dog. Not your usual "To Do" list and certainly not part of any plan I had. But the way my life has been going, I'm starting to doubt the value of having any sort of plan in the first place.

19

I DON'T see Jem for the rest of the day. Instead, I fall into bed early and wake up at five the next morning, exhausted but unable to sleep a moment longer. After going through Dad's ordeal and finally ending things with Mark, every part of my body feels charged with frenetic energy. I want to grab life with two hands and make it do exactly what I want. But I'm not entirely sure how to go about it.

I jump up and grab my running clothes. Thankfully, George is snoozing in his resting station and doesn't sense me tiptoe past. I quietly close the door behind me and take off into the streaky pink of the early morning.

The background fades as I switch my focus to Alyssa and who she really is, what happened in her past. Are both her parents alive? Has she had her heart broken? Would she run every day, like this? I reckon she might be someone who prefers to go to the gym, but then again, her life's so busy, when would she have time?

I head down to the beach and along the coastal track, desperately trying to fixate on Alyssa's world, despite the constant churn of worry over Dad. So much so that when a familiar flash of blonde speeds by, it takes me a moment to register who it is.

I stop and call, 'Charlie Reynolds!'

'Hey.' Charlie looks back but barely stops. 'Sorry, Indie, gotta keep going.'

'Speak soon?' I call after him.

Charlie waves and jogs off.

That was weird. He really didn't want to chat. Very unlike Charlie. I slowly pick up my pace but stop dead, a stab of guilt pinning my feet to the concrete path. I never called Charlie to apologise about the other night. I meant to ring him but what happened? Somewhere between getting a film audition, kissing Jem, and nearly losing Dad, I let it slip. I start running again but stop with a jolt. I've been so selfish recently. I haven't spent much time with my parents, and I almost lost Dad. I should have been more upfront with Mark. I wasn't fair to Jazz, then I hurt Charlie's feelings and did nothing about it.

Standing alone, staring across the endless blue of the water, a sense of unease creeps over me. I've been busy playing the role of the hurt girlfriend without realising that I've doubled up as the selfish diva who takes advantage of everyone around her. What about playing the best friend, excellent housemate, thoughtful daughter? What about those great roles?

I tap out Charlie's number. It rings a few times and just when I'm wondering if he'll take my call, he picks up.

'What's up? Realised you're not as fit as me?'

'Charlie, I'm sorry I haven't called you. I went to do it the other day, but I had to see Michelle—'

'It's okay, Indie.'

'No, it's not, I've been a hopeless friend. I haven't apologised about that night, but since then I lost the dog, then Dad had a heart attack.'

I still find it hard to say those words, which feel like they are someone else's, not mine.

'What? Is he okay?'

'Dad or George?'

'Ha! I meant your dad?'

'He pulled through, thank God, but it was terrifying. I'm still in shock.'

'That's awful. No wonder you haven't had time to call.'

'I would say it was the worst moment of my life, but still, I feel bad about us.'

'It's okay, Indigo James, your dad having a heart attack is an excuse I'll accept. Besides, we're friends, we always will be.'

I start tearing up. 'Forgive me?'

'Just this once.'

'You're the best, Charlie Reynolds.'

'True. Do you want to me to turn around so we can finish the run together?'

'I would, but I've got to get back to work on my audition for *Not Missing Out.*'

'Hey, that's great. I auditioned for a role too, Ben Caine, the defence lawyer. You going for Alyssa?'

'Yep.'

'When?'

'Tuesday.'

'Do you want to run a few lines.'

'That'd be awesome!' I'm at that point when it's hard to keep working in isolation. Rehearsing my scenes with Charlie would make a huge difference. 'Later this afternoon?'

'Sure, I'm free.'

'Come over to my place – Jazz's place, I mean – around five? I'll text you the address. That'll give me time to do some more work on the scenes. I know how tough you can be.'

Charlie and I have worked together so often he knows my little tricks and will pull me up if I'm the slightest bit lazy. I feel comfortable with him. A bit too comfortable, judging from recent behaviour, but I think we're past that.

Jem is up making coffee when I arrive home. Wearing a singlet that showcases his beautiful arms. I can't keep my eyes off them. Strong, well-defined. Imagine how they might feel if he grabbed me from a burning building and carried me to safety. Or swung in on a tree vine to save me from a pack of wild animals, or if he—

'Indie?'

'Huh?'

'I asked about your dad.'

'Oh, he's doing well. I'm seeing him today.' My voice is strangely upbeat, while my eyes home in on the gentle ripple in his bicep as he stirs his coffee.

'That's good.' He takes his coffee and walks back to his bedroom.

'Are you in tonight?' I call after him.

'Not sure.'

He shuts his door and that's that. Looks like we're not going to discuss the kiss right now. And with my audition looming, it's probably just as well.

After a shower, I drive to the hospital and text Mum when I'm at reception. She meets me looking drained, but the hug she gives me feels like I'm pulling on a favourite jumper. Warm, comforting, and lovely.

'He's looking forward to seeing you, darling, but you can't stay too long as he needs to rest. The nurses are very strict.'

We arrive at Dad's room and I'm catapulted into shock. I thought I was prepared for the worst, but seeing him here, surrounded by machines, looking so small and old, a grey tinge to his face, my heart splinters into a million little pieces.

His face lights up when he sees me. 'Indie, my love, how are you?'

'Me?' I force back the tears. 'Dad, how are you? That's more the question to be asked here.'

'I'm fine, fit as a fiddle.'

Mum scoffs.

'Okay, maybe not a fiddle, maybe something small and percussive. A maraca perhaps?'

I giggle and squeeze Dad's hand, glad he hasn't loss his sense of humour. I try to focus on that, rather than the trauma of the situation.

'When do you come home, Dad?'

'In a few days' time, they reckon. Maybe a week.'

'And life is going to change, let me tell you,' Mum jumps in. 'He's taking two months off work and starting a new diet and exercise regime. Then he's not taking any more Saturday appointments. No more trans fats, processed foods, red meat, wine…'

Dad looks at me mournfully.

'It's for the best, Dad. You gave us a real fright and we don't want to lose you.'

'I'm not going anywhere.'

'And I'm making sure of that.' Mum looks fraught.

'Pam, everything's going to be fine.'

Mum nods, and they share a brief tender look that reminds me how much they love each other. Will I ever find someone with whom I can share a moment like that? Not the heart attack bit, naturally, but that unfailing connection through life's tumultuous ups and downs?

Mum and I chat about this and that while Dad lies there listening until a serious-looking nurse with jet black hair dragged back into a bun comes to kick me out.

'Time to go now, Pam,' she says in a voice you don't want to argue with. 'David needs to rest.'

'This is Veena, the bossiest nurse in the hospital,' says Mum.

'Someone has to be, especially with cheeky patients like this one here,' says Veena with an efficient smile. 'Now off you go, please.'

I give Dad a hug. 'Try to be good – and no boring lectures to the nurses about the importance of thorough flossing.'

'But it's vital, Indie, I was only saying to Veena—'

'Bye, Dad, love you.' My throat catches on a simple phrase I say all the time, but somehow now has more significance. What if something goes wrong and I never get to say it again?

'I love you too.' His voice thickens and his eyes dampen.

'Now, no need to get upset, David. We need to keep calm, remember?' Veena turns to us. 'Sorry, but it's time to go.'

I creep out before I get into trouble. Mum's right, Veena *is* bossy. I walk to the lifts in a daze. Life is so unpredictable. Like an ice cube, seemingly clear, strong, and reliable, but left in the sun on a hot summer's day it disappears in minutes. Still, you can't guard it in the freezer, cautious and fearful. What's the use of that? You need to bring it out, enjoy what it has to offer. Pop it in your drink and relish every delicious drop. Because if you don't, it slips away and you're left with nothing but a lukewarm beverage in the searing heat.

20

BACK home, I'm met with what must be the most hopeful eyes ever seen on a dog. A walk is the last thing I feel like but it might help raise my flailing spirits and George is unlikely to give up trying.

'Okay, okay, let's go.'

I look for something to wear but my (very limited) activewear is in the dirty clothes pile. And none of it translates to proper dog walking attire. I rummage around Jazz's wardrobe for something more appropriate. Casual, sporty yet stylish – from what I see at the dog park, something I never seem to achieve. Of course, Jazz has plenty of options and I put together an outfit that screams "experienced dog-owner". I even find a puffer vest. It's a bit hot to wear at this time of year, but it's about time I take this dog thing seriously and look the part.

Next, determined not to be beaten by an inanimate object, I grab George's harness. I check out yet another YouTube video, attempt to slip it over George's head and, after a couple of tries, I succeed, only to find it's inside out. I get there in the end and feel like I've put a flag at the top of Mount Everest.

I strut to the dog park, like someone who knows what they're doing. When I let George off his leash, he runs off to play and sniff and… well whatever dogs do. I haven't been to the park since the night I lost him. How could I show my face after failing so badly? Not that anyone would know. But I knew, and that was enough to put me off. Now I'm back on track, taking on the dog community with a vengeance. Well, going for a walk in a puffer, but still, it's progress.

I also haven't seen Alex since that night. To be honest, I don't want to. Sure, Jazz is the one who kissed him, but why is he spending so much time with a happily married woman? Although maybe that's the problem. Maybe Jazz isn't happy and went looking elsewhere. I don't feel comfortable about the situation but thankfully, there's no sign of Alex and Roxie.

'Never mind!' I say to a downcast George. 'There are other friends here to play with.'

I flick through messages on my phone. Mostly Michelle suggesting potential roles, a few from Lucy, who wants to catch up for coffee. I go onto Instagram and almost drop my phone to see a photo of Mark and Kourtney, arms around each other, laughing at some joke. Wow, that was quick. I don't want Mark, but I also don't want to see him so happy. Especially in the arms of Kourtney Layne.

'Hey, you,' a voice says behind me, making me jump at least half a metre off the ground.

I turn to see Alex in his crisp workout gear and crinkly smile. 'Sorry, I didn't mean to startle you.'

'That's okay, I was a million miles away. Didn't think you were turning up.'

'I'm a little behind schedule today.' Alex bends down to give George a pat. 'Good to see you haven't lost George again.'

'Don't even joke about it. I still feel terrible. Please don't ever tell Jazz.'

'It's our secret.' Alex pretends to lock up his mouth and throw away the key, something I haven't seen done since primary school. But then, teaching Year Three, maybe it's part of his every day.

'So, how are you?' he asks.

'Well, as you said, I haven't lost George again, so that's something. I did try to bath him – disastrously I might add.' I pause. 'Actually, my dad had a heart attack, which has been a shock to say the least.'

'I'm so sorry.' Alex looks concerned. 'Is he okay?'

'He should be fine, fingers crossed.' My voice catches. 'But it was awful. I still can't believe how close we came to losing him.'

'But you didn't.'

Tears sting my eyes so I change the subject before I embarrass myself in front of the entire dog community. 'I'd better go, I've got an audition on Tuesday and I need to work on my scenes. Can you see those cheeky dogs?'

Alex calls Roxie, and George follows close behind, looking at me like I'm the meanest dog-sitter in the entire world.

'Sorry, George, I've got work to do.'

'Woof,' he says grumpily.

'Don't worry, George, we're not staying long either.' Alex turns to me. 'Fancy a drink Tuesday night? Celebrate your audition, which is bound to go very well.'

I don't know what to say. Feels like I'd be fraternising with the enemy, but maybe after a few drinks, he'll share crucial details about Jazz. And I know I won't feel like staying home participating in super polite question-and-answer conversations with Jem.

'Sure.'

Alex says he'll text to confirm a venue as I drag George from the park. I wish it were Tuesday night now and the audition was well and truly done.

'Earth to Indie?'

'Huh?' I look up to see Charlie, script in arm, clearly waiting for a response.

We're in the lounge room, going through one of the scenes. My mind must have drifted. Not a good sign.

'Sorry, lost my concentration. Where were we?'

'What were you thinking about? Something more interesting than this audition by the looks of it.'

Heat surges through my cheeks. An image of Jem's arm stirring coffee had randomly popped into my head. Come on, Indie. Focus, please – and not on that.

'Just tired. It's been a big week.'

He nods. 'Why don't we go from where Alyssa first meets Ryan and they have a huge fight about how the case should be run.'

'And are clearly attracted to each other,' I add.

'Exactly.' Charlie's eyes sparkle. 'Do you think you can manage that?'

I giggle. 'I'm a pretty good actor, you know, but not sure if I'm that good.'

We spend a couple of hours working on the scenes and I start to feel more confident. Charlie is an enormous help and immediately picks up when I'm not connecting with the character.

'Let's do the third scene one more time, from where Alyssa comes to the police station to talk to Ryan,' I say.

This scene is pivotal, as it's where Alyssa realises she's in love with Ryan but isn't sure he feels the same. Honestly, it's like someone's been watching my life and put it in a script. Except in this script, everything works out perfectly. It also includes two murders, a few gunshots, and a psychopath serial killer who died about a decade ago. Apart from that, I could be looking into a mirror.

'Okay,' Charlie says, 'I'm here at the police station. Enter when you're ready.'

My character comes to give Ryan a piece of her mind, to tell him what she really thinks, but Ryan has just received bad news and is close to tears. Alyssa is so moved and falls in love on the spot. The only trouble is, the scene's been feeling dull and boring, it even puts *me* to sleep. I need to find something to increase the tension and raise the stakes.

I focus on the fury I felt for Mark when I discovered the truth. How dare he lie to me. And Jem, how dare he kiss me and ignore me? *Again*. He needs to know how I feel. And Ryan needs to know how Alyssa feels.

I start the scene, determined to say what I want to say. I'm so focused that when Charlie speaks Ryan's lines about discovering a second murder, a close friend of his, I'm shocked into silence. Fuelled with passion, I walk up to Ryan (in fact, Charlie) and kiss him full on the lips. I kiss as if my life depends on it, and Charlie responds. It's not a gentle kiss like Jem and I shared in the garden, but a fiery wild kiss, filled with promise and fervour. I pull away and leave the scene.

'Wow!' Charlie doesn't seem to be able to say anything but that for a while. 'Wow, that was… wow!'

'Too much, Charlie Reynolds?'

'Just enough, Indie James.'

A noise at the door drags my attention and I see Jem standing there staring at me, hurt and confused. When did he walk in? Did he see that? Judging by the look on his face, he caught the whole scene. Which was acting but might not have looked that way to him.

'Jem, hi we're just—'

'Sorry,' he mutters. 'Didn't mean to intrude.'

He leaves as quietly as he arrived.

Charlie looks at me. 'What's going on?'

'I'm not sure.'

Actually, I know exactly what's happening. Jem walked in to see me passionately kissing Charlie. A kiss that was nothing but a tool to help me work out my character's underlying feelings. The tension between Alyssa and Ryan. The intense dislike she feels for him masking the passion beneath the surface. Much like me and Jem.

After Charlie leaves, I gently tap on Jem's closed door. Not that I need to defend my actions but it must have looked bad to the outside eye. Or Jem's eye, I should say.

'Yeah?' he calls.

'Just me,' I say nervously. 'Have you got a minute?'

He opens the door and leans against the doorway. 'Sure.'

'Before, with Charlie, we were rehearsing for my audition.'

'You don't have to explain yourself. None of my business.'

'Jem, it was work.'

'Really? Didn't look like work to me, but I guess it's part and parcel of being an actor.'

'What's that supposed to mean?'

'Pretty easy to cross the line between work and well… just kissing your co-star.'

'That's not true!' My voice jumps so many octaves, I give myself a fright.

'Looked that way to me.'

Just like that and we're back to when we first moved in. How dare he say that to me? And be so judgemental? But I think how Mark and I got together, and then Mark and Kourtney. Okay, it happens, but this was different. There's nothing between me and Charlie, not anymore. Besides, I don't have to explain myself to Jem.

'Look, Indie, who you kiss, or should I say, "work with", has nothing to do with me. I've never thought much of actors and their world and I'd rather not be a part of it.'

He closes his door and I'm left fuming. How dare he judge me! I was rehearsing a scene. And there are times when I have to kiss other actors. It's part of the job. Besides, Jem is in no position to tell me who I can or can't kiss. We're not even together. And if he can't stop for five minutes to get off his ridiculously high horse and be a normal human being, then quite frankly, we never will be.

21

TUESDAY morning, I'm sitting in the waiting room of the casting agency trying to blank out the world around me and focus on the task at hand, which is all about Alyssa. My thoughts stray to Dad and my stomach swirls like I've been reading in the car. But as always, I hear his happy voice cheering me on as if he were in the room. 'You can do it, Indie, I know you can.'

Okay, Dad, this one's for you, I silently tell the voice. Now, just get out of my head for the next fifteen minutes and let me get on with it.

Noise filters through from the audition room. The actress before me must be finishing up. I close my eyes and breathe, feeling prepared and focused. But open them to see Tia walk out of the door, my insides dropping like a super-fast lift going down a sky rise building. Damn, of course she's going for the same role.

It's so easy to get freaked out in the waiting room when you see other actors going for the same job. Often people you know, sometimes friends. You immediately think how great they'd be in the role and that they'll probably get it. But the minute you let yourself go there, it's absolute death for your audition. You're basically handing the power over to your colleague and saying 'Here, I'll stand aside, the part is yours'.

I'm not doing that today. I know Tia gets roles I go for, and she's at least a foot taller than me, and let's face it, gorgeous – but I keep hearing Michelle's deafening voice reverberating in my head, insisting that Tia and I are very different. And that this is a role I can definitely play.

Tia says goodbye to the casting agent like they're the best of friends, and flashes me her most dazzling smile.

'Have fun in there.' Her silky voice grates on my already delicate nerves as she glides out the door.

My hands start to quiver and I clench my fists. Just focus on the task at hand.

The casting agent, who looks vaguely familiar, disappears back into the room.

Two minutes later, she pops her head around the door. 'Indigo? Come through, thanks.'

I pick myself up, take a deep breath and follow her through the door. No turning back now.

'Thanks for coming in, I'm Zoe. I think we've met before, and this is Nina the director, who you already know.'

'Indie, how are you?'

'Great, thanks.' I step forward to shake the director's hand. 'Lovely to see you again.'

'And you, how's life in La La Land?'

'It's okay.' I remain determined to appear upbeat. 'But to be honest, it's good to be home.'

'I always feel like that after being away, especially after a stint in LA. So, Alyssa – any thoughts? Pretty strong character, isn't she?'

'She's awesome,' I say.

Zoe steps out from behind the camera and I notice a guy standing with her.

'This is Jasper. He'll be reading opposite you today.'

'Hi, how are you?' I flash Jasper a smile, hoping he has a handle on the scene. A good reader is worth their weight in gold.

'Do you have any questions about Alyssa?' Nina asks. 'Or

would you like to run the first scene? See what comes up.'

'Happy to have a run through.'

'We might film it, but we'll go through it few times so just relax into it.'

I clear my head and focus on the first scene, a disagreement over a new piece of evidence between Alyssa and Ryan, which develops into a fiery argument. There's an intense connection between the pair, but Ryan is hot headed and arrogant, and Alyssa refuses to be pushed around by him.

After the past couple of months, I feel I've been living this scene – dealing with arrogant men who think they're better than me. Something stirs deep down, and it's not just my stomach growling with hunger, which unfortunately often happens during an audition. No, this is stronger, boiling from the bottom of my soul. Anger bubbles up like a flash flood, surging through my body, sharpening my focus and fuelling my passion.

I use my nerves and take control of the scene right from the start. I have a job to do, and I do it. It's as simple as that. And because I'm centred and able to tap into real emotions, I bring Alyssa to life without losing a sense of myself.

I finish the scene and there's a slight pause as my final words, charged with electricity, hang in the air.

What seems like an eternity ticks by before Nina finally says, 'Thanks, Indie, that was a great start.' She doesn't give much away, but I've clearly piqued her interest. I still may not get the job but it makes for an enjoyable audition. And that's all I'm worrying about right now.

'Great sense of what Alyssa's going through. This time, let's try and see a little more sadness from her past.'

'Sure, I feel she struggles with that, always trying to maintain a tough façade, especially around Ryan.'

'Exactly. Right, let's take it from the top.'

We run through the scene a couple more times, the turmoil brought about by Dad and his heart attack egging me on. Honestly, I have so many emotions fighting for attention, it's hard to know which way to look. I stay centred and with each take, I absorb Nina's different directions into my body and bring the lines to life. I forget to be nervous. In fact, I'm enjoying myself, if that's at all possible. By the time we do the next two scenes, I'm calm yet totally energised, soaring like an eagle, ready to swoop at a moment's notice. While nothing over the past week has made any sense at all, now I have absolute clarity, as if the demister in the car has finally kicked in and I have perfect vision of what's ahead. Everything I've ever done has brought me to this moment and every piece of the usually annoying puzzle is coming together like a dream.

'Right,' says Nina after the final scene has been done. 'I think we'll leave it there. Thanks so much for coming in.'

'Lovely to see you again. Best of luck for the film.'

The casting director escorts me back out to the waiting room. 'Well done,' she whispers. 'That was amazing.'

I smile gratefully. 'Thanks, Zoe.'

And I walk to the door with my head high, not even pausing to see who is waiting to go in after me. I don't want to know. It's all over. That went far better than I could have hoped, but now I must let it go. It's out of my hands. I gave it my best shot. Let's just hope it's enough.

22

WHEN I say, 'I must let it go', this of course never happens. I don't know why I even bother saying it. I never let auditions go. Instead, I cling to them with two hands, painfully reliving every minute detail (usually in the middle of the night), wondering why on earth I did what I did. While it's a relief to get a big audition like this one out of the way, an empty (and often panicked) feeling usually follows close behind.

Back home, I feel at such a loose and unsettled end I even consider baking a cake. But as my mother never fails to point out, cooking is not my thing. And fair enough, I've concocted a few disasters in my time. I can never remember what comes after the sugar. Eggs or butter? Luckily, Charlie calls before I inevitably pick the wrong one.

'How'd you go?'

'Pretty good, I reckon.' I pause. 'What are you up to? Feel like a run?'

I'm not sure if I want to run but I need to do something. And I'm better at running than baking. Charlie agrees to come by in about fifteen minutes. I change into my running gear, grab a glass of water and take it out to the garden where George is lazing in the sun.

'Hello there, what a good boy you are.'

'Why, thank you.'

I turn to see Jem, reading at the table, his unexpected presence throwing me into a whirl. We haven't talked since the whole kissing argument. 'Sorry, I was… just saw George and…'

'Oh, you weren't talking to me?' He pretends to be disappointed.

'Definitely not. I wouldn't call you a good boy.'

'Really? What then?' There's a slight twinkle in Jem's eye I haven't seen since before we went to the hospital, like the heavy oak door is opening just the tiniest bit. Except, I have to tread carefully as it can shut in the blink of an eye.

'Sarcastic, rude, and a little judgemental. And that's just for starters.'

'Don't hold back.'

'I never do.' What's going on? Are we flirting?

Jem says nothing for a moment and I wonder if I said too much. We were just joking around. He started it.

'Hey, I'm sorry for overreacting yesterday. It was none of my business.'

'Oh… um.' I wasn't expecting an apology. 'There's really nothing between Charlie and me.'

'Sure, whatever, but I had no right to say that to you.' He smiles. 'Thought I might take George for a walk, wanna come?'

Jem's offer makes my heart beat faster. Shit, why did I say I'd go for a run with Charlie?

'Would love to, but I'm meeting Charlie for a run. He's about to arrive, so I can't really cancel.'

'Oh, right.' I can almost hear the bang of the door slamming shut.

'Maybe later?'

'Sure.'

What has officially become an awkward moment disintegrates further when the side gate clicks and Charlie appears, dressed in his sleek running attire. Jem's energy shifts downward so fast it could have been a contender for the next Olympics. If that were a category.

'Hi, Indie.' Charlie leans in and kisses me on the cheek and extends his hand to Jem. 'Hi, Jem, we sort of met the other day.'

Jem smiles and shakes it politely. 'Hi, mate.' He eyes Charlie up and down.

It's not like Charlie has an amazing body but for some reason, today, in his shorts and singlet, he looks picturesque. And being an actor, he has that sort of face people notice.

'Let's go.' I want to leave as soon as possible.

'That was weird.' Charlie turns to me as we run along the coastal track. 'What's going on with Jem?'

'Nothing.' I nearly trip and hurtle into the water below.

'Come on, Indie James, he wasn't impressed when he saw us kissing. He's totally into you. Has anything happened?'

'Yes and no. We've kissed. Twice. Once at Jazz and Stu's wedding, years ago. Then the other night, just before we had to race to hospital for Dad.'

'And then he saw us "running lines" the other day? Poor Jem.'

'Poor Jem! Why do you say that?'

'He likes you. He sees you and me kissing. Probably thinks he doesn't stand a chance.'

'He's had every chance, but he's not interested.'

'Indie, you know he's interested. I could tell within about five seconds.' Charlie runs ahead. 'Now move it, slow coach. We're never going to get that coffee the way you're running.'

I speed ahead, overtaking Charlie in a flash. 'See you there!'

We stop at my favourite Bronte Beach café, where I usually love to sit and stare. Not just at the mix of passers-by with young mums pushing fancy prams and elderly swimmers heading to do laps in the little ocean pool, but also that magnificent stretch of sea and the horizon beyond. I could look at it all day, and have done many times, but right now, we've got to go. Charlie needs to get ready for an ad casting. And I must go and… well, do nothing much.

As I head home, I mull over what Charlie said about Jem. That kiss with Charlie was purely a stage kiss, but today, he turned up for a run looking all handsome. Jem probably feels like he can't compete. If only he knew the truth.

Thankfully, my phone pulls me back to reality with a text from Alex. *Meet for a drink at The Bondi Hotel 6:30pm? Hope you aced audition.*

I completely forgot about our drink tonight. It's the last thing I feel like doing, but I'll be able to pump him for information about Jazz. I text back to say I'll see him there, and he shoots back a "thumbs up" emoji. Such a nice guy. That's the sort of boyfriend I need. Someone who makes dates, follows up, and sends cute emojis. No wonder Jazz kissed him.

Back home, Jem is nowhere to be seen, which is a relief. Just easier if our paths don't cross for a while. Especially if I'm meeting Alex. We're only friends but Jem will think the worst. And I don't want to explain why I'm trying to find out what's going on with Jazz.

George is still luxuriating in the warmth of the sun, so Jem's not out walking. Maybe he's gone to work. Soon this house situation will be over and I'll be back in LA. Unless I get that film. God, I hope I do, just to get away from Jem and the weirdness between us.

My eyes fall on Alex the minute I walk into the pub. Hard to miss him when he's as tall as a giraffe. Alex sees me almost at the same time and waves. Although he's not in his perfect dog park gear, he looks equally smart in black jeans and checked shirt.

'Almost didn't recognise you away from the dog park,' he says as I walk up to the table.

'Maybe I should have bought some poop bags to jog your memory.'

'Very funny. You look great. Aren't they Jazz's shoes?'

I look down at the leopard skin pumps on my feet. 'Very observant.'

'I helped her buy them. Drink?'

'Thanks, I'll have a glass of sauv blanc.' Shoe shopping? Pretty intimate.

Alex arrives back at the table, drinks in hand. Before I can talk about Jazz, he asks me about my audition, not that there's much to tell. Then I find out snippets of his life, that he lives in his own house in North Bondi with Roxie. No mention of a flatmate, but he was in a long-term relationship until a few months ago. Maybe that's why he kissed Jazz? He works at a local primary school, grows his own veggies, and spends a lot of time walking his dog.

The world of Alex sounds calm and organised. Makes a pleasant change from my chaos. Life is never calm for me. Work's either full-on or non-existent, and my situation can change in a flash. One phone call and I might have a job the week after next in the Blue Mountains. The ups and downs are exhilarating but exhausting. And there's no time to plant so much as a pot of herbs. I find myself listening wistfully to Alex talk about the local soccer team he's played with for eight years, and his passionfruit vine, which is finally producing fruit. A real life in a proper home. I want that.

'Surely that's enough information about me,' he says after a while. 'There's not much more to tell. Your life is more exciting.'

'Not at all.' I sigh. 'There are exciting moments, sure. But that's it. A whole lot of moments with long stretches of nothing in between.'

This is not exactly true. Before LA, it was constant work and much excitement. I was being paid to do what I love. A dream come true. But now that's on hold, it's hard to feel positive. And I'm not sure where I belong or which place I call home.

I steer the conversation towards Jazz but Alex's responses are vague. I've re-enacted enough police investigations to know when someone's being evasive. Okay, so they were scenes in a TV show and carefully scripted to go a certain way, but still, I feel more than qualified to gauge when someone's avoiding the truth.

'Do you know when they get back?' I ask.

'Who?'

'Jazz and Stu.' I try to keep the impatience out of my voice but it's proving a challenge.

'You're her best friend. Don't you know?'

I pretend to think back. 'They weren't exactly sure. It was supposed to be a three-month trip.'

'Sorry, I'm no help.'

Time for a more direct approach. 'Alex, about you and Jazz, what's going on?'

'What do you mean?'

'Is there something between you?' Enough being polite. I need to know why Alex is going after a married woman.

'No, we're dog park friends, I guess.'

'Dog park friends that kiss?'

'What?' Alex looks confused.

'You and Jazz kissing, buying shoes, knowing to come around to the sliding door, knowing what's going on in her marriage. You're quite handsome, you know, so maybe you should keep away from Jazz's marriage instead of confusing the situation. It's not fair,

Alex, not on Jazz and not on Stu, and in the long run, not fair on yourself.' Words tumble out of my mouth, not making much sense.

'Indie, what are you talking about?' Clearly Alex is attempting to maintain a façade of innocence.

'You're saying you didn't kiss Jazz?'

'No—'

'What?'

'She kissed me. And it was a mistake.'

'But you hang out so often, you've obviously given her the wrong idea.'

'No, I haven't—'

'Is that why you broke up from your relationship?

'No—'

'To be with Jazz? Moving on pretty quick, don't you think?'

'From Geoff? No, that was—'

'Sorry?' What did he say? Geoff?

'Geoff and I broke up a while ago—'

'You're gay?'

'Didn't Jazz tell you?'

I recall our last phone conversation. I didn't let her get a word in, too busy telling her off her for cheating on Stu. Obviously not the case.

'So, you're not trying to break up Jazz and Stu?'

'Not at all. Jazz was upset and looking for comfort. I happened to be there. We'd been spending more time together, she confided how her marriage feels in a rut and wanted to talk it through.'

I think back to our angry conversation and my cheeks bristle with shame. I was being judgemental. Poor Jazz, she needed a friend not a lecture.

'Why didn't she talk to Stu about it?' I ask.

'He didn't want to know, and when they did talk, they ended

up fighting.'

Jazz and Stu were usually so happy, but then I think of their constant bickering. Maybe there's some truth in what Alex is saying.

'As I said before, the trouble is George.'

'But I don't get it.' How could their beloved dog be a problem?

'It may seem weird to you as a non-pet person,' Alex says. 'But ever since they got George, they've been fighting over how they should look after him. They don't really agree on anything, and they're always competing over who gets to spend more time with him.'

'Is that normal?' I mean, is it a thing?'

'It happens to couples all the time. They have different ideas about how to look after a pet.'

'But Jazz and Stu are both mad about George and treat him like he's a member of the royal family come to stay.'

'Yeah, but Jazz is very structured and disciplined about George's training and care. She likes George to sleep in his own bed, and Stu is much more relaxed and laid back, letting him sleep on their bed or the sofa, giving him leftovers. He thinks Jazz is a bit full on. Same sorts of things parents go through with kids.'

'Jazz is full on with George, but she usually gets her way with Stu.'

'Not always, it seems.' Alex is sounding more like a psychologist with every passing second. 'The other thing that can happen is partners get jealous of each other's attention towards the pet. Jazz always says that Stu would rather hang out with George than her. And when they do hang out, she gets upset because Stu does all the wrong things. I reckon she's trying to keep control of her life and Stu by controlling George, and it's not working.'

'She's always joking about how hopeless Stu is, usually just to be funny.'

'She says it a lot, and maybe Stu doesn't like it.' Alex is even looking like a psychologist. I feel like I should be lying on a couch for this date. And not for the reason one might think.

'Poor Jazz.'

'Stu often lets George sleep on their bed, which she doesn't approve of,' Alex continues. 'And I have to agree with her, once your dog is in or even on the bed, you'll never get him out.'

I guiltily think how George has slept on both my bed and the sofa. What if I've encouraged a bad habit that helps bring about the downfall of their marriage?

'That afternoon, when I picked up Roxie, Jazz was crying after having a huge fight with Stu. She desperately wants a baby but Stu thinks they're not coping with parenting a dog, let alone anything else. She offered me a glass of wine. She'd already had a few, and we chatted for a while. I suggested she and Stu see a counsellor. Maybe go on a holiday without George, have some dog-free time together. Geoff and I broke up for similar reasons. I wanted a family, he wasn't interested. I can relate to what Jazz is going through. When it was time to go, Jazz kissed me on the lips, out of the blue, saying it's a pity we're not together as we have a dog each and agree about everything.'

I can't believe I'm hearing all this from Alex. Why hasn't Jazz confided in me? Maybe she thinks I wouldn't understand the baby thing. She always says I'm too career focused to have a baby and that I should be careful as the opportunity could pass me by. Am I too career orientated? Charlie said I was ambitious, but is that such a bad thing? I guess when you don't know what's going on in your best friend's life, it can't be good.

'What did you do?' I ask.

'I pulled away.'

'Sounds like she was drunk and confused.'

'She was, but I hope they work it out,' Alex says. 'And I hope we can stay friends. Jazz is great. I really enjoy her company. She's given me some great tips on my home décor. And I even started looking into studying psychology part-time thanks to her advice.'

He doesn't have to tell me. I know Jazz is great. Thank God we've cleared the air since our fight and we can move on, the sign of a true friendship.

'What about teaching?'

'I don't want to be a primary school teacher forever. But I love kids, so maybe I'll major in child psychology. Hey, I'm starving, do you want to grab some dinner?'

I look at the time. Suddenly, I want to get home to my trackie pants. 'Ah, sorry, I'm going to get an early night. I'm exhausted.'

'So, what about you? What's going on with Jem?' Alex looks me straight in the eye and I almost fall off my stool.

'Jem? What do you mean?'

Someone like Alex with a leaning towards psychology would immediately interpret my reaction as confirmation that something most definitely is going on.

'Jazz told me there was nothing between you but when I came over that time, I definitely saw something.'

'We were just super relieved to see George and avoid the very real possibility of being murdered by Jazz and Stu.' I laugh nervously. 'Mind you, if we'd lost George, maybe we could have saved their marriage.'

'Don't even joke about it,' Alex says. 'That would've been even more disastrous, as they'd have to deal with the guilt of leaving their "baby" with someone else. Someone who wasn't up for the job.'

I pretend to be deeply hurt. 'Hey, I happen to think I'm doing a fantastic job.'

'I'm joking. You are. So's Jem.' Alex smiles ruefully. 'Maybe you should talk to him about it.'

'About how we're looking after George?'

'About what's going on between you.'

My God, Alex is good, he sees everything. Imagine being in a relationship with him, you'd hardly have to talk. Just get up in the morning and he'd say, 'Hmm you feel like muesli for breakfast today, don't you?'

We finish our drinks and call it a night. I give Alex a hug as we part ways with a vague plan of meeting at the dog park. It's still light, so I stroll home, picking up a Pad Thai on my way, glad to be on my own.

I've never been as keen to have a baby as Jazz. One day, perhaps. Work always makes me happy but now I wonder if it's enough. Alex's life looks so tranquil. Normal. Is that what I want? Suddenly, Jem pops into the scene, mowing the front lawn, walking the dog and picking vegetables.

Alex is right. I need to talk to Jem. But about what? Lately, I've had trouble knowing what's right for me. I thought Mark was the one. Jazz thought Stu was the one. Maybe there's no perfect fit and I'm better off alone. Then I think how I nearly lost Dad. What if he's not so lucky next time? And Mum, what if something happened to her? I can't bear to think about it. I realise I won't always have my parents around, but without them, I'd be well and truly on my own. My body feels limp at the thought. Then the image of Jem pushing the lawn mower flashes in my head once again, and I glance down at my hand, holding the single serve of Pad Thai in a white plastic bag. Being on my own is more straightforward and less confusing, but is that what I really want?

23

OVER the next few days, I google "pets interfering with relationships" and "how my dog is coming between us" type stories. Mostly to distract me from angsting over my audition. And it's definitely a thing. Pets interfering with relationships, that is. Although actors angsting over auditions is also very much a thing. People really do argue over what they feed their pet, where their pet should sleep, and in one case, the thickness of their pet's winter jacket. They compete over who's the better parent. Conflict over pets has led to divorce and custody battles. It's a whole new world – one that has put me off ever getting a pet. Not that I have a relationship for it to break up.

The following week, I meet up with Lucy for a walk along the beach and I bring it up, without mentioning Jazz, of course.

'I've heard about that.' Lucy stops to take her slides off as we walk down onto the sand. 'Pets come between owners all the time. I read one story where the wife didn't want their dog sleeping on the sofa, but when she was out, the husband let the dog on the sofa all the time. One day, she came home early and caught them in the act. She moved out that afternoon.'

'No!'

'True story.'

'Unbelievable.'

We fall into a comfortable silence as we stroll along the water's edge, waves gently lapping at our ankles.

'So, what's going on with you?' Lucy gives me a sideways stare. 'Is George causing you relationship problems?'

'No,' I say lightly. 'There's no relationship to ruin.'

'Not getting back with Mark?'

'Definitely not.'

'Charlie?'

'Mistake, never really happened.'

'What about your hot housemate?'

'Jem?'

'Is there another one?'

'He's not for me. No, I'm well and truly single, which is better. Who knows when I'll be leaving?'

'Didn't you get the film? I heard they've cast it now.'

Energy wooshes out of me, like a balloon released of air, instantly lifeless on the ground. 'Really?'

'You didn't hear?'

I shake my head.

'Apparently Tia got a role.' Lucy stops dead, realising she said the wrong thing. 'Oh, sorry.'

My heart drags on the sand, about two feet behind. She must have got Alyssa. Damn.

We walk in silence as I digest this news. I look out across the sparkling water, wishing a boat would suddenly appear to sail me away. I really thought I had a chance and I didn't believe Tia was right for Alyssa. But what do I know? Clearly nothing.

'I didn't even get an audition.' Lucy tries her best to make me feel better. 'And you never know when that director might think of you for something else.'

'I know, I know.' Although hard to hear, Lucy's right. More times than not, you might not be right for that role but for something else further down the track. I've worked with that director and I know she likes me. Our paths will cross again.

But still.

Big bummer.

I struggle to enjoy the rest of our walk, feeling like a blanket left out in the rain, heavy and unloved. I'm thrilled to hear Lucy and Jesse are looking for a place together. And I try to be interested as Lucy chats excitedly about the houses they've seen, but deep down I'm wallowing in utter devastation.

My phone rings. Michelle. I let the call go to voicemail. Once I hear it from Michelle, it's official. I'm not ready for that.

'My agent. I'll call her back.'

Lucy says nothing, knowing exactly how I'm feeling. Awful. At least I was happy with my audition. But that's somehow worse. I don't think I could have done better, so I'm simply not right. Or not good enough.

'When are you planning to go back to LA?' Lucy asks. 'When does Jazz come back?'

'Not for a while yet.'

I take a moment to consider my plans. I could go back sooner if I wanted. Jem can look after George. I didn't get the ad. I didn't get the film role. Perhaps I'd be better getting back to LA. Get on with it, instead of waiting around for a lot of "what ifs".

But then I think of my parents. After everything that's happened, I'm not sure I can leave so soon. I want to stick around a little longer while Dad recovers. Be there for Mum. I wish someone would just tell me what to do. Like a director in a movie who yells 'Cut!' when I go wrong. 'No, Indie, I didn't believe that. Is there a better choice you could make?'

I get home to be absolutely rumbled by George. A couple of months ago, I'd have freaked out, but now, I couldn't care less. It's lovely to be welcomed with such enthusiasm.

I call Mum to check in.

'Hello, darling, how was your audition?'

I try to sound upbeat, which feels even harder than doing that stupid audition. 'Good but didn't go my way.'

'Oh, I'm sorry to hear that, so ridiculous, they obviously don't know a good thing when it walks in and acts in front of them.'

Mum always gets angry when I don't get cast in something. She takes it personally, as if her mothering skills are being criticised. Or maybe she's just being protective.

'How's Dad?'

'Much better, he's coming home tomorrow.'

'That's great, can I speak to him?'

'Of course… it's Indie, she wants to speak to you, yes she is, I'm not sure… Indie, just passing you over.'

There's a lot of rustling and hushed voices as my parents navigate what sounds to be a major operation.

'Indie, here I am.' Dad's tone is surprisingly chipper. 'How are you, what audition was that?'

'Oh, just a film role, would have been great, but it's not for me.'

'Something else will come along, you know that.' Dad offers words of comfort but shouldn't it be the other way around? I guess a parent can't help themself, even after having a heart attack. But, right now, everything should not be about me.

'How are you feeling, Dad?'

'Right as rain and ready for bungy jumping.'

I can hear Mum squawking in the background, and Veena too by the sounds of it.

'I'd better go now, sweetheart, there's a few tests I have to do,' says Dad. 'And just quietly, I'm a bit scared of Veena. Wish me luck.'

I hear more laughter as I hang up. I definitely need to spend more time with my parents, especially while Dad recuperates. But what about work? There's nothing here for me. Apart from dog-sitting, and I'm not very good at that. And a wedding I don't want to go to.

I briefly skim ticket specials online but deep down, I know I can't leave yet. I promised Jazz I'd look after George until she got back. And I don't want to leave Dad after nearly losing him.

My mobile rings and I glance at the screen. I guess it's time to face the rejection music.

'Hi there.' If there was an Oscar for the "flattest sounding voice when talking to your agent", I'd be in the running.

'Darling, I called before, did you hear my message?' Michelle sounds impatient. 'Why didn't you call back?'

'Sorry, I was just out, look I know that—'

'Such great news, my lovely! Well done!'

'What are you talking about?'

'The film.' Her voice is increasingly insistent, but I still don't understand. 'I told you this one was yours.'

My cloudy brain manages to register the word 'film'. 'But I heard it's already been cast.'

'Yes, you. You've been cast in the role of Alyssa.' She sounds like an excited mother whose child has finally tied a bow. 'Did you listen to the message I left you? You got Alyssa!'

I can hear what Michelle is saying, and I recognise individual words, but altogether it just doesn't make sense.

'But... but... I thought that... didn't Tia get it?'

'She got the role of Jane Ross, the victim's mother.'

'So, I got the role? I got Alyssa?'

'Yes, my darling, you did.'

'I thought I hadn't.'

'Clearly, but if you'd answered your phone you'd know otherwise.'

Blood rushes to my head at breakneck speed. I feel like I'm going to faint.

'I got the role?'

'Yes, you got the role.' Michelle speaks slowly and distinctly as if giving vital life-saving instructions to passengers on a plane that's about to crash. And, like a blocked pipe finally cleared, everything falls into place.

'But I thought I hadn't got it. I mean, I did a good audition, I thought I was in with a chance, I really did, the audition went well but you never know and then I heard Tia was cast and... I REALLY GOT IT? I just can't BELIEVE it! Wow, that's just... WOW!'

My voice gets increasingly louder. Poor Michelle must be deaf from having to tell over-emotional actors this sort of news, but I can't help it. It's not like I haven't had these sorts of conversations before but in my current situation, the relief is overwhelming. I have a lead role in an amazing film and it's shooting in Australia near my parents.

Two minutes ago, I felt like I was lying face down in a muddy puddle. Now, I'm standing on the top of a mountain, my superhero cape flying behind me. If not getting a job is the worst feeling in the world, then getting a job is truly the most spectacular. The moment an actor lives for. If I could bottle the feeling and sell it, I'd make a fortune. I got the job! I got the job! I got the job! But what if I can't do the job? What if I'm no good? What if they realise I can't act and have to fire me?

My emotional rollercoaster reaches the peak, teeters at the edge of the downward leg and plunges even more quickly than it flew up.

I can't do this job. I can't do it. What am I going to do?

I take a deep breath before I hyperventilate. And I remind myself to let it out and breathe in again. And out. In. Out. Just keep breathing, Indie.

'Are you still there?' Michelle has been waiting patiently while I lurch through the highs and lows of this life-changing news in the space of about thirty seconds.

'Yes, sorry, it's just… I didn't… and now, and then my dad… but now…'

My sentences seem to be getting less comprehensible by the second.

'I've just emailed you the latest version of the script.' Michelle ignores my ramble and pushes on. 'I'm still negotiating a few terms and pushing for a bit more money, but we should have a deal memo in the next few days. I'll send you the current schedule but as you know, it could drastically change at a moment's notice.'

Michelle runs through a few details, things like travel days, per diems, all of which roll off my back like a slippery piece of silk. I got the job. I got the job. I got the job. A great film role, earning decent money, and shooting in the Blue Mountains. Which means I won't be able to help look after George as much. I'm sure I'll come back and forth, but I better check that with Jem. After all, he's going through a tough time at the moment and working all hours. Still, I must take this job. Even Jazz would agree.

I text Lucy my news and she calls immediately, screaming down the phone as loudly as I'd done to Michelle. We plan to meet for a drink later to celebrate. I also ring Charlie to tell him and thank him for running lines with me.

'Great news! Would you believe I got cast, too?'

'That's fantastic!' And it really is. Charlie is a wonderful actor and should be working, as with so many of my friends. But there's never enough work to go around. Charlie agrees to join Lucy, Jesse, and me for a drink tonight.

Next, I ring Mum and Dad. After supporting me through the ups and downs of my tumultuous life, they deserve to share every win. Mum always thinks it's thanks to her when I get a job anyway. If I ever win an Oscar or Golden Globe, she'll expect it to go on their mantlepiece at home to show everyone what she achieved. Up until twenty minutes ago, I wouldn't have thought such an award possible. But now I feel I can do anything. That's the addictive nature of the industry. You go for months, even a year with nothing, no jobs, no positive affirmations whatsoever. Then you land a role, and it lures you back like a drug you thought you'd given up.

'Sweetheart, that's WONDERFUL!' Mum also screams like me and Lucy. 'David, she got the part after all, oh, not even sure… Indie, tell me again what it's for?'

'An Australian film, high profile. I'm playing the female lead.'

'And they're paying you?'

'Yes, Mum!' I say impatiently. It doesn't matter how many jobs I've done, Mum always asks the same question, not quite understanding that I do get paid for my work.

'Well, that's great. Dad looks very happy, he's cheering. Can you hear him?'

I hear Dad and Veena clapping and cheering. Then Veena telling him to quieten down. My heart tears slightly. It's just as well I'm staying in Australia. I'll be busy in the Blue Mountains but at least it's closer than LA.

Just as we hang up, I hear footsteps down the hall and a door closing. Jem must have just got home and gone to his bedroom. He spends a lot of time in there. Not that I can talk, but he's often in there for hours, well into the night, but not streaming shows like I do. Or sleeping for that matter, as I can usually see light crawling out from under the door. I have no idea what he's doing.

I'd love to tell him my news. And not just so I can prove I'm a worthy actor who earns decent money (okay, I admit that's part of it), but also, I just want to share it with him.

My moment comes later as I'm walking out the door to meet Lucy and Jesse for a drink.

'Going out?' he asks politely, stepping out of his room.

'Ah, yes. Meeting friends for a drink.' I pause. 'I got that film in the Blue Mountains.'

'Great.' His eyes light up for the briefest of moments. 'Well deserved.'

'Thanks.' I'm so thrown by his genuine response, I start talking like a running tap. 'But it means I'll have to stay a few nights a week up in Katoomba. I haven't got the schedule yet, but I'm so sorry to leave you in the lurch. I promise to make sure I do double the dog caring when I'm here. It's not like you have to do absolutely every item on Jazz's list—'

'I can look after George.'

'Are you sure?'

'Yep, he likes me better anyway.'

'Oh, really?' I smile. 'You shouldn't joke about things like that. I've heard competition over pets can break couples up.'

'Lucky we're not a couple then, isn't it?'

'Yes, lucky.' God, why did I say that? 'But that doesn't mean you're the fun one. George and I have fun too, you know.'

'If you say so.' Jem almost smirks. 'But if you hot foot it up to the mountains, there'll only be me and I'll become the centre of his world.'

I giggle, knowing a film is way more important than being George's favourite carer but somewhere in the back of my mind, hidden behind a whole lot of other unacknowledged thoughts, is a little voice saying that it's Jem I might miss. I tell the voice to get back in the dark corner where it belongs and focus on the present.

I check the time on my phone. 'I'd better go.'

'Have a great night. Enjoy your celebration.' Jem sounds like he means it.

'Thanks.' I head for the door, then turn back. 'Hey, do you want to come?'

He pauses. 'Thanks, but… raincheck?'

'Sure.'

I wander out onto the street feeling topsy-turvy. Why does he have to go and be so nice? It confuses everything. At least when he's rude and cranky, I know where I stand. Now he's being pleasant again, I don't know how to respond.

I meet up with Lucy, Jesse, and Charlie to toast my success. But it feels a little empty. I think of Jem, and not for the first time, wish he were right here by my side.

24

OVER the next two weeks, my days are consumed by rehearsals, camera checks, and wardrobe and make-up calls. I go through some scenes with the guy playing Ryan, whose name is Will, a fantastic actor I've never worked with before. Fortunately, he's down to earth with his ego in check and we hit it off straightaway.

'I loved you in *Time on the Line*,' he says when we go and grab coffees in a break. 'That was a great show.'

'Thanks, but weren't you a regular in *Country Doctors*?'

'That's right, for a few years. I'm thinking of heading to LA after this, maybe you could give me a few hints?'

Shooting starts next Monday. The schedule looks hectic, but I'll be able to come back to Sydney some weekends to help with George. Not that Jem really needs my "expert" dog-wrangling skills.

I sit up on a stool at the island bench and flick through my shoot dates. My heart sags when I realise I'm free the weekend of Emily's wedding. I could always say I'm not. No one would know. But I've already RSVP'd, and it would be rude. I'd have pulled out if I'd gone back to LA early, or if I was shooting, but I'm here and available. The only thing is, I don't have a plus one.

For a split second, I wish Mark was around so I could turn up with my handsome American actor boyfriend, whom people would recognise from half a dozen Netflix shows. I'd look like I'd got my life together instead of being a sad, nowhere-near-getting-married type of woman.

No, Indie, Mark isn't the answer. Glossy on the outside, but away from the glitz of Hollywood, he's just an unreliable guy, and life is hard enough without having to deal with that.

I'm so deep in my thoughts that I don't hear Jem come through the sliding door with George. Until I feel a wet tongue on my ankles. George's, that is, not Jem's.

'Oh, George, don't pash my legs, it's disgusting.' I giggle as George then jumps up, trying to lick my cheek.

'You can't blame him,' says Jem, making my cheeks prickle with instant heat. What did he mean by that? Nothing. Just his humour.

'How are you going?' he asks. 'Looks like you're in another world.'

'Oh, yes, sorry, just thinking.'

'Don't do that.' The tiniest of twinkles appears in his eye. 'Might be dangerous.'

'I'm trying to get out of a wedding.'

'Another one? You don't waste time. Who proposed now?'

'Very funny.' I'm relieved to see the return of our banter. 'Emily Carter, a friend of Jazz and mine from school. Well, she used to be a friend, but we're not that close anymore. Jazz got out of it by conveniently going to France. I thought living in LA would be my excuse, but that's all changed. Then I hoped I'd be booked for a job, which I am, but as luck would have it, I'm free that weekend.'

'Oh yeah, I've met Emily. And I remember her at Jazz and Stu's wedding.'

'She got completely drunk and made an idiot of herself.'

'I had to help her into a cab. I always wondered if she got home safely – or threw up on the back seat.'

'I think she did both.' I smile. 'And now she's marrying a

millionaire banker in a big society wedding. It even got a mention in the paper.'

'Why don't you want to go? Weddings are usually fun. And this sounds like it might be a big one.'

'It'll be totally over the top.'

'What's the problem then?'

I look at Jem, embarrassed to say the real reason. He wouldn't understand. 'I was supposed to be taking Mark, but now…'

'You don't want to go alone?'

Wow, he does understand. 'Normally I wouldn't mind. It's just I haven't had much to do with Emily for years. I don't know why she even asked me.'

'She invited you to her wedding, so maybe she needs her old friends around. It's a big moment and she wants to share it with you.'

Rub my nose in it more likely. 'I'll go. I'm just not looking forward to it.' I look at Jem with an eye roll. 'What are you doing four weeks from today? Wanna come to a wedding?'

'What?' Jem almost steps back in surprise.

Oh, my goodness, where did that come from? Why did I say that? I had no intention of asking Jem. In fact, if there were a list of tasks I was least likely to do, inviting Jem to a wedding would be at the top of the page. But I've said it and put Jem on the spot. And he sort of recoiled at the thought of it.

'Sorry, I'm joking.' I guffaw an over-enthusiastic laugh that leads to a highly embarrassing snort. Oh my God, where did *that* come from? And why does it keep happening around Jem? His lips twitch slightly, but all I can do is push on. 'You don't want to be my date at a wedding for someone you shoved drunk into a cab. Not that it would be a date as such, well it would be, but just as friends, which would be great don't get me wrong, but I don't want to put you out. Probably be really boring anyway.' I close my mouth, as that's the only way to stop words (and snorts) tumbling out of it, making the situation even more awkward than it has already become.

'Are you asking me or not?' Jem looks directly at me, his velvety eyes momentarily freezing my senses.

'Ah, not,' I say quickly. 'Just forget I even said it.'

'Right.' Jem turns to the sink. Was he disappointed? Relieved?

'Unless you want to go,' I say before I can stop myself.

He turns back in a flash. 'Do you want me to go?'

I don't know if it's the directness of the question or what he's asking, but it's like a packet of Fruit Tingles has exploded inside my stomach, a sensation that seems to be venturing down my thighs.

'I do!' I blurt out, before realising how that sounds, considering we're talking about a wedding. 'I mean, if you're free, that would be great. Really appreciate it.'

'Then I'll come,' Jem says, as if he simply agreed to going to the supermarket for a few groceries.

'Thanks.'

'No problem.'

'It's probably going to be a bit fancy. I think it's black tie.'

'Cool. Okay, gotta go. Are you in tonight?'

'Yeah, think so. But I'm going to the Blue Mountains on Monday, remember?'

'That's right.'

'I'll walk George every day until I leave.' I feel bad about dumping the dog duties on him.

'It'll be fine. I can manage George.' Jem gives me a quick smile. 'Just going to Bondi Junction, need anything?'

'No.' I realise I haven't had much spare cash to buy groceries lately. 'I'll be getting paid soon, so I'll be able to do a few more shops.'

'Sure.'

Jem heads out the door as quickly as he came in, making me wonder if I didn't dream the whole encounter. Did he just agree to be my date at Emily's wedding? If you'd told me three months ago, firstly, that I'd be going to Emily Carter's wedding, and secondly, with Jeremy Taylor as my plus one, I'd have suggested you seek professional medical help. But now, it feels normal. Unexpected, yes, but exciting. After not wanting to even go, I'm now looking forward to it and thinking about what to wear. One thing is for sure: I need to look amazing.

The few times I've seen Emily over the years, I've always felt inadequate. A little rough around the edges next to her expensive designer image. But for some reason, it's Jem that springs to mind when contemplating outfits. I feel an overwhelming need to make a good impression, and one that doesn't involve sweaty running gear, grey trackie pants, or Jazz's pink fluffy dressing gown. If there's any chance of re-visiting that kiss from the other night, surely a wedding might speed up the process? Look at what happened at Jazz and Stu's.

I ring Mum to see if I can come up to Pymble for dinner on Saturday night, as I won't be able to get up there much during the shoot. I also check with Emily about bringing Jem to the wedding.

'Of course, I've met him before. I spent a long time chatting to him at Jazz and Stu's wedding. Did we share a cab? Or maybe he drove me home. Anyway, I remember him being very charming.'

I smile as I mentally file Emily's memory of the wedding to share with Jem later. 'Thanks for that, we're both house-sitting for Jazz and Stu at the moment.'

'No problem, I'm just happy you'll be there, Indie. I've really missed you.' Emily sounds genuine. Surprising.

'Well, I'm glad I could come in the end.'

And I *am* glad to be going. Maybe Emily does want me there after all. And I have to say, with Jem by my side, the society wedding of the year just got a lot more appealing.

25

SATURDAY morning arrives, and although I'm not leaving for the mountains until Monday, I'm all ready to go. Mum checks in to see if I'm still coming over for dinner.

'I'll leave here about three-thirty, so should be in Pymble by, what, mid next week?'

'Very funny,' Mum says. 'It's not that far, you know. Pymble is central to everything and moments from the city.'

All Pymble people go on about how convenient the suburb is, not to mention green and leafy. I'm about to disagree with this wholeheartedly when Jem walks in with George, making the usual racket.

'What's going on there?' Mum asks.

'Jem just got back from walking George.' I mouth to Jem that it's my mum.

'How's Jem?' Mum gushes. 'Does he want to come over for dinner, too?'

I almost drop the phone. 'I don't think he does. I think he's working.'

Jem looks at me enquiringly. I cover the phone and whisper, 'Mum's asking you over for dinner with me tonight. Don't worry, I said you're not free.'

'I'll come,' he says without hesitation.

'What?' My whisper turns into a squawk.

'I'm not working. I'll come with you. I'll drive so you can have a few celebratory drinks.'

I wish I could see my face, which is bound to be as white as Jazz's crisp French bed linen. Not after George jumped on it of course, but after being soaked for a few days. First Emily's wedding, and now dinner with my parents. What's going on?

'Hello? Darling, are you there? I can't hear anything,' Mum's voice pipes out.

'Sorry, Mum, here I am. Um, Jem says he'd love to come to dinner.'

'Great news. Looking forward to it.' I can tell Mum is beaming down the phone. 'Any dietary requirements?'

Jem has gone out to the garden, so I can't check. 'Don't think so.'

'Great, see you both later on.' And with that, she hangs up.

'Are you sure you want to go to Pymble tonight?' I ask as Jem walks back into the kitchen.

'Yep, do I need my passport?'

'Hah! Bring it in case. Leave around half past three?'

'See you then.'

Five hours later, we're in Jem's car heading to the depths of the Upper North Shore. Jem has brought a bottle of wine. Thoughtful. Mum will be even more impressed.

'Darling.' Mum embraces me with even more intensity than usual. 'Hello, Jem, lovely to see you again.'

Mum gives Jem a hug too, which catches him unaware and makes me want to giggle. 'And this is my husband, David, you didn't see him the other night of course. And Jazz and Stu's wedding was so long ago.'

Dad struggles to get up and move across the lounge room and

I'm even more thrown than when I saw him at hospital. In my mind, he was on the mend, all better. But he still looks so frail as he shuffles along. Like he might break in two. He gives me a big hug and I don't want to let him go.

'Hello, my love. I'm alright, you can let go of me now.' He then turns to hug Jem. 'Of course, I remember Jem. Thanks for looking after my girls the other night.'

'My pleasure. How are you feeling?'

'Happy to be alive.'

My parents have always been huggers. Sometimes it's embarrassing, but Jem seems to be coping just fine. He hands Dad the wine.

'How thoughtful.' Mum looks thrilled. What did I say?

We head to the back deck while Dad brings out a bottle of bubbly. 'A night for celebration.' He pours us each a glass. 'Here's to your new job, Indie.'

Mum is instantly concerned. 'Darling, you're not supposed to be—'

'Just a sip, Pam. No one will know.'

Mum and I both give him a look that says exactly what we think about him having "just a sip" and his shoulders droop.

'You're all as bad as Veena,' he says mournfully, putting his glass on the table.

Jem clinks his glass to mine and our eyes meet. 'Congratulations.'

'Here's to keeping you in Sydney a little longer,' Mum adds.

Jem gives me a nod and the tiniest of smiles. My heart backflips. The fact that he's here, standing on my back deck, chatting with my parents, is weird. But good weird. Mum and Dad look like they're about to burst. On one occasion, Mum looks over with shining eyes and mouths, 'He's so nice!'

Once again, Jem reveals his knack of charming everyone around him. I don't know why it's taken ages for us to become mildly compatible.

'So how is it sharing with Indie, Jem?' Mum asks. 'She's not the best cook.'

'Thanks, Mum!' Honestly, nothing like parents to point out your faults. 'Luckily Jem is an excellent cook, so I don't have to worry.'

'But you're much better at cleaning than me.' The corners of Jem's mouth twitch into a smile. 'And bathing the dog.'

Heat pulsates from my cheeks. Obviously, he's recalling me, semi-naked, clutching a wet dog.

'How's the dog-minding?' Mum asks.

'Pretty good, apart from losing him one night,' Jem says.

He doesn't say anything about me leaving the gate open and before I can admit my fault, it's time to clear the table for dessert. I'll have to thank him later.

Mum and I take the plates to the kitchen. I start stacking the dishwasher while Mum gets out a pavlova, a bowl of chopped fruit, and some whipped cream and starts tossing everything together like an overzealous toddler making mud pies.

'Mum, are you okay?'

She looks up from her "creation", face fraught. 'Oh, Indie, I don't know what to do. I'm so relieved Dad's better but I'm also angry because he acts like nothing happened. He won't face the fact that he needs to take things easy now, and I'm terrified he's going to have another heart attack. You've seen him, he can barely move about the house, yet all he talks about is "getting into jogging". And not just a casual saunter around the block. He's decided to train for the City to Surf and every time he mentions it, I go into a panic.'

'You know Dad's all talk.'

'Well, it's upsetting and infuriating. His recovery is going to take a while, yet he wants to do the Seven Bridges Walk next year in preparation for a trek through the Himalayas. Normally, he doesn't even walk to the shops, but suddenly he's looking up plane tickets to Nepal and googling those stick things that walkers use. I think he's got an eye on a second-hand pair on Gumtree.'

'Hiking poles.'

'Sorry?'

'They're called hiking poles.'

'I don't care what they're called. He doesn't need them.'

'Take no notice,' I say gently. 'He's probably got a new lease on life after almost… well, you know.'

Mum's eyes fill with tears. 'He should be trying to get better. Gentle exercise. Stretch class or yoga. Not hiking up mountains.'

I stop my stacking and give Mum a hug. 'Everything is going to be fine. Dad didn't die, he's still here. And from the look of him, he won't be climbing mountains for a while.'

'I know, darling.' Mum sniffs. 'I just don't want it to happen again.'

'Me neither.'

'Will you talk to him?' Mum's eyes brighten. 'He'll listen to you. Just try to get him to see sense. Explain that he got away with it this time but needs to be careful.'

I sigh, knowing there's probably nothing I can do to make Dad not buy a plane ticket to Nepal. Nor do I want him to not buy a ticket to Nepal. He probably wants to live life to the fullest, or at least plan to, and I'm not going to stand in his way. But Mum's fraught expression tweaks my heart.

'Sure, Mum, I'll talk to him.'

Eventually we escape my parents' clutches, although I didn't think Jem was ever going to leave. And I could tell Mum was ready to make up the spare beds so we could stay.

'I have to get going, I start my job on Monday,' I had to tell all three of them. 'I need to finish packing and go over my scenes for the week.'

'Yes, of course, darling.' Mum pulled me into an extra firm hug then turned to Jem, who looked more prepared this time. 'And so nice to see you again, Jem, hopefully we'll see you soon.'

'Your parents are great,' Jem says as we drive back.

'Yeah. A bit full on sometimes, but they mean well.'

'They're so proud of you.'

'They are, although Mum will suggest at least twice a month that I follow a more reliable career.' I glance across at Jem. 'They definitely like you, that's for sure.'

Jem smiles, eyes ahead, as he stuck to his offer of driving. 'I remember them both from the wedding. I couldn't get away from your dad.'

Back at Bondi, George bounds on us like we've been gone for a year.

'Thanks for coming tonight,' I say as we stand at the back door waiting for George to do his business before bed. 'Is George doing a wee, I can't see.'

'No problem, I enjoyed it.' Jem looks at me, holding my eyes in his for what seems like a fortnight but is probably no more than three seconds.

'You enjoyed dinner with my *parents*?'

'I don't get out much.' Jem laughs. 'But I did enjoy the company.'

Does he mean mine? My parents? He's probably just being nice.

George scampers in. Who knows what he does out there?

'Night.' Jem locks the sliding door and heads to his bedroom.

I don't feel tired so I settle into bed, looking over my scene for Monday morning. But my thoughts meander to my conversation with Mum. She's still in shock, Dad too, by the sounds of things. And fair enough. They both glimpsed the end and it's devastating. Overwhelming. I always felt like my parents would live forever. Always be around at the end of the phone when I needed them. Now I know that's not the case. I've always known it rationally but after coming so close, I *really* know. And it's heart-breaking. It didn't happen this time but eventually… my eyes burn with emotion. I know it's life, but I'll never be ready.

I wipe away a tear and force my attention back to the script. Alyssa's car has broken down just outside of town and Ryan stops to help her. She doesn't know who he is and instantly dislikes him. Like me and Jem. Except with Alyssa and Ryan, she's a forensic scientist and he's a detective, it all works out, and they fall in love. They also solve a gruesome cold case and crack the mystery of a copycat killer at the same time. So, in fact, nothing like our situation.

That's the luxury of a script. For the next six weeks, I can live my life through Alyssa. I know exactly the direction she's heading and how her situation will turn out. Unlike my own. I may have an awesome job doing what I love, much like Alyssa, but beyond that there's very little structure or certainty and absolutely no leading man whatsoever.

26

MONDAY morning, I bounce out of bed like a pogo stick, despite the fact it's still dark. I have a six o'clock call, so I need to get on the road as soon as possible. Like any job, the first day is always a little stressful. Unlike other jobs, every acting gig means starting over at a brand-new workplace with new colleagues, cast, and crew to navigate. My tummy fizzes with nerves as I speed up the highway into the unknown. The outer Sydney suburbs melt into the rugged backdrop of the iconic Blue Mountains. Even in the car, the air chills as I capture wild and breathtaking vistas of escarpments, valleys, and bush. What a place to work. I suddenly feel like the luckiest person in the world. But the feeling quickly passes as those first-day nerves launch what feels like a fiery street protest in my stomach.

Fortunately, I've worked with Nina and a few of the actors so it's not a complete mystery. But a niggle in the back of my head worries they might discover I'm not very talented and should never have been cast.

As it happens, I have nothing to worry about. The first day goes off without any dramas. After hair, make-up, and a quick egg and bacon roll, Will and I are shooting the car scene on a deserted road on the outskirts of a fictitious town (actually near Katoomba). The location is divine. There's not a soul to be seen (apart from the film crew of course) and the air, scented with eucalypts, feels fresh and comforting. I never felt that in LA. Nothing was familiar there, whereas this unique landscape is like an old friend.

It's a long day, but so great to be working that I hardly notice the passing hours, many of which are spent doing very little. Nina seems happy so far, so maybe she'll keep me on after all. At least another day, I hope.

I get back to my motel room, which is fine. Clean, reasonably comfortable, a little sterile. Not quite Jazz's lovely room. I'm not complaining. There's nothing worse than actors who whinge all the time about not having work, then when they get a job, complain about said job, the accommodation, or having to get up early. It's a bed and I'm happy to sleep in it. And I don't have to think about cooking. We'll be eating most of our meals on set, which will be far better than anything I can rustle up.

I shower and snuggle into my lumpy mattress, exhausted. I wonder how Jem and George are getting on without me. Probably out for a last-wee-of-the-night stroll. My eyes slowly close, that image in mind, and before I know what's what, my alarm goes off in the early morning darkness.

I have early starts all week, where I'm in the make-up chair by four thirty. Louise, the hair and make-up artist, is lovely and soon becomes my new best friend.

'God, I love your hair,' she says one dark and early morning.

'I love yours.'

'No way. It's an absolute nightmare.' She puts my hair back into Alyssa's tight bun. 'But yours is a bit dry. You should try this fantastic hair mask. It'll really help.'

That's one of the perks about having hair and make-up done on set. I always pick up the latest beauty tips. Plus, my hair always looks great. I just wish I had someone like Louise by my side on a full-time basis. I never look as good in real life.

By Thursday, more actors are called in to rehearse a big court scene, and it's lovely to see Charlie's familiar face. Tia turns up, too. Hopefully, we'll get on okay. We've rarely been cast side-by-side since drama school.

'Congratulations on getting Alyssa,' she says, as Paul the sound guy puts on our radio mikes, an intimate job that requires attaching a microphone somewhere under our clothes. 'Perfect for you.'

I look at Tia, not quite trusting the compliment. She probably wanted the role herself and is secretly jealous.

'Can you say a few words, Indie?' Paul asks.

'Hello, hello.'

'Perfect, thanks.'

'Hi, you two.' Charlie walks in, looking handsome and every bit the defence lawyer dressed in a slick suit.

'Hey, Charlie.' I smile. 'Ready for today?'

'Sure.' He glances at Tia, who's gone quiet. 'Well done on *The Three Sisters*.'

Tia turns pink in the cheeks. 'Did you end up seeing it?'

'Yeah, you were the best thing in it, just quietly.'

Tia giggles, looking pleased.

'Always the charmer, Charlie,' I say with an eye roll.

I catch a sag in Charlie's shoulders. 'No, Indie, I meant it, didn't you think Tia was great?'

'Oh, Indie would've acted circles around that part,' Tia says, smiling.

'You did a great job, Tia.' And I mean it. I'd like to think I'd have done better but to be honest, I don't think that would have been the case. 'You were awesome.'

Tia seems genuinely touched. Maybe she isn't the person she was back at drama school. Maybe I'm not either.

We don't get to chat much after that as the entire day is taken up with a few intense scenes to shoot and a few technical problems to deal with – one of which is my radio mike falling in the toilet.

'I am so sorry,' I say to Paul, mortified, as he mikes me up with a new one. 'I don't know how that happened.'

'Don't worry.' He chuckles. 'You're not the first. At least the mike was off when you went in there. Can't tell you how many people leave it on. I hear absolutely everything!'

The day is long and tedious and doesn't end until nearly nine that night. Everyone heads to their motel rooms in Katoomba to get some sleep before another long day.

Friday's shoot runs a lot more smoothly. Charlie does a great job, and overall, Nina seems happy.

'Thanks for yesterday and today everyone. Long days, but really great work.'

Later, Nina approaches me for a private chat and I slide into panic mode. What if I'm no good? What if everything is wrong?

'Great work, Indie, I like where Alyssa is going.'

'Thanks.' I smile as my insides almost collapse with relief. In the frantic buzz of shooting, you only know if you're doing something wrong when you're asked to do another take. Compliments come infrequently, so Nina's words are like honey to my over-tired and needy ears.

Before I know what's what, I'm driving back down the highway to Sydney, surprised by how much I'm looking forward to getting back to Jazz and Stu's place. It's not like it's my home, but my heart feels light and fluttery as I pull up out the front.

I walk in through the sliding door to see Jem sitting up at the island, reading a newspaper, a plate with the remains of some sort of rice dish pushed to one side.

He looks up immediately. 'You're back.'

'Miss me?' I dump my bags on the floor.

'George has.'

At the mention of his name, George almost flies in from the living room, jumping up on me and barking excitedly.

'Hello, there.' I give the huge dog a big cuddle, thrilled by his enthusiastic welcome. 'Hasn't Jem been looking after you? Never mind, Auntie Indie is back.'

'I think you'll find I've been looking after him extraordinarily well. We've done every item on Jazz's list.'

'Really? Ten minutes of dog yoga every day and his teeth cleaning? With that funny finger brush?'

'Yep.'

'Liar. What about his bedtime story?'

'Even that, and every time we got to a raunchy bit, George started to howl.'

'He did not.'

Jem smiles, a cheeky sparkle in his eyes. 'We also went to the dog park and saw Alex. I told him you got the film. He was happy for you.'

In all my excitement, I hadn't told Alex my news. 'How is he?

'Good, I think. We didn't share life stories or anything.'

'Did he mention Jazz at all?'

'No, why?'

'No reason.' Stop talking, Indie.

Jem moves to the stove, turning on a hotplate. 'Mushroom risotto?'

'My God, love some.'

While heating a serve of delicious looking risotto, Jem grates fresh Parmesan, tosses a green salad together, and pours me a glass of wine.

'What great service.'

He grins. 'After a week on set, you're probably used to being waited on hand and foot.'

'Hardly. It's not like that at all. Although the catering is amazing.'

'I hope this is up to scratch.' Jem shifts uncomfortably on the spot as if he doesn't know whether to sit or stand.

'Do you want to join me?'

Jem hesitates slightly. 'Sure, why not?'

He pours himself a wine and sits opposite me on a stool at the island bench, while I tuck into the very delicious risotto.

'Excuse me stuffing my face.'

'Is it okay?'

'You kidding? This is delicious – but then again, I'm starving so anything would be good to me right now.'

He laughs. 'Thanks very much. So, glad to be working?'

'It's only the first week, but yes, it's a great role, I've worked with the director before, fantastic cast, can't say enough good things about it.'

'You're lucky you love your job so much.'

'True, but it comes in fits and starts. You don't always get to do it and not every job is amazing. There's a lot of boring bits to being an actor. Sometimes I feel like the actual acting part of it is like the tiny tip of a massive iceberg.'

'Well, you're doing it now.'

'Yes, for another five weeks, I get to sunbake on the tip of the iceberg.'

Jem drains the last of his wine. 'I was happy opening my own bar. It certainly felt like the tip of the iceberg.'

'Do you think you'll try again, maybe with a better business partner and much nicer girlfriend?'

Jem shakes his head. 'I really picked the worst people to trust, didn't I? No, that's it for me. That was my one chance, and I blew it.'

I smile. 'If I had even five cents for every time I said that I'd be a millionaire.'

'Really? But you're so successful, you get everything you go for according to Jazz.'

'Jazz is more positive about my career than I am. Sure, I've been lucky, but I've missed out on a lot, too. Especially leaving and going to LA. I might have had lots more work here, but I left to start from scratch in another country. Then I missed out on that huge job, but coming home led me to this film.'

We look at each other for one super-charged second. I just want to put my arms around him and tell him how great he is, but he'd probably bolt out the door.

Jem breaks eye contact. 'Do you mind if I go to bed? I've already taken George for his evening stroll so don't let him sway you with his sneaky doggie charm.'

George, while crashed out at my feet, opens one eye, forever hopeful that another walk might be on the cards.

'Great, thanks for doing that,' I say through a mouthful of creamy risotto. 'And thanks for dinner, it's delicious.'

Jem smiles self-consciously and heads off to bed.

I finish my dinner, drink my wine, and clean up the dishes. That was unexpected. Maybe Jem and I are on the way to becoming friends. First agreeing to be my wedding plus one and then coming to my parents. Now a gourmet dinner upon my return. And he's polite, charming, and open about his past. I'll make the most of it before the tables turn and we're thrown back into our usual awkwardness. Or have we moved on from that? Who knows? Jem is like a puzzle you avoid buying in a shop because it's categorised as "Very Hard". And not being good at puzzles at the best of times, I'm struggling to work him out.

27

SATURDAY dawns bright and sunny and I'm thrilled to have a day free. I plan to walk George, get a coffee, do my washing, and run through scenes for the next week. I go to the kitchen, looking for my script, pick up a sheaf of papers lying on the bench and start reading. Hang on, this isn't mine. I flick through. Looks interesting. But where did it come from?

Confused, I turn back to the cover page and get the surprise of my life to see the writer is none other than Jeremy Taylor. Since when does he write scripts? Now I must read it. I have no choice. Jem left it out in plain view, so surely he won't mind. He should put his manuscript away if he doesn't want anyone to see it, particularly when he lives with an actress. What does he expect?

I make a pot of tea and take the script out to the garden. Cup in hand, I start to read. But the tea goes cold because I forget it's there. I can't lift my eyes from the page. The story is so compelling, the writing so strong. I'm hooked from the very start. The central character, tough detective Tara McCreadie, has found herself on the wrong side of the law. A great premise, strong central character. And goodness, Jem can write. That must be what he's been doing in his room every night.

I continue to read, that sensation I get when I find a great part I absolutely want to play sparkling in my tummy. It's like Tara has been specifically written for me but maybe that's just my enthusiasm for the role. Actors always think they're right for every role. It could be a giant three-headed zombie set to take over the world who needs to be an experienced mountain climber and able to speak with a perfect Scottish accent – and an actor would think, 'I can do that!'

I wonder if Jem has plans to develop the script further, or even shoot it – with me playing the lead role, of course. He might not know how to go about it, but I could help. I could talk to Michelle for advice on casting, maybe get a casting agent onboard. We'll need money though, which neither of us have. Maybe we could pitch it to producers and also apply for funding.

Three hours later, I've mentally cast, shot, edited, and screened the film without even talking to Jem. I've even planned the wrap party and drinks for the premiere screening. And accepted a few awards at film festivals.

Okay, slow down, Indie. This belongs to Jem and right now, he has no idea I've even read it. He's obviously private about his scriptwriting. I doubt Jazz even knew. If she had, she'd have told me. In fact, it would have been one of her selling points to convince me to house-sit with Jem.

'Come on, Indie, move in and he'll write you a fabulous role,' she'd have said. And now it looks like she'd have been right.

I think back to that lunch with Jazz and Stu and how awful Jem was to me. He's like a different person now, one I increasingly want to be around. And this script, the fact it came out of his head, is making me long to know what else is going on in there. I'm intrigued. All that aside, I must decide what to do with it.

Before I can even think about it, Benji from LA contacts me with an AMAZING AUDITION for a guest role on a Netflix series. He says it's FANTASTIC and that he's SUPER EXCITED.

As I'm in Sydney, I need to film the scenes myself and upload them. It's set in a high school and revolves around the teachers and their personal dramas. I'm up for a role as a substitute teacher who upsets the equilibrium of the group and has a brief affair with the geography teacher. There are three scenes to prepare and put down. There goes my weekend. I'll have to spend today working on the scenes, then organise someone to shoot them. And find another actor to read opposite me.

I call Charlie, who's happy to help. He has some days off from shooting next week, so doesn't mind giving up some time. He also suggests I call a friend of his, Rob, who has a studio set up in his backyard for actors to do exactly this.

'He'll charge a fee for the use of the studio and his time, not a huge amount, but it's worth it because he does such a good job,' says Charlie.

I think about my over-used credit card. Oh well, at least I'm earning now. 'Will you be my reader?'

'Of course.' I hear the smile in Charlie's voice. 'Look what happened last time I helped with your audition – you got the lead. Guest role on a Netflix series? Piece of cake.'

I call Rob, who's available on Sunday afternoon. I tee it up with Charlie and we arrange to meet in the morning for a run-through.

Next, I call Michelle to update her on the first week on set and to let her know about the LA audition.

'By the way, I have a script I'd like you to read.' I decide there and then to share Jem's script with Michelle.

'Oh yeah?'

'Actually, my housemate wrote it, and it's impressive. Might be a good role for me. I'd love your opinion, maybe Hal's too, if he's interested.' I'm sure Jem would value the opinion of a well-known and respected writer like Hal Franks.

'Sure, send it through, although hubby's inundated with students at the moment, plus he's getting a fair bit of TV writing.'

'Great, thanks, no hurry.'

A little voice in the back of my brain, the one that usually stops me from making regrettable mistakes (and sounds like Miss Tonkins, my Year 7 teacher) suggests that perhaps I should talk to Jem first. Am I doing the wrong thing? Surely Jem won't mind if my agent reads his script? And what if she loves it? Wouldn't he be thrilled? I would be if I'd written such an awesome film script and Jem secretly showed it to his agent and her writer husband. Isn't it better that his story gets out in the world, read, and made into a film? I'm doing Jem a favour, and I'm sure he'll thank me for it when we're on set shooting his film.

I ignore Miss Tonkins for once, confident that I know better. I'm doing this for Jem and his script, so it's the right thing to do. Dismissing any doubt, I make a copy at Officeworks and drop it off on Michelle's doorstep, then place the original exactly where I found it.

After spending Saturday night learning lines and Sunday morning running scenes with Charlie, we finally finish filming with Rob. In the end, it was quite fun. Charlie was an enormous help, and Rob has a great eye for detail.

'You've got at least five useable takes of each scene to choose from,' Rob says. 'Great work, by the way.'

We're sitting outside Rob's studio in the shade, having a chat and a cool drink. It's a great set-up, more like a stylish yoga retreat than a film studio. I wish all auditions took place in such relaxing surrounds.

'Thanks.' I sigh, relieved to have got to the end of it. 'And thanks for fitting me in.'

'You going back up the mountains this week?' Charlie asks.

'Yep, I'm driving up tomorrow morning.'

'I'll be up later in the week. I have one scene on Thursday and a couple on Friday.'

'We have a scene together, don't we?' I think back over the schedule.

'Yes, another big court scene.'

'That's right, the evil solicitor working for the dark side.'

'Now, now, Alyssa, everyone deserves a fair trial, even suspected serial killers.'

'Spoken like a true actor/lawyer.' I laugh. 'Thanks for your help today, I always feel calm working opposite you.'

'That's because I'm an incredible human being.'

'Really?' I pretend to be surprised. 'I thought it was because you're a generous actor.'

'That too.'

I drop Charlie off at his place then arrive home, exhausted. Not exactly what I'd planned for this weekend but I had to give it a shot. The ridiculous life of an actor. I didn't even get to see my parents; hopefully next weekend. I've been texting Mum every day to get updates, but I need to see for myself.

I make a cup of tea and email Michelle my scenes to see what she thinks before I upload them to my LA agent. She has a great eye and is brutally honest. She must be on the computer (does she never stop working?) because she calls me straight away.

'Great scenes, darling. Well done. I'll send you back my choices.'

'Thanks, Michelle, appreciate that.'

'Not that I necessarily want you back in LA, but this would be a good job. Excellent money. And who knows where it might lead?'

I say nothing, as I don't want to jinx it by getting my hopes up. The chance of getting this role is minimal.

'By the way,' she continues. 'I had a quick squiz at that film script. Amazing! Did your housemate really write it? Who is he, and has he written anything else?'

'Not that I know of,' I say. 'I didn't even know he was a writer. He usually works in hospitality and recently tried to open his own bar, which failed miserably.'

'Writers can be sneaky like that, you never know who they are, as they generally have other jobs to fund their habit.'

'Did you show it to Hal?'

'I did. He wishes he wrote something like that when he first started out,' Michelle says. 'Thinks your housemate might have a promising career.'

'Really? Wow, that's fantastic.'

'So, what now? Will you try to find a producer?' Michelle pauses. 'I can cast it, although the lead role is clearly written for you.'

'Do you think?'

'I'd say it's custom made, and the film has real potential.'

The script is finding a life of its own, and Jem is completely unaware.

'I haven't actually talked to him about it yet.' I fidget nervously.

'He knows I've read it though?'

'Not exactly.'

'What?' Michelle's normally energetic tone jumps up half a dozen notches. I almost have to pull the phone away from my ear.

'I know, I know, I found it in the kitchen. It's not like it was under lock and key.'

'Okay, my love, you need to have a conversation with him,' Michelle says briskly. 'Let him work out what he wants. Only Hal and I have seen it, so still completely under wraps. But try to convince him to take it to the next stage and tell him I'd be happy to help make it happen.'

I see Jem briefly in the morning before I leave for the mountains and there isn't the time to get into the whole "I read your manuscript without permission" conversation. Or rather, I'm too scared to go there.

'You off again?' Jem arrives home just as I'm about to walk out the door.

'Heading up now. I'll be back Friday night.'

Our chat will have to wait until next weekend. A growing sense of unease niggles my insides. I must tell him that I found and read his manuscript. And passed it onto Michelle. Who passed it onto Hal… oh well, the feedback's been so positive, won't he be happy about it? I'd be over the moon if it were me. But Jem isn't me and he might not see things the same way. But he can't be angry for too long. Not when the film becomes a box office-breaking success. He'll be thrilled – and he'll have me to thank for it.

28

AFTER another huge yet exhilarating week, it's finally Friday and I head back to Sydney. Luckily, I finish at a reasonable hour so I dash to the shops on the way to buy ingredients for a chicken salad, a fresh baguette, and a bottle of sauv blanc. Hopefully Jem is around. I need to talk to him about his manuscript as soon as possible. I figure making him dinner might soften the blow.

I get back to an empty house with no Jem or George. Obviously out walking. I put the wine in the fridge, throw my salad together, and set the table, while trying to appear as casual as possible. Should I text him? No, I don't want to look like I'm waiting around for him. Even though I am. Instead, I give Mum a quick call to check up on Dad (all going fine, except he's planning to do some famous walk in Japan), then settle on the sofa with a glass of wine.

My patience pays off because thirty minutes later, in walks Jem.

'You're back?'

I look up to see Jem grinning. My heart skips a beat. How could I not have thought he was good-looking? What am I saying? I always knew he was good-looking, I just thought I was immune. Now one glance at him gives me heart palpitations. Then again, maybe I'm anxious about the script situation.

'Yes, home for the weekend.' George bounds in and jumps onto the sofa next to me. 'George, get down! You know that's not allowed.'

'I don't think Stu minds, but don't tell Jazz,' Jem gives a cheeky smile.

I say nothing, not wanting to explain how George sitting on the sofa might be a marriage-breaking issue for Jazz and Stu.

'Have you heard from Stu?' I ask

'No, why?'

'Just wondering how they're going,' I say quickly. 'Haven't had any news lately.'

'Jazz not checking up on George?'

'Not in a while, surprisingly. I thought she'd call to see how Dad is going too. Maybe she's been too busy. George, stop walking all over me, please.' I look back at Jem. 'You in for dinner? I've made a chicken salad, one of my very few specialties.'

'Yes, I'm in and hadn't thought about dinner.' He looks pleased. 'Do you need me to do anything?'

'No, all sorted.'

An hour later, we're sitting outside clinking our wine glasses and enjoying big bowls of chicken salad.

'This is good.' Rare praise coming from Mr Chef extraordinaire.

'As I said, it's one of my go-to meals. Perfected over years. The secret is in the aoli, which comes from a jar. And the chicken, which I got from the gourmet chicken shop on Bondi Road.'

'What?' Jem drops his fork. 'None of it's homemade?'

'Well, I put it together.' My cheeks flare with heat. 'As Mum told you, I'm not the best cook.'

'I'm joking, it tastes great.'

'It's just you made a point about homemade dishes when you ate my pasta that time.'

'Sorry, I was a dick that night.'

'You said it!'

'The pasta was actually delicious.'

It's hard to remember any of the original tension between us as we chat about our weeks. Jem tells me about George and their trips to the dog park, and I tell him about the week on set, the long days, the delicious catering, the funny things that happened, like when all of a sudden, I couldn't say the word "specifically" and it took six takes for me to get it right.

'Really? You couldn't say "specifically"?'

'Normally, it's not a problem, but it became a thing. Another day, we had to do at least fifteen takes of one scene because things kept going wrong. I walked into a chair, the other actor in the scene had a sneezing fit, we both got the giggles. Anyway, how was your week with George?'

'That dog community's pretty tight, isn't it?' Jem says. 'I feel like an outsider who has to prove he's worthy before being welcomed in.'

'I feel the same. I don't have the right clothes and I clearly don't know what I'm doing. I'm sure they could smell my fear. Luckily, Alex is often there, otherwise I'd never go back.'

We fall into a comfortable silence. Now, Indie! This is the moment to bring up his film script. Just tell him. How can he be upset when I (and Michelle and Hal) love his script so much? My nerves fray and I almost back out, but I can feel Michelle looking down on me, eyebrows raised, waiting for me to do the right thing.

I take a breath and hope for the best. 'Jem, can I talk to you about something?'

Jem's cheeks redden slightly and he almost looks nervous. 'Sure, what's up? Should I be worried?'

'Nothing bad,' I say quickly. 'But I absolutely have to say something.'

'What is it? I'm on the edge of my alfresco dining bench seat.'

I giggle. 'It's just, well… I don't know how to say it so maybe I'll just come out with it.'

'You've fallen head over heels in love with me, haven't you?' Jem says. 'That's okay, completely understandable, you're only human.'

I almost fall off *my* alfresco dining bench seat. That's not what I was going to say, of course, but it touches a nerve. Or maybe something a little further down. I feel more flummoxed than ever.

I quickly pull myself back together. 'I know you secretly wish that were true. I'm afraid it's something else.'

Jem shrugs. 'Pity for you.'

'I read your script.' The words catapult into the air before I can stop them. And for some fluky reason, they fall in the correct order so at least they make sense. Good start.

Jem's grin fades and he falls silent. I'm not sure what he's thinking, so I power on, trying to liven what feels like a party where no one has turned up. 'It was on the kitchen bench. I was looking for my script and accidently picked up yours. And it's awesome. That's what I'm trying to say. Your film's fantastic, I love it, and I want to play Tara!'

'You read my script?'

'Yes.'

'Without my permission?'

The impact of my error crashes down on me like a clap of thunder. Panic rises in my stomach. I did the wrong thing! What was I thinking? I never should have read it without talking to him.

'It was there,' I falter. 'And I didn't realise it was yours until I'd started reading, and by then, I was hooked. Great opening, by the way.'

'It's just… I haven't shown the final draft to anyone yet. Not even my teacher.' Jem's voice is quiet but steely. Unnerving.

'Your teacher? Are you doing a course?'

'Yes.'

'I didn't know you wanted to write film scripts.' A comment Jazz made before she left pops into my head, something about how creative Jem is, how he and I have so much in common. Maybe we do. Except I could never write such a great script.

'I've always liked writing but never took it seriously.' Jem pauses, looking down at his clenched fists. 'I wished you'd asked me first.'

'What would you have said if I'd asked?'

'Probably, no.'

'Exactly,' I say brightly. 'It was better I just read it.'

'Maybe I didn't want you to read it, Indie.' Fury creeps into his voice. 'The world doesn't revolve around you and what you think.'

I'm shocked into silence as Jem grits his teeth, his frowning face now a deep, angry red.

'I'm so sorry, Jem. But it's great. Really, really great. I showed my agent, and she was excited about it, too. Her husband is a writer called Hal Franks, don't know if you know him. He's really impressed, and he knows what he's talking about.'

'Of course I've heard of Hal Franks,' Jem's voice jumps a decibel, making me flinch. 'You showed it to your agent? And Hal Franks?'

'I know I should've asked you first,' I say quietly. 'But we were chatting on the phone not long after I'd read it and I couldn't help myself. I wanted to see what she thought of the central character…' I trail off because Jem has gone into a sullen silence with a fiery look on his face.

'Why? Thinking about yourself again, to see if you could play it?' Jem's hardened voice is more upsetting than if he were screaming at me. 'You had no right to do that, complete invasion of privacy.'

Panic now flooding my body, I backpedal like mad but to absolutely no end. Like I've found myself in a soggy ditch and every time I try to stand up, I slip on my face.

'Sorry, Jem, just forget I read it. I'll forget all about it. I won't mention it again to Michelle. I was just so excited about it and the central character – she's awesome and I know I could play her. It's like she was written with me in mind!'

Jem jumps up as a pink blush sweeps over his cheeks. I feel the floor slipping under me. Oh my God! He did write it with me in mind. But he can't have. It's dated way before we moved in together. We hadn't seen each other in years. Maybe I didn't inspire him. Probably a coincidence. There's no way he'd have given me a second thought, let alone created a story around a character I was born to play.

'Just keep out of my stuff, okay? This is private and not ready for reading.' Jem turns his back on me and marches out the kitchen. His footsteps disappear into his room and the door bangs shut.

I stay where I am, scared we might cross paths in the hallway. Honestly, if the script is that private, maybe he should have put it in a high security safe, or at least in his bedroom. Of course I'd pick up a script left lying around. Occupational hazard. It's his fault for writing such an incredible script with such an awesome central character. Can't blame me for that.

The front door slams. I exhale slowly, discomfort seeping through every cell in my body. Deep down, I know I should never have read his script. What was I thinking? I should have waited until he came home and asked his permission. The trouble is, he'd never have let me, he'd probably never have shown anyone. And it's too good not to be read, brought to life and enjoyed.

I feel like I'm on a sinking boat with nothing but a novelty egg cup to scoop out water. If I'd written that script, I'd have shot it by now. But it's not about me. In fact, this has nothing to do with me. But then I think of Tara, the tough Robin Hood-style detective in his story, and I wonder if it does after all.

I've thrown a spanner into the works. Not just one, but the complete twelve pack. And it's short-fused the whole system. Just when I thought we were becoming friends… maybe even something more? Well, not now. Any feelings growing inside me have dissipated like bubbles in a bath. They looked good to start with but then all they do is melt into nothing. Sure, I made a mistake, and I'm genuinely sorry. But quite frankly, his reaction is a little over the top.

After a fretful sleep, I drag myself up the next day to take George for a walk. There's no noise from behind Jem's tightly shut door. I heard him come in last night as I rolled uncomfortably from one side of the bed to the other but didn't dare venture out of my room.

I don't see him the next day or night, so I can't even apologise. He clearly doesn't want to talk to me, and I don't want to hang around the house, so I get up early Sunday morning and head over to Mum and Dad's. I want to check in and see how Dad's going anyway. And I can drive on from there to the mountains.

When I get out of Jazz's car, Mum is still in her dressing gown, watering the plants out the front. 'This is a lovely surprise. You didn't mention you were coming over when we spoke yesterday.'

'Last minute decision.'

'Doesn't matter, good to see you, darling. Where's that housemate of yours?'

'I don't know.' My tone is slightly curt and Mum eyes me suspiciously but thankfully lets it go.

'Dad's inside on the computer. I think he's researching walking the Camino for next year. I tell you, that man will be the death of me – and himself the way he's going!'

I smile and wander inside to the kitchen.

Dad looks up from his laptop. 'Indie, my love, this is a lovely surprise. Where's that housemate of yours?' Honestly, it's like Mum and Dad work from the same script.

'What are you doing?'

'Just planning our next walking holiday.'

'About that, Dad, how are you going?'

'Terrific. Never better.' He does actually look a bit better. Maybe all the travel planning is helping him recover.

'Dad, it's great that you're feeling so well, but just go easy on planning all the adventure holidays and activities.'

'I'll be fine, love.'

'I know you will be, but it's upsetting Mum.'

'Oh, you know what she's like, always worrying.'

'It's a little more than that. She nearly lost you and it terrified her. She doesn't want it to happen again.'

Dad looks up, his cheerful expression softening. 'Did she say that to you?'

'It's really stressing her out. All this planning and talk of overseas trips.'

Dad says nothing for a few moments. Not one for big emotional outbursts, I figure that's all we'll say on the subject.

'Indie, life is so short. Mine was nearly shorter. I don't want to waste a single day.' Seems Dad is in the mood for a big emotional outburst. 'What if I were to go tomorrow? I'd want to know that I lived every minute of today to the absolute fullest. Mum has to understand how I feel. I can't go back to how I was. I need to make more of my life. We all do.'

What Dad's saying makes sense. I've felt the same since it happened. And as a result, I finally cut Mark out of my life and got an awesome film role. Dad survived a near death experience and is now full of energy and determination. On the other hand, poor Mum, the carer who had to be so strong, is feeling the despair of "what if".

'You're right, Dad. It's amazing to have got through it and, yes, you need to make the most of every second, but still, you have a way to go with your recovery. And remember, Mum was by your side and saw you at your absolute worst. And saw what life might become. Just spare her a thought and I'm sure she'll be back on track in no time, planning to walk the Camino with you. She'll have it all mapped out, where you'll stop each night and where you'll eat every meal. You know how she is.'

'Yep, I do.' Dad sighs affectionately and gets up to give me a hug. 'Thanks love. We're so lucky to have such a wonderful daughter, wise beyond her years.'

I feel the sting of tears but shake it away. Not now. Now is for moving forward and being positive. For my dad's sake.

In the end, after a peaceful day far away from the drama that's called Jem Taylor, I drive to the mountains around six.

'Are you sure you don't want to stay over?' Mum busies herself with chopping carrots so she doesn't look too desperate.

'I'd love to Mum, but I start at five in the morning. It's better if I go tonight. Get a good sleep.'

Later, sitting in my little motel room, I write Jem a letter, explaining once again how it all happened, and how much Michelle and Hal love his screenplay. I'm still knocked sideways by his reaction. I thought he'd be happy. Obviously, I know nothing about Jem Taylor.

He may not even read it, but writing the letter is cathartic and allows me to re-focus on my job. I jump back into the shoot and surprisingly, my scenes with Tia turn out to be some of the best days so far. We haven't worked together since drama school and it was rarely enjoyable back then. This week, we click, and our scenes spark. Acting can do that. It throws you into close proximity with people you'd never usually share time with. You work so intensely together, emotionally and physically, and often in extreme situations, in bizarre locations. You might be outdoors on a freezing day, up all night in a supermarket, or stuck in a car in the middle of nowhere. Tia and I share a couple of days in a tiny cottage where her character lived until her daughter went missing ten years before. By the end of the first ten hours, we're lifelong buddies.

'I'm sorry if I was a bit stand-offish at drama school,' she said to me one day as we were being driven back to our motel.

'You weren't,' I say, even though she was. 'It was drama school. Everyone was going through something.'

'No, I was a bitch, and I don't even know why,' she says. 'You were so amazing, everyone loved you. I guess I was jealous and let it get the better of me.'

I'm so taken by Tia's frank apology I don't quite know how to respond. I instead look out the window as the countryside flies by under an inky black sky. She *was* a bit of a bitch, but now in the black of night after a long day that started at five in the morning, it all seems a century ago. And no longer relevant.

'I was probably the same,' I say. 'Don't worry about it.'

'I just want to say sorry.'

'Please, it's fine, Tia. No need.'

'Thanks, Indie.'

We fall into silence, side by side in the back seat of the car, but Tia is far from comfortable. Wow, she's really been fretting about this.

'It also had something to do with Charlie.'

'Charlie?' I look up in surprise.

'I was jealous of your relationship.'

'Charlie and I were just friends,' I say, puzzled. 'Still are.'

'Really?' Tia asks. 'I heard something was going on before you went to LA. Word was that you broke Charlie's heart. He didn't go out with anyone after that.'

'We did get together back then, but it was a mistake. I thought Charlie wasn't interested in anything serious, and I was about to go overseas.' Once again, I feel the guilt of my ambition. I was so focused on myself I didn't even see how much I hurt Charlie.

'And now you're back, what do you think?'

'Of Charlie?' Where is this conversation going? And why is Tia so concerned about Charlie? 'We're just friends. In fact, Charlie's one of my best friends.'

The release of tension in Tia's body is noticeable.

It suddenly hits me. 'You like him!'

I look at Tia's bright eyes. She's in love with Charlie. No wonder she never liked me. She was angry because I was in the way. Maybe it wasn't that we were competitive over acting jobs, rather, she couldn't get past me to Charlie.

'It's silly. He's never even noticed me. You guys were such good friends, and so funny together, I didn't think I could compete. I could never be myself around the pair of you. And now we're working together, I didn't know if I should say anything. You broke up with your American boyfriend and you and Charlie seem close again – but yes, I do, I always have.'

'Does he know?'

'No!' Tia says quickly. 'And he doesn't need to. It's all too long ago, and we've become friends since then, which is probably better.'

'Just tell him how you feel. What do you have to lose?' Even I can hear the hypocrisy as the words come out of my mouth. I'm not prepared to tell Jem how I feel, so I'm hardly the one to advise Tia.

'Would you tell a guy how you feel if you'd liked him for ages?' she asks as if reading my thoughts.

We pull up at the motel so I give a quick shrug as we say goodnight and head to our rooms. The thing is, I'm sure Charlie would be thrilled to know the truth about Tia. But would Jem want to know about my feelings for him? Not since I stole his script and showed it to Michelle without permission. Hardly the same situation. Tia would never do anything so thoughtless and completely unhinged.

Lying in my not-so-comfy motel bed, the enormity of my actions hits like a hurricane devastating a small defenceless town. I'd like to think I did the best thing for Jem. But if I'm honest, I wanted to be the one to make it happen and I wanted to play the lead role. I saw an opportunity and was only thinking of myself. That comment Charlie made about my career being more important keeps tapping me on the shoulder. It wasn't only about helping Jem, although I do want to do that. Deep down, I was really only thinking of how I could boost my flailing self-esteem and shine once more.

Despite the solitary darkness, my face flushes with shame. It doesn't look like Jem wants to forgive me. And fair enough. Who'd forgive someone that invades their privacy and expects them to be fine with it? And while we're on the subject, what if that same someone neglects her best friend, kisses someone else before officially ending her engagement, holds onto past tensions with a classmate from drama school, and unfairly judges an old school friend?

I definitely wouldn't want to be with someone like that, so why on earth would Jem?

29

THE next two weeks of filming roll by and I stay in Katoomba, drowning my guilt in a sea of scones and tea. I don't know if Jem read my letter, so I decide to call but hang up when I get his voicemail. He probably doesn't want to pick up. I write a text instead.

I'm so sorry for reading your script and showing it to my agent. I was too busy thinking of playing that (awesome) role. I didn't consider what you want nor how you feel. I'm a complete idiot. Just as I was enjoying spending time with you! I don't expect you to forgive me, and I don't expect you want to come to Emily's wedding. But I want to let you know how sorry I am. If I could take it all back, I'd do it in a second.

I also ring Emily to let her know that I'm still looking forward to seeing her but that my date may not be able to make it.

'No problem, I'm just glad you can come,' she gushes. 'It's been ages.'

'I know. Sorry I haven't been in contact, I'm suddenly busy shooting a film in the Blue Mountains.'

'How exciting! Your life's always so glamorous.'

I smile down the phone, if only she knew the truth. 'You're the one getting married, that's pretty exciting.'

'I know, can you believe it?'

I can't believe it. The Emily I knew was in no hurry to get married. 'It's fantastic and I'm sure you'll look beautiful.'

'Let's hope so, otherwise Hamish might change his mind!'

'I doubt that.'

'How's Jazz going on her trip? I wish she was coming too.'

I murmur agreement. I definitely wish she was coming.

'I'd better go, Indie,' Emily says. 'Looking forward to seeing you soon.'

It's nearly eleven when I arrive home the following Friday night. I creep in, unsure whether Jem is there or not. Doesn't seem to be. His bedroom door is shut and the light is out. George, on the other hand, greets me with a satisfying amount of enthusiasm.

'Hello there, haven't forgotten me?' I give him a big hug. 'It's been so long.'

He jumps to lick my face with fervour as if to say, 'Aunty Indie, I could never ever forget you!'

I look around the darkened kitchen. I'm not sure Jem would agree. Probably only too happy to forget me. Maybe he already has. I think about tomorrow's wedding and my heart drops like the swift curtain at the end of a play. Surely, I can face this day alone. People manage to go to weddings all the time without a plus one. I've done far more challenging gigs than "solo at an ex-best friend's wedding full of ultra-beautiful people". Hell, in LA it's tougher simply going out for brunch.

There'll be some girls from school, probably all the cool ones, but maybe they're not cool now. Maybe they're tired-out mums with nothing to discuss but sugar-free lunchbox snacks and what's a safe age for kids to go on social media.

In the morning, I get up early, make a cup of tea and book in to have my hair done at ten. After that, I'll have time to come home and get ready for the three-thirty service at a church in town.

Three hours later, feeling a little more glamorous thanks to a chic salon hairdo, I'm sitting in the garden trying to calm my anxious thoughts. Luckily, we already sorted out a gift. Jazz, being super organised, picked out some towels from their wedding registry. You'd think they'd have plenty of towels but it was on the list, and Jazz assured me that if it's on the list, then they want it.

I can't believe I was engaged only a few months ago. I'd have been opening presents of towels and saucepans, thinking happily about my future with Mark. The thought of it now is like jumping on a roller coaster that's missing a crucial bolt. Seemed like a safe bet on the surface, yet possibly the biggest mistake of my life.

I look in the bedroom mirror for the millionth time. My dress is divine (thanks to Jazz and her wonderful wardrobe), my hair is movie star wavy, but my heart is flat as an ironing board. Come on, Indie, you can do this. You've been onstage in front of countless audiences of absolute strangers for God's sake. Being one of a few hundred wedding guests should be a walk in the park.

I grab my purse, check my lipstick, then head down the hall. A movement from Jem's room stops me in my tracks. He's probably hiding in there until I go. He was the one that offered to come in the first place. I'd never have asked him. Now it feels like he's turning me down, which he kind of is. So annoying. I quickly reach the front door to avoid any awkward interaction. As much as I don't want to go to the wedding, I certainly don't want to bump into Jem.

'Indie!' His voice behind me makes me jump. Damn.

I turn to see Jem standing outside his bedroom door and my heart backflips. Not only because that's what happens every time I look at him, but the sight of him dressed in a beautiful dinner suit, looking like James Bond, is enough to make my insides melt like chocolate in the microwave.

'Ready to go?' he asks, as easily as if he's been waiting for me to finish getting dressed while he calls a cab. 'You look fantastic by the way.'

'Oh, thanks, um, you too, yes, ready, yes.' I'm not forming proper sentences. I'd assumed Jem was leaving me in the lurch to deal with the society-wedding-of-the-year alone. But no, here he is, looking amazing, on time and ready to go.

He holds out his arm, a shy smile on his face. 'Shall we?'

I link my arm through his and we make our way out the front where a cab is waiting.

'I didn't think you'd come.'

'I very nearly didn't show. But I said I would, so here I am.'

'You don't have to.'

'I want to.'

We say nothing more on the matter. There's nothing more to say. He said he'd be my plus one and here he is. An almost unbearable night might now be fun. He may not have the wild and uncontrollable feelings for me that I seem to have inconveniently developed for him, but I can practice self-restraint for one night.

I smile as Jem opens the taxi door for me. I climb in then he does the same, sitting so close that the sides of our legs touch. I gasp (as quietly as possible), inhaling the familiar scent of the shampoo from Jazz and Stu's bathroom. Coconut. Like a tropical holiday.

He turns his head sideways. 'How are you?'

'I'm great, thanks for asking.' And I am. I don't think I've felt this happy for a long time. Not that I really know why I'm so happy. I tell myself it's probably because Jem followed through, which means he's not completely furious with me for reading his script. But actually, I'm thrilled to be spending an entire evening with my hot housemate. And for now, I'm going to pretend he wants to spend the evening with me. It may not pan out the way I want because, unlike the movie I'm shooting where I know exactly what will unfold for Alyssa, real life is annoyingly unpredictable.

I glance across at Jem, who's facing out the window. He's never looked more divine than he does right now, although for me, it wouldn't have mattered if he'd turned up in his ripped jeans and crumpled white t-shirt.

'Thanks for coming.'

He grins. 'Thanks for asking me.'

For a moment, all seems forgiven as the cab speeds into the city. Or maybe he's had a bump on the head and has forgotten. That must be it.

Ten minutes later, we pull up outside the church. Jem reaches for his wallet and I stop him. 'This is my shout. You're the one doing me the favour, remember?'

We step onto the street and I take a big breath and release it slowly. This moment feels more nerve-wracking than any opening night performance. Although I wouldn't want Emily's life for the world. Okay, so I'm single and only have a job for a couple more weeks. After that, who knows? Anything could happen. Another job here? A job back in LA? Spielberg might even finally call…

'Are you ready?' Fortunately, Jem interrupts my fanciful thoughts.

'Yes, I think so.'

'You look gorgeous,' Jem says. 'You've got a happening career, and as far as everyone else is concerned, an awesome boyfriend. What more could you ask for?'

I smile. 'Apparently, I have it all!'

'Who cares anyway?' Jem says. 'We'll have a great night. Better than sitting at home watching TV.'

He's right, but half of me wishes that's exactly what we were doing right now: trackies, pizza, and a new Netflix series to binge.

As we stroll into the church, a few unfamiliar faces nod at me and smile at Jem. Several girls check him out, not that I blame them. He's looking particularly breathtaking today and he's single and fancy-free so they're in with a chance. More than they realise.

The packed church feels cramped and stuffy until anticipation of the bride's entrance pulls all focus. Emily's husband-to-be is waiting nervously at the altar with three burly groomsmen who all look the same. The organ breaks into a rousing hymn and the first bridesmaid appears. After the last one makes her way down the aisle, Emily enters, looking magnificent. Brides always look beautiful, but Emily positively shimmers down the aisle.

The ceremony goes as smoothly as her arrival. Knowing Emily, everything would be micro-managed to within an inch of its life. She probably has a wedding organiser with a headset outside saying, 'Cue the bride, and go!'

Eventually, we file out of the church and mill around the front. I make my way to congratulate the euphoric bride and say what every bride wants to hear. 'Hi, Emily, you look beautiful.'

'Thank you so much for coming.' She looks at Jem, her beautifully made-up eyes widening by the second. 'Hi. Jem, isn't it? We met at Jazz and Stu's wedding.'

'That's right. Good to see you and congratulations.' He grabs my hand in his. 'We'll get out of your way. There's a bit of a queue.'

Emily giggles. 'It's great getting married, you feel so popular.'

'I'll have to give it a go,' Jem returns breezily as we walk off, the feel of his skin against mine shooting an electric bolt up my arm.

Out of the corner of my eye, I see Emily's look of approval. At least people think I have a beautiful boyfriend, even if it's lightyears from the truth.

'Thanks for that,' I whisper.

'My pleasure.' Jem drops my hand and it's business as usual.

It was nice while it lasted.

'Do you think she remembers you helping her into a taxi?'

'And asking me to come home with her? Absolutely not, and I didn't want to remind her.'

I giggle. Of course, Emily tried to lure Jem into the taxi. Thank God he didn't go.

With two hours to kill between ceremony and reception, everyone assembles at a nearby pub for a drink. Emily and Hamish embark on what looks to be an epic scale professional photo shoot. They're probably selling the story to *New Idea*.

Jem buys two beers and we search for a secluded corner, only to get caught up with wedding guests – a couple from Orange, who are convinced they know me. We try to trace any possible friend connections to no avail because I don't know them. They've probably just seen me on telly, but I don't like to say. Jem and I don't get a chance to discuss our fight and his unexpected appearance. We can talk later, I guess.

Jem squeezes my hand. 'You okay, you look a million miles away.'

'No, I'm right here.' I smile, very much aware of heat creeping up my neck and a tingle in my fingers that are nestled in his palm. As if suddenly aware of his action, he drops my hand.

All too soon, it's time to go to the reception and we walk there with our new best friends from Orange.

'How long have you known the happy couple?' gushes the woman. I can't even remember her name, despite our super-glue-wedding-guest bond.

'I went to school with Emily,' I say.

'Oh, she always says how she was miserable at school,' the woman says. 'Not very fond memories.'

'Really?' I'm surprised because Emily always looked happy in the cool group. And she certainly didn't want anything more to do with Jazz and me once she got an in with the tall, leggy, beach-babe set.

'Apparently she was badly bullied,' the woman continues. 'The girls weren't very nice. She's very open about it. You must have been one of the good ones. I don't think she invited many from school.'

I haven't seen any of the blond beach gang strutting around. There was only me and another girl, Fiona, who lived next door to Emily. They were more like sisters or cousins but didn't hang out at school. Jazz was also invited, so maybe we do mean something to Emily. It's not like she was limited with numbers at her wedding. She probably could have invited the whole year if she'd wanted to.

'How long have you two been together?' the woman asks with a knowing smile.

'Oh we—'

'Only a few months,' Jem interrupts. 'Early days, but we've been friends for a long time and I finally convinced her to go out with me.'

I look at Jem in surprise.

'What? That's the truth, isn't it?' He laughs when he sees my bemused expression and turns back to the woman who looks desperate for every detail. 'We actually kissed at our friends' wedding years ago and never spoke again until our paths crossed earlier this year – and the rest, as they say, is history. It took a while for her to agree to come on a date, but I wore her down in the end.'

I desperately want to giggle and punch Jem in the arm to stop the lies coming out of his mouth, but to be honest, I'm loving every moment. And I wish it were true. I'm also grateful to him for saving me from having to explain our somewhat unique situation.

Easier to say what people want to hear rather than explain my mess of a life.

We grab a glass of sparkling on our way into the reception room which looks like a wedding shop just exploded, leaving an aftermath of bows, flowers, and shiny balloons strewn from one end to the other. Every table has a floral centrepiece as big as me and every surface is white as snow. We make our way to our table (luckily Jem's name is still on the list) and do the obligatory introductions to the other guests. From there, the night slips away like a dream. Jem chats easily to everyone on the table. He's fun and entertaining, and I haven't laughed so much in ages.

'Where have you been hiding your sense of humour all this time?' I ask in a mock serious tone.

'I only pull it out for special occasions.'

'This is a special occasion?' I say with a wry smile. 'Pretending to be my date so I don't lose face at my school friend's wedding?'

Jem hesitates, as if about to say something, but our main courses arrive and the moment disappears. What was he going to say? Maybe something about the film script debacle, which we still haven't addressed. Hopefully, we don't have to. Tonight is wonderful, I don't want to spoil it by raking over my inexcusable mistake.

Eventually, the groom gets up, pulling out a sheaf of papers which look like they've been sat on for the last two days. Shifting uncomfortably on his feet, he looks around the room with a timid smile. He starts off haphazardly but warms into it when speaking of Emily and how they met. He mentions his surprise when Emily agreed to go to the movies with him, a feeling that has never left as she continually wants to see him again, and now forever after.

The speech is beautiful, touching, and not what I expected. Not that I was really expecting anything. I don't know Hamish, but I'm so used to Emily hanging out with Sydney's elite, I thought he'd be the same as the rest. Rich, arrogant, and superficial. Maybe I got it all wrong. Maybe Emily really has met the love of her life, who just happens to be a rich banker. Maybe the money wasn't the main attraction. The Emily I first knew would have only married for true love, if ever, and it looks like she's done exactly that. My eyes ache with tears as he leans over to give his new wife a gentle kiss and the crowd madly applauds.

Finally, speeches done, the band strikes up a rendition of *Walking on Sunshine* and the happy bride takes her groom by the hand and leads him to the dance floor. A surprising song for a bridal dance but when I think of Emily, it makes total sense. We watch as they dance, laughter on their faces, as husband and wife, with bridesmaids and groomsmen slowly joining in.

Jem takes my hand. 'I believe I owe you a bridal dance.'

I nod, not wanting to remind him of our backyard dance and yet another interrupted kiss.

We share not one, but many dances together. It turns out Jem isn't at all self-conscious on the dance floor as I assumed back at Jazz and Stu's wedding. He has some hilarious moves up his sleeve that keep me in fits of laughter. In fact, we're a hit, and end up leading everyone around in a conga line. No wonder everyone loves Jem. He's incredibly charming and so much fun. By the time he's waltzing the mother-of-the-bride around the room, I signal to say I'm exhausted and going to take a break. However, the music quietens to a slow and moody number and Jem excuses himself from Emily's mum, who's looking positively radiant, and grabs my hand.

'Where are you going?' Jem pulls me close, the firmness of his body against mine, the smell of his skin, the strength of his grasp whisking the air from my lungs. The crisp cotton of his dinner shirt brushes against my cheek as I rest my head against his shoulder while we sway to the music, barely covering any ground. It feels like we're the only ones in the room, despite the other two hundred wedding guests. I want to snatch this moment and keep it in my pocket forever.

At last, we take a break and head out to the terrace to cool off in the crisp night air.

'Don't feel like you have to stay,' I say, in case he's wondering when he can make his escape.

'Do you want me to go? Did I completely embarrass you on the dance floor? I tend to get carried away.' Jem looks at me slyly. 'Or have you got an eye on that best man?'

'The groom's brother? Hardly. Besides, he's married with four kids.'

'Homewrecker!'

'I'm not interested in him!'

'Who then?'

I look away, scared of what might come out of my mouth and ruin a wonderful evening, to say nothing of the remaining time in the house. I want to shout Jem's name at the top of my voice, but then I'd need the floor to swallow me up and I doubt that would happen.

'No one, I'm afraid. I'm happy on my own right now.'

I look back to see a flash of something in Jem's eyes. Disappointment, maybe? Relief?

'I doubt you'll be single for long.' A slight breeze makes me shiver and Jem moves in closer. 'Are you cold?'

'A little.' My voice is almost a whisper.

Our faces are inches apart. I take a breath. 'Jem, I'm sorry for reading your film script without permission and showing it to my agent.'

'I know you are and it's fine. I'm over it.'

'It's very good.'

'Did Hal Franks really like it?'

'I think his words were, "I wish I'd written it".'

'Wow!'

I'm standing close to Jem, like he's a magnet and I'm a random piece of metal, powerless in his presence. I want to sneak my arms around his waist and pull him even closer, but I don't know what's going on and if that's acceptable behaviour for housemates who've had a fight, haven't spoken in weeks, but clearly find each other incredibly attractive. Well, one of the housemates finds the other incredibly attractive. It's a whole new (and unorthodox) world to navigate.

'Indie, about the script, the central character—'

'It's okay, you don't have to tell me, I understand about finding inspiration for characters—'

'It's you.'

I open my mouth to speak. Nothing comes out.

'The character, Tara, I wrote it with you in mind. Way before we moved in together. It's something I've been working on for ages. You've always been the central character in my head. Even my scriptwriting teacher told me I tend to write my female leads the same way.'

I stare at Jem in surprise. He squirms uncomfortably and abruptly changes the subject. 'I might go. You don't have to go but it's close to midnight and it's been a long day.'

'I'll grab my purse,' I say without hesitation.

We call an Uber and leave, looking like any couple after a wonderful evening out. Except we're not like most couples because we're not a couple. And I have no idea what's going on. He bases his characters on me, so I must mean something. There's so much

I want to say, but we don't speak all the way home, the air heavy with new information and unanswered questions.

Does he think of me? He must do. But does he actually like me? And that kiss we had once, no twice… does he want to do it again?

30

BACK home, we're distracted by the usual routine. Getting tackled by George, filling his water bowl, giving him some after-dinner biscuits and a big cuddle.

'I'll take George around the block.' Jem puts the harness on the over-excited dog. 'He's been cooped up all afternoon.'

'Want some company?' I ask before I can stop myself.

'Sure, you can protect me from muggers.' He smiles. 'Have you got your trusty broom?'

I giggle. 'I think George will be more use than that.'

'He'll try to lick them to death, but then you could trip them up while they're distracted.'

We shed our wedding clothes and pop on our comfy trackies. George is thrilled to be taken for a late-night stroll. As we step onto the pavement and head down the street, Jem seems to be deep in thought.

'So, what happened at Jazz and Stu's wedding?' I struggle to find a way to talk about what we're not talking about. 'You clearly like dancing. But it was like you hated me.' The question has been burning in the back of my mind since we hit the dance floor tonight.

Jem takes a breath. He looks so uncomfortable that I immediately regret my question. God, he must have really hated me.

'Sorry, dumb question, just forget I asked.'

I try to recover from an awkward moment by giving Jem a

casual friendly pat on the arm but misjudge my nervous energy (off the charts) and arm strength (better than I thought) and it turns into a swift punch. Jem staggers slightly.

'Go easy, it was a long time ago.'

'Oops, sorry, I didn't mean to do that.' My attempt to alleviate discomfort has merely highlighted it with fluorescent pen and even then, I keep talking. 'It's so fine, I mean if you didn't find me attractive, that's not your fault, it's not like I was attracted to you either, I mean we hardly knew each other, it's just I feel like you made some snap decision about the sort of person I am, and I think that was a bit unfair…'

It's like I'm competing in a speed talking competition and pulling up in first place. Jem can't get a word in, but I don't really want to hear what he has to say.

'No, Indie, it's not—'

'I mean, if you think I'm a terrible actress, that's one thing, and there's not much I can do about that, but really, it's a bit judgemental and also completely subjective and doesn't have anything to do with me as a person…'

Even I don't understand what I'm saying now. I just wish I'd stop speaking altogether. If I put Jem off at Jazz and Stu's wedding, I'm doing an even better job of it now.

'Indie!' Jem's raised voice silences me immediately. 'I should've explained before, but I didn't want to make things awkward living together. Now, after everything I've been through lately, I no longer care, so here goes.'

I feel like sticking my fingers in my ears, but that's probably a bit juvenile.

Jem takes another deep breath. 'I was such an idiot that night because I was instantly attracted to you, and it freaked me out. I still am. Attracted to you that is, a bit less freaked out. I'd seen a couple of your plays and TV shows with Stu and Jazz before we met and was blown away. I figured it was just some fan thing I'd get over. But when I met you at the wedding rehearsal dinner, I realised how amazing you really are but was too scared to say. I couldn't believe someone like you would even consider someone like me, who was nowhere near your world. I'd started writing in secret back then but never imagined I could write something you'd read, let alone like.'

I accidently trip over George, who's sitting patiently at my feet, and he gives a little yelp. That's not what I expected Jem to say.

'I thought the best thing to do was act tough and keep away. Then I started going out with Alice, which was a disaster. I didn't know you were moving in until that lunch, and I was angry. I'd been through such a rough time and had nowhere else to go. But it meant living with you. I didn't know how I was going to get through it. I hoped I wouldn't find you attractive anymore and that by living together, I'd discover some annoying habit that would put me off. But you have none. Well, you do, but even the annoying and frustrating things about you are adorable…'

Now Jem's in the speed talking competition, qualifying for state championships, while I'm left completely speechless. As we stand stock still on the pavement, George stares up at us, probably thinking this is the strangest night he's ever had and secretly hoping his real mum and dad might come home soon. Our faces are millimetres apart, Jem's dark eyes are sad and resigned, like he shared everything and has no secrets left.

'Indie, can you say something?'

I don't say anything. I simply stand on my tippy toes and put my lips to his in a gentle kiss. Jem pulls back and looks at me and then in less than a second, he returns my kiss with fervour, his hands cupping my cheeks. I wrap my arms around his waist as I lose myself in the moment. In our kiss. Hungry and passionate, fuelled by months of tension. We pull away, but only because George is over the lack of attention and starts barking madly.

'Come on, mate,' Jem says to George. 'It's late, let's get you into bed.'

I secretly wish he were saying that to me, just not addressing me as "mate" of course. Jem grabs the leash, takes my hand, and we walk home in silence. Rather than releasing the mounting tension between us, the kiss merely intensified it.

Jem pops the leash and harness on the hall table and I check the water bowl. George snuggles into his "resting station" in the hallway. He doesn't even try to come into one of our rooms. Maybe he senses something's up and is giving us some space. What now? It's all very well kissing in the street but back home, everything has changed. We're not purely housemates anymore but not exactly anything else.

Jem also appears unsure but tentatively puts his arms around me, a simple action that thrills my body no end and our eyes lock as securely as Jazz and Stu's side gate.

'Indie, I had a great time tonight.'

'Me too.' Again, heat ripples up my neck. 'Thanks for being my wedding date.'

'Anytime.'

'I doubt there'll be another one soon.' I start to ramble. 'I don't know too many people getting married.'

'That's a pity.'

'Just me, really, and that didn't work out.'

'Lucky for me.' Jem pulls me closer with an unexpected confidence that makes my insides gasp.

All I want is to press my lips against Jem's, but instead, I continue chattering with what seems to be a case of opening night nerves. 'Unless we just turn up at random weddings.' Honestly, what am I saying?

Jem's chocolaty eyes spark up. 'Whatever it takes.'

We lean in and our lips meet once more. This time, there's no impatient George to pat, walk, or feed. Thank God, because I don't think I'd be able to stop, and George would just have to do without. And somehow, I don't think Jazz would mind in this particular circumstance. In fact, she'd be delighted.

Jem pulls away. 'Is there anything I should be aware of? Any more ex-boyfriends waiting in LA for your return?'

'No,' I say hotly. 'I don't have that many. You're the one I should be worried about. Jazz is constantly telling me how women throw themselves at your feet.'

'You know Jazz, she exaggerates.'

I do know that. I think about her and Stu and the happy picture she's always painted of their life together. I desperately want to talk to Jem about it, but now's not the time.

'So, where were we? I think you were telling me how you've been in love with me for a million years and—'

Whatever else I say is lost as Jem kisses me then pulls away. 'That seems to be the only way to shut you up.'

'So, if I keep talking, you'll keep kissing me?'

'Unless you want me to stop?'

I most definitely do not want him to stop, so I take a breath as well as Jem's hand and head in the direction of my bedroom. 'My room's nicer than yours.'

Jem doesn't need to be told twice. In a flash we're on the bed kissing, every minute we've shared over the past weeks driving our desire to be as close to each other as humanly possible.

I pull Jem's t-shirt over his shoulders and almost fall backwards off the bed. My God, he's incredible. Sure, I saw him that time in the hallway, dressed in nothing but a towel, but I was so stressed I didn't know where to look. Now I'm taking in every curve, every muscle, every single millimetre of his body, as if it's the first time I've laid eyes on it.

Thankfully, my not-so-sexy trackies are discarded, revealing my fancy wedding underwear (so glad I wore it). Jem swiftly unclasps my bra, letting out a little moan as he takes each of my nipples in his mouth, until I can bear it no longer. Slowly, sensuously, he explores every intimate corner of my body as if he's found himself in some wondrous new land made of gold and precious jewels. Making his way past my stomach, gently stroking the lacy silk of my underwear, he audibly releases a breath as he sees what's underneath.

'God Indie, every part of you is beautiful.'

'You're not so bad yourself.' My response falls on deaf ears as Jem skilfully caresses and teases with his tongue, building an almost painful sense of anticipation like I'm climbing a magnificent mountain with no end in sight. Exhilarating and amazing. Almost unbearable as every touch ignites my body like flashing lights on a Christmas tree. And just when I feel like I can't take anymore, like I'm about to burst, I'm suddenly free-falling down the other side, an overwhelming sense of heat and pleasure flooding every cell of my body.

Oh, my goodness. Jem certainly knows what he's doing. I wish I'd been aware of that when he moved in. Not that it's something you really advertise to your housemate who you can't stand to be around.

I impatiently reach for Jem, feeling more turned on than ever, and far from done.

'Indie…' Jem speaks, but I don't want to hear words right now. My mouth meets his before he can say another word, until he pulls away. 'Do you have a condom?'

'Oh, no,' I try to catch my breath. 'Last thing I thought I'd need living with you.'

'Thanks.' He smiles. 'Wait here.'

In less than thirty seconds, all is sorted.

'That was quick.'

'Are you kidding?' he says, his eyes inhaling every part of me as I lay back against Jazz's big white pillows. 'I don't want to rush you but I can't wait a moment longer.'

'Me neither.' I pull Jem towards me, desperate to feel the weight of his body against mine, and we seamlessly meld like the two final and glorious pieces of a puzzle. We move in unison as if speaking our own language and it's not long before I'm once again rising on a magnificent wave, this time at a more furious rate, and Jem's right there, pushing me higher and higher. Unable to stop and not wanting to, I give over to its intoxicating power until I hear myself gasp, all my senses exploding like champagne glasses dropping onto concrete. Jem holds me close as my body melts, liquid velvet flowing through my veins. As if I've been swept back to shore and am now luxuriating on soft warm sand in the glow of a tropical sun.

We lie there motionless, our breathing heavy, as if not quite believing what just happened. One of Jem's arms is draped across my stomach as if it always belonged there. I shift my head slightly and see his eyes are closed. What's he thinking? Was his experience equal to the truly extraordinary one I just had?

I think back to sex with Mark. It was never like that. It was good, don't get me wrong, but a little too organised and efficient, much like his apartment. Just now, with Jem, was nothing like I'd ever known. What a shame we were interrupted at Jazz and Stu's wedding. Although, the wait has definitely been worth it.

'That went pretty well, didn't it?' I nervously ask.

'Not bad.' Jem slowly props himself on his elbow. 'Not bad at all.'

I smile, secretly relieved. 'Is that all you can say?'

Jem kisses me tenderly on the lips. 'As I've probably said many times, you're extraordinary, Indie.'

'I don't think you've ever said that to me.'

'Not to your face.' He stops to look at me for a moment. 'But I'm saying it now.'

I don't think I can possibly sleep after the evening we've had. I don't want to in case I wake up to find it was all a hopeful dream. But as Jem wraps me in his arms, my eyelids droop like heavy weights.

All too soon, the sun is creeping its way through the timber venetians. I snuggle deep under the covers. It can't be morning yet. The previous night flashes before my sleepy eyes and I glimpse the top of Jem's head poking out from the doona. It did happen. I did have the most amazing sex with Jem Taylor. We didn't just kiss and fall into a cloud of awkwardness. We finally connected in a way I never thought possible.

I lie back, recounting every glorious moment from when Jem turned up in his dinner suit, to the moment he peeled off my unglamorous t-shirt and sent my heart spinning in every direction.

What will happen now as daylight creeps in and the wedding magic dissipates? We're supposed to be housemates, but it's safe to say we've moved on from there. Did Jem really want to? Or is he going to run away like he's done every other time? Didn't he mention that I was extraordinary? I definitely remember something along those lines. But maybe it was just that. A line. God knows, I've heard a few of those before, and not just onstage.

'Hey there.' Jem jolts me away from the voice in my head,

which is already mapping out how badly this situation might unfold. 'Hi.'

'You look worried.' Jem shifts closer to me. 'What's wrong?'

I want to say that I'm worried this will all end once we get up and go about our days. Walking George, cooking dinner, cleaning up. Where does this fit into our life of humdrum domesticity? And what about my film? Or worse, what about LA? I don't even want to think about that.

A concerned expression brushes Jem's face. 'Having second thoughts about last night?'

'Not at all. I'm worried you might be.'

'Me? No, last night was great.' He pauses, his rich coloured eyes staring right into mine, melting my heart and turning me on all at the same time. 'Well, I was great, you were okay.'

I giggle. 'I think I was pretty awesome. We both were.'

'Perfect wedding guests.'

An image of Jem dancing with Emily's mum lights up in my mind. 'You were definitely a hit.'

'Well, we know who the real star was,' Jem says. 'People kept telling me that my girlfriend was on telly.'

'What did you say?'

'I said that yes she was and I was very proud of her.'

'Nice. You didn't say that we were just friends? Housemates?'

'No way, I wanted people to think we were together,' Jem says, suddenly a little more serious. 'I've wanted this for so long, Indie. Last night it felt like it was real.'

This is the moment in a musical when the couple would break into song, and I can understand why. But being an average singer at best, I leave well alone. Instead, I focus on the fact that Jem is here and isn't going to ignore me nor pretend it didn't happen. Doesn't sound like much, but considering our past encounters, it's a huge achievement.

'Coffee? Jem pulls his boxers on and moves towards the bedroom door.

'Yes, please.'

I give my cheek a light slap. Ow. Yes, this is real. Just checking. But will it happen again? All I know is I have a few more weeks of shooting to get through before I come back to Sydney. As much as I want to stay in bed with Jem and never get out, I must stay focused and finish the job. And what about LA? That question keeps jumping out in front of me. Last night has turned everything upside down. I had a plan but now I can barely remember my middle name.

I take a breath. All I need to do now is my job. Be in the moment and don't think beyond it. That sounds like a plan. Well, a new one anyway. One that's good enough for now.

We eventually get up and take George for a walk down to the beach. Absolutely starving, thanks to the combination of a wedding followed by a night of passion, we stop at a café for breakfast, taking an outside table so George can loll next to our chairs.

'When do you go to the mountains?'

'This afternoon.'

'Unless you can't find the car keys.' Jem smiles mischievously. 'Or you have a flat tyre?'

'Unfortunately, I'm still expected on set at six tomorrow morning. Lost keys or a flat tyre is no excuse.'

'Oh well.'

'But I'll be back Friday night. You around?'

'Maybe,' he says. 'I'll have to check my very busy schedule.'

'Hopefully there's a small window for me to squeeze into.'

'Don't worry, I'll be waiting next to an open door.'

I smile. In this moment I could not be happier. I have the

trifecta – a job, a lover, and a beautiful home. It rarely comes together and never for very long. Definitely the job will end, and the house. Jem too, knowing our history. For the moment, I have it all, and I'm going to make the most of every second before the next dramatic and inevitable scene change.

31

ALL too quickly, I'm back at work. It's Monday morning and I'm trying to get my head around the first scene of the day.

'What's going on with you, Indie James?' Charlie is up for a few days of work and is looking at me suspiciously.

'What?' I say with a smile I just can't help. 'Nothing at all.'

Charlie is far from convinced. 'It's pretty early in the morning and you look all glowy and radiant.'

'I've been into make-up,' I say quickly. 'Louise is amazing.'

'No, it's something else.'

'Just happy to be working, you know how it is.'

Charlie isn't convinced but thankfully leaves it there. Mind you, I saw a few loaded smiles between him and Tia at breakfast, so maybe he knows exactly how it is.

The week goes exceptionally well, despite my love-struck haze. I feel like everyone is looking at me as if they know I've had amazing sex with my incredibly hot housemate. Even Nina eyes me suspiciously when she says I've found 'a lightness in Alyssa that hasn't been there before'. It must be written all over my face.

By the end of the week, I'm ridiculously excited to be seeing Jem. Also, incredibly nervous. It's a lifetime since the morning after our night together and I suddenly feel shy to see him in person.

'Hello, there,' Jem greets me as I walk into the kitchen, sending my insides into a whirl.

'Hi,' I say in a weird sing-song voice that should only be used for teaching pre-schoolers craft, not for greeting my new lover. 'Wow, the kitchen looks clean. Good to be back. How are you? How's George? Hopefully not lost. What have you been up to? Yeah, really good to be back.'

Words eject from my mouth as if filling awkward silences on a first date. Jem says nothing, well how can he? I'm talking for the two of us. He has a slightly bemused look on his handsome face. Even more good-looking than I remember. But what if he's realised this was all a huge mistake and he's preparing to have a difficult conversation? Why do I always get carried away? Mark and now Jem. What was I thinking?

Luckily, George bounds his way through my nervous thoughts with such force he nearly knocks me over.

'Whoa, George, did you miss me?'

At least the dog gives me a big welcome. Good old George. I give him a cuddle to calm him down.

'He has missed you,' Jem says. 'We both have, though probably not for the same reasons.'

Warmth spreads over my cheeks as Jem moves towards me. My worries disappear like smoke in a breeze. He puts his arms around me and for the first time in I can't remember how long, I feel like I'm really home.

We spend the entire weekend together. Occasionally, we put on clothes and go out to walk George or grab something to eat. But mostly we stay in bed, talking, laughing, making love, and playing Scrabble. It's like we've known each other for years. Which we sort of have. Not that we were even friends until a few weeks ago, but somehow it feels normal for us to spend every moment in each other's presence.

I feel bad that I haven't made time to visit my parents, but I blame Jem and his distracting ways and give them a call instead.

According to Mum, Dad's doing well and is taking his recovery a little more seriously. It seems it has hit home, just how long it's all going to take. He's even slowed down on the adventure planning.

'That's good, isn't it?'

'Yes, I guess so.' Mum sounds a little unsteady. 'But now he seems a little low. I think I prefer him planning to hike mountains and jump out of planes.'

'I'll come over soon,' I say, feeling even more guilty. 'This is the last week of the shoot, then I'll be back in Sydney so will have time to visit.'

'Perfect, that'll give Dad something to look forward to.' I can hear Mum flipping through her calendar. 'Jazz and Stu will be back soon, won't they? You might need to move home anyway.'

Mum's right. She obviously has it marked down, whereas I've completely lost track of time (again, thanks, Jem). I knew it was coming up, but now it dawns on me what that actually means. Jazz and Stu will want their house and dog back. So, what happens to Jem and me? We're not living in the real world right now – will we survive when we do?

I try to put it out of my head but later, as we lie, legs and arms entwined, under Jazz's French linen sheets, I can't help but worry.

'What's up?' Jem interrupts my thoughts. 'You look stressed?'

'What are we going to do now?' I ask.

'I don't know… maybe you could do that manoeuvre you just did which was pretty awesome, but then again, I could devour some poached eggs.'

'No, when Jazz and Stu come back. Us, this, what will we do?'

'Let's not think about it until it happens,' says Jem. 'Instead, let's focus on re-doing that manoeuvre, then afterwards cooking eggs.'

I giggle, only too happy to oblige. I'm going to keep living in the moment, not dwell on the inevitable. Right now is one of those rare moments of pure perfection and I'm going to enjoy it. Before it ends. One thing I've learnt from recent events is that nothing stays perfect for long. Especially the precious things. Not work, not love, not family. You just have to live in the moment and make the most of it – because the very minute you think something is perfect, everything goes horribly wrong.

I somehow prise myself from Jem and get to work on Monday morning. When I finally crawl into bed that night after a massive day, I tap out an email to Jazz.

Hi there,

How are you? Haven't heard from you for ages. Hope all is okay. Dad's recovering nicely and finally stopped planning extreme sports activities. Just realised you must be coming home soon? Let us know so we can clean up and pretend that George never slept on the sofa – only joking!

I xxx

I put it out of my mind for now and throw myself into the last week of the shoot. We have to finish up on Friday, so the days are long and extremely packed. But we get there, and the first assistant director finally says the words we want to hear (but don't want to hear), 'That's a wrap!'

Everyone cheers and applauds. A double-edged sword – while it's great to finish the job, it also means we've finished the job. And that means unemployment for the un-foreseeable future.

Secretly, I'm thrilled. It's been fantastic, but I can't wait to get back to Jem. I've never been so happy to finish up on a shoot. Goodness, what's happening to me? Is my personal life becoming more important than work? I've never felt that before. This time, I'm really looking forward to the next chapter, which means spending time with Jem. And hanging out with Mum and Dad. That little voice in my head (Miss Tonkins again) keeps asking me what I'm going to do about returning to LA, but I tell her firmly that she's not my teacher anymore and to not interfere.

Instead, I shut the door on my motel room and jump into Jazz's car. Jazz hasn't replied with a return date, so perhaps Jem and I will have one more weekend where I don't have to think about migrating to Pymble.

Jem sweeps me into his arms the minute I walk in the door. 'Hi, gorgeous lady.'

'Hello there, have you been waiting at the door for my return?'

'Since Monday morning.'

'Yeah, sure.

'Good to see you.'

'Better to see you.'

Our bodies sink into each other as we kiss and just like that, we're back in our bubble, a sense of relief sweeping over me like a delicious summer breeze.

While I was away, Hal and Jem met for coffee, which sounded more like eight hours of non-stop talking and Scotch drinking. Hal gave Jem copious notes, and he's been re-writing with great enthusiasm ever since. Michelle and I discuss the cast at length, and I start working on a pitch for producers. I've never gone down this path before, having only ever worked on the actor's side of the camera. So much needs to happen before filming even starts and I love being a part of it. Naturally, when and if we ever shoot it, I'm cast in the lead role.

I ring my parents every day to check on Dad and to make sure Mum is coping. Which means I chat to Mum, while Dad throws in a few comments over the top. He seems to have cheered up a little and re-discovered his zest for life, but now, rather than trekking through Nepal, he's focusing on cooking the healthiest recipes possible.

'You should try my vegan lentil bolognese, Indie,' he calls out one time as Mum and I discuss her latest shopping expedition. 'It's incredible.'

'That's one word for it, David,' says Mum. 'Now where were we, Indie, I lost my train of thought.'

'You were telling me about an orange shirt you bought but are thinking of returning because it clashes with your hair.'

'Is no one interested in my wellbeing anymore?' Dad jumps in.

'Of course we are, stop being ridiculous.' Mum then whispers down the phone, 'I almost wish he would jump on a plane to Nepal.'

I smile, feeling reassured by my parents' usual banter. Dad must be well and truly on recovery's road.

Apart from that, Jem and I spend our days working on the script, playing Scrabble of course, and wearing very few clothes. Often all at the same time. Lost in our own "Indie and Jem" world, we can't get enough of each other. I haven't told anyone, although I'm sure Lucy suspects something's going on as I'm never available. And I don't seem to do anything but "stay home" or "walk George". Even though I do both those things with some regularity, I think she assumes they must be some sort of euphemism.

One morning the following week, after having sex, walking George then going back to bed and having sex again, we start up yet another game of Scrabble, this time coming up with words to describe each other in intimate detail. Naturally, I'm way out in front in no time.

'You're proving an enormous distraction in my life,' Jem says. 'And not just because I keep letting you win at Scrabble.'

I smile as I add on 32 points from one particularly sexy word.

'Tell me about it, I'm not getting anything done.'

'Don't let me get in your way.' Jem pulls back the covers, as if allowing me out the bed. I make a move, and he tackles me playfully, narrowly missing the Scrabble board.

'See what I mean, you're right in my way.' I laugh. 'But I don't mind *too* much. Besides, it's your turn and you deserve the chance to win at least one game.'

We haven't talked seriously about our newfound relationship, nor have we discussed moving out of Jazz and Stu's, so this short, casual exchange seems momentous. We start kissing again and lose ourselves in each other for yet another time today. So much so, we don't hear the key in the front door until too late.

'Who's that?' I pull away from Jem.

'Don't know.' Jem drops his voice to a hush. 'Next door?'

We listen intently but the noise is undoubtedly in the house and coming down the hall. I wish I had the trusty broom close at hand.

'Hello?' calls a familiar voice. 'Anyone home?'

We look at each other in shock. Jazz!

George realises his real mum is finally home and yelps excitedly. We hear Jazz open the sliding door and George racing around the garden with happy barks. Thank goodness Jazz is distracted.

My brain switches into panic mode and I speak in a frantic hiss, like I've pressed fast-forward on my own personal remote. 'I'll go. No, you go. No, I'll go, and you stay here. Then come out. As if you were in your own room.'

'Why don't we just tell them the truth?' Jem says far too loudly.

'Shh, we will, just not yet. Jazz will go bananas if she knows about this, probably leak it to the press or even put her own announcement in the local paper.'

Jem snickers quietly. 'True. Okay, off you go, see you out there.'

I give Jem a quick kiss on the lips and reluctantly leave his gorgeous body, grab Jazz's dressing gown, and head outside.

'Jazz! You're back.' I give my friend a hug. 'Sorry, I didn't realise it was today. You should've let me know. I'd have cleaned up a bit, done some food shopping and moved my stuff out of your room. Did you email? I must have missed it.'

I'm painfully aware that I'm talking too much and too quickly for someone who's clearly been sleeping in all morning.

'My fault. It was all very sudden.' Jazz eyes me up and down suspiciously. 'It's nearly eleven thirty, why are you still in bed?'

'Oh, I sat up last night, reading a script for a new film project, don't know what time I went to bed, it was pretty late.' I make a conscious effort to slow down my words. 'I've been awake for a while.'

'Fair enough.'

'Where's Stu?'

Jazz starts to crumple in front of my eyes, tears rolling down her pale cheeks. 'We went our separate ways in France. I stayed down south doing some buying and he went to…' Where Stu went was lost in a wash of tears and sobs.

I pull my friend into a hug while she cries into my shoulder. 'Jazz, what happened?'

'I don't know,' she splutters. 'Well, I do, but I can't do anything about it.'

'Tea?'

Jazz nods and turns to George who is whimpering beside her. 'I'm alright, Georgie, Mummy's just a bit sad.'

Even so, a noise from the bathroom snatches her attention. 'Who's that?'

'Jem, probably,' I answer dismissively. 'I haven't seen him today.'

'Looks like he slept in, too.'

'Yep.'

'You haven't killed each other yet?'

'Not yet.' I pause. 'Jazz, I know we talked about it at the hospital, but I'm so sorry I've been such a hopeless friend.'

'That's okay, you can't help that you were away in my hours of need and I was forced to roam dog parks looking for replacement best friends.' Jazz smiles. 'But what about your dad? I was so devastated I wanted to fly home immediately. I'm sorry I haven't been in contact. I've been thinking of you and your mum and dad every day.'

'It was awful, I've never been so scared in my life.'

'I bet. I was too.' Jazz pauses. 'It certainly put everything in perspective for me. What's important and what's not.'

'So, what *has* been going on with you?'

Jazz takes a breath and pours out every detail from fighting over George, to hanging out with Alex. I don't mention that Alex has already filled me in on the situation. I wouldn't have been able to get a word in anyway. It's like someone turned on a tap and Jazz can't stop until the bath is full.

'We wanted to go away without George but spent all our time missing him – and fighting about it. It was like Stu preferred to be with George than me.'

'That's ridiculous!'

'And he doesn't want a baby.' Jazz looks down at her hands. 'Stu's scared if we have so much trouble dealing with a dog, we'd be even worse trying to manage a child.'

'But you two are meant for each other.' I squeeze Jazz's hand. 'Of course, you can handle a child.'

'But I kissed Alex, didn't I?'

'You were upset and apparently quite drunk, plus he's gay.'

'It meant nothing, but I told Stu, and he went ballistic. Caught a train to Paris and said he might see me at home. I waited a couple of days, but he didn't come back, so I left.'

'You guys'll work it out.'

'But that's not the end of it.'

'There's more?'

'I'm pregnant.'

'Jazz!'

'I was going to tell Stu, but we'd been arguing so much about having a baby that I wondered whether I should keep it.'

'It's great news.' I give Jazz yet another hug. 'Of course, you'll keep it.'

'What's such great news?' a voice says from the doorway.

'Jem!' Jazz jumps up and throws her arms around him.

'How are you? Where's Stu? Did you lose him? Is that the good news?'

I flash Jem a look to say "don't joke about it" but he just gives me a puzzled expression. I guess we don't know each other well enough to be able to communicate telepathically yet.

Jazz dissolves into tears and Jem looks more confused than ever.

'Stu's heading back soon,' I say quickly. 'We're not sure when.'

Finally absorbing the scene of Jazz sobbing into a cup of tea with Stu somewhere in Europe, Jem leaves us to it, muttering something about having a shower.

I sit with Jazz for two hours while she cries and talks, mostly at the same time, while I give plenty more hugs and make three pots of tea. I'm about to suggest yoga poses that help in times of trauma when Jazz announces she needs to lie down.

'Let me put fresh sheets on.' I think how Jem and I were rolling around in them only a few hours earlier.

'Don't bother, I'm sure you're very clean. I just really want my own bed.'

'I'll be five seconds.'

I race around the room, packing up the Scrabble game, grabbing discarded underwear, Jem's boxers, his trainers, and a few random condom wrappers. Anything that alludes to a night (and morning) of passion between two housemates who supposedly hate each other. Then I strip the bed and put on fresh sheets.

'Thanks. Looks great.' Jazz literally falls onto the bed fully clothed and almost immediately lets out a gentle snore. I take off her shoes, pull a vintage patchwork quilt over her, close the plantation shutters, and tiptoe out.

I make my way back to the kitchen, feeling guilty about having not told Jem the information that Alex revealed about Jazz and Stu. I didn't want Jem to think badly of Jazz. We don't know the full story, so it's too soon to make any judgements.

'What's up with Jazz and Stu?'

Drained by the day's turn of events, I simply put my arms around Jem's neck and sink into his chest, drawing on his calm strength like a parasite. 'Let's cook brunch first. I'm starving. Or rather you cook brunch, while I watch.'

Half an hour later, I'm sitting at the kitchen table while Jem serves eggs benedict with spinach and sauteed mushrooms on sour dough toast (don't know how he whipped that up).

'Stu's said nothing to me.' Jem piles a mountain of mushrooms on my plate. 'I can't believe you didn't tell me what Alex said.'

'Sorry, but you and I were hardly talking then. Besides, I was worried Jazz might have had an affair and I didn't want you angry with her. Stu's your friend, remember?'

'Yeah, but he can be annoying, too.' Jem smiles. 'I love them both and can't imagine them not together.'

'I know.' I stick a forkful of creamy egg in my mouth. 'My God, this is delicious! You should've made this for me in the first week we moved in. I'd have jumped into bed sooner.'

Jem's eyes light up. 'If only I'd known you were that easy!'

'Not easy,' I say seriously. 'Eggs benedict is a hard dish to perfect.'

Despite my anxiety for Jazz and the state of her marriage, I feel like I'm sitting on a cloud as Jem and I eat breakfast and chat, knowing that later we'll rip each other's clothes off and… hang on, what do we do now? Jazz is home and will want my, well, her bed. And fair enough. I'll have to go back to Pymble. At least I can be there for Dad, help Mum out as he recovers. But still, teenage memories tell me that nothing sexy happens there.

'What's wrong, you look like you lost your wallet at the supermarket.' Jem brings my attention back to breakfast.

'Nothing, just tired out.'

Jem looks at me, questioningly.

'Okay, with Jazz home, it's like we're back on Planet Real World.'

'What's wrong with that?'

'We're going to have to move out. I mean, Jazz and Stu need their own space right now.'

'I'm sure there's no hurry… hey, feel like seeing a movie?'

I sigh. Clearly, Jem is avoiding the inevitable too. 'Love to.'

'It's not too much like work for you?'

I shake my head. Going to the movies never feels like work. Acting is not clear cut, like a nine-to-five office job. Not the same boundaries. You have other challenges, mind you. You go through that "interview process" a few times a week, more in LA – and usually get rejected. There's no financial security and some of the jobs are taxing with long hours and busy schedules. And, unless you're a regular on a long-running soap, most jobs come to an end. In fact, the "not working" is more stressful than the working part. And acting in a movie is definitely better than sitting in a cinema watching one. But right now, a movie and popcorn with Jem sounds divine. And nothing at all like work.

We choose a Hollywood action film that's just come out and I keep digging my elbow into Jem's side and pointing out the actors I know.

'See that woman with the gun, in the florist shop, she goes to my yoga class,' I whisper. 'And that guy playing the undercover cop was in a workshop I did earlier in the year. Pain in the bum.'

'Are you going to name drop through the entire movie?' Jem asks. 'Because if so, I'll have to move away from you.'

I giggle. 'Sorry, my lips are sealed.'

'Not too tightly I hope.' Jem kisses me gently on the lips.

'Never.'

We hear an impatient huff behind us and look at each other, trying not to laugh. There's nothing more annoying than people talking through a film, but it feels like we're in our own mini-universe and I keep forgetting we're sharing a space with fifty other movie-goers.

We get through the film with no more disturbances and dissect it over wine and an antipasto plate in a nearby bar.

Jem sighs wistfully. 'I wonder if I could ever write a script like that?'

'I'm sure you could, but there has to be one condition.'

'And what's that?'

'You cast me as your leading lady.'

'Done. Although you're already my own personal leading lady.'

I smile but can't help wondering what will happen now we're no longer required to house sit.

Back home, we creep in to see that the door to Jazz's bedroom is still closed. Maybe she got up and went back to bed? Maybe she's still asleep, jetlagged and exhausted.

'Should I knock?' I ask.

'Nah, leave her a little longer. Let's take George for his evening stroll.'

'Yes, we shouldn't abandon our duties just yet.'

We're back home in a flash as George had no intention of having a "stroll", rather a gallop around the block with me and Jem trying to keep up. Jazz's door is still closed.

'Finish what we started earlier?' I ask.

'Sure, might be weird with Jazz in the next room but we could be quiet, well I could, don't know about you—'

'I'm talking about Scrabble, you idiot.' I set up the board on the coffee table.

'Oh, sure, I think I was going to finally beat you.' Jem pours two glasses of red wine.

'Yeah, right.'

It doesn't take long to get into the zone, and I have to say, I'm outdoing even myself. Dad would be so proud. As always, I can hear his voice in my head, advising me on my every move. 'Aim for at least 30 to 40 points each turn, Indie,' he'd say. 'The words are out there; you just have to find them.' My heart feels like a twig about to snap. Thank God he's around for me to tell him that I just scored 48 points for JEWELS.

'I can't believe you're winning yet again.' Jem huffs over his letters.

'Don't feel bad, I told you I played it all the time when I was growing up. If I failed as a Scrabble player, I'd have been kicked out of home.'

I retrieve my replacement letters while Jem struggles to make his next word. Just as he's about to (finally) put something down, George charges in like a hurricane, barking excitedly and trying to jump on my lap.

'George! Be quiet! Get down!'

George chooses not to listen, or rather can't hear me over his own yapping. I haven't seen him so frenetic since bath day. And he seems to be taking up even more space than usual, like he just grew a metre in length. Either that or the lounge room has shrunk. He leaps about, all legs and noise, throwing his paws onto the coffee table, like a clumsy giraffe. Quick-as-a-flash, Jem grabs our two glasses, however he doesn't save the Scrabble board, which flips into mid-air, sending my precious letters soaring.

'George! Noooooo!'

Through the chaos, we hear the front door opening. Judging from George's super strength enthusiasm, it could only be one of two people and one of them was already asleep in bed.

'Anyone here?' a familiar voice calls from the hall.

We look at each with a start and Jem shouts over the barking, 'Stu, mate, we're in the lounge.'

Stu walks in looking haggard and grey-faced. George, beside himself, lunges on his long-lost parent.

'Hey, George, how are you buddy?' He hugs his dog like his life depends on it.

Jem jumps up to grab his friend's bags. 'Been a long day, has it?'

'I left Jazz in France.' Stu sits on the couch and puts his head in his hands. 'Long story, but I don't know where she is. I'm so worried. Have you heard from her?'

George jumps up beside him, licking his face and whimpering, obviously sensing that something is amiss.

'She's here,' I say quickly. 'Asleep in bed.'

Stu looks at us, lost for words. He gives George another cuddle, gets up and goes straight to the bedroom. The door closes behind him, and we don't hear another sound. Even George quietens down easily, settling into his resting station. Probably tired himself out.

'I think our work here is done.' I yawn. 'Now I've got to go to bed. Lucky you in the spare room, looks like I'm on the couch.'

'You don't have to be.'

'But Jazz and Stu are here.'

'So? They're going to find out sooner or later, why not let them find out in the morning?'

'You don't mind if they know?'

Jem pulls me into his arms. 'I want the world to know. But Jazz and Stu make a good start.'

'Are you inviting me into your messy room?'

'It's actually clean.' Jem looks sheepish. 'I did a tidy up in the hope you might visit one night.'

I peek in and it's true. His room is immaculate, the bed crisply made, the clothes picked up off the floor.

'It's a miracle.' I jump on the bed. 'But it won't stay neat for long if I have anything to do with it.'

'Big words.' Jem climbs next to me. 'But actions speak louder.'

I giggle as he pulls the doona over the top of me. For this briefest of moments, I can't even remember what LA looks like, let alone my plan to head back there as soon as possible.

32

JEM and I sleep in. I wake first, staying still as a photo, relishing the sensation of his smooth skin against mine for as long as possible. Except I desperately need to go to the bathroom. And even more desperately need a cup of tea.

I wonder how Jazz and Stu are going. The house sounds quiet. Maybe they're asleep? Or out with George?

Eventually, I decide it's safe and silently creep into the kitchen to put the kettle on. I grab a cup and slowly place it on the stone benchtop so it doesn't make a sound. Then I carefully open the cupboard and retrieve a teabag, as if handling a delicate prehistoric artefact.

'Good morning, missy.'

I freeze, then slowly turn around, like a character in a sitcom, milking the moment of being caught in a surprising situation. Jazz is sitting at the dining room table on the other side of the vast island bench. Toast and tea in front of her. With Stu sitting beside her. I wasn't expecting that. Probably because Jem and I never really use the dining room table and just sit at the island. I wonder how long it will be before Jazz asks where I slept last night.

'Where did you sleep last night, young lady?' Not long at all, it seems. 'And don't say the couch because we know that's not true.'

'You had my bed,' I say breezily. 'Jem said I could bunk in with him.'

'Really?' Jazz's eyebrows are so arched they look like two

tepees. 'Is that what you kids call it these days?'

'Yeah, we crashed that's all…' whatever excuse I had lined up after that was lost as I look up at Jazz and Stu to see them smiling at me like they'd won the lottery. 'We're just friends.'

Before I can say another word, Jem appears looking suitably dishevelled as if he'd had a particularly rigorous night of passion, which he did. He doesn't notice Jazz and Stu sitting at the dining room table either as he leans in and kisses me gently on the lips.

'It's nice to see you guys are such good friends.' Jazz's smile stretches even further across her face.

'Oh… hi.' Jem looks around and gives me an apologetic grin. 'Sorry, habit I guess.'

'It's fine, as you say, they're going to find out sooner or later.'

Jazz looks like she's about to self-combust. 'Oh my God, this is fantastic, you guys are perfect for each other. I've always said that, haven't I, Stu?'

'Yes, many times. Have to admit, I agree.'

'Enough about us. What's going on with you two?' I'm determined to not pussyfoot around the issue.

'We're good.' Stu gives a triumphant nod.

'Better than good.' Jazz looks at Stu in a way that reminds me of their early relationship days.

Stu stands up as if making a formal announcement. 'We have something to tell you both, we're having—'

'They know already, Stu.'

'What? You told them before me?'

'You were goodness knows where, I had to tell someone!' Jazz smiles affectionately at Stu's devastated expression. 'Besides, Indie and Jem are like family, I didn't think you'd mind.'

Stu beams. 'Of course not.'

'Such great news,' I say. 'I'm so happy for you both.'

Jem gives his friend a big bear hug. 'Congrats, mate.'

'I'd been so worried about us having a baby, but the minute I found out, I was thrilled.'

'You're going to be awesome parents,' Jem says.

'I agree.' Stu smiles proudly. 'Should've done it ages ago.'

Jazz throws me an exasperated look as if to say, 'Men, am I right?'

Later, the boys take George for a run and I grab the chance to speak to Jazz alone.

'So, you and Stu?'

'Madly in love as always,' she says with a shy grin. 'And thrilled to be having a baby.'

'That's good to hear.'

'Well, not initially, mind you. I got the fright of my life when I woke up to him snoring beside me. I was angry and woke him instantly for an explanation. He said he couldn't live without me. He thought about it but realised he didn't want to. Then I told him about the baby, and he started happy crying.'

'Really?' I can't remember Stu ever crying, happy or sad. 'What about Alex?'

'I explained it meant nothing.' Jazz's cheeks redden at the mention of his name. 'I explained that I wanted my husband, who seemed to have lost interest in me. He thought I loved George more than I loved him, while I thought he preferred George over me.'

I grin. 'Fair enough, George doesn't talk as much as you.'

'Hey! You're supposed to be on my side. Anyway, all a big misunderstanding. Going away without George was the best thing we did.'

'Alex's advice?'

'It was, actually.' Jazz eyes sparkle. 'Now… Jem. You guys are so right for each other. It's been tedious waiting for you to work it out. But then you're both so stubborn and single-minded, I was worried it might never happen. I can now admit I might have had a hand in the housemate/dog sharing situation.'

'I knew it!'

Jazz shrugs. 'How else was I going to get you together? It makes life easier if the people I love are in close proximity.'

'Emily's wedding helped. It was like she took over match-making duties while you were away. So, I have both you girls to thank.'

'How *was* the wedding?'

I told the story of our terrible fight over his film and then Jem turning up looking divine in a dinner suit and being the best wedding date ever.

'I knew he wanted to write but I didn't know he was any good at it,' Jazz says. 'And what about Emily?'

'I spoke to her before the wedding and she was lovely, like the old Emily. And do you know, I chatted to a woman on the day who told me what a hard time Emily had at school.'

'Really?' Jazz almost chokes on her tea.

'Seems like the cool long-legged gang wasn't that nice to her,' I say. 'In fact, none of them were there. Just Fiona and me. And you, if you'd been able to come.'

'Who'd have thought? She never said anything, even the times when we've caught up over the years.'

'Maybe she felt embarrassed. Ditching us and it not working out so well.'

'Anyway, more importantly, between the two of us, we've managed to keep you in Sydney,' Jazz says. 'Couldn't have planned it better if we tried.'

'Not so sure about that. I'm going to have to go back soon.' My heart sags. The thought of leaving Jem is unbearable.

'Really?' Jazz is genuinely surprised. 'What about Jem?'

'I haven't talked to him about it yet.'

'You'd better. He's already been badly hurt.'

'I know that!' I snap, immediately regretting my tone. 'Sorry, Jazz, I don't want to hurt him, far from it. But I have to think of my career. After I do a few pick-ups for the film, there's nothing happening here.'

'Some things are more important than work and career, Indie.'

I look at Jazz. Are they? Work has always been the most important thing in the world. Succeeding as an actress. Giving it absolutely everything. Nothing holding me back. Does this mean I now have to choose? If I don't follow my passion, I'll be regretful and resentful. But isn't Jem now my passion, too? Why can't I have both?

'We'll work it out,' I say casually.

Jazz doesn't look so sure. But she's hardly in a position to criticise after what she's just been through. One step at a time. I'll cross that rickety bridge when it appears in front of me.

It appears sooner than anticipated when I turn on my computer the next day. I flick through my emails and almost fall backwards off the kitchen stool when I read a message from Benji, the words bouncing off the screen so enthusiastically it's like he's doing jumping jacks right here in the room. I didn't get that guest role I auditioned for, that self-test Charlie helped me film, but apparently one of the producers remembered me from the last show I auditioned for – the job that got away into the fiancé-stealing hands of Kourtney Lane. Apparently, they're now SERIOUSLY CONSIDERING me for an ON-GOING ROLE in another new series. I can almost hear Benji's overly enthusiastic voice from the other side of the world.

It's exciting news, but Jazz is right. I'm going to have to talk to Jem. But about what? That I might have a big screen test? That some producer likes me? All that happened last time, and it went nowhere. Nothing is definite, so how do I explain that I might or might not be leaving Sydney?

For a split second, I want it all to go away. If this were a story in a script, I'd simply tell my agent I wasn't interested. But in life, there's no picking and choosing scenarios. There's no cutting and doing another take. Which way do I go? I badly want a career, but now it's not just the possibility of losing a major TV role that brings tears to my eyes, it's also the possibility of losing Jem. However, the alternative doesn't fit into my plan at all. And that makes me want to cry even more.

33

FORTUNATELY, Jazz and Stu are in no hurry for us to leave, in fact, they insist we stay in the spare room as long as we want. I'd like to say we've been too busy to discuss the future, but there have been many lazy moments of idle chatter when I could have broached the subject. Every microsecond we spend in each other's company is so divine, the last thing I want to do is bring up a conversation that will rain on our love parade. Trouble is, if I'm not careful, I'll be having the "talk" as I'm waiting for an uber to take me to the airport. Especially as another message comes through from Benji.

The producers want me to come back IMMEDIATELY for a chemistry test, which is huge. It sounds like a science exam, which it sort of is, but not the sort you do at school. This test is to see if you have chemistry with the leading man they're considering. To see if sparks fly. Or not. As I read on, despite the enormity of the request, there's a growing heaviness cramping my stomach. Like a piece of cement is stuck down there. Then I see the actor I'm testing the chemistry with and I start to hyperventilate. The leading man is none other than my ex-fiancé, Mark.

How can I do that audition? But how can I say no to that audition? Will Mark and I have any chemistry? What if it's all gone now? But what if we do have chemistry? What will that mean? I don't want to be with Mark, but how will Jem deal with the fact that if there's a suitable amount of chemistry between my ex-fiancé and me, we'll be working together, living in each other's space, practically breathing the same air indefinitely?

I've longed to be in the privileged position of being seriously considered for a big job in LA. Now I'm there, it's like being caught in the surf when the shark siren goes off. A moment of utter panic out of nowhere on a calm blue day. And the way I see it, there's little chance of me achieving a positive outcome. Either I leave and Jem hates me and wants nothing to do with me, or I stay and resent him for standing in the way of my big break.

And what about Dad? I can't leave him now. If I get the job, I won't be back for ages. He wouldn't want me to stay for him, but how can I seriously go?

'Did you hear me?' Jem appears as I battle my chaotic thoughts. 'I was calling out to see if you want a cup of tea.'

'Oh?' Panic rises in my stomach like an ocean swell but I force a smile on my face. Not that Jem buys it at all. Quite the opposite in fact.

'Do you want to tell me what's going on?' Jem looks as if he's about to walk across hot coals at some confidence-building retreat.

Come on Indie, big breath.

'I have to go back to LA. I'm being considered for a big TV role and the producers want me to fly back for a screen test.'

The words plummet out of my mouth in one go.

The light in Jem's eyes disappears in a flash. 'Oh, right.'

'I need to book a flight for Sunday or Monday.'

'So soon?'

Panic surges through my every vein. What am I doing? How can I leave Jem?

'I'm going back for a chemistry test. It's a massive deal, it means I'm very close.'

'A what?'

'They literally test the chemistry between you and the actor you're playing against. To see if we're a good match on screen. My manager, Benji, emailed, firstly last week to tell me that it was only—'

'Wait!' Jem says sharply. 'Last week? You knew about this all week and didn't tell me?'

'All Benji said last week was that the producers were considering me. And frankly, after getting so close last time and then falling short, I didn't think anything would come of it. The fact they want to test me against the male lead character is super exciting. It means I'm in with a shot.'

Jem falls into a heavy silence that makes me feel like I've just boarded the Titanic.

'I'm sorry, it's all happened so quickly, I haven't had a chance to think it through.'

'Well, maybe you should.'

'Sorry?'

'Think it through. Give it some thought. Give us some thought.'

I don't know what to say. Jem is a priority, but this is my career, and a chance like this only comes about once in a lifetime, or never at all. There's nothing to think about, really. I must do the chemistry test. Jem must understand.

'You've obviously made up your mind.'

Looks like Jem can read my thoughts now. Weird.

'It's my work. What else can I do?'

'Stay here. Don't go.'

'It's only a screen test.'

'And if you get the job? What then?'

'I'm not going to get the job.'

'Then why even go?' Jem becomes angrier by the second.

'If I did, by some stroke of luck, get this role, you could come with me. There are fantastic writing courses over there. You might even get some interest in your script.'

'I can't just pack up and go to LA.' Jem is positively fuming now. 'Have you considered what I might want to do or how this affects me?'

I fall silent. I should have talked to Jem earlier. Maybe we could have planned this together. But it didn't work out that way and there's not much I can do about it now.

'This is my career, Jem. It's an amazing opportunity.'

'Who are you testing your chemistry with anyway? Do you know this actor?'

My hands dampen with nerves and perspiration beads on my forehead. Damn. Something else I should have mentioned before now.

'Would you believe it's Mark?' I try to lighten the mood with a comic eye roll, which has zero effect. Probably makes things worse.

'Great,' he says quietly. 'That's perfect, you two should really hit it off. At least you know there's chemistry. You won't even have to act. Just pick up where you left off.'

'Jem, that's not fair—'

'Not fair?' Jem jumps up from the couch. 'You're the one who's not being fair, Indie! Were you ever going to discuss this with me? Or just leave a note on your way to the airport?'

'No, I—'

'And what about my film, I thought you were helping me? We were going to organise a read-through.'

'Of course, I'm still helping you. And organising a read-through. And I'm still going to be in it.'

Jem furiously paces up and down the living room. I wish I'd listened to Jazz and told him earlier, but I was scared of losing him and now I've ruined everything.

'I guess we could re-cast if you're not available. Maybe Tia would step into your role. Get someone else for hers.'

'What?'

Out of anything Jem could have said in that moment, that was the most hurtful. Not that I mind Tia, she's a talented actress but that part was written for me. Or so I thought. He has every right to be upset but something inside me starts to boil. Without me, this film would still be locked away in Jazz and Stu's spare room. I guess that counts for nothing. I'm completely replaceable after all.

'What do you expect, Indie?' Jem stops still and looks straight at me, his eyes like lasers boring through to the back of my head. 'I need certainty in my life. I'm not waiting around for a flighty actress who doesn't know where she is from one day to the next. You might be able to live in chaos, but I can't.'

I get up, unable to speak. My eyes ache with determined tears but I don't want to cry here. Jem's words cut through my heart like a five-star chef's knife. I'm falling in love with him but I didn't consider how leaving would make him feel. If I had, I might have been able to have both work and love in my life – but now, I've carelessly tossed any hope of that out the window. But something tells me, however I approached this, Jem would have reacted the same way. I can't throw away this audition and if he expects me to, then he can't possibly love me.

Neither of us speak until George bounds in with his big, round, please-walk-me eyes, causing a much-needed distraction.

'Come on, mate, I'll take you for a run.' Jem beats me to the door without a sideward glance.

George, unaware of what he walked into, follows, thrilled to be granted an outing so easily. He didn't even need to beg. Life doesn't get better than that when you're a dog. Right now, for me, it couldn't get much worse. I hear the side gate click and now alone, I can't hold it together a moment longer. Tears tumble down my cheeks, hot, wet, and never-ending. Normally, a little part of me would stand aside and note my every feeling and reaction. I'd save it up, so I could hook into it when playing an emotional role down the track. Today, I can't separate myself from the despair washing over me. That scene with Jem was completely unexpected and unfortunately there's little chance of anyone saying, 'Cut, let's go again.' And absolutely no chance of any re-writes, especially as the in-house writer just stormed out the door.

34

AFTER a torpedo-like conversation with Benji, it's settled, and my flight is booked for the day after tomorrow. No turning back now. On one hand, I'm ecstatic about this mind-blowing opportunity. On the other, I'm devastated that Jem isn't speaking to me. I text him to say I've booked a return ticket, thinking that might warm his heart. I hear nothing back. I guess it's much too little, far too late.

Next, I have a conversation with Mark about the fact we will be testing our chemistry once more. If he feels weird, he doesn't let on.

'I think you've got a good chance at getting this one, Indie.' He skirts around the fact that if I get this job, we'll be living in each other's pocket. Literally.

'Are you sure you're okay about it?'

'I think I'll cope. I'm a professional, remember?'

And he is. Just one that tends to sleep with his leading ladies. Well, not this leading lady.

The following morning, Jazz marches me off to do the coastal walk to Bronte. It really is spectacular, overlooking the water beneath the early morning pink-tinged sky. But even an awe-inspiring view like that isn't enough to raise my lead-like spirits.

'I did suggest you talk to him about your plans.' Jazz takes her usual not-so-subtle approach.

'It wouldn't have made any difference when I told him. He'd

still have flipped out.'

'Has he spoken to you since?'

'Not yet.' Heat pinpricks my eyes as I think back to yesterday afternoon. He texted to say he was staying at Mick's last night but that was it.

'Do you want me to drive you over to Pymble tomorrow?'

'No that's okay, I'll get the train.'

I've planned to stay with Mum and Dad. We'll have dinner together and then they'll drop me at the airport the next morning. I probably won't see Jem before I leave.

'It's been great spending time with you,' says Jazz. 'Wish it was for longer.'

'Don't you start on me. I feel bad enough as it is. Guilty for being plucked out of almost obscurity to play the lead in a huge TV series, and finally earn some decent money. Go figure.'

'Now you're sounding like an LA actress.'

'Jazz, this is a really big deal.'

'It is, and Stu and I are over the moon, but Jem's feeling hurt and rejected. And fair enough. He really likes you.'

'I'm coming back, it's a return ticket. I probably won't even get this job. Even though I'm close, it's a long shot. Look at that last one. It was between me and Kourtney, of all people. She'll probably get this job, too. I'm sure she'll have more chemistry with Mark than me.'

'What about Jem's film?'

'I'm still going to help him, and play the lead role, although I think he's having second thoughts about that.' I pause. 'It takes ages to get a film up and running, years even. He should come over to LA with me. Do some writing workshops, get a script assessment, talk to a few people.'

Jazz's face lights up. 'That's a great idea, did you suggest that to him?'

'Of course, but I'd only just told him about the audition so he wasn't very receptive.'

'He can be a little hot-headed.'

'A little?'

'Okay, a lot, but do you blame him?'

'This is my career, Jazz. Why should I have to sacrifice everything I've worked for?'

'You shouldn't have to. Go back to LA. Do what you need to do. Let him miss you. He just needs time.'

Back home, we find George in the garden and Stu cooking up a huge batch of his famous tomato chutney.

'Where's Jem?' Jazz asks.

'Gone out. Maybe a shift at the bar?' Stu says distractedly. 'Or with George?'

Jazz sighs impatiently. Since George is snoozing on the grass, Jem is clearly not with him. 'Did he say anything?'

Stu looks up with a mildly surprised look on his face. 'No, he was a bit quiet. Why?'

'Oh, no reason, Indie's just gone and broken his heart.'

'Huh?' Stu glances from Jazz to me, taking in my blotchy eyes. 'Do you want me to text him?'

'Yes, Stu, immediately!' Jazz gives me a look that indicates how ridiculous men can be. 'But be casual. Ask if he's home for dinner tonight.'

Stu texts Jem but hears nothing back. He calls, but the phone is dead. Or purposely turned off. Wherever Jem is, he doesn't want to be contactable and he doesn't want to see me. Later, Stu and Jazz do their best to cheer me up, cooking a delicious dinner and opening a bottle of French red wine. It's all they drink now, in an attempt to keep their holiday vibe going. It could be fruit juice for all I care. I don't feel like eating, so eventually, I excuse myself and go to pack my stuff. The sooner I'm out of here, the better. Jem can come back and have the spare room.

In the morning, Jazz and I take George for one final walk to the dog park. I know it's not the last time I'll see George or walk him, but everything feels so gloomy, despite the sparkling blue sky. I should be over the moon about going back to LA for this audition, but I don't think I've ever felt so low.

We reach the dog park gate and George jumps and barks excitedly. Through the fence grills, he sees Roxie and whines, pulling on Jazz's arm with all his doggie strength. Roxie barks back with equal enthusiasm. Oh, to be a dog in love. So straightforward.

'Hang on, mate, give me a second.' Jazz tries to unlatch the lead while George struggles impatiently. 'Roxie's bum isn't going anywhere. Plenty of time to give it a sniff.'

She lets him go and he bounds up to his friend. When Alex sees George running over, he looks up and waves.

'How do you feel about seeing Alex?' I whisper.

'Fine, why?'

'Maybe something to do with getting drunk and kissing him while being married to someone else?'

'I've seen Alex since, it's as if it never happened. In fact, he's started seeing someone.'

'Really?'

'Another dog owner from the park. You might have seen him. He's even taller than Alex and has two very cute cavoodles. I'm not sure what's going on, but they seem to be walking their dogs together a lot and arriving at the park at the exact same time. And from my experience, that sort of thing is never platonic.'

Alex walks over, his dog-walking outfit as pristine as always.

'Hello, you two. What's happening?'

'I'm off to LA tomorrow.' My voice sounds unnaturally upbeat, even Jazz looks at me strangely.

'That's come around quickly,' he says. 'Are you ready?'

'Sort of. I wouldn't be going so soon except I've got an audition. A big one, and I'm in with a chance.'

'That's fantastic.'

'I may not even get it. Probably won't. And I don't know if I want to go. I mean, I do… but then I don't.'

'See what happens,' Alex says calmly, picking up on my slightly manic vibe. Or maybe Jazz already filled him in on the details while hanging at the dog park.

I'm going to miss this bit: walking George, chatting to Alex. I've always been a bit wary of dog people, who seem slightly obsessive, to say the least. When Jazz got George, I saw a side to her I never knew existed. Now I realise what a close bond dog people have. Like one big family you can only be part of if you have a dog. I've been lucky enough to have a temporary membership. True, I was never keen, but now I feel sad to be leaving. Maybe if I come back to Sydney, Jem and I can get a puppy and then we… I quickly let that thought go before I get carried away. I don't think Jem will even be talking to me, never mind considering co-parenting a dog.

35

BACK at Jazz and Stu's, I finish packing my stuff, which seems to have quadrupled in size, especially as Jazz keeps throwing in clothes from her to-be-thrown-out-when-I'm-completely-sure bag.

'You're doing me a favour,' she explains. 'It gives me a little more time to consider if I need them or not. I can get them back from you a lot more easily than I can from Vinnie's.'

I think back to the time when Jazz accidently threw an original sixties cocktail dress into her Vinnie's bag and had to negotiate a hefty price to get it back from the volunteer working in the shop that day.

'She drove a tough bargain,' Jazz said to me after she'd retrieved said dress. 'You'd think she'd have given it back to me, being a charity shop, but the minute it went through the door, I'd relinquished ownership.'

As a result, Jazz throws nothing out. Or very little. Apparently, it drives Stu crazy but now she's nesting, she's decluttering with a little more enthusiasm. And it's certainly not doing my paltry wardrobe any harm.

I finally agree to let Jazz drive me to Mum and Dad's. Jem is nowhere to be seen when we leave, which is devastating. This audition could change my life and career trajectory, but my heart is so heavy I'm finding it hard to be cheery. I wish I could rewind and play out last week differently, but I can't. Maybe there was a better way of handling the situation, but things just happen sometimes that are not part of any plan. I can't not go back to LA. This is everything I've been striving for. If Jem can't understand that and try to find a way to make it work between us, then we don't stand a chance.

'Jazz, so lovely to see you.' Mum almost pushes me over to sweep Jazz into a big hug. 'How was your trip?'

'Hi, Mum. Your real daughter is here too.'

'Oh, sorry darling.' She puts her arms around me, her hair about two shades more vibrant than the last time I was here.

'Pam, I was so shocked to hear about David. Is he okay?'

'Looks like I'll survive,' says a voice from the front lounge room.

Dad appears in the hall and Jazz throws herself at him in a big bear hug. 'Make sure you do, please. Gave us all a nasty shock.'

'Yes, I've told him, that's quite enough of that,' Mum says. 'Besides, now we need to focus on you-know-what!'

'Sorry, I told her,' I say to Jazz.

'Congratulations!' Mum pulls Jazz into another hug. 'So exciting.'

'Thanks, Pam.' Jazz grins happily. 'It is, although I'm very tired.'

Mum and Jazz immediately delve headfirst into the many intricacies of the first trimester of pregnancy, a conversation to which I can't contribute. Dad smiles and helps bring in my luggage from the car. My suitcase is now too small, so I have an endless trail of green shopping bags. How I'm going to get on the plane is beyond me.

'Stay for dinner, Jazz?' I hear Mum say as we come back into the kitchen.

'Would love to Pam, but I've got to get back. Stu and I have plans.' Jazz turns to me. 'In fact, I'd better get going straight away if I'm going to battle the after-work traffic back to Bondi.'

'Thanks for the lift,' I say. 'And the house, George and… well everything.'

Jazz gives me a hug and whispers, 'Don't fret, you guys will work it out.'

It's nice of her to say, but that's something that happens in rom coms, not real life.

'Let me know how the ultrasound goes, I want to see pictures.' I try to hold back the tears that so want to make their grand entrance.

'Of course,' Jazz says. 'And you need to let me know how you go with the audition. Hopefully you do a terrible job and are back in Sydney next week.'

'Gee, thanks!' I laugh. 'It would be nice to come back, but hopefully, I'll nail the audition, too.'

'Of course you will, not a doubt in my mind.' Jazz turns to Mum who's just walked back into the hallway. 'Bye, Pam, hopefully we can catch up for a coffee soon?'

'That'd be lovely, text me next week. And give my love to the father-to-be. We're so happy for you both.'

'I will. He'll be sorry not to have seen you.'

Jazz has always been a big part of my family. Mum will probably claim their baby as her own grandchild. Fair enough, she'll be hard pressed to get one from me.

Jazz speeds off back to her beautiful Bondi cottage and lovely husband. Jazz's life is not as perfect as I always thought, but at least she's heading in the right direction.

'Thanks, Mum, I love it.'

I pull away the last of the paper to reveal a beautiful new

suitcase, much larger than the one I had and far more stylish. I'll be the envy of the luggage claim at LAX.

'As long as you let me throw that other one straight into the bin.' Mum pulls it out of my reach. She probably wants to turn it out on the street this very minute.

We sit in the dining room for dinner, as it's what Mum refers to as "a special occasion". Not that it feels very special right now. Saying goodbye to Jazz, not speaking to Jem, Dad's heart attack, even the new suitcase sends silent tears sliding down my cheeks. Mum and Dad are discussing how delicious the eggplant dish is (one of Dad's "amazing" low-fat vegetarian recipes) before they realise our happy farewell dinner has dramatically dropped in mood.

'Indie, what's up?' Mum says, surprised. I've never been sad about going to LA or going anywhere. I've always known what I've wanted and always kept on task to make it happen.

'I… it's just—' But whatever I'd planned on saying is lost in never-ending sobs and snotty sniffs.

'You don't have to go, sweetheart, you know that, don't you?' Mum says.

I take a breath and wipe my face with a napkin. 'Mum, I do have to go. I want to go. It's an amazing opportunity. Even if I don't get it, the fact I've been called in for a chemistry test is extraordinary.'

'I keep thinking you're doing some sort of science exam,' Dad chips in.

Mum gives me a look, as if to say, 'Just ignore your father with his bad jokes.'

'You know I'd never seriously try to stop you,' she says. 'But if the thought of going is making you this upset, maybe it's not right. Maybe you don't want this job?'

Mum's trying to help, but I absolutely want this job. I want Jem, too. But that's not possible. Things usually have a way of working out, but not today. I've had to make a hard decision, and while I really had no choice, something in the pit of my stomach is suggesting, or rather loudly announcing, that maybe I've done the wrong thing.

'No, I do, but what about you and Dad? Maybe I should be around for you?'

'Don't be ridiculous, we're fine!' Mum says. 'Well, I am, and your father will be too if he does what he's told.'

I attempt a smile through my tears.

'Is there something else, darling?' Mum knows me too well. 'Is this about Mark? Are you worried about auditioning with him?'

'Mark? No, I called him, and we had a good talk about it, we'll be fine.'

'Is it Jem?'

'What?' How does she always know what's going on? So annoying.

'Jem, your lovely housemate, handsome, good fun, friend of Jazz and Stu's that you brought over for dinner—'

'Yes, I know who Jem is,' I say. 'And yes, okay, we're more than housemates now, but it's over. I can't possibly choose between him and my career.'

Dad sees this is going to become an "emotional discussion" and excuses himself to 'go check on the sugar-free, dairy-free tiramisu'.

Mum looks at me expectantly.

'I organised to go back before telling him.' I give a little sniff. 'I didn't consider his feelings and I don't think he'll ever forgive me.'

'Then he's not the one,' Mum says firmly. 'If it's right, it's right.

If it's not, it's not.'

Trust Mum to simplify my love life into a few sensible words.

'You're amazing and you deserve success.' Mum pulls me into a hug. 'I'm sure Jem thinks that, too. If not, he's not the one for you.'

It's nice of Mum to say, but I have a sneaky suspicion that Jem doesn't think I'm amazing anymore. More like thoughtless and selfish, which is so unfair. How can I be with someone who doesn't understand what I do for a living? I've worked too hard to achieve what I have. Mum's right, I do deserve success. I deserve love too, but why should I be the one to give up my dream, especially when there's a very real possibility of my dream coming true?

36

THE alarm goes off at five and I force my body out of bed with all the energy of a slow-moving goods train. It's not like I'm tired. I went to bed early and I'm used to five o'clock starts since the shoot, but every bone in my body feels like it weighs a tonne and putting one foot after the other is a chore.

'Indie?' Mum knocks gently on the door.

'I'm up, just about to jump into the shower.'

Mum and Dad insisted on taking me to the airport. It's not necessary, but now I'm glad they were so adamant.

Twenty minutes later, I'm downstairs with my new bag neatly packed. It looks much smarter and fits in so much more. I've taken other clothes from home that I'd forgotten about and thrown in a few of my favourite acting technique books. Maybe I can brush up in time for the audition.

'Ready to go, love?' Dad is sitting at the dining room table finishing his coffee.

'Yep, I think so.' I look around. 'How about Mum?'

'Yes, yes, here I am,' she sing-songs from the kitchen, a voice that tells me she's pretending to be happy.

The flowery streets of Pymble race by, reminding me of my teenage years. I couldn't wait to move out, but now I long for those simpler days when all I worried about was getting a part in the school play and being picked to play GA for netball. But I know this isn't where I want to be. I felt more torn leaving Jazz and Stu's house, and George, surprisingly. I didn't think I'd get so attached to him. I'm getting a dog one day. When I'm settled. Wherever that is. Maybe that's what's making me sad. That sense of home. All this travelling from one side of the world to another, one suburb of Sydney to the next. It was a treat being briefly settled in my own space. Except I know now that it wasn't the space. It was the person in my space. Something I never felt with Mark. Jazz and Stu's house is lovely, but with Jem there, it felt more like home than any house I've lived in. My eyes sting at the thought of it.

As we get closer to the airport, my parents turn into the car park. Unusual. Normally, they'd drop me off.

'You don't have to stop. It's too expensive to park.'

'Don't be silly, we want to wave you off,' Mum says.

'Just want to make sure you get on that plane and out of our hair,' Dad throws in.

'Rubbish. Don't listen to your father, we don't want you to get on the plane at all.'

I smile at Mum's last desperate attempt to keep me home.

'I have to go, Mum. It's my job. People are expecting me.'

'And Jem?'

'If he can't see that then he can't be part of my life.'

I see my father shoot Mum a warning look as she's about to say something. She obediently closes her mouth even though the effort is clearly a challenge.

I hug my parents one last time and make my way through the departure gate. This is it; I'm really going. Coming to Sydney was about taking time out, getting physically and emotionally strong, and I've achieved that. When I arrived, the thought of even a small audition was too much. Now, I've shot a film and I'm ready for the next chapter. I guess I stuck to my plan and achieved what I wanted to do. Despite repeating this to myself, I feel empty without Jem. I ruined my chances of a relationship with him and I'm going to have to close that door. Well, wait outside that door which, for now, is shut and locked.

I turn back to see Mum and Dad waving madly at me. I wave back, then see that my mother is pointing towards a nearby crowd of people. What is she trying to say? Did Jazz come to say goodbye? I can't see anyone I know, so I give them one last wave and grab the handle on my bag. She probably saw an acquaintance and is trying to explain some detailed story about them in waving language. I'm about to walk off but pause and turn back to the crowd. I don't know why. A flash of recognition, maybe? Instinct? I cast my eyes from face to face and stand still, completely frozen, as if someone came along and cemented my feet into the airport floor. A familiar shape emerges from the noisy clutch of farewellers and my heart turns inside out.

Jem. Here at the airport. Walking towards me.

The bustle around me slows to a standstill. It's as if every part of him has been put under the microscope: his eyes, his nose, the ripple of every muscle in his arms. I want to run towards him, but maybe it's not him, maybe I'm imagining it. It looks like him, and he's smiling at me. But it doesn't make any sense. He's not meant to be here. Maybe it's my wishful subconscious conjuring up an image of what I want to appear. Think it and it will come. I did a workshop in LA on that once, which seemed a waste of time and money but now I see there may be some point to the technique.

I stand still as a wax works statue, trying to sort through all the reasonable explanations as to why I think I see Jem, when reality hits me on the head with a loud bang. I think I see Jem because he's actually here. In the flesh. Putting his arms around me, pulling me towards him in one of those all-familiar embraces that leaves me breathless.

'Jem.' My voice is almost a whisper. 'What are you doing here?'

Without answering, Jem holds me close. I smell the delicious shampoo from Jazz and Stu's bathroom. I'll never be able to buy anything coconut-scented again.

Jem pulls away, takes my face in his hands and puts his lips to mine. I respond without even thinking as if it's the most natural thing in the world. Jem has turned up to say goodbye. Maybe there *is* some hope for us. But hang on. This just makes it harder. How can I say goodbye now?

'Why are you doing this?' I'm almost angry at the control he has over me. Despite my decision to go, one kiss and I'm likely to forget to board the plane.

'Indie, I'm sorry. You shouldn't have to choose between your career and us. Your work is part of you, a part that I love, respect, and admire. I never should've expected you to choose. I fell in love with you, seeing you onstage all those years ago, why should it be different now?'

I rest my head against his chest, his heart beating like a percussive band. 'I don't actually want to leave you at all.'

'I know, and you tried to explain, but I thought it was Alice all over again.'

'But I'm not Alice. Far from it.'

'I know, well I know now, ever since Jazz got stuck into me and told me how I was being "absolutely ridiculous".'

I laugh, despite the fact my entire body is shaking like I've been stuck in the snow in a summer dress. 'No, you weren't, I behaved selfishly, but I'm glad you listened to Jazz.'

'I had no choice. She was going to ban me from ever seeing George again.'

'Wow, tough love.'

'I know.'

'So, that's the only reason you're here?' I ask shyly. 'To be George's favourite fun uncle?'

'Of course,' he says. 'That – and because I can't stop thinking about his favourite fun auntie.'

My insides beam like the Harbour Bridge on New Year's Eve. But where does this leave us? I'm about to board a plane and be away for a couple of months. Maybe longer. Despite the warmth spreading through my veins, my heart sags like an air mattress with a slow leak on the first night of a camping trip.

'I have to go.'

'Well, come on then,' Jem says impatiently.

I look at him and realise there's an over-packed backpack at his feet. He slings it onto his shoulder, straining under the effort. 'I've never been good at packing light.'

I stare at Jem like he's speaking some obscure foreign language. His face breaks into that wide smile that I tried so hard not to fall for back at Jazz and Stu's wedding.

'I'm coming too. Jazz lent me the money. No, let me re-phrase that. She stood over me while I booked a flight, and then she read out her credit card number. I didn't want to, but she and Stu insisted. I'll pay them back. I seriously think they were going to disown me if I let you fly away. So really, I had no choice.'

'Are you sure?'

'I am, but I do have a return flight booked for three weeks' time, so I have an out.' Jem grins. 'On the other hand, it can always be extended if things work out with us and your audition.'

'And if things don't work out with my audition, I'll be on that flight home with you.' I hesitate. 'So, you're sure? Really, really sure?'

Jem takes my hand in his and squeezes my fingers. 'This is what I want to do. Besides, as you suggested, I'm going to check out some writing workshops and spend time on my script – we can make plans together.'

I throw my arms around him, almost bowling him over, what with the extra weight of his backpack, then pull sharply away. 'Are you only here because Jazz made you buy a ticket?'

'Are you going to stop asking unnecessary questions? I'm here because there's nowhere else I could imagine being right now.'

'But I'm still a flighty actress who never knows where she'll be from one day to the next.'

'As long as that flighty actress includes me in her plans, however chaotic they might be.'

'Of course. Jem, I'm sorry I've been so selfish. I don't deserve you.'

'No, you don't.'

'I love you.' I can't believe I just said that, but it's true. I know that now.

'Indie, I've always loved you.'

'Really? What about my inability to cook and look after a dog?'

'I love you even more for all those things. Even your penchant for rosters and competitive approach to Scrabble.'

'What about my lack of respecting boundaries, stealing my housemate's manuscript, sending it to my agent, casting myself in it, and expecting him to be cool with it?'

'Yeah, well you need a bit of work.'

'And what about the thoughtless way I dealt with this audition?'

'Yep, okay, you almost blew it there.' Jem stops and laughs. 'Are you trying to talk me out of it?'

'I'm surprised you want me back at all.'

'I never let you go in the first place.'

We lean towards each other, our lips merging in a firm yet sensual kiss. I look away to see my mother waving madly.

Jem gives me an apologetic smile. 'Jazz told me your flight details, and she found out from your mum what time you'd be at the airport. She may have mentioned my plans. Apparently, your mum said that she knew right from the start that we were "meant to be together".'

'She reckons she can "feel" these things. I've never believed her, but maybe she does have "the gift" after all.'

'I didn't want to miss you and have to find you on the plane. Then explain in front of all the passengers. Or miss the plane, catch the next one, and track you down in LA.'

I smile and give Mum and Dad a big wave. Mum responds by patting her heart and then pointing at Jem.

'We'd better hurry,' I say. 'Before Mum breaks through the departure barrier to hug us both. Are you absolutely sure you want to get on this plane with me? Last chance to back out.'

'I don't know about you, but I'm getting on the plane,' Jem says in a business-like voice. 'I've got plans in LA.'

'Can I join you?'

'I might be really busy.'

'I can be flexible, fit in with you.'

'That could work.' Jem puts his hand out for me. 'See how it goes.'

I can't believe how things have turned out. Three and a half months ago, I arrived at this airport heartbroken, rejected, and unemployed. My relationship was over, my Dad had a heart attack, I couldn't even look after a dog very well. My world and everything in it turned battleship grey.

Now I've shot a fabulous film, found a truly amazing boyfriend, Dad survived, and I'm going back to LA with the possibility of scoring my dream job. And with Jem by my side, everything is even more sparkly. I close my eyes and breathe in the enormity of the situation.

The right place, the right time, the right person. Doesn't happen often but when it does you have to box it up and treasure it forever. One of life's moments of pure perfection I constantly strive for. So much for my plan. Perhaps you have to make plans so they can be broken. Or maybe it's about being open to opportunities and adapting your plans when a better path presents.

Jem is waiting. 'Ready?'

This is the moment in a film when the credits would start to roll, but this isn't a film, it's real life and it's just the beginning. I don't know exactly where it's going, but I can't wait to find out.

I take a big breath and put my hand in his. Then breathe out so I don't hyperventilate.

'Definitely.'

The End

ABOUT THE AUTHOR

Photo by Sally Flegg

Rom com author, Susannah Hardy, writes comic stories on flawed characters navigating their way through life and love.

Susannah was originally an actor who completed a Bachelor of Arts at the University of New South Wales before running away to study theatre in Paris. Returning to Australia, her work has involved anything from film and television roles to being one of two singing/rollerblading Carmen Mirandas, *Tutti & Frutti*, and creating sketch comedy for Foxtel.

Through performance, Susannah discovered a passion for writing and has spent many years creating feature articles and content for magazines, with a focus on parenting, home interiors, and real estate. However, Susannah's main area of interest is fiction writing and her first novel, *Loving Lizzie March,* was published in 2021 (Pan Macmillan Australia). Susannah lives in Sydney's inner west with her husband, two teenage daughters, and very needy puppy.

ACKNOWLEDGEMENTS

Having a book published is a dream come true, but getting a second one published is unbelievable – and doesn't happen without the help of many people. Thanks to my wonderful publisher, Carolyn Martinez, and the dedicated team at Hawkeye Publishing, Anne, Rikki, Isabelle, Bek, and Lara, for taking on *My Hot Housemate*, and for being so passionate about bringing it to life. Thank you, Lily Qistina, for the gorgeous cover jacket that so perfectly represents my work.

Thanks to my agent, Michael Cybulski, at NAC, you've made so much happen and your faith in my work has been remarkable. My very talented editor, Andrea Barton, thanks for your sharp eye and hours of work that went into creating this book. My lovely friend, Lisa Heidke, thanks for tackling an early (and later) draft, and always being on hand for advice or a chat.

To Valerie Khoo, CEO of the Australian Writers' Centre, thanks for twenty years of never-ending support, positivity, and tough love. I would not be a published author without you.

Diana Glenn, thanks for reading random excerpts, offering feedback, and filling me in on what it is like to play a lead in a film. Sophie Gregg, for the constant friendship, many coffee catch-ups and for doing a very early read. And all my readers who gave up their time – Pilar Mitchell, Alicia Ash, Edel Murray, Lisa Heidke, Anne Freeman, Karina May, Penelope Janu, Natalie Murray, Amy Hutton, Sarah Bourne, Sarah Hawthorn, Holly Brunnbauer, and Kaneana May. Thanks to Kelly Morton from Looking Glass Creative for her continual belief and amazing web designing skills. As always, thanks to Margaret Megard who played a significant role in my becoming a writer, and my wonderful acting agent,

Sue Morris who (much like Indie's agent) has been a constant support and friend.

Karen McDonald and Boon Lim Yeo, thanks for generously sharing your dog care tips – I learnt a lot. And thanks Roshan Sahukar for introducing me to you. Thanks also to vet and friend, Michelle Lawler, for her helpful dog advice. Any dog related errors are my own.

Writing can be a lonely job and I'm lucky to be part of Romance Writers of Australia, where I've found a welcoming and supportive community of writers. And the Scribblers, an online writers group run by Sandie Docker, that also introduced me to so many fantastic writers and now friends.

My parents, Liz and Peter Hardy – thanks for everything including a lifetime of love and encouragement. Dad, your support has been above and beyond, and Mum, I know you would have loved to be here for this. Thanks to the best two brothers you can get, Sean and Simon Hardy, and their families who I'm pretty sure secretly buy up as many copies of my books as they can.

Massive thanks to my lovely husband and very own hero, Andrew Crowley, for so much love, support, patience, and free legal advice – you're amazing, I couldn't do this without you – and to our beautiful girls Maggie and Phoebe, for putting up with me as I tap away on my laptop, and for being a constant source of delight, inspiration, and excellent plot ideas.

And finally, my readers, the booksellers, librarians, bookstagrammers, and everyone who reads, reviews, posts or recommends my book – my appreciation is endless.

BOOK CLUB QUESTIONS

1. Romance novels usually contain one or more "tropes" or overriding themes. This novel leans into the enemy-to-lovers trope, with Indie and Jem disliking each other intensely. Do you think this is an effective set-up for a romance? Do you like this trope? What is your favourite trope and why?

2. Even though Indie is a successful actress, her work life is not easy. Jem is scathing of what she does. Do you think the general public understand what it means to be an actor? Does Indie's life fit your perception of the acting industry?

3. Indie has never had a pet in her life but suddenly finds herself dog minding. Do you think she benefits from this emotionally? How do you think looking after George helps Indie grow as a person? Is this something you can relate to?

4. Indie has a set plan to get her life back on track but finds nothing turns out as she hopes. Is it worth having life plans? Should you stick to them no matter what, or is there a time to let go?

5. Indie is shocked when her father has a serious health scare. For the first time, she realises her parents won't always be around. How does this change her outlook on life? How do serious themes such as this work in a rom com?

6. Through the novel, we see that nothing is as it appears on the surface, such as Jazz and Stu's relationship, Charlie's

feelings for Indie, Indie's relationship with Mark. How do you think Indie keeps missing what's really going on in people's lives? Is this something we all do?

7. Indie's drama school friend, Charlie, describes Indie as being ambitious, which comes as a surprise to her. Do you agree with Charlie? Do you think ambition is heathy?

8. Indie is forced to choose between love and career. Do you think this is fair? Do you believe you can have both?

9. The novel looks at Indie's relationships, not just with Jem but also with her friends and family. She feels guilty as she has been caught up in her life and feels like she has neglected those closest to her. Do you think is this is true?

10. Indie often talks about perfect moments when everything comes together. Do you recognise this feeling? When has this happened to you?

If you enjoyed *My Hot Housemate*, you'll also enjoy:

Loving Lizzie March by Susannah Hardy
New Year's Eve by Sarah Todman
Me That You See by Anne Freeman
Forgotten by Casey Nott
Returning to Adelaide by Anne Freeman
Rosanna by Annie O'Moon-Browning

Book reviews can make or break a book. If you liked what you read today, please do consider posting a review on Goodreads or your favourite forum.

My Hot Housemate is available at hawkeyebooks.com.au
and all good bookstores and libraries.